TWIST AND SHOUT

A Decade of Feminist Writing in
This Magazine

TWIST AND SHOUT
A Decade of Feminist Writing in
This Magazine

Edited by
SUSAN CREAN

SECOND
STORY
Press
FEMINIST
PUBLISHERS

CANADIAN CATALOGUING IN PUBLICATION DATA

Main Entry under title:
Twist and shout: a decade of feminist writing in This magazine
ISBN 0-929005-27-9

1. Women – Social Conditions.
2. Feminism. I. Crean, Susan, 1945-

HQ1206.T93 1992   305.4   C91-094899-2

Printed and bound in Canada

Second Story gratefully acknowledges the assistance of
the Ontario Arts Council and the Canada Council

Published by
SECOND STORY PRESS
760 Bathurst St.
Toronto, Ontario
M5S 2R6

CONTENTS

Introduction

NATIONALISM, SOCIALISM AND FEMINISM
Margaret Atwood
I

REFLECTIONS OF REALITY
A Canadian Reporter in the West Bank
Linda McQuaig
17

CREATIVITY AND MOTHERHOOD
Having the Baby *and* the Book
Libby Scheier
25

ROOTS OF DISSENT
Pursuing Bitter History in Basque Country
Theodora Jensen
34

THE ADVERTISED INFANT:
Ivan's Adventures in Babyland
Carole Corbeil
44

FOR AS LONG AS THE RIVERS FLOW
An Apocalyptic Preview of Free Trade
Lenore Keeshig-Tobias and David McLaren
52

IMAGES FOR A STORY THAT ISN'T
Sandy Frances Duncan
65

THE CALGARY TIME MACHINE
In Olympic City the contest between winners and losers is as
old as the town itself
Katherine Govier
74

THE BIRTH OF A MURDERER
Fauzia Rafiq
81

WOMEN, VIOLENCE AND THE MONTREAL MASSACRE
Lee Lakeman
92

DANGEROUS DETERMINATION
Moira Farr
103

FEMALE COMPLAINTS
▼

MUSE IN A FEMALE GHETTO
A Portrait of Elizabeth Smart
Rosemary Sullivan
115

POST-FEMINISM AND POWER DRESSING
Who Says the Women's Movement has Run Out of Steam
Susan Crean
123

PEACE AND THE FEMALE PRINCIPLE
A Feminist Look at the Politics of Power
Bonnie Sherr Klein
134

WILL THE REAL NATASHA PLEASE STAND UP?
Women in the Soviet Union
Myrna Kostash
143

IN HIS IMAGE:
Science and Technology
Heather Menzies
156

OF MUFFINS AND MISOGYNY
REAL Women Get Real
Susan G. Cole
166

MONEY, SEX AND DEATH
The Return of the Warrior
Donna E. Smyth
177

THE MEECH BOYS
Are Women Up the Lake Without a Paddle?
Susan Riley
185

LANA SPEAKS!
C-54, Where Are You?
Timothy Findley
194

TRUE NORSE
Iceland's Women Show the Way for Newfoundland
Dorothy Inglis
202

"NELLIE, WE'VE *GOT* WASHING MACHINES"
Working Out on the Family Farm
Susan Glover
209

HUNGER
Maggie Helwig
217

EXAMINING THE ELECTION ENTRAILS:
Whatever Happened to the Gender Gap?
Thelma McCormack
224

SCRAPING THE SURFACE:
Politics and the Pap Smear
Alison Dickie
237

ABORTION JUSTICE AND THE RISE
OF THE RIGHT
Dionne Brand
246

OF MICE AND BATMEN
(or Woman as Wimp)
Judy MacDonald
252

JOCK TRAPS:
The Locker-room Door is Still Closed to Women
Helen Lenskyj
260

THE SAGA OF SPACE DORKS:
Technophilic Flying Boys from Planet Earth
Joyce Nelson
267

Chronology
274

INTRODUCTION

Dreaming the Dance

IT WAS APRIL 1972, two years after the Royal Commission on the Status of Women submitted its report to Parliament, when six hundred women from across the country met in a downtown Toronto hotel to discuss Strategies for Change. Drawn from every nook and cranny of the organized women's movement of the time, there were traditionalists and radicals alike. Alongside the stalwart ladies of the IODE were radical feminists who had more than good deeds on their minds, who had, in fact, already set up women's shelters, rape crisis centres, legal and health care clinics across the country, and were beginning to publish their own tabloids and magazines to air feminist views and raise women's voices. What came to be known as the Second Wave of feminism was well launched, gathering strength and opposition.

In political orientation as well as life experience these women might have come from different planets as well as generations and time zones. I was there as a delegate from Toronto Women's Liberation, and immediately joined with about sixty others to form a Radical Caucus. We met continually between sessions, after hours and long into the night, discussing tactics, working out an analysis of what was happening and plotting a response, among other things, to the unannounced agenda. Organized by the fledgling National Action Committee on the Status of Women (NAC), the Strategy For Change conference was funded by the federal government and had on its Steering Committee a number of powerful women with Party (Liberal and Conservative) connections and who had, many of them, been part of the force which created the RCSW in the first place. The Liberals were then in office and were definitely interested in seeing such a conference endorse the idea of a federal advisory council on the Status of Women. To the Radical Caucus, though, the whole idea was a blatant pitch to harness the activism and co-opt our desire for social change. We weren't interested in tame councils or piece-meal programs.

It was Madeleine Parent who said it. The women of Canada do not need an advisory council responsible to Parliament; they need a Parliament responsible to the women of Canada. Just as I remember Parent's clear-eyed definition of the issue twenty years later, so I remember her in that smoky caucus room. The only one over forty (never mind thirty), the one with the experience to match the analysis (on picket lines, in jail in Duplessis' Québec, and latterly on the front lines of the Canadian union movement and the formation of the Confederation of Canadian Unions). Early in life Parent had crossed class and gender lines to help organize workers, mostly women, in the textile mills of Québec. Now here she was crossing the age barrier to make common cause with a bunch of "women's libbers" who could be described as middle-class dropouts, products of the sixties counterculture, the politics of community activism and the anti-war movement's non-violent direct action. I remember being amazed by the role Parent played that weekend, moved by her easy grasp of the political and her unassailable sense of democracy. I had never met anyone like her before though I'd read about them: people who have light and know how to share it.

The conference went on, as I recall, to vote down a recommendation endorsing a government sponsored council. At just the right moment Ursula Franklin — whose name along with Madeleine Parent's I heard for the first time that day — rose and gave one of the most stunning speeches I have ever heard. She simply reminded everyone they had an obligation to listen and to respect our point of view. "They are we," she said, and with that drew the room together.

Apparently the assent of the conference was a political nicety, not a necessity. The Liberal Government went right ahead and created its Advisory Council the following year, endowing it with a minister responsible for the status of women. (The occupants of this rather archly titled cabinet post, usually male, never have seemed bothered by the double entendre.) Of course, long before the federal Advisory Council was a possibility, let alone a controversy, the need for a national focus for action and advocacy had been obvious to many women, as had the need for such a body to be completely independent and entirely controlled by women. Madeleine Parent was among those early visionaries. And in its twenty years of activism, NAC has indeed proven time and again how and why it is that women still need to speak with an independent and collective voice, to weigh into national debates, be they about free trade, the constitution, daycare or reproductive rights.

In fact, this anthology is Madeleine Parent's legacy and the connection is more than sisterslip. Around the time I first met her, Madeleine and a group of friends (including Mel Watkins, Danny Drache, Rick Salutin and later, managing editor, Lorraine Filyer) joined the collective which was publishing a very successful, small magazine about education. *This Magazine Is About Schools* began in 1966 on a Company of Young Canadians (remember?) grant, and rode the wave of the free school movement sweeping North America from California to Cabbagetown in the late sixties. The new collective took the magazine into a larger fray, shortened the name to *This Magazine* and broadened the scope to include political and cultural journalism, short fiction and poetry. The perspective, left and nationalist; the sensibility, critical and irreverent; the voice, acerbic, witty and frequently female.

So it is that Madeleine Parent had a hand in creating the magazine which welcomed the voices of feminism, which encouraged the wonderfully loud, shrill and strident opinion of women, and eventually invented a column (first called Female Complaints, now called Gender Bender) to feature that perspective. Her name hasn't been on the masthead for some years now, but it was there through most of the 1970s and 1980s.

All the writers in this volume are politically active and, like Madeleine, self-described citizens of the world and keepers of history. In our individual search for social justice and knowledge we have been shaped by quite different forces and cultural formations. We come from and belong to many communities which are, in one way or another, struggling for survival, articulation, and self-definition: the lesbian and gay communities, the women's movement, the union/peace/environmental movements, the communities of family, gender and culture. In a sense we are all marginals and seekers after alternatives: alternative solutions, alternative ways of organizing, alternative journalism. *This Magazine* allowed us a place to write what we think. Call it a vehicle for exposing the status rot, for engendering new insights, angles and tools for surviving it, the magazine's most important function has been to publish voices and stories that otherwise wouldn't be heard or seen.

It often takes an anthology to see these things. And the special pleasure of the anthologist is that she gets to see the whole cloth and to appeciate the full tapestry. This collection of feminist writing spans a decade (a baker's decade), from 1979 to 1991 and is selected from a list four times as long and as various. A list which demonstrates that women have been writing all over the map in *This Magazine*: Chile, Nicaragua, Israel, the West Bank, Greece, Russia, Yugoslavia, Granada, Cuba, outer space. The survey also reveals that women in our pages have as likely as not been there writing about nitty gritty, hard edge boy stuff (economics, the Middle East, defence policy) as nitty gritty, serrated girl stuff (reproductive rights, male violence, racism, child custody). We have written as foreign correspondents, as investigative reporters and commentators; as participants, poets, lovers and mothers.

In the eighties women published major pieces in the magazine on tax reform (Neil Brooks and Linda McQuaig's "Taxing Our Intelligence" and "OK Michael Wilson, Here's the Alternative"), on the origins of the Free Trade Deal (Joyce Nelson's "Losing it in the Lobby"), on Latin American politics (Rosemary Sullivan's "Nicaragua: Four Years After" and "Fighting Words: The Opposition Press in Chile"), and on modern Greece (Myrna Kostash's "Of Orange Pickers and Authors"). As might be expected, we have also dealt with feminist subjects and so-called women's issues, (abortion, pornography) as well as familiar themes and pleasures (art and literature, the movies). We have written about sexism in the art world, about dead poets (Joyce Wayne's "Shouting Love: Milton Acorn Remembered"), about multiculturalism and CanLit (Rosemary Sullivan's "The Mulitcultural Divide"); we've relived our experience of female sexuality, childbirth, abortion, rape, murder and death; and we've analysed the messages of the media.

Twist and Shout is, of course, borrowed from the Beatles album which came out a few months after the first *This Magazine Is About Schools* appeared. It is emblematic of an era when people celebrated political life rather than endured it like a religious duty, when people insisted we should dance at the revolution, at least occasionally. The collection consists of the Female Complaints columns which ran in the magazine between 1986 and 1991, preceeded by a section of feature pieces beginning with Margaret Atwood's "Nationalism, Socialism and Feminism in Scotland" which reads the way a radio documentary sounds, and likewise uses interviews or dialogue knit together with narration. It concludes with Moira Farr's expert investigation of the politics and pitfalls surrounding the new reproductive technologies.

In terms of the "features section," tight focus naturally limits scope and diversity, but not the acuity and invention of the writing, or the range and intensity of the intellectual engagement. Here the post-modern "female gaze" belongs to the curious traveller. Thea Jensen delves back into history to find herstory, accompanied by a present-day Basque separatist — parallels to Québec intended. Linda McQuaig takes a trip behind the Looking Glass to see the West Bank as the Israeli Government would rather a Globe and Mail reporter not see it. The past creeps into the present in other ways too. The murder of a native woman in Calgary over a century ago haunts Katherine Govier as she contemplates the meaning of Olympic Square in a city which has no centre. Lenore Keeshig-Tobias and David McLaren, native and non-native collaborators, reconstruct the moment of contact between European and native cultures drawing lessons about Free Trade and what happens when such deals are made among unequals.

Occasionally the point of view takes you by surprise. Carole Corbeil's wonderful sendup of commercialized Babyland is written from the vantage point of the innocent (?) kid in the crib. Lee Lakeman and Libby Scheier, on the other hand, return to the vast hidden territory of female experience. Scheier looks at childbirth and artistic creation in "Creativity and Motherhood: Having the Baby *and* the Book." She ruminates on the conflict women feel about their creative capacities, instincts and inspiration, while examining her own experience after the birth of her son when she exploded into poetry.

On the dark side is Lee Lakeman's diary of the Montreal Massacre, written within days of the event, in which she follows the media reportage of Marc Lepine's rampage at the Ecole Polytechnique. How he lined up fourteen women and shot them dead, blaming feminism for ruining his life. The first political assassination of feminists, Lakeman thinks, as she grapples with the enormity of it. Asking the awful questions, expressing the well-deep rage.

Sandy Frances Duncan and Fauzia Rafiq take us on another sort of journey. Though labelled fiction, "Images For A Story That Isn't" and "The Birth of a Murderer" zigzag over the line normally separating fiction from journalism. And although the voice of the narrator is quite different (close, anguished and subjective in Duncan, distant and somehow calm — which is not to say dispassionate — in Rafiq), both fold real events into an interior narrative.

Female Complaints was created at a regular Friday afternoon editorial board meeting in Rick Salutin's kitchen sometime in the winter of 1986. It was launched the following summer in the August/September issue of the magazine where Editorial Notes described it as regular feature presenting "a feminist perspective on current events in the patriarchy." Female Complaints was not intended as one writer's preserve, to be turned over occasionally to guest writers as in the case of Mel Watkins' Innis Memorial Column, Joyce Nelson's Media Tedia, and Salutin's Culture Vulture. Female Complaints was meant to circulate; its voice would be plural, its persona an amalgam of the attitudes and preoccupations of all those joining the circle.

The eighteen columns in *Twist and Shout* are not quite the entire set. Six have been pruned either because the author contributed more than one, or because the piece has been recently anthologized — a compliment to the perspecacity of editors, but a curse to anthologists. By this time you may also have noticed that not all the columnists here gathered are women. Timothy Findley was, as it happens, the only man to have offered. And as the author of one of the most profoundly feminist novels in Canadian literature (*Not Wanted On the Voyage*), and a gay man, we thought him singularly qualified to comment on male mythology and the Female Icon. "Lana Speaks" is constructed as an interview between alter egos (Findley's and Lana Turner's) and indulges in a genre ambiguity which leaves much to the reader and a good deal more to context. The piece acquires its journalistic pitch as much from the setting as a "Complaint" as from the real life reference to the government's proposed pornography (censorship) bill, C-54.

Female Complaints arrived with a bang followed by a loud clatter. The very first column, Rosemary Sullivan's "Muse in a

Female Ghetto," won a magazine award in 1987 which was unexpected and pleasant recognition. But, frankly, the feedback publications like *This Magazine* thrive on is readers' responses. And there was no doubt that our readers, regulars and irregulars, were reading Female Complaints. People loved or hated the columns. They wrote in to praise the writers and they wrote in with equal vigour to denouce them and all their works. Our intention always had been to to stir things up. We also hoped to use Female Complaints to highlight the feminist slant of the magazine as a way of attracting readers, in particular those reached through women's bookstores which often exclude books and magazines which aren't exclusively by and about women.

Hardly a column went by without reaction. Allan Chamberlain wrote in high dudgeon to accuse Donna Smyth of trotting out "trite Freudian symbolism" in "Money, Sex and Death: the Return of the Warrior" which suggests that the cause of the arms race are psycho-sexual and thus rooted in the nature of males. Lieutenant-Colonel (ret'd) Shirley M. Robinson also had a few words for Smyth. "Those of us who espouse employment equity for women cannot afford to be judgemental as to the ethics of individual job choice since we do not all share identical moral views." David Rankin cancelled his subscription after reading Myrna Kostash's "Will the Real Natasha Please Stand Up". And Heather Robertson sent a short withering note to say "This sort of strident polemic based on false assumptions is typical of Soviet and Canadian journalism at its worst". Robert Fulford wrote to say that he didn't think he'd ever said that "women's liberation had run out of steam" as I'd stated in "Post-feminism and Power Dressing". (Fulford was right. He had actually written "women protested in various polite and not polite ways; their protests were heard; and the world changed.") Adonica Huggins took both the magazine and Susan G. Cole to task for the racial stereotype repeated in the last paragraph of "Of Muffins and Misogyny". "What kind of anti-racist editorial policy exists if it allows this kind of language to be published?" she asked. Answered Cole, "It does smack of intellectual tokenism — incorporating the issue of racism for my own purposes in an article that really had nothing to do with race. I say this even though I suspect the analogy wound up being quite eloquent. But if the sensibilities of black readers ... are violated in the process of convincing readers of something, then I agree that such a casual use of stereotypes is not appropriate."

Without doubt, what really irked readers was the title. The letters and calls didn't let up for months. People told us they weren't amused, that they found it demeaning, too flip. Mary Ambrose declared it would reinforce the image of women as whiners and complainers suggesting that these reactions of anger are held by women only. "Why didn't you just call it the Bitch Box?" Eventually we felt obliged to answer. We realized not everyone would like the title but we hope(d) that the content of the column would, in time, redefine the term. Just as lesbians have taken words like "dyke" and "cunt" and invested them with positive wit and dignity, so we imagine the quality of the thinking and writing in our "Female Complaints" column will effectively reinvent the term.

Female Complaints was the creation of 21 women (and Timothy Findley); women of three generations, women living at both ends of the country on islands, and in between, in cities, small towns and on farms. They are teachers, novelists, editors, farmers, filmmakers, journalists and scholars. Because of this Female Complaints became just what we wanted it to become: a moving feminist focus on issues and ideas, positive and negative, occurring in the culture. Women and technology, sports and party politics; women in the peace movement, in the doctor's office, in the workplace, in the movies. Sometimes the view looks outwards (to Iceland, Russia), sometimes it goes inward (Maggie Helwig's new approach to anorexia in "Hunger"). The Complaints described things, asked impertinent questions, made history and occasionally offered comments on male culture, as in Joyce Nelson's "The Saga of Space Dorks: Technophilic Flying Boys from Planet Earth".

Twist and Shout is a collection of essays, observations and

fantasies, writing which, until recently, has been lumped unceremoniously together in a category called non-fiction. A no-name genre if ever there was one; described in reverse, with reference to what it isn't, like calling women non-men. During the last century "belles lettres" flourished and was understood to include a vast variety of material: memoire, travel, adventure, biography, criticism, history, essay, humour, philosophy and so on. One objective in publishing the anthology, then, has been to check for patterns and narratives and to see what sort of writing *This Magazine* has produced over the years. It could also be called a reclamation job, for while it's not unusual in Canadian letters to publish collections of journalism, it's almost unheard of to publish magazine journalism as literature.

The current resurgence of interest in the forms of documentary expression has certainly found its way into *This Magazine*, though it has gone virtually unnoticed in the literary circles. Recognition has come by the inch. Creative writing courses, workshops, and authors' festivals routinely omit both the writing and the writers, and it has taken fifteen years to persuade the Canada Council to provide the same level of support as afforded writers of other genres. Nevertheless, creative documentary has evolved over the last three decades into a tradition.

What is interesting, and what this anthology tells us, is that "non-fiction" has ceased to be regarded as a means to an end, or merely a way of funnelling information, images and messages to the public. The documentary tradition in Canadian film provides an intriguing aesthetic and formal parallel. Moreover, women have taken to it with alacrity and in large numbers. Is it possible that creative documentary is one place women have found to write their experience with some safety? Is it possible that there our voice is least adulterated and mediated? Is this the place where new methods as well as perspectives can be explored? Do they not, in fact, demand a idiosyncratic approach to research as well as language? Heather Menzies' in "In His Image" writes about the struggle to resist the de-feminization of her own research, the pressure to close off individual experience and replace it with the impersonal. And she begins with her own body, in a hospital bed following surgery for an ectopic pregnancy. Joyce Nelson is equally unafraid of the Big Topics and questions of high moral moment, as "Space Dorks" shows us. In the same vein, Dionne Brand rages with implacable and measured purpose against the fragility of women's reproductive rights and our imagined freedom of control over our own bodies. In "Abortion Justice and the Rise of the Right" she laments the fad — to be crass about it — of arrogant and determined ex-boyfriends deciding to use the courts to force their ex-lovers to have their babies. "Daigle is not a political activist but simply a woman who was forced to fight for her life. In defying the injunction against her, however, she has shown us that women's rights are not given, but taken and at high cost."

For Brand and for all of us, writing is a political act. Publishing can be too, and so it was with *Twist and Shout*. Racism has moved onto the political agenda in this country with tremendous power and urgency in the last few years. (Images of Oka, Elijah Harper and Ovide Mercredi, Ethel Blondin and Helen Betty Osborne flash across the contemporary screen.) The women's movement, no less than the left, no less than the trade union movement, no less than the artistic community, has heard the demands that barriers be removed and systematic racism confronted. And one of the venues where confrontation took place, the Women's Press in Toronto, led directly to the creation of a second press and sparked a debate which continues still about cultural appropriation and voice. Because of this recent history, the choice of publisher for this anthology led to discussion with two Black writers about their presence in it. For Lillian Allen the wounds of that debate are not yet healed and her choice was not to appear here. Dionne Brand accepted because of her commitment to *This Magazine*, despite misgivings.

And so the process unfolds. Like the creative itch in the brain Sandy Frances Duncan writes of, I believe in the efficacy of cultural knocks. When real political differences are acted out there usually is pain and dislocation. And there aren't any shortcuts to understanding, enlightenment or poetry. In the end, we have to believe in the positive purpose of those mistakes, trust the irritation to produce changes in language, to create awareness.

So, let's dance to that dream.

Susan Crean
Gabriola Island, British Columbia
April, 1992

NATIONALISM, SOCIALISM AND FEMINISM

Margaret Atwood in Scotland

Margaret Atwood

I SPENT THE WINTER AND SPRING of 1978-79 in Scotland. Before this sojourn, my image of Scotland was straight out of Walter Scott novels and tourist brochures: mists, castles, bagpipes and haggises, and quaint people who recited Robbie Burns poems and pinched pennies. I knew about the massacre at Glencoe, Bonnie Prince Charlie and the battle of Culloden, and the Highland Clearances, but these were history book events to me; I could not imagine what consequences they might have had for present-day Scotland.

Spending time in a country plays havoc with your clichés. Yes, the stores on Princes Street in Edinburgh were full of kilts and woolies and, for those of us with dubious taste, tinned tartan underpants; yes, taxi drivers did say — occasionally — "Cheerio the noo." But these things bore about the same relation to Scotland as plastic Mounties and ersatz Inuit carvings in airport junkshops bear to Canada.

It was tempting, initially, to draw parallels between Scotland and Canada. Apart from the obvious influence Scotland had on Canada, through its immigrants, in the 19th century (one calculation has it that for every thirteen English immigrants, there were ten Scotsmen: high in view of their relative populations), there was the self-evident paradigm: a small nation struggling against the odds (roughly ten to one in both cases) and against the overwhelming economic and cultural influence of a large southern neighbour to maintain or regain its independence.

But the parallels are not exact. Scotland has centuries of recorded history and a distinct (though largely unspoken) language to fall back on. On the other hand, it's politically one with England. Although it has its own legal tradition, educational establishment, and local governing units, it is *de facto* ruled from London. As Scots pointed out over and over again, Canada has one advantage: its separate political structure. Canadians, looking at the content of that structure, may smile ironically; but the structure does exist.

While I was in Scotland, two events of significance — the Welsh-Scottish football match aside — took place there: (1) Scots voted on a proposal for Devolution, a scheme that would have given Scotland its own political structure in the form of a National Assembly, and, by Westminster's reckoning anyway, they lost; (2) Mrs. Thatcher won the British election, over the heaped-up electoral bodies of the Scots.

I talked with several Scottish Nationalists about these developments: among them an academic, a Scottish Nationalist Capitalist, a Vice-Chairman of the Scottish National Party (SNP), and a Scottish Nationalist Feminist. I've reproduced the latter two here. I was trying to make sense of what had just happened, for my own benefit as well as for that of the Canadian reader. What was going on? Whither Scotland?

In June I talked with Stephen Maxwell, who is one of the five Vice-Chairmen of the Scottish National Party. He seems very young to hold such an exalted position, and though he walked thirty miles, pushing a man in a wheelchair, to the traditional SNP celebration of the Battle of Bannockburn, he's hardly the image of the kilted eccentric I'd associated with the SNP before I came to Scotland. As usual, I wanted to know how he'd ended up where he was.

When I was growing up in England, I'd always had a sentimental interest in Scotland, a sort of Jacobite interest if you like. It wasn't until I was at University — again in England — that I was introduced to the first volume of collected poems published by Hugh MacDiarmid, and in the same year to a volume called *The Democratic Intellect* by George Elver-Davie, which was an attempt to describe a tradition of democratic access to university education in Scotland. Reading them convinced me that perhaps there was more to the Scottish identity than the sort of Jacobite sentimentality which had attracted me a few years earlier.

Could you explain "Jacobite sentimentality"?

In the 18th century there were two revolts in Scotland against the Hanoverian English dynasty. Walter Scott and other 19th century Scottish writers romanticized the Jacobite rebellion and made it a part of the Scottish romantic identity in the 19th century, and it lived on as that into the 20th century.

What are your views on the Devolution vote? Why was it a No vote?

Well, in fact it *was* a *Yes* vote by the principle of the bare majority, because 52 percent of those who actually used their vote voted *Yes*. It was interpreted by Westminster and by sections of opinion in Scotland as a *No* vote because Westminster had imposed something called the 40 percent rule (which was opposed in Westminster by the majority of Scottish MPs — it was imposed by the English MPs). It required that 40 percent of all those eligible to vote would have to vote *Yes* before the legislation setting up the Scottish assembly would be implemented. And in fact in the end just 33 percent of those who were qualified to vote voted *Yes*.

As for why — the legislation had been very long in gestation. It was mooted way back in 1975, shortly after the SNP's breakthrough in the general elections of 1974, when we got just over 30 percent of the vote and forced the Labour and Conservative parties to make concessions to nationalist feeling in Scotland.

Both parties then came forward with proposals to set up an elected Scottish legislature. The first bill was defeated in the House of Commons, voted down by a majority of English MPs against the wishes of the majority of Scottish MPs. The second bill was an even weaker bill than the first. It had a very long and troubled parliamentary career and was amended several times, making it even less attractive, and I think in the end wide sections of Scottish opinion just got bored with it. During the referendum campaign itself the Assembly was identified as a source of more bureaucracy, more jobs for the boys, and more expenditure.

There's a section of opinion that feels that faulty though the legislation was, one still ought to have voted Yes *and then worked out the problems afterwards; that a* Yes *vote would have been an emotional affirmation of separate government for Scotland.*

Yes. The fact is, the bill as it finally emerged from Parliament had very few firm supporters, that is, people who were prepared to argue for it strictly on its merits. Most people are prepared to argue for it as a necessary expedient to satisfy nationalism or from the nationalist side — from the SNP side — as a first step on the road to independence. So the bill had few defenders on its own merits. The Conservatives, who had previously been committed to the principle of an elected Scottish legislature, in fact campaigned very vigorously in the end for a *No* vote on the grounds that this particular bill was inadequate as an expression of their support for Devolution.

Do you think that Labour made a crummy bill on purpose so that they would get a No *vote?*

Well, I think that if Westminster had deliberately set out to bore the pants off the Scottish voter through Devolution, then they pursued the right strategy. I think quite a lot of people in Westminster and perhaps in the Labour Party in Scotland were hoping that there'd be a *No* vote. Certainly I shouldn't think more than perhaps a third of the activists in the Labour Party actually campaigned for a *Yes* vote.

*Then came the national election in which Mrs. Thatcher won, and the
SNP lost all but two of their previous seats. Do you connect the loss of the
referendum with the subsequent loss of seats for the SNP?*

I don't think it's the whole explanation. Throughout the
United Kingdom, perhaps throughout Western Europe, there is
at the moment a swing to the right in politics. In England that
expressed itself through a considerable switch of the Labour vote
to the Conservative party. In Scotland, because of rather different
economic conditions, it expressed itself as a swing to the traditional opponent of the Conservative party, the Labour party, as a
reaction against the right wing move in England and the pros-
pect of another right wing government which would probably
cut subsidies of aid to the Scottish economy. The SNP, against the
background of the referendum, just didn't have enough purchase
on the working class votes that it had won in the period 1974-76
to prevent that swing back to Labour.

*I've heard it argued that the SNP is a kind of double party. On the one
hand you have the Tartan Tories, who are essentially conservative, and I
guess Jacobite sentimentalists, and on the other hand you have a left wing
element. Can you say a few words about this division and the party's
relation to socialism?*

I think until about 1967 — certainly until the late 1960s —
the SNP was seen predominantly as a conservative party, a small
"c" conservative party. It was accused of being Tartan Tory in the
party political sense, though it was also accused of being Tartan
Socialist. It shouted the odds for independence without feeling
an obligation to spell out just what independence would mean in
terms of the sort of economy and society Scotland would be. And
then around the late 1960s into the 1970s, the SNP did manage
to strike a more radical position in the Scottish electorate and
from 1973-76 established itself as a credible alternative to the
Labour Party, for many working class voters in Scotland. What
has happened in the last two or three years is that, partly as a
response to the disillusionment with Westminster's treatment of
the Devolution issue, and partly as a reaction to the disappoint-

ing electoral fortunes of the party, there's been a fairly strong swing within the SNP *back* to a fundamentalist position — away from the more radical position which the party adopted for three or four years. At the moment the fundamentalists are very much in the ascendency in the party.

Independence, nothing less, as they say.
　　But also nothing *more*. Not for the sake of doing something else with it.

Would I be putting you on the spot to ask you about your feelings on that?
　　No, not in the least. My own feelings are that the party will never consolidate its votes to create a solid mandate for self-government unless it establishes a firm social base, and that firm social base — given Scotland's particular problems and history — can only lie in the working class of Scotland.

Let's move to a problem which is also Canada's. If your recent history and your recent identity have been one of a colony — a cultural colony — and if other elements in your tradition don't seem particularly desirable, what is nationalism for?
　　I think in any country in the modern world nationalism has got to be basically innovative, and it's got to be concerned with creating a new identity, rather than simply defending an identity handed down by history. Even the earlier phase of cultural nationalism in Scotland, in the 1920s and 1930s, as represented by Hugh MacDiarmid, was an attempt not simply to preserve or to recover a language which had been used in the 14th to 16th centuries for Scottish literature, but also to reinterpret or apply that language to dealing with modern dilemmas, and Hugh MacDiarmid's achievement was that he almost accomplished that. He did not recreate Scots as a language through which one could discuss the problems of the 20th century.

Let me ask you a Utopian question. Suppose the SNP had won by some overwhelming majority and that Scotland also at the same time had got the Assembly; how would you redesign Scotland if you were in charge of it?

That certainly seems, in the light of recent election results, Utopian. In the economy, the private sector in Scotland is very, very weak; the Scottish economy is dominated by either public corporations controlled by London, or multinational corporations, so that *if* the Scottish sector was to be expanded, as presumably almost any sort of Scottish government would wish to see happen, it could only be through a massive extension of the public sector, and of course the Scottish government controlling the oil revenues would have to provide the capital to finance this. Similarly, if the Scottish government had any social conscience at all, then it would have to take a fairly radical action to solve some of the problems of poverty that exist as a result of the industrial revolution. In Scotland we still have something like one fifth of the population living on or very close to the official poverty line; that's the level of income at which you qualify for supplementary benefits, and obviously to cure a problem of *that* scale you'd need a very large diversion of money into the public sector. So I think a Scottish government — unless it was ideologically of the right, which would be a bit unlikely in view of Scotland's voting history, would be a government which would be committed to fairly massive extensions of the public sector.

Let me finish with a practical question. How do you see the future of the SNP, say within the next ten years?

Well, assuming that the fundamentalists are dominant, as it looks as if they will be, for the next few years anyway...

Unless you raid Labour again...

Well, yes, that's the thing. I think as a fundamentalist party we will be in a position to get the protest vote again, and the circumstances we face now in Scotland are not unlike those we faced in 1970 when a Tory government was returned on the back of the English vote. Scotland voted predominantly Labour and, within eighteen months of that election result, the SNP was picking up support, predominantly from Labour voters, on a fairly dramatic scale. Now, assuming the party's in a fundamentalist mood, I think we'll still be able to get that protest vote. The problem will be how we consolidate it, and I would be very frightened if we simply go through much the same cycle we've been through *since* 1970. If we follow that sort of cycle it's going to be a long time before we get a large enough base to claim a mandate for self-government. That's why I think there's got to be a debate over the next five years or so as to how we do consolidate. It'll be a debate between people to the left of centre in the party, who are a minority at the moment, and the fundamentalists.

The last person I talked with was Aileen Christianson, who is connected with the Rape Crisis Centre in Edinburgh and has just begun to write a book on women in Scotland. Scotland is not exactly a hotbed of feminism; in fact, in the pinky-white English-speaking world, it probably ranks second only to Australia. (It also ranks second in the consumption of sweets, which raises disturbing questions on the linkage between male chauvinism and sugar consumption.) I knew Aileen much better than I knew the three others I interviewed; she was, for instance, an unfailing guide to cheap eateries, strange films, and other delights. Our conversation was thus more informal, and there was some hooting and cackling, as well as more self-expression on the part of the interviewer. I started by asking Aileen how she'd become a nationalist and a feminist.

It may have to do with being an adopted Scot in the sense of having been brought up in Scotland by English parents, but educated totally in Scotland, in the Scottish system, so there was a lot of Scottish stuff getting fed into me, but there's also a lot of North of England obsessions, like social equality; there's the fact of being a girl brought up in an almost all-female household, in an all-girl's school, who just assumed she was equal because there was no evidence to the contrary. So there were a lot of hangups that didn't get fed in, because of the protectiveness.

But then when you came out of the cocoon and encountered reality...

Well, I still figured I was equal. At University I was more than equal to most of the blokes, frankly, because I had the advantage of articulation which may have come from my middle classness, or it may have come from my English parents. A lot of the blokes were Scottish and fairly inarticulate; I could talk circles around them. But when the whole women's movement happened, basically from 1970 on in Scotland, here was what I believed all my life being expressed externally for the first time. It was a great relief. Suddenly there's an external theory for it, but it *had* existed incoherently in my head before that. The Scottish thing didn't become certain until later because I had always been beaten about the head with my Englishness by my Scottish contemporaries — "you can't be Scottish because you've got English parents" — and it wasn't until I was in my late twenties that I thought, this is ridiculous, of course I'm Scottish — I don't want to live anywhere else, I've never lived anywhere else — I've got all the hangups and all the guilt complexes the Scots have got.

So from then on you've got the two together. And the nationalist thing, again, also comes along with the Scottishness — though I'm not a member of the Scottish National Party; I never voted for them until this year.

So you see it as the logical consequence of your Scottishness...

Yeah, yeah, everything follows along neatly. The Rape Centre involvement happened this year because I had avoided it like the plague earlier; it's hard work and it's depressing and takes a lot of energy, but there came a point when it was time to get involved in something practical. Just like the book on Scottish women — again, it was the logical conclusion after the Devolution referendum was lost, and I had been cracking myself up to try to get into straight politics because I thought it was necessary for women to get into the Assembly right at the beginning. Couldn't do that — it's been ruined by the way the vote went, and the anger I felt about that actually led into what I could *do*. I'm a researcher, I'm a historian, I'm a Scot, I'm a feminist.

Now, being a socialist, a feminist, and a nationalist, I wonder whether you have the problems here *that other socialists, feminists, and nationalists sometimes have across the water, notably in Québec and English-*

speaking Canada. Or I should say that I have these problems. If you're a socialist, the feminists and nationalists get after you. Why waste your time on those other things? If you're a feminist, the nationalists and socialists come after you and tell you that feminism's an Americanized movement or a bourgeois movement and you really ought to be spending time on their thing, and if you're a nationalist both the others get after you and say it's fascist or it's regressive or it's petty bourgeois or it's male-dominated, and you ought to give that up and put your energies in with us. Do you find this happening to you, and do you find any conflict within yourself among these three things?

Yup, absolutely, absolutely.

Absolutely what?

Absolutely all three. The women's movement, because it's the newest, is still going through a lot of splits — very much along these sorts of lines — because there aren't enough women to do the work which needs to be done, and so if you become distracted by other tasks you're seen as taking energy away.

Just the other week I was told by another woman who wanted to stand for the Assembly that I could not be objective about, for example, the Scottish National Party, because I had friends in it and therefore I couldn't see that they were actually patriarchal, too straight, whatever.

Well, it must be admitted that most of the people running those movements are men.

Oh absolutely. My resentment was that she couldn't see that I was quite capable of being objective about them, but that one uses what's available.

Do you find any sort of ideological conflict between...

In myself?

Do you think it's real conflict or a conflict imposed by the people who happen to be partisans of one or more movements?

I think it's both, I think it's a real conflict and it's imposed.

On the socialist side there are women I know who are much more committed to left politics, who are committed to a class analysis and who *therefore* do not necessarily see Scottish women as being any worse off than English women, Canadian, American, whichever women — they see Scottish working women being *as* badly *off* as North of England working class women, suffering from the same kinds of oppressions, but they would see the class struggle as being *more* important and would have very little sympathy with, for instance, a lot of feminist consciousness-raising which they see as middle class...

Chit-chat?

Yes. I get that conflict in myself, between the pulls toward practical action and the pulls toward analysis — self-analysis.

I'm more naturally inclined to the analysis because it's easier; it's less outrageous to my system, whereas practical work is hard work, you have to go out and face people and they're frightening. Like leafleting in Edinburgh, on issues like abortion or rape. It's horrendous; it reminds you of what ordinary people can be like — how nasty they can be in their responses to you, how stereotyped, how sexist, how...

Rude?

Rude — but also how oddly nice and open others can be. I mean, if you're handing out feminist leaflets in the street in Edinburgh, the number of couples — the man will grab for it when you're giving it to the woman and not let the woman see it or insist that he should see it first. There's no real awareness of the fact that now there are things which we would want to give just to women; there's no grasp of that in the bulk of the people...

I don't feel that the conflict is necessary. I don't feel it's a real conflict; on the most abstract level it seems to me that each of these things is a function of the other, that you can't have — in Canada anyway — you can't have a real feminism if you allow it to be dominated by American feminism. On the other hand you can't have a real socialism unless both of those other things are taken into consideration — it just becomes another piece of cultural imperialism in which you are dominated by an ideology from abroad...

Yes...

...whether it be from Germany or from Russia or from the States; if you just take the Marxism of somewhere else and try to squeeze your own country into it, you get a distortion; you've got to start with what is there.

Yeah, I agree with that.

I don't think it's a necessary conflict but it's certainly seen as a conflict by other people.

I do agree with all of that, but for agreeing with that I would be seen by each of those three groups — hardliners in each of those three groups — as a liberal liker, someone who sees both sides of questions and sits on fences and does balancing acts and so on and so forth — and it's only the hardliners — I mean there's a number of blurred people on the edges, and there's lots of us who actually belong in all these camps, with slightly different viewpoints, but the hardliners, they don't like it when we straddle madly...

Yes, well I grew up being told what I should be, and I'm not too amenable to that any more whether it be by the Girl Guides or by anyone else. I think women are brought up thinking that they have to make sacrifices, and I think it's an imposition really to expect you to cut off your arms in favour of your legs — which is what all this is. Anyway, I shouldn't talk so much — I'm interviewing you. Let's go on to practical views, the actual position of women in Scotland, if you can make such a broad generalization. First, their political position in relation to, for instance, England. Are they actually involved in politics; are they recognized as much as they are in England?

It's difficult, some people say, in fact they are *not* more oppressed, that up and until the 1960s the legal position of women in Scotland was often better than the position of women in England, and what has happened since then is that certain legal improvements which have happened in England have not yet been implemented in Scotland, and so they have fallen back — for instance, the domestic violence bill has been lost because of the elections and so it will take more time for that to come back in. There does seem to be an assumption which seems to be true, that a lot of wife battering goes on in Scotland, and that's mixed up with things like alcoholism and economic deprivation...

I was talking to someone who felt that possibly the incidence of rape was lower because women aren't allowed out on their own as much, but that wife battering and domestic rape were a lot higher.

It's extremely high. In the 19th century times and earlier I don't think women were any worse off than anywhere else, but at the moment probably legally they *are*, and it's reinforced simply because of the anomaly of Scottish law not being amended at the same time as English law. This comes back to why we should have had the Assembly in Scotland; there would have been opportunity to change the law in Scotland *as* it affects women, rather than having to wait for the MPs in Westminster to get round to it. But, for instance, they did not have abortion legislation proposed for the Assembly, because they were afraid the Scots would be more conservative than the English. They're all frightened of this, the so-called Catholic vote in the West of Scotland, but it hasn't been proven really, that Scotland would necessarily have been more conservative where women are concerned.

In terms of social attitudes, I think that Scotland is more conservative; women are more put down. Just as England is behind the United States, so Scotland is behind England — London anyway.

I've heard the view expressed that Scotland is really a matriarchy.

Ach yes, that's one of their favourites, and that Scottish women bring up their sons to be pigs, they, they — what's the favourite thing?... that they are more than partly responsible for it, in just the way in which Black women are supposed to be bringing up their sons in a matriarchy; I mean the blame is always on the women.

In other words, if there's streetfighting you might as well make sure that your son can streetfight, otherwise he's going to get killed?
Right, right.

They say things like, the working man comes home and gives his wife all his money for housekeeping money, and therefore she runs him...
There's an awful lot of drinking and an awful lot of money going on. And the same wife they supposedly give the money to is the same wife they beat up when they get drunk — so what are they getting drunk with before they beat her up? I mean it's all the same woman who's being given all this money and controlling everything, and also being beaten up.

It's a matriarchy like Jewish society is a matriarchy; the women have no real power so they have the power in the home, but they've got no real power outside, so to hell with that kind of matriarchy.

Okay, here's a lay it on the line question. Do you think it would be better for women in an independent Scotland than it is now? In other words, what do you think feminists would get out of supporting the movement for independence?
What we would gain — we mightn't gain a lot — what we have got is a very hard fight at the moment; it's really tiring, it's like beating your head against a brick wall...

This as a feminist?
As a feminist, *also* as a socialist *and* as a nationalist. Particularly as a feminist because you're beating your head against *all* the brick walls and the fact that it is still a very male-dominated society, and even if Scottish women aren't necessarily worse off than English women, despite one's suspicions. So you do it because, though it is like beating your head against a brick wall, on the other hand there's the water on the stone theory, and you keep

dripping away on it — eventually you'll wear it away. Independence wouldn't be any different in that sense. There would still be a lot of hard work to be done, against the men — or maybe with the men, if one was optimistic. Those attitudes — the male attitudes — would not be changed by independence. They might be hardened; they might be just the same.

However, with either, say, independence *or* greater legislative autonomy within the United Kingdom as a whole, there would be a better chance for agitating, for pressurizing, for working through the system, which would be right here on our doorstep. It's *expensive* to go to London and lobby and so on and so forth. Also, the English women's movement, they have their own problems; they can support us in a very *general* sense but they're not really gonna have time for our campaigns when they've got their *own* to run. So in *that* sense it's closer to home; it's easier to agitate, your rail fares are less, in practical terms. It would also be a newer system, whether it was independence or Devolution, and there might be some chance of getting in there, getting more women in at the beginning, things might be less jelled, less solidified; so there might be some chance of starting from the beginning to change attitudes — not necessarily — I mean, they were called Assemblymen *already* — they were being called Assemblymen before the referendum, instead of members of the Assembly or whatever...

Here too you can say two things about women in relation to men who are themselves colonialized and oppressed. One is to say well, forget about feminism for now and stand...
No Way!

stand by your men, that was once the Black women's position in the States — because the men are such downtrodden creatures, so that you've got to support them and be a mother figure and buoy them up and inject energy into them and...
Yes, yes...

...their balls are falling off anyway so why should you cut away at them any more. And the answer to that is why should women be the whipping boy, the whipping girl *for that particular one; in other words why should they sacrifice any more than they already have, to inject a bit of adrenalin into some men. Let the men cook up their own adrenalin...*

That's where feminism comes first, that's where it would come for me anyway.

So sex precedes class and nation...?

In that way, yeah — it's like the socialists being offered pie in the sky by the Christians in the 19th century — there's no way we want it; we're not prepared to wait till after the revolution because — besides, our revolution if we're just straight feminists is different anyway; it's to do with getting rid of *men,* in lots of ways...

So, if we're not straight feminist, if we're feminist socialists, there's really no way that we can have the pie in the sky; it's not possible any more to work for the revolution and *then* get sexual equality afterwards, because it wouldn't come of course, it wouldn't follow — there's no way it would follow...

So you're not gonna lick envelopes for the SNP?

Hell, no!

Margaret Atwood is the author of *The Handmaid's Tale* and *Cat's Eye.* Her most recent book, *Wilderness Tips,* is a collection of short stories.

REFLECTIONS OF REALITY

A Canadian Reporter in the West Bank

Linda McQuaig

ON THE ISRAELI GOVERNMENT TOUR of the West Bank, one sees few Arabs. This is no small feat since the tiny strip of land contains some 750,000 of them. As the government van winds its way through the dry, rolling hills, the guide for the press tour of visiting journalists — two South Africans and myself — points out the spanking-white Jewish settlements which come into view. He makes no mention of the Arab communities in the distance — more earth-toned in colour and tucked into the side of the hills instead of standing commandingly on top of them.

The tour guide — kind of a hip New York-born Israeli in his early thirties — doesn't talk much about the Arabs. He's more interested in telling us about life in the new Jewish settlements Israel is building on the West Bank — the Arab-populated land which Israel seized from Jordan in the 1967 Arab-Israeli war. One of the few references he makes to the Arabs comes at the outset of the trip when he puts a rifle in the front of the van. This is just to protect us in case Arab youths on the West Bank throw stones at us, he explains. I'd read about this stone throwing before and even knew the Israelis carried guns in their cars. But still it takes me aback to see the rifle right there with us in the van. As we drive along roads near Arab settlements, I find myself flinching, half expecting a stone. (One never comes.)

I feel much more at ease when we stop for lunch at one of the Jewish settlements. It's cool and sunny, and we sit on a patio eating falafels and humus. It's really nice here. Occasionally an Israeli soldier strolls by with a machine gun slung over his shoulder. But the sight of him isn't scary; strangely it's almost comforting. Our guide points to the underground bunker on the settlement where the settlers will hide if an Arab country invades the West Bank. Jets flash noisily across the sky above us, but I am assured that they are only Israeli planes on maneouvre. Nothing to worry about. And at the end of the day when the van passes back into Israel, the guide jokes that now we can all relax; nobody's going to throw stones. To my surprise, I do suddenly feel relaxed.

But I am also left with the disturbing feeling that I am seeing things inside out, that the Israelis, with their tanks and guns and warplanes, have managed to make themselves look like they are the victims here. The Palestinian youths — often children — who throw stones somehow look like the aggressors. Inside the Israeli van it is easy to forget that Israel has imposed a strict military dictatorship on the Palestinian Arabs here for 17 years. And in recent years Israel has mounted an extremely costly campaign to move Jews into state-subsidized settlements throughout the West Bank. There are now some 40,000 Jewish settlers living here — all heavily armed — who seem to consider this their land. Certainly Israel appears to have no plans to leave.

But it is easy to forget all this when a stone is coming at you, or when you think a stone may be coming at you. From the van, the Palestinians look undeniably foreign, don't speak English, wear funny clothes and, above all, look at us in the same hostile way that they regard the Israelis.

The Israelis, on the other hand, seem incredibly North American and easy to relate to. The tour guide with his American accent keeps up a friendly banter throughout the trip and reminds me of a number of people I knew at university. At the Jewish settlement of Ariel we are given a tour by Dina Salit, a thirty-five-year-old Canadian from Montreal who moved to the West

Bank with her husband and three children last year. "If you have a right to the land, you've got to exercise it," she explains, as she points out Ariel's new townhouses and the site where the settlement's country club will be built.

But I get that down home Canadian feeling most sharply when I go for an interview set up by the Israeli press office, with a spokeswoman for the West Bank's civilian administration — the Israeli government body that oversees the West Bank. The building that houses the civilian administration is surrounded by walls and barbed wire and men with machine guns — which I guess indicates just how civilian it is. Inside, I am shown to the office of Captain Elise Shazar — a young woman who grew up in none other than Port Credit, about twenty miles from Toronto, where I grew up. Before we settle down to the interview, we talk about what Port Credit was like before it became the present sprawling suburban community of Mississauga, best known for a dramatic train derailment. Is this Israel or did I make a wrong turn and end up at Yorkdale Shopping Centre? Am I paranoid or is there reason to suspect that the Israeli press office is planting these Canadians in my path?

Certainly the image of the hostile Palestinian and the friendly Canadian-born Israeli can't help but make me feel sympathetic to Israelis and their concerns — a major step forward for Israel in getting across its message. So maybe it's not so wild to think that Israel plans it this way. Certainly, having experienced the efficiency of the Israeli press office, nothing would surprise me.

I was told to check in at the foreign press office as soon as I arrived. (There is a whole division of the foreign press office which deals exclusively with visiting foreign press.) I explain who I'd like to interview and on which subjects. By the next day, a press officer has lined up a long list of interviews, including some that I hadn't asked for. He keeps arranging more and, within a few days, all of my ten days here are virtually booked. He's drawn up a schedule for me which will keep me running constantly between Israeli government offices and universities. But wait. One of the things I really wanted to check out over here was the fate of the West Bank Palestinians. Apparently there's no time for that. I suggest to my press officer that some of the interviews he's booked aren't necessary. He doesn't argue, just indicates that they had been difficult to arrange. In the end, I get tremendous satisfaction out of canceling the interview with an Israeli cabinet minister — a minor one, but still a cabinet minister — in order to make time to see Bassam Shaka'a, the Palestinian mayor who lost his legs in a car bomb attack.

The press office plays a key role in explaining Israeli actions to the world. And it goes to considerable lengths to make those actions look acceptable by western standards. Take the prickly issue of land seizure, for instance. Apart from its overall military occupation of the West Bank, Israel has been seizing individual Arab-owned properties there since 1967. And while it can more easily argue that its military occupation is necessary for self-defence, it is harder for Israel to explain why it must take land from Arab farmers and hand it over to Jews to build bedroom communities for Israeli cities. When I ask about these land seizures, the press office gives me a long, detailed bulletin that explains there has been a misunderstanding: Israel does not seize private lands, it only takes over "state lands." This sounds better.

But the concept of state lands turns out to be just a tricky legalistic device. Under old laws dating back to the Ottoman Empire, which controlled the West Bank in the 19th century, property owners who cultivate less than 50 percent of their land or who do not cultivate it for a certain period of time automatically lose it to the Sultan. Israel, which now controls the area, has substituted itself for the Sultan and laid claim to land that does not meet cultivation requirements — which is common on the rocky slopes of the West Bank. Israel also claims that property is state land if the owners are unable to provide adequate documentation to prove it is theirs. Palestinian lawyer Elias Khoury explains that proof of ownership is hard to establish since West Bank inhabitants traditionally defined their boundaries informally. "They would say the land stretches to Mohammed's property on the south, the valley to the east, Ishmail's to the west and so on," he explains.

A Palestinian who suddenly finds his land declared state land can appeal — to a tribunal appointed by the Israeli military. There is no appeal above the tribunal. Khoury, who argues cases before the tribunal, says he cannot remember a Palestinian ever winning one of these appeals.

I suppose it is not surprising that Israel is obsessed with the image it presents to the western world through the press. After all, it owes its survival largely to the enormous military and economic aid it receives each year from the U.S. government, as well as the private donations from the North American Jewish community. It is important to maintain public sympathy in Canada and the U.S. Much of the task will be accomplished if Israel can convince North American readers that Israelis are, after all, just like them and Palestinians are all members of a Moslem terrorist band. By keeping the Palestinians largely out of view — a distant, dark people who throw stones at passing cars — it is possible to portray them this way. The image breaks down almost immediately upon meeting them.

At the Kalandia refugee camp on the West Bank it is hard not to be struck by an overwhelming sense of injustice. The refugees, many of them second and third generation homeless, once lived in towns and villages in what is now Israel but were driven out in the Israeli war of independence. Many of them have lived here since then, cared for largely by the United Nations' Relief and Works Agency. They live in shacks and rely on the UN body for food, but UN funding is being cut back now. Outside the spartan lunchroom, children wait to be admitted for a UN-subsidized meal. When I go to take their picture, they eagerly pose, a few of them raising their fingers in a V for Victory to the Palestine Liberation Organization (PLO), while covering their faces so they won't be identifiable. It is illegal to show support for the PLO. The small building at the camp that serves as a community centre has been shut for months. The Israeli military ordered it closed after complaints that children from the camp had thrown stones at passing Israeli cars. There is an Israeli jeep parked on the main road that runs through the camp, and soldiers with machine guns lounge inside it, listening to transistor radios. The main entrance to the camp has been sealed off, and rolls of barbed wire spread in front of it.

Nearby, in the village of El Jeep, the Israeli army has recently bulldozed the home of a widow whose twenty year old son was arrested for questioning about the murder of a Jewish settler. The woman, Najeh Sha'alan, is now staying at a neighbour's house with her five children. She says that the night her son was arrested, she woke up to find her house surrounded by the army. They gave her five minutes to get out and then flattened the place. Two weeks later, there are still no charges against her son. We walk through the rubble and she points out bits of furniture, clothing, parts of a bed.

In Nablus, the legless mayor, Bassam Shaka'a, lives in a pretty stone house high up on a hill. He greets me from his wheelchair. The Palestinian taxi driver who has brought me is clearly thrilled to meet Shaka'a, one of the revered figures on the West Bank. The three of us and Shaka'a's wife sit down for tea. In the west, Shaka'a is considered something of a radical, so I was surprised to discover him to be a fifty-three-year-old businessman. His family owns a successful local soap factory and he and his wife look like a conservative middle class couple. With an appropriate business suit and a pair of legs, he could pass for president of the Brampton Chamber of Commerce.

Shaka'a's troubles began shortly after he was elected mayor of the West Bank city of Nablus in 1976. He recalls that he found himself under constant pressure from Israeli authorities to stop his people from demonstrating or expressing discontent with the Israeli occupation. Rather than letting him represent his people, the Israelis wanted him to police them, he says. The bomb that tore off his legs one June morning in 1980 was probably the work of Jewish terrorists. But Shaka'a remains convinced that the Israeli authorities were involved. Whether they were or not, they have harassed him before and since in just about every conceivable way, he says. His house is under twenty-four-hour police guard, and police follow him every time he leaves. They also follow Arab visitors who come to see him. In 1982, two years after the bombing, Israel dismissed him as mayor along with six other elected West Bank mayors who refused to cooperate.

I also visited the home of the Abu Taa family in East Jerusalem — part of the West Bank which Israel unilaterally annexed in 1967. A year later Israel expropriated nine acres of the Abu Taa property without compensation, bulldozing the family's olive groves to erect a six-storey government office building and parking lot. The Abu Taa family is now used to the sight of bulldozers on their property, knocking over a fence or clearing out some more olive trees. When I visited the family, the bulldozers had just claimed a few more yards for the parking lot.

The eighty-four-year-old grandmother shows me where her trees have been uprooted. The scene is strangely reminiscent of the kinds of situations championed in North American newspapers — an elderly person vowing never to leave, bulldozers ready to roll. It could be a tenant somewhere in Canada being kicked out of her home by an insensitive developer. I don't know why, but I find it particularly moving to watch this old woman look so longingly at her gnarled trees lying on the ground. Maybe the real terror — car bombs and midnight house demolitions — are just too remote to seem real. But there is something so simple and familiar in this scene.

Back at the King David Hotel, Israel's beautiful old palace-like hotel in downtown Jerusalem, I am having drinks with a South African journalist I met on the government press tour of the West Bank. The drinks are expensive and the decor in the bar makes it look like any downtown Toronto hotel. The clientele also seems very North American. The South African journalist works for a liberal anti-apartheid publication and seems liberal himself. He's almost at the end of his five week assignment here to prepare a large special report on Israel. But I am surprised to discover that in five weeks, the only time he has spent on the

West Bank was with the government press tour. He has met no Palestinians. It seems the Israeli press office has kept him busy talking, I guess, to every official and professor in the country. I ask him if he would like to come with me to visit Bassam Shaka'a. He's never heard of Shaka'a, which is odd since the mayor is quite well known both inside and outside Israel. He finds the story of Shaka'a interesting, but declines to come, explaining that an Israeli hotel in the pleasant seaside town of Eilat has offered him free accommodation. He figures he can write a travel piece and get in a little sun-bathing.

And so it is that the liberal audience in South Africa will get a travel piece on the beaches of Eilat instead of a few ugly details of what its ally Israel is doing on the West Bank. Thank God for the free press.

In 17 years as a journalist, Linda McQuaig has covered a wide range of subjects, from the revolution in Iran to the financial dealings of Canada's establishment. She has worked for *Maclean's*, CBC Radio and *The Globe and Mail*, where she was most recently a national political reporter. Her investigation of what became known as the Patti Starr affair won her a National Newspaper Award in 1989. Her first book, *Behind Closed Doors: How the Rich Won Control of Canada's Tax System...and Ended Up Richer*, was an exposé of the inequities in Canada's tax system. In 1991 she published *The Quick and the Dead: Brian Mulroney, Big Business and the Seduction of Canada*.

CREATIVITY AND MOTHERHOOD

Having the Baby AND the Book

Libby Scheier

"THAT WOMEN SHOULD HAVE BABIES rather than books is the considered opinion of Western civilization," the American poet Alicia Ostriker notes in her 1983 book *Writing Like a Woman*. "That women should have books rather than babies is a variation on that theme," she continues. Like many women, I was influenced by this two-headed myth. Looking over my notebooks recently, I saw that six years ago when I was debating with myself about whether to become pregnant, I actually wrote, "Sometimes it seems to me that I will either have a baby or have a novel." Despite this fear, I decided to become pregnant, feeling an intense mental and physical drive to have a child, and not wanting to give it up, *even if* I thought it might be at the expense of some of my work as a writer. But quite the opposite occurred. My pregnancy and my son's first two years were very creative times for me as a writer, probably more so than any previous periods in my life.

This was on my mind when the 1983 Women & Words Conference was being organized. I wrote to the conference organizers in Vancouver suggesting a workshop on "creativity and childbearing and rearing," and a draft program was mailed back to me including a workshop entitled "creativity and motherhood." I started when I saw the word "motherhood," wincing with embarrassment or revulsion or...I'm not sure what exactly. I wrote back suggesting a change and it was retitled "creativity and childbearing, childrearing."

In business and politics there's the expression, "It's a motherhood issue," meaning that it's so obviously good, something favoured by everyone, that it's not even worth discussing. It's taken for granted. Everybody has a mother. Mothers are wonderful. We all love our mothers. *Now* let's talk about the important and contentious issues.

Or, there's the embarrassment some adults feel talking about their mothers in public. It reminds me of Aldous Huxley's forecast in *Brave New World* about the day when the mention of biological motherhood will evoke universal disgust.

Certainly some of all this was at work in me when I flinched at the word "motherhood." I feel ashamed of my reaction, but I think it has to do with my sense of what the word generally connotes, and to whom, these days. Birthing and mothering have in the past inhabited a shadowy realm in language — hovering somewhere between delicacy and disgust. This has been true not only of the mainstream but, until relatively recently, of the feminist movement too.

A significant stream of the women's movement has in the past found motherhood at best an unpleasant concept and at worst the *sine qua non* of female oppression. Many feminists reacted to the oppression women have undergone in the *institution* of motherhood by declaring there can be no freedom if one has children. There can be no power. And there can be no creativity. This attitude has changed somewhat in recent years. But it's still around. Not too long ago, feminist Joanne Kates wrote in *The Globe and Mail* that there have never been any great women writers who had children, or scarcely any. Kates was uninformed on the issue — her statement is patently untrue of the last thirty to forty years, though it is pretty true before that — at least in terms of *known* writers. But for the post World War II period, there have been many fine women writers who had children (see Tillie Olsen's list of names in *Silences*).

Olsen refers to the "moldy theory that women have no need, some say no capacity, to create art, because they can 'create' babies." The theory is indeed mouldy. But sometimes we spend too much time with like-minded people and forget how much currency this theory still has. The viewpoint continues to exist that something destructive happens to a woman's creative forces when she gives so much physical and mental energy to pregnancy and motherhood.

When I was pregnant I wrote a great deal of poetry, including "Fetal Suite," a long poem about my pregnancy. After my son was born, I did not write for three or four months, partly because I was absorbed in this amazing new experience and partly because I was exhausted from lack of sleep. I was fortunate that my son began to sleep for long stretches earlier than most babies, and I began writing again soon, completing two short stories, a novella, and many poems in his first two years. I wrote about childbirth, new motherhood, and my baby, but mainly my work ranged widely over many subjects, more in fact than before my son's birth.

Rather than use up my creative juices, so to speak, pregnancy and motherhood got new ones flowing. I felt that a long-dormant piece of my brain had been uncovered. I had ideas and feelings I'd never had before. And they found a natural outlet in my work. But it wasn't simply a new series of subjects. I felt more in touch with the realities of nature, the world, even the universe — and with human things like love or fear. My mind and heart had been expanded, and I was able to put some of that, sometimes, into my work.

I still found inspiration, or the muse, or whatever you like to call it, as quixotic and difficult to summon or control as ever. But when it was there, it was changed from before and, I think, changed for the better.

Some time after I had given the Vancouver workshop on "creativity and childbearing, childrearing" (along with workshop co-leaders Marian Engel and Joan Haggerty), I came across "A Wild

Surmise — Motherhood and Poetry," an essay in Ostriker's *Writing Like a Woman.*

"The advantage of motherhood for a woman artist," Ostriker writes, "is that it puts her in immediate and inescapable contact with the sources of life, death, beauty, growth, and corruption. If she is a theoretician it teaches her things she could not learn otherwise; if she is a romantic it constitutes an adventure which cannot be duplicated by any other, and which is guaranteed to supply her with experiences of utter joy and utter misery; if she is a classicist it will nicely illustrate the vanity of human wishes."

Ostriker places herself in a list of American women poets who pioneered in writing about childbirth, pregnancy, and children in the early sixties, naming works like Sylvia Plath's *Three Women,* Adrienne Rich's *Snapshots of a Daughter-in-Law,* Ann Sexton's *To Bedlam and Part Way Back* and *All My Pretty Ones,* Diane Wakoski's *Inside the Blood Factory,* and Carolyn Kizer's *Pro Femina.*

Her own poem about pregnancy, "Once More Out of Darkness" (dubbed by a colleague, "A Poem in Nine Parts and a Post-Partum") was written in 1965 and published in 1970. Hostile reactions were divided between male critics who found such subject matter narrow and radical feminists who felt that motherhood "was a burden imposed on women by patriarchy."

Ostriker found both schools of criticism wanting and continued to pursue this and other subjects she found worthy of poetry.

To women and men who raise the issue, "How can you write with children taking up your time," Ostriker notes that people have managed to write despite the "drain" of sex and love on their mental and physical energy. "Can you imagine," she asks, "Petrarch, Dante, Keats, bemoaning their lot — 'God, I'm so involved with this *woman,* how can I write?'" This passage reminded me of a friend who responds to the query about children eating into writing time and energy by saying, "Yes, my children are demanding, but my ex-husband was much more so. I have more energy for my writing now, as a single parent, than I did when I was part of your typical nuclear famly."

So if motherhood is so terrific and such a boon to creativity, *why* were there almost no great women writers who had children until recent decades? I don't think it has anything to do with the nature of biological motherhood as such — but the *social institution* as it has mostly existed. This meant having a lot of children, bearing full responsibility for them, and succumbing to social and family pressure to limit activities to hearth and home. While having one or two children may stir up new ideas, having five will exhaust you completely and use you up, I think (but Carol Shields has five...).

Daycare, some enlightened male partners, babysitters, and shared households for single mothers (and couples too) have all helped to give more "free" time to mothers.

The crunch still comes, predictably, around economic questions. For one thing, who can afford daycare and babysitters? Many women who have children find that they still must get a job just to pay the bills. This can definitely interfere with writing. You can work full time and write, and you can have a child and write, but you cannot work full time, have a small child, and write. When my son was three, I took a full time job as an editor for a year and wrote only five poems, all during Christmas week when I was off work. Working full time and being a mother eliminates what Tillie Olsen calls "the simplest circumstances for creativity."

It's often a matter of choosing risks. It's a risk, if you have children, to abandon the full time job and live on a small amount of money, doing freelance work, part-time teaching, getting grants when you can. But if writing is part of your necessary physical and mental life, it may be a greater risk to put yourself in a situation where you can't write. Much has been said about Sylvia Plath's suicide, but the main point is often missed, that a compulsive writer/single parent had two small children and had to work to support herself. She was reduced to getting up at four A.M. in an attempt to find time to write. That's a very hard situation to sustain.

So motherhood does not produce some sort of psycho-physical dislocation which rechannels the urge to write into breastfeeding and singing lullabies. These activities, wonderful in themselves, can exist right alongside artistic production, enhancing the conditions for creative work. Motherhood *can* introduce some enormous practical problems relating to time and money, and resulting from the failure of men to take their share of responsibility in raising their own children, and from the failure of society to place as much value on the welfare of its future citizens as it does on producing weapons and fast food.

A reflection of how having and raising children is undervalued by society can be found in the discrimination still practiced by many editors and critics against subject matter like pregnancy, childbirth, and bringing up children. Such subjects tend to be judged as narrow, personal — *domestic* — that supposedly most damning of all words. Confined to the home, not part of the world outside, not part of the main action, invisible. But it is precisely by bringing those subjects out of the closet and into the written word — "de-privatizing" them, if you will — that we make them visible and insist that they *are* part of the main action, part of the larger life. It is only relatively recently (the last 20 years and increasingly in the past five) that we see some of these subjects in literature and the visual arts. Some good poetry on birthing and mothering has appeared in Canada in the last two or three years, for example, work by Lola Lemire Tostevin, Jeni Couzyn, Mary di Michele, and myself. As women, we are trying to reinvent language which emerges from the reality of our lives, rather than reflect the perceived impressions of men.

Judy Chicago's critical writing and art opened many eyes to the fact that in the entire history of art there are very few female genital or birth images. Chicago especially noted the absence of images of "the crowning," the ecstatic moment in childbirth when the newborn's head appears and comes out of the vaginal opening. If the experience were a male one, Chicago said, images of this triumphant, joyous moment would be seen in many works of art.

It took me three years to bring my long poem on pregnancy to the surface, partly for fear of its being judged "personal" or "domestic." This was compounded by reactions of some friends to the poem when it was completed. One, a feminist and a good poet, told me the poem was not as good as my other work, adding that "it is a hard subject to write about." A male writer friend discouraged me from including it in a book I was about to publish. He felt it was too personal, not sufficiently artistically controlled. I decided to publish it and it has been well received by several critics and writers (Robert Fulford and Erin Mouré, for two), perhaps reflecting some change in social and critical viewpoints.

But the prejudice against this type of subject matter is still widespread, as can be seen in the continued use of terms like "a woman's novel." One could reverse this and refer to certain books, such as Farley Mowat's or Ernest Hemingway's novels as "men's novels" or "chewy male fiction," (to borrow Charlotte Vale Allen's phrase). I've always been amazed that mountain climbing, for example, could be considered a "universal" theme, while childbearing might be viewed as a narrowly individual experience. How many people do you know who have climbed mountains compared to the number who have had children? What is a more universal experience than giving birth and nurturing a child? It's once again a case of "universal" meaning an experience in the domain of the dominant sex and culture, "personal" meaning an experience in the domain of a "marginal" sex or culture.

"If [a] woman artist has been trained to believe that the activities of motherhood are trivial, tangential to main issues of life, irrelevant to the great themes of literature, she should untrain herself," says Ostriker. "The training is misogynist...and it is a lie."

An example of a bias against "female" themes appeared in an ad placed last year in *Books in Canada* by Quadrant Editions for *A Sad Device* by Roo Borson. The blurb said, "one of the most refreshing woman writers in Canada." Now, you don't have to be paranoid to get the meaning of this ad. Fortunately, we *have* come too far for the ad to have said, "she writes like a man" or "unlike most women, she doesn't slobber her personal emotions all over the page" or "she writes about mountains, not babies." If you can tell me what else was meant by "refreshing" when combined with "woman writer," I'd like to hear it. (Borson, of course, is not to blame for the ad.)

Adrienne Rich in *Of Woman Born* talks eloquently of the difficulties of surviving as a writer within the institution of motherhood as defined by men. She describes suffering from the role thrust upon her as a housewife in an academic community, but she makes no statements about motherhood as such being stifling. On the contrary, she describes a summer when her husband spent several weeks abroad and she and her three small sons lived in a house on the beach. She recounts the wonderful time they had playing in the sand and water in the day, exploring the coastline. They ignored the clock, rising when they wanted to, the boys going to sleep when they were tired, eating hand to mouth when they were hungry. It was a very creative time for Rich as a writer. In the evenings when the boys were in bed, she wrote with much energy, often late into the night without feeling tired. When she was able to carry out her mothering according to what was natural for her rather than fit into the needs of someone else's system (her husband's and the academic community's), she found that it enhanced her ability to write.

Everyone has been reacting strongly, one way or another, to Germaine Greer's new book *Sex and Destiny*, which comes out in favour of motherhood. While Greer makes many cogent points, for example about the hostility to children in North American and European social life, her book is marred by an idealization of the existing extended family system in the Third World. It is more than disconcerting to read Greer's claims that the horribly oppressed women in traditional Islamic societies are not discriminated against but have parallel and equal societies to those of men.

The reaction to Greer's book is as interesting as the book itself. Some critics (for example, Paul Stuewe in the June 1984 issue of *Quill & Quire*) see this as part of a swing back to traditional family values, while others have noted that Greer is making a gee-whiz discovery which others have known for some time — that having children is nice. What is missed here is that Greer is writing as a long-time participant in the feminist movement, and she is in many ways speaking to other feminists. She represents a viewpoint finding currency among an increasing number of women these days, that the popular feminist wisdom on motherhood was definitely throwing the baby out with the bath water, if you'll excuse the expression. There is a re-evaluation of mothering occurring within the feminist movement which does not represent a reactionary trend but a re-defining and re-possessing of this womanly activity by women, or by enlightened women and men both. The more innovative, "revolutionary" if you will, feminist thinkers look toward a new type of extended family, a more liberated parenthood. Paul Stuewe finds it amusing to watch the passing "trends"; he thinks it's all a question of "lifestyle." But for some of us it's a question, simply, of life.

Because a portion of the feminist movement confused the existing institution of motherhood with the activity itself, it saw parenting as destroying creativity and power. But parenting can be a source of creativity and power, if it is part of a new approach defined by women and enlightened men.

Libby Scheier is the author of three books of poetry, most recently *SKY — A Poem in Four Pieces* (The Mercury Press, 1990) and co-editor of *Language in Her Eye — Writing and Gender (Views by Canadian Women Writing in English)* (Coach House, 1990). A collection of short fiction is forthcoming from Mercury in 1993. Scheier's poetry, short fiction, and criticism have appeared in numerous periodicals and anthologies. She teaches creative writing and women's studies at York University, is Consulting Editor of *paragraph - The Fiction Magazine,* and editor of recent books of poetry by Dionne Brand and Di Brandt.

ROOTS OF DISSENT

Pursuing Bitter History in Basque Country

Theadora Jensen

THE SUBJECT OF THE WITCH TRIALS has fascinated me for more than a dozen years. Perverse charges detailing sex with the devil. Nine million women executed throughout Europe. Some towns left with only a handful of women or maybe none. All burned (hanged in England).

It was a 300-year-long Dachau. It is *the* fundamental event in women's history. And it's my roots.

I found out about it gradually, coming across the odd reference or two, following them up, reading eclectically. I proposed a documentary series to CBC television where I worked. It was turned down.

I began a novel — the story of a young Canadian woman who has "gender memory" of the witch hunt which peaked in the 16th and 17th centuries.

The worst persecutions were in Germany, closely followed by France. I chose to set the historical section of the book in Labourd, one of the Basque provinces on the south Atlantic coast of France, near the Spanish border. There was a ferocious witch hunt in Labourd in 1609 conducted by a pedantic, pious pervert — Judge Pierre de Lancre. He burned 600 women in four months. And he wrote a book about it, which provides not only the details of the "confessions" of the "witches" but insight into the character of the well-educated judge and the pornographic nature of the persecution of women. De Lancre was also a racist, despising the Basques, so this additional element in the Labourd trials helps focus the true nature and motivation of the witch hunts. I decided to go to Labourd for on site research.

My first stop is Bayonne, a large town near Biarritz. I have read that there's a witch museum here but it turns out to be the Musée des *Basques,* not witches. I am shocked to find it has a three foot by eight foot closet dedicated to the subject of the "superstition" of witchcraft and the "intelligent" Judge de Lancre. But it also has original 1612 and 1614 editions of de Lancre's verbose account of the witch trials.

The museum's man in charge of the exhibits (a former *pelote* champion, he informs me) is indulgent. He shows me an iron cage that was used to duck adulterous women in the river to purify them, he says, although this was a well-known test for witches. (If they floated, they were witches and were executed; if they sank and drowned, they weren't.) He also shows me a kind of doll of rags and feathers which is said to have powers and he photocopies some material for me in the small library section of the museum.

This is when I see Lucien. He's seated at one of the several tables — early thirties, long wild hair, dressed all in black and bent over a Uher tape recorder, speaking breathlessly in a language I've never heard. The photocopying is interfering with his recording and he scowls occasionally at the *pelote* champion. I figure him for a Basque nationalist and a journalist, given the professional model tape recorder, and introduce myself.

I end up spending about half my week there with him. He is, he says, on the radical fringe but not a bomber, and he knows more about Basque culture than anyone I meet there. He's even read de Lancre. Best of all he's full of intellectual and physical energy and has a well-developed sense of irony.

Lucien first drives me to the cemetery of a nearby village. (Many of the Basques live in small villages scattered throughout the almost unbearably benign and beautiful countryside — whitewashed houses with red shutters amid green, rolling hills and ever-present bird song.) He explains that Basques have a preoccupation with death — *Orhait hilceaz,* Remember death — and he points out the various kinds of grave stones which during the period of my research were circular *stele,* not crosses.

We talk about the witch trials, and I'm surprised to find he doesn't share my outrage at the museum's favourable presentation of de Lancre. Lucien says the Basques are superstitious and live too much in their imaginations. Like many people and almost all men, Lucien seems bothered by the notion of witchcraft.

This is, at the first level, a language problem which constantly frustrates me. The entire language of witchcraft has been corrupted by the Christian Church as a strategy for eliminating the Old Religion that witchcraft was. It's hard to talk about a forgotten holocaust when the word "witch" conjures up a Walt Disney cartoon or weird groups with looney rituals. The survivors and descendants of the Nazi holocaust, at least, don't have this problem with the words "Jew" or "Judaism." They can talk about their history in language that others understand.

I suggest to Lucien that he think of the historical events free of the connotations the word "witchcraft" now conveys. But, as a Basque, he's got other connotations. He says it's dangerous to believe in witches. I assure him I don't, except in the historical sense of the Old Religion, now called witchcraft, which was originally the religion of the Great Goddess, going back through Greece and Egypt and into prehistory.

But he goes on to tell me about a local witch who told a credulous woman that she should get rid of everything that was red. So the woman burned everything in her house that was red.

Language is an essential part of Lucien's struggle for his culture as it is of mine or of Quebeckers. Only old people and those young people born in villages, like Lucien, speak Basque. It's an impenetrable and very ancient language, though many Basque names are instantly recognizable. Lucien's surname is Etchezaharreta. Throughout the area you see spray-painted messages in Basque on walls and buildings. Whenever I ask what one says, it turns out to be nationalist. Some are bilingual with French — the stencilled head and shoulders of a young man — *"Didier assassiné par la police."*

On the Saturday, Lucien is covering the *korrika* for the tiny Basque language radio station where he works. The *korrika* is a symbolic relay race, run day and night through the Basque country of France and Spain. It has a fund-raising function attached to participation, like Miles for Millions, with the money going to fund the teaching of Basque in the schools. It's not presently taught.

Lucien arrives at my hotel in St. Jean de Luz with a young friend, having worked a twelve-hour day of live broadcasts. His rusting car is plastered with posters for the *korrika* and has two loudspeakers strapped on its roof. We career down the road to Bayonne on our way to a rock music concert which is to feature Basque groups.

Lucien mentions three times that evening how moved he was when he arrived with the race at the Spanish border. A huge crowd of Spanish Basques was there to greet them. It was clearly an emotional event of cultural oneness for him that eliminated political boundaries. He makes me think of how I felt talking to a German woman filmmaker in a theatre filled with women at a festival of women's films in Toronto. It's a tremendously emotional feeling of connectedness.

At the concert, the nationalists are there *en masse* — hundreds of young people who express a warm, open friendship for one another which reminds me of the relationship I've noticed among the younger Québec nationalists in the cafés on St. Denis Street in Montreal.

I'll never forget the setting of the concert. It's in the ramparts of a 13th century castle. And it actually *is* a dark and stormy night. We get drenched before the concert begins, leave and come back later. The concert finally starts four hours late at midnight — not without historical reason called the bewitching hour. There are about 500 Basques, average age about twenty-eight or thirty, gathered inside the thirty-foot-high ancient walls open to the sky. The stage for the musicians is set up at one end, the red, green, and white Basque flag above it. Further up, over the top of the wall are the towers of the chateau, silhouetted in the moonlight — a full moon, issuing thin, yellow light through the black strips of clouds racing across the sky.

The first group up is from Spain. They play mostly ballads. The lyrics of one song consist of poetry smuggled out of a Spanish prison, written by a friend of the singer/guitarist. Lucien says they talk about a feeling of losing his country, losing his people. Another song is written by a leading Basque writer, also in jail.

I'm thinking about jail during the couple of days I spend visiting churches — the 13th century church in St. Jean de Luz where, in my novel, the heroine's mother is kept and tortured — and other old churches in the villages I visit. Entering them I always feel an instant sense of oppression as I step from warm sunlight into the cavernous chill of Christian history.

In St. Jean de Luz I made several attempts to find out if the church still has a dungeon or the tiny cells in the stone walls which I'd read about. My questions were met with looks of utter incomprehension by people connected with the church or at the municipal library. Cells? What torture instruments? *Strappado?* They couldn't make the link between jail and the church. I finally concluded that the cells and any dungeon had been eliminated during renovations for the arrival of Louis XIV, some years after the time of de Lancre.

It was, however, the Church and the Inquisition which provided the law and the momentum of the beginnings of the witch craze in Europe. The principal theological basis was the writing of St. Thomas Aquinas who showed a twisted interest in sex and a fear of female sexuality. This fear is, I believe, at the basis of the executions. A key phrase in the *Malleus Maleficarum* — the handbook for witch trials written by two Dominicans in 1468 at the request of the pope of the day — is "All witchcraft comes from lust, which in women is insatiable."

The witch craze was carried to its heights by Catholics and

Protestants alike, with the executions being carried out by the civil authorities.

The "church" of the Old Religion was often a mountain top where sabbats were held, starting at midnight, often under a full moon. They involved the induction of new members of covens, trading of pharmacological recipes and joyous amounts of eating, drinking, and sex. The free sexuality between men and women and among women was the way in the Old Religion of communing with the group — a religious expression totally free of any concept of Christian sin.

There's a 3,000 foot mountain called La Rhune which dominates the coastal landscape in Labourd. Religious ceremonies were held here as far back as one can imagine. There are prehistoric menhirs and dolmens on the mountain dating, perhaps, from the time of Stonehenge.

I made two trips up the mountain, the first on an old cogwheel railway in open wooden cars filled with some of the touring senior citizens whom you see in busloads throughout the area. At the top there's a telecommunications installation with microwave dishes transmitting signals between France and Spain and a souvenir shop-cum-bar. The seniors rushed into the bar. I spent most of the time looking across the breath-taking landscape below. You can see half of Spain from the summit — all misted, indigo mountains.

A couple of days later I went back to the mountain alone in search of its ancient spirituality. I took a bus to Ascain and asked directions for climbing La Rhune from the *patronne* of a bar-restaurant (who also pointed out several plants in the area which her grandfather used as medicines). I climbed up to a plateau. Here are the notes I made, seated on the wild grass and ferns, below a craggy summit of rock and in a degree of peaceful solitude I've never before experienced:

> You really do feel in a sacred place. The rock formations, outcroppings are huge and powerful, very old, and weather-beaten. I can see the bay of St. Jean de Luz in the distance.

An eagle is floating, circling overhead. Sound of crickets everywhere. Some birds. Sheep bells. The feeling — late afternoon — is enormously benign.

This mountain is so much more spiritual than the churches!

I had several experiences of "being there." Another was on the beach at St. Jean de Luz where so many of the women had been burned. It's a beautiful fine-sand beach on a wide cove. I was there just before the tourist season so there was only a scattering of people sun-bathing or swimming at any time. The first day I walked its length it was just a very pretty, clean beach. But subsequent days — I walked the beach every day — I thought about the burnings.

I saw the pyres. Black scars along the beach. Not burning, but bent and blackened after it was all over for the day. Charred limbs. Skulls hanging forward, features consumed by lingering flames from green wood. The acrid peat still smoking and the sweet, sick stench of seared flesh. Then I realized there would have been women there removing the bodies, cleaning up for the next day, the men being away at sea.

After a few days I made an effort NOT to think of the pyres. My own grim face was scarring the beach.

On my final day in France, Lucien calls to say he has the day off and we drive to St. Pee, a village where de Lancre conducted trials. Lucien shows me a farmhouse of the style that would have been common 400 years ago, and we visit a ruin known as the Witches' Castle.

Lucien at this stage has loosened up a lot about witchcraft. After the owner of the ruin gently disagrees with Lucien's arguments for restoring historical buildings, saying that his children's education is more important, Lucien whispers, "We'd have to get a witch up here to cast a spell in order to get this place restored." As we scramble around the old church — I think I've found an area where cells have been sealed up — Lucien dips his hand in the holy water, crosses himself, and says with a gleam in his eye, "For the devil!"

We spend several hours just talking, Lucien stuffing me with facts about the Basques before I leave, then apologizing for his constant rant about his people. I remind him that I hold forth rather frequently on witches. I ask, is it difficult for him to understand why I feel my roots are in his country? He nods.

But we suddenly connect when I point out the continuity from the suppression of witches as the doctors of their time, to the control of abortion and birth control today. He has followed the recent case of the French woman, whose husband died of cancer and who was refused — following his death — the sperm they had placed in a sperm bank so she could have his child.

I ask Lucien what he'll be doing in a few years. Will he stay in the Basque country and make revolution, I ask. Not forever, he says. You have to eat. He's also too intellectually curious, I think to myself, to stay put forever. And he's stylish in his own way and enjoys the cachet the radio work gives him. He may move on. Then again, he may get drawn even further into the current politics of his people which, he says, are so obsessive that they exclude all other interests.

We talk about the bombings and where they're leading. Lucien says the Basques have to be given independence beyond the degree of home rule they have on the Spanish side of the border. But he agrees with me that this will not happen. So what's the future? It will get worse, he says. There'll be more acts of violence.

He gives me a book, *Concerto Guerrillero*, a lament for the Basques written with a humour that satirizes their rural and "superstitious" background:

In this inexistent country — the last rampart of which is the starstruck brain of incurable lunatics — the wakeful dreamers who give it life have baptized the full moon *Ilargizaharra, la vieille lune* (the old moon) and attribute to it all sorts of beneficent influences. So it's under the old moon that one cuts short all hesitation, carves rifle butts from chestnut trees, and moves the harvest of arms and ammunition into the barn.

When I arrive home in Toronto I find a report in the pile of *Globe and Mails* which have accumulated during my absence: "Three people are killed in Basque violence." Almost as I talked with Lucien a boy and a policeman were killed by a bomb in Pamplona, and a munitions factory manager was shot dead in Bilbao. Ten days later as I write this article, the *Globe* reports an upsurge of Basque violence, and two more people shot dead in Madrid.

Personally, I'm still waiting to see what directions I will take in my own search for roots. Or, where the roots will take me, is a more accurate way of stating it. I am, like Lucien, beyond any point where I can opt to ignore them.

For a long time I had trouble accepting the history of my sex which I have come to see as gynocyde.

The witch hunts are almost impossible to deal with since they allow no rationalization. Is their lesson that most men really don't like women? Or that most men fear what they perceive as women's sexual and spiritual power? Or that most men need a sense of power at any cost? And are the caring relationships with fathers, sons, men friends and lovers the exceptions to a terrible rule? The heart wants to shout, no! But the head persists.

Perhaps the most important question for women and men is, how will women deal with these issues which are emerging from the relatively new area of women's history? And, as a consequence, what direction might the dissent of women take? Already, growing numbers of women are not marrying or marrying late, not having children or having them on our own, or at least on our own terms. And I have to admit to occasionally wanting, like Lucien, our own state.

It's this feeling of wanting — the emotional juice — that I share with Lucien. Our situations are, otherwise, quite different. His culture still exists but is in the process of disappearing. The culture of women is not only long gone, but has been, in effect, erased from history. Nowhere is it taught that the Renaissance was about killing women.

Lucien's roots are nurturing whereas mine are tough, even poisonous. Men often don't understand why women want to pursue such bitter history, seeing the process as an attempt to dig up a lot of dirt about men. And not understanding that this needn't muddy individual men.

But it simply is important to know. Poison, dirt and all. And once that's swallowed, it feels better to know. To understand where the anger comes from. To recover the feelings of culture among women. And to experience the kind of warmth and energy I saw among the Basque nationalists.

Because the mere act of pursuing roots is, for women, an exhilarating, free-style chase outside the boundaries of patriarchal culture. It lets you know you're alive — like the guy we saw on the motorcycle.

Lucien is driving me back to St. Jean de Luz after the concert in the old castle. It's almost three o'clock in the morning. We come across a young man on a motorcycle, traveling at top speed along the winding road — standing up! Is there something wrong with his knees, I ask. Maybe they don't bend.

"No," cries Lucien, delighted by the sight. "C'est le bonheur d'être!"

Jensen soon abandoned the novel which sent her on a research trip to the Basque country. Since writing "Roots of Dissent," she's continued to peer into the past with a female eye, finding our roots are deeper than the witch hunts. She's currently preparing a thematic work, covering some 25,000 years of theocratic beliefs and the effects of change on the patriarchy.

Jensen spent her earlier working life in television. She created and ran the first public access channel on cable television and went on to spend 12 years at CBC Television in Vancouver and Toronto, most of that time as an Executive Producer of documentaries. Today she believes television is a destructive force and is directing her energy towards fundamental change and the rediscovery of non-patriarchal ideas and lifeways. She lives on Hornby Island, British Colombia and continues her field research abroad.

THE ADVERTISED INFANT

Ivan's Adventures in Babyland

Carole Corbeil

WHEN IVAN TURNED THREE MONTHS, the Big Ones took him out of a basket and put him behind bars. Like most babies, Ivan hates to sleep alone so the Big Ones got him a red plastic battery-operated heart which was recommended for "sleep-resistant"* infants. The artificial heart beat did, there's no getting around it, remind Ivan of better times.

Ivan is napping now, big head close to the red plastic heart, tiny body looking like a little invalid in a terry sleeper. The bars of his Bauhaus model crib are white, his sleeper is pale blue, and everything around him has the germ-free aura of a new town house. (From the window you can see that the front yard has yet to be sodded, and that a small thin maple awaits burial in a burlap earth bag.) Near Ivan, on the chest of drawers which matches his crib, there is a coffee-coloured plastic contraption with an orange-tipped antenna. The Big One always turns it on before leaving the room. Ivan senses that this is an ear, somehow. There is another ear like it in the kitchen. The unit is, in fact, called "a nursery monitor," or "a nursery listening system for parents' peace of mind." It "lets parents be in two places at once," and it retails for $64.95.

All the products in Ivan's world are real, and all quotes are from advertising or packaging material.

Ivan doesn't want the Big One to be in two places at once. He wants to be with, or be carried by, the Big One at all times.

The Big One sometimes puts him down on the floor where he can't see a goddamn thing (it's the ceiling if he's on his back, the screaming colours of an "alphabetized learning blanket" if he's on his belly, and he can't turn over yet.) The last time the Big One put him on the floor, he managed to hold his head up the whole time, he was so pissed off. Both Big Ones went bananas. They looked at their copy of *The First Twelve Months of Life* and said he was right on time and wasn't that great; they were beginning to worry because Marlene who's such a screamer but the same age was already holding up her head.

Now, Ivan is waking up. He opens his eyes. He cries. The happy faces on the "voice-activated crib mobile" above him start to move at a frenetic rate; the more he cries the more the happy faces spin.

He knows the routine. The Big One takes an eternity to come and see him. Then the Big One winds the music box of another mobile, where clowns this time spin around to sickening music. If he cries in esthetic protest, the Big One sticks an "orthodontic pacifier-exerciser recommended by leading dentists and pediatricians" in his mouth, or a bottle with a silicone nipple which is said to be made "of the same material used for making artificial heart valves."

"Look at those clowns," the Big One says, "those pretty, pretty clowns." There is a tag on the bar from which the clown mobile hangs. "Caution," it says, "mobile for visual entertainment. Not intended to be handled by children."

Now the Big One is going to take him downstairs for a bout with a "shared development system." Babycise, a one hour follow-along video with workout accessories, "was created by leading pediatricians and physical therapists." The Big One identified with this ad: "Chances are you won't be able to spend as much special time with your baby as you want. We're talking about Discovery Time. Learning Time. Doing Things Together Time. It's the time your hectic schedule makes very very scarce." (The Y is part of the Big One's hectic schedule.)

Now the Big One lies Ivan down by the TV, pushes the tape in, hands him a yellow barbell with red, blue and green balls, and one-two-three, they're off on a ride which will help him, at three months, to "develop physically and grow in self-confidence."

By the time he's six months, Ivan sits up and plays with an "activity centre" which is full of things that make "rewarding sounds," and with European-designed objects which spruce up "his eye and hand coordination." He also has numerous encounters with a "glow worm," a strange, worm-shaped object which lights up when it is hugged. It is not until later, when he begins to crawl and then finally to walk, that the Big Ones, anxious and fearful for his safety, get into another major consumeristic panic. (Ivan has let it be known that the playpen, with its "chew-proof vinyl rails" is anathema.)

"BabySafetronics" enter the home. Now when Ivan, using great cunning, manages to open the pantry door where foul tasting detergent is kept, a loud, electronic alarm goes off, shaking him to his very foundation. This is called "Door Alert." Occasionally, Ivan is equipped with a beeper, called "The Nanny, an electronic Babysitter." ("The function of The Nanny," in case you haven't guessed, "is to assist in informing you that your child might be out of your immediate presence. It attaches easily to your child and monitors up to 50 feet.")

When the Big One takes Ivan for a walk, Ivan attempts to teach the Big One that private property is a rather odd concept. He explores other people's front yards and ends up on neighbours' front porches. The Big One finds this tiresome and humiliating and therefore buys a "safety harness." ("As your child starts to walk, you have the facility to restrain his movements.") For "a more secure feeling" in "shopping centres, airports, crowded places or anywhere" the Big One handcuffs Ivan to his/her self with Hug & Tug, a multicoloured rope that yanks Ivan from what interests and pleases him.

Ivan will probably never know what wondrous things he learned in his first year. He may wonder, when he gets older, why he has to sleep with a walkman, why he wants to suck on artificial heart valves, why going through physical and metaphorical doors fills him with anxiety, why he likes to be restrained during sex, and why he is aflutter with shocks of recognition when he reads Kafka. But never mind. For now Ivan the Investment is Safe & Secure. And that's what really matters.

Babyland is a world of substitutes, a world in which nothing is the real thing, a world where everything is surreal, fantastical, cartoonish, sentimental, exaggerated, excessive. The inhabitants of Babyland moreover are perceived as having the dullest, bluntest, most embryonic senses imaginable. In the daytime, colours not only have to be bold, they have to scream with day-glo pain. At night, everything turns into pastels, with teddies and puppies and tarted-up ABCs dancing on sheets and blankets and nightgowns and sleepers.

How, you have to ask yourself, when you first encounter this stuff in baby stores or in the hitherto invisible baby aisle of Shoppers' Drug Mart, did Babyland come to be? How did the world of babies come to resemble a derailed acid trip? Why is it that baby ads turn human infants into Disneyfied cuddlies or into chubby ids to be harnessed and restrained?

Western technological culture is certainly unique in this respect. No other culture creates such a separate, hermetic, bizarre world for its babies. In tribal and agricultural societies, babies are simply carried about in slings or papooses and take part in the productive life around them through the comfortable mediation of the mother's body.

In our society, however, Babyland is so separate from the rest of the world that it is entirely possible to grow to child-bearing age and have no idea how to take care of a baby. Most people now take courses to prepare for the main event, but what happens after the birth is hardly discussed.

The first thing you notice then, when you go through the gates of Babyland, is that you've entered a realm apart, a realm that remains invisible to all but those confined to it. Eventually, you begin to understand, in a visceral way, that the system you live under owes its existence to a rigid separation between the private (home and babies and children) and the public (the "work place.") This separation of spheres is economically rooted; it infects every aspect of our lives by organizing what we will experience and how. Most distressing, however, is discovering how we've internalized this division. No matter how many women join the work force, no matter how many babies and young children end up in daycare, the public and the private continue to exist as two distinct realms, with two distinct sets of values, not to mention degrees of reality. "Out in the real" world used to refer to the world of men; now it refers to a world bereft of babies and children.

This definition of reality reminds me of *Who's Real?*, a book I bought for my daughter when she was a year old. She was very fond of books with flaps at that point and *Who's Real?* had plenty of them. It wasn't until I got home that I realized what it was about. An illustration of a toy graces the flap, while underneath, there is a drawing of the animal the toy is based on. One flap, for example, shows a rocking horse; lift the flap and you find a so-called real horse. "So-called" because it is, after all, nothing more than a stylized representation of a horse. A real horse exists only in the skin-rippling flesh. The question *Who's Real?* obviously can't be answered under these circumstances.

Who's Real? is a kind of paradigm for what goes on in Babyland. The most stunning thing about baby toys is that they introduce babies to imitations way before they've had the chance to experience the real thing. All animals, for instance, are perceived as stuffed first and alive later. Real animals must seem like nastier, less evolved versions of the prettified, defanged, pastel cuddlies.

The same kind of polarized qualities define the private and the public world. It may be that Babyland is the way it is because "the real world" is the way it is. It may be that Babyland screams with colour and is drenched with sentimentality because it is a split-off; it's the distorted reflection of everything which is repressed in the "real world." Maybe if the two worlds were more integrated, we'd start to see true colour in both realms. It's just a theory, mind you, just a theory.

The Advertised Infant

According to critic Raymond Williams, the early uses of the word culture all had something to do with process: culture referred to the tending of something, crops or animals. So baby culture can be defined as how we tend to tend babies in the heated, isolated boxes we call home, or in the more heavily populated boxes we call daycare centres. ("Tend to tend" because there are a lot of variations here — there's a mainstream, high tech baby culture, an alternate, low tech baby culture, and an achievement-oriented baby-yuppie culture. The mainstream is most likely to use the products Ivan is subjected to.)

While in our society fashions of baby tending come and go, human infants don't; they have strict biological expectations which are either frustrated by the fashions of the day, or fulfilled. The history of western infants is of necessity tied to the history of women, and the technologically oriented obstetrics and pediatrics of modern medicine have made both unconscionably miserable. (Male doctors invented formula — an "improvement on breastmilk," for example, or drove both baby and mother crazy by advising scheduled feedings every four hours.) What newborns expect is simple — to be held, carried, to feel the same motion and heartbeat as in the womb, to be fed from the breast whenever hunger strikes, and, as they get older, to learn from the activity of those around them, while returning periodically to the mockwomb protection of the parents' arms. (It is a product of our evolution that babies expect to be carried at all times; predators would have made mincemeat out of them otherwise.)

The expectation of taking part in a culture is also a product of our evolution, and the mores we absorb from the earliest moments of life correspond to the inborn ways of other species. What babies first encounter, in other words, is "imprinted" as rigidly as the instincts of animals. (In the rare instances where children have been raised by animals, they cannot be broken from their first imprintings; animals raised by different animals, however, are much more flexible when it comes to adapting to their own species because so many of their responses are innate.)

How a baby is cared for, then, is crucial. It is certainly more crucial than the objects and toys that make up Babyland. (Babies, in any case, are rarely interested in toys. They're interested in playing with what adults play with, or use, and adults rarely use baby toys. Wooden spoons, pots and pans, little brooms, real telephones, and especially tape decks are big hits.)

In terms of marketing, however, what fascinates a baby is irrelevant. Babies don't buy baby products; adults do. And it's not just anxious, insecure, learning on the job first-time parents who buy baby products. The triumph of consumerism is that it has transformed life into a series of stackable markets (the baby, kid, teen, marriage, middle age, senior, dying markets), and transformed all rituals with orgies of product giving.

Baby toys are not, moreover, the most lucrative part of the baby market. The lion's share of the baby market goes to "instruments of infant care," as one manufacturer of high chairs, swingomatics, playpens and walkers, puts it. These products are aimed at people, you understand, who are in a profound state of shock (nothing has prepared them for the bloody sensorama of birth) and who now spend most of their waking hours obsessing about crib death (some have been known to dangle feathers in front of their babies' mouths to make sure they're "still breathing").

Today's parents, moreover, are in an unenviable and historically unique situation. They must bring up children without the physical and emotional support of an extended family. An awful lot of baby products "extend" or try to duplicate the mother's body because an extra pair of arms, or eyes, or ears, are rarely available. In fact, a baby store is a kind of body shop. (All the body parts, not too surprisingly, are recommended by leading white male pediatricians.)

Baby culture is, in fact, a lot like sports culture. In sports culture it is impossible to do the simplest thing, like running, without buying lots of equipment (head bands, track suits, wrist guards), and most activities depend on the validation of medical experts for their pleasure.

A baby store, moreover, is not just a body shop, it's also a projection shop. Baby products perfectly reflect the neuroses, obsessions and trends of this, our twilight zone. Even the twin preoccupation of the eighties — "security systems" and "fitness systems" — have found their way into baby culture.

Looked at from an infant's point of view, however, baby products are a very poignant kind of code. What products proclaim, if they are used as advertised, is that it is preferable and "safer" to bond with objects than with human beings because objects do not disappear the way human beings do; that the body is inadequate and must be supplemented if not supplanted by technology; that the visual sense is the most important sense; that knowing how to use tools — beep horns, push levers, dial phones, rattle bells — is the foundation of human society; that approval and therefore well-being is dependent on the mastery of such skills. Last but not least, the restraining equipment makes it clear that the Big One's agenda is vastly more important than one's own.

You have to admit that the above provides a masterful kind of imprinting. Looked at from this perspective, the baby market could set in motion the obsessive-compulsive attachment to objects which makes all other markets possible. An added feature of this advertised baby tending is that infants are so traumatized by the cold void they encounter that memory of those early years is completely wiped out. As adults they are likely to scoff at the notion that babies have real feelings and real expectations; the cycle may then perpetuate itself.

It's just a theory, mind you, just a theory.

Carole Corbeil has written for *The Globe and Mail* as well as for magazines such as *Saturday Night, This Magazine, Canadian Art*, and *Impulse*. Her piece, "Ivan the Advertised Infant", won a national magazine award in 1987. Her short stories have appeared in literary magazines, and in the Second Story anthology, *Frictions*. Her first novel, *Voice-Over*, has just been published by Stoddart. She lives in Toronto with her husband and child.

▼

FOR AS LONG AS THE RIVERS FLOW

An Apocalyptic Preview of Free Trade

Lenore Keeshig-Tobias and David McLaren

HISTORY, SOME SAY, has a habit of coming around again. Today, Canada seems determined to sign away what its indigenous nations are struggling to regain. Konrad Sioui, Québec regional chief for the Assembly of First Nations, summed up the lessons of history in a speech to the "Canada Summit" in Ottawa this April. He said, "Our opposition to a free-trade agreement arises out of our own historical experience.... The things we've endured over the last four-and-a-half centuries will certainly be the fate of the majority of Canadians in the future should we be tricked into any kind of a free-trade agreement with the United States."

Native nations controlled their own affairs before European contact. Each occupied a defined territory and was organized under a grand council — a sovereign government largely independent and free from external control. Of course, not every nation was completely independent. Sovereignty is a relative thing, and some native states were more sovereign than others.

It is the same today. Largely because of its tremendous military and economic clout, the U.S. is more sovereign than Canada. So are Japan and West Germany, mostly because of their economic strength. Both have favourable balances of trade, both have industries of comparable advantage, and neither is as reliant on a single trading partner as Canada is (and as native states became with Britain).

NATIVE CULTURAL SOVEREIGNTY

Culture is everything, the sociologists say. It is the sum of the activities of all the institutions of a nation — the total of what a nation does and how it does it. Culture means a lot more than an evening at the theatre, and cultural sovereignty means a lot more than going to watch a Canadian play.

Before the the first treaties were signed, the native peoples of this country had what Canadians have today: the ability and the collective will to determine their own path in all aspects of their culture. As sovereign states, the first nations had control over their own political, economic, religious, familial, and educational institutions. And with this control, they developed a society whose institutions were as diverse and sophisticated as anything the Europeans imported.

The village or band was the basic political unit of the native nation-state — a kind of municipal government. There were those who were charged with keeping the peace and bringing offenders to justice. The harshest penalty was, in most native societies, banishment for life. The chief and village headman were hereditary positions, but their power was extremely limited, for major decisions were made by consensus at every level of the political structure.

First five, then six nations formed an alliance called the Iroquois Confederacy which, by the time the Europeans arrived, was a real political force in the territory draining into the St. Lawrence River and Lake Ontario. Iroquois society was matriarchal; lineage was passed on from the mother's clan. Chiefs and headmen were still men, but the real power lay with the women who nominated them and, if they proved unfit leaders, impeached them. They also held the power of veto, and could nix everything from war to a wasteful hunt.

The land was the economic base of every native nation-state as it still is for Canada. Natives respected the land — harm it, the crops which it supports or the game, and you harm yourself. No one could derive power from owning land because the idea of one person, a village, or even a nation owning land was inconceivable. Tecumseh, in a confrontation with W. H. Harrison, governor of the Indiana Territory in 1810, stated the native attitude precisely: "It [the land] was never divided, but belongs to all. No tribe has the right to sell, even to each other, much less to strangers... Sell a country! Why not sell the air, the great sea, as well as the earth? Did not the Great Spirit make them all for the use of his children?"

The same kind of communal regard in which the land was held extended to other facets of native culture. Families were extended, and everyone had a role to play in the rearing of the children. Grandparents taught; aunts and uncles disciplined; parents provided the love. Everyone, including the children, was expected to assist in the hunt for food and in the cultivation of the land. The fruits of their labours were shared with the rest of the village.

Among the Haida and other nations of the Pacific coast, entire families gave away all their possessions in potlatch ceremonies. Aside from being a great excuse for a party, the potlatch was an effective means for redistributing the wealth in a village. The ceremony was well established long before income taxes and charities (and tax deductions for charitable donations) had become a tradition in European societies. In fact, the first real income tax was levied in Great Britain in 1799 — not to redistribute the wealth, but to raise money for the Napoleonic Wars.

One can see, in all societies, how inextricably bound one institution is with another — like the weave in a tapestry. Undo one and the whole of society will unravel. Native religion was (and still is) geocentric. The circle ceremony is, in one form or another, as common to all native cultures as the Eucharist is to Christianity — with much the same goal.

The definitions of "cultured" and "sovereign" which white societies apply to themselves also applied to native societies before the Europeans came. In their initial attitudes of respect and gratitude, the Europeans seemed to recognize this themselves. They needed the "Indians" to survive the harsh conditions in the New World and were grateful for their help.

The very fact that the Europeans (English, Dutch, and French) treated with the natives at all is evidence that they considered their chiefs to be the leaders of sovereign nation-states. How else were two sovereign nations to deal fairly with one another?

THE FIRST FREE-TRADE DEAL

And I (Joseph Shabecholouct) do promise for myself and my Tribe that I nor they shall not molest any of His Majesty's Subjects... in carrying on their Commerce, or in any things whatever within this the Province of His said Majesty or elsewhere.

And I do further Engage that we will not Traffick, Barter, or Exchange any Commodities in any manner, but with such person or the Managers of such Truckhouse as shall be appointed or established by his Majesty's Governor at Fort Cumberland or elsewhere in Nova Scotia.

Thus reads the Treaty of Peace and Friendship between the Merimichi and the British Crown. The treaty, at first glance, appears to be simple promises on the part of the native nations not to "molest, interrupt or disturb" British subjects and their settlements, and to patronize only British trading posts. In reality, this treaty and all so called "peace and friendship" treaties were effective bilateral free-trade agreements.

Generally, native nations made five promises with far reaching consequences:

1. Natives promise not to interrupt commerce.
2. Natives promise to trade only with Britain.

3. Natives promise strategic military alliance.
4. Natives agree to submit to British laws in the arbitration of disputes.
5. Natives agree to send hostages to ensure cooperation.

To put it crudely, the promises of peace and friendship and military alliance removed the major barrier to trade between the signatories — war. The natives had the furs that the British wanted and England made the manufactured goods the natives learned to want. Each had what may be called "industries of comparative advantage" and, while the fur trade lasted, that made them equal trading partners.

It's no different now. The U.S. needs Canada, not only as a strategic ally, but also as a secure supplier of raw materials for its industry. The natives kept the English in furs. To the Americans, we are a source of cheap lumber, hydro, oil. In return, we're considered to be a northern extension of the U.S. domestic manufacturing market.

The trouble was, the old peace and friendship treaties restricted one of the "partners" to exclusive dealing with the other. Each native nation agreed to deal exclusively with the British.

As any corporate executive will tell you, it is fiscal suicide to rely too heavily on one customer, as the native nation-states did and as Canada would under a bilateral free-trade deal with the U.S. Some would argue that we rely too heavily on the U.S. already — that we have already lost control of our economy. Does not our dollar rise and fall on the world market with the U.S. dollar? Did not our government obligingly impose a 15 percent tax on our own softwood lumber under threat of a 30 percent tariff?

By the peace and friendship treaties, the British developed a whole network of different suppliers. In this way they could dictate trade and treaty terms to suit their own needs. If one nation grew dissatisfied, or if white settlements scared away the animals in one territory, English traders simply took their business further up the river.

This is not to say the British were "evil" and the natives

"good." It was just the way the English did business.

Despite the cultural differences, it is difficult to understand how the native nations could agree to the terms of the peace and friendship treaties. There is evidence from the records of the later land treaty negotiations that the natives were told one thing during the oral negotiations but put their mark to a different, written version. Certainly the natives could not read what they signed, and even if they could read, how could they understand the notion of ownership? Land was not something anyone owned, so how could it be given up, let alone sold? The oral histories of many nations say the chiefs who negotiated the treaties thought they were only leasing the land to the whites.

Native ideas differed dramatically from white notions. Attitude toward the land is the best example, but there are others. Exchanging "hostages" was one way natives ensured a lasting peace between warring nations. The hostages were not prisoners, but members of each nation sent to live with the other as citizens with full rights, privileges, and obligations. As they were adopted into the villages of their old enemies, it became difficult for either side to make war on the other — each now having relatives in the other's camp. It is interesting to note that none of the peace-and-friendship treaties required English hostages to live among the natives.

Anyone who has traveled will understand the culture shock both natives and whites experienced on meeting one another for the first time. It is certain the natives did not understand many of the ways of the whites — just as Canadians have trouble understanding the U.S. attitude that peace and security come from exercising a right to bear arms. And it is certain that many in the U.S. (especially TV and film producers) fail to understand that our cultural industries are more than entertainment.

History does not record the date when white attitudes toward natives first began to change. It may have been when the Europeans no longer needed their help to survive in the New World. Perhaps it was after the signing of the first peace and friendship treaty, when the whites saw how easy it was to trick the natives into economic bondage. Or perhaps it was in October of 1783 after Captain Redford Crawford of the Kings' Royal Regiment of New York purchased from Mynass of the Mississaugi a large tract of land to the east of what is now Kingston, Ontario for "some clothing, ammunition and coloured cloth." But one thing is certain, attitudes to natives did change, and with the change came the notorious land treaties.

FROM FREE TRADE TO DEPENDENCE

The British Board of Trade and Plantations was essentially a committee of bureaucrats who advised the British government in matters of economic concern to the Empire. This board formulated the Royal Proclamation of October 7, 1763 which directed that all lands for future settlement and development in British America must first be cleared of the "Indian title" by Crown purchase; native "ownership" of the land was recognized, but not native sovereignty. Settlements expanded as the immigrant population increased, and attitudes toward the native peoples worsened. Treaties were now expected to lead the native nations into Christianity and civilization, as well as to take their land.

But treaties served a political function as well. By the time the Canadian Parliament voted to adopt the Indian Act in 1876, the government was worried about the possibility of U.S. expansion into the vast and "empty" Canadian West. Sir John A. Macdonald put native land treaties on the "fast-track" to establish Canadian title to the lands in the West and to clear the way for immigrant settlers who were clamouring for land of their own. The situation for Canada then was not unlike the situation the U.S. finds itself in today — not politically, but economically. The U.S. finds itself today with a severe imbalance of trade. It fears economic domination by the Japanese and Germans whose economies continue to expand, especially in those areas where the U.S. used to hold a comparative advantage — technology and cars.

The U.S. is responding to the pressure by, on the one hand, erecting trade barriers to manufactured goods of the kind the

German and Japanese export and, on the other hand, by pursuing a bilateral free-trade deal with Canada. A deal with Canada would guarantee the U.S. at least one secure market and would be an example that free-trade works. And it will work — for the U.S.

The expansion of white settlement into the West in the last half of the 19th century was an economic disaster for the natives. The encroachment of white settlers drove away the game on which the natives depended for food. Facing starvation and an uncertain future, the Ojibway Nation was only one of many native nations which found itself under a great deal of pressure to sign the treaties quickly. In 1873, the Saulteaux tribe of the Ojibway came to the negotiation table wanting only peace and land on which to continue their way of life in relative security.

In a land treaty now known as Treaty Number Three, the Saulteaux agreed to: "cede, release, surrender, and yield up" 55,000 square miles in northwest Ontario; "transfere and relinquish" title to the Crown; maintain peace, law, and good order.

The Crown agreed to: reserve one square mile for each family of five; supply the natives with farm implements, seeds, and "for each band one yoke of oxen, one bull and four cows"; maintain a school on each reserve, as advisable, at the people's request; pay $1,500 a year for ammunition and twine; purchase a suit of clothes for the chiefs and headmen every three years; pay $25 per chief, $15 per headman and $5 per Indian every year; prohibit liquor on reserves until authorized by legislation in order to protect Indians from evils of intoxicants.

Disposition of resources found on the reserves is not mentioned. However, some treaties, the Robinson-Superior Treaty for example, stipulated that natives are not to dispose of reserve "minerals or other valuable production" unless the superintendent-general of Indian Affairs consented.

Treaty negotiations were, by terms of the Royal Proclamation, to be held at a public meeting of the natives affected. Nevertheless, what was said during public negotiations was often at odds with the written document.

Verbal assurances made by government negotiators to protect the culture and way of life of the native signatories did not always find their way into the signed treaty. The agents of the Crown often engaged in this kind of trickery in order to speed things up a bit and to win the best deal for their government.

Both the earlier peace and friendship land treaties were words placed in the mouths of the natives. The language, prepared by white negotiators, is conveniently contrite and grateful. In the treaty ceding the Lake Huron-Georgian Bay area to the Crown, native leaders signed away one-and-a-half million acres in a deal, "which we consider highly conducive to our general interests." What did the native nations think they were signing?

In fact, what they were signing were economic treaties with the most serious of cultural ramifications. The treaties destroyed the economic land base of the natives and left no hope they would ever regain any of the land they ceded to Canada — even for hunting. The reserve lands were too small to support an adequate game supply.

They were not too small for farming, however, and it was with farming that Canadians hoped to assimilate and civilize the natives (the twin goals of the Indian Act, in all its amendments). But natives, especially on the prairies, knew nothing of farming. They had been hunters and good ones at that. What did they know of raising crops and cattle? When they got hungry, they butchered the animals the treaties left them.

The annual payments began a system of government grants which helped to keep the natives dependent on the Canadian state. And the new suits encouraged the people to give up their traditional dress (which was outlawed later anyway). Schools on the reserve (and later the residential schools) were denominational. Not only were native children punished for using their language and customs, but also those who taught them did their best to proselytize for white religions and values.

By the time the land treaties were negotiated (and renegotiated), the economic base on which native culture rested had eroded to the point where all native institutions were threatened. One of the first things to go (after economic independence) was their political sovereignty. By the treaties, native people agreed "to conduct themselves as good and loyal subjects" and abide by Canadian law. It was then a simple matter for the law to finish the job of cultural annihilation.

LOSS OF CULTURAL SOVEREIGNTY

"The first question is why is there an Indian Act? The white man did not acquire the Indian and his lands through conquest, the white man acquired [them] by mutual agreement as is manifested in the Indian treaties."
— Chief Yellowfly, representative of
the unaffiliated Indians of Alberta, April 21,1947.

The function of the Indian Act has always been to integrate and civilize the native peoples of Canada and to implement the terms of the treaties that were being signed. By the time the Indian Act had been voted into law by the Canadian Parliament, native nations were not any longer recognized as being sovereign. Natives who, at one time, considered themselves citizens of independent nation-states now found themselves wards of another state which they could neither understand nor participate in, even if they wanted to.

Natives could not vote in Canadian elections, a law that remained on the books until 1960. They could not be doctors or lawyers or get any kind of higher education without first renouncing their "Indian" status. These provisions were enshrined in the act under a section entitled, "enfranchisement." What double-speak — only by denying who you were could you be treated as a full-fledged member of Canadian society. That section was not repealed until 1986.

The potlatch was outlawed in 1884 as "debauchery of the worst kind." Earlier legislation made it an offence for western Canadian natives to leave the reserve in native costume. In fact, a system of passes was officially introduced in 1886. Natives in the old Northwest Territories (now Manitoba and Saskatchewan) were not permitted off their reserves without a pass, and to get one they had to present a letter of recommendation from their farm instructors. The pass system originated from fears that natives would support the Riel rebellion. But it stayed on the books well into the 1930s.

Residential schools were born out of an 1888 amendment to the Indian Act. They took native children off the reserves and put them into white facilities far away from their families. There they were punished for speaking their native language and practicing their native customs. The culture shock was tremendous for both parents and their children. It took the children away from their grandparents who now had no one to teach the old ways to.

It also took them away from the traplines. Available manpower for hunting and gathering in the traditional way was suddenly reduced by 50 to 80 percent. The residential school system survived into the second half of this century.

The elective system, which finds its legislative roots in laws passed in 1869 but which was incorporated into the 1876 Indian Act, abolished the traditional, hereditary way natives chose their government. Initially it simply made provision for an elective procedure for "band councils." When the Canadian government discovered most native nations were continuing with their traditional forms of government, legislation was passed to force the adoption of the elective system. The law forcing its use is still on the books.

The history of the Indian Act reveals how Canada came to utterly dominate native nations first through the terms of land treaties and then through the articles of legislation. There is not a single institution of native culture which has not come under the control of the Indian Act. The status of native women; limitations on inheritances; control over logging and mineral rights on reserves; legislation against native religious ceremonies, customs, and government; regulations on native education — everything they did and the way they did it was controlled by Canada.

These things are what the current native struggle for self-government is all about. Natives are fighting to regain something of what they never agreed to give away — their cultural sovereignty.

THE SAME FOR CANADA?

When the Canadian Mint decided last year to discontinue the old two dollar bill, *The Globe and Mail* carried an interview with Herodier Kalluk. Mr. Kalluk is one of five Inuit hunters pictured on the back of the bill. The engraving is from a photo taken in 1952 of an actual whale hunt. Mr. Kalluk is the third hunter from the left, just stepping into a kayak. His reaction to the change was quoted: "It's the printer's money so it's the printer's decision. But it's part of Canadian history so I would like very much to stay on the money. It's part of our old way of life. I think people should know about it." The robins which stand proudly on our new two dollar bill are more indigenous to the Eastern United States than to Canada.

The irony shouldn't be lost on those who would negotiate a free-trade treaty with the United States. The very treaties by which the Europeans recognized native sovereignty were also the instruments of native subjugation. Natives have learned what a fragile thing cultural sovereignty is, how easily lost, how difficult to win back.

The capitulation of a single institution can undo an entire nation. And it will not matter a jot that Canada has a brand new constitution, or that our family ties are stronger, or that our our religions are more righteous, or that our educational system is more intelligent, or that our social assistance programs are more progressive, or that our Auto Pact is a good deal. Even if everything in this list were true, it wouldn't matter. Canada's "resolve" to keep cultural sovereignty out of the free-trade talks is as thin as the rhetoric which defends us.

The U.S. has warned us, but we refuse to listen. Everything — all that we do and how we do it — is fair game at the free-trade table. Once Canada's economy goes on the table, all our institutions will come under the imperious eye of a slicker, more resourceful trader who promises fidelity and the good life for "as long the sun shines and the rivers flow."

Lenore Keeshing-Tobias is an Ojibway writer-storyteller from the Bruce Peninsula. She works to consolidate and gain recognition for Native contributions to Canadian writing — to reclaim the Native voice in literature. Her work has appeared in a number of literary journals and anthologies (mostly Native). Her first book of poetry will appear in 1992 in a bilingual format. Keeshig-Tobias is a member of the Writers' Union of Canada and chair for the Racial Minority Writers' Committee.

David McLaren is currently working with the Saugeen Ojibway Nation on the Bruce Peninsula of Ontario. He is helping to coordinate land claims and Native rights negotiations and to publicize their view of history. Previously, he was employed by a small ad agency in Toronto. He is also a freelance writer with radio and television dramas to his credit.

IMAGES FOR A STORY THAT ISN'T

Sandy Frances Duncan

OUTSIDE THE MUSEUM OF ANTHROPOLOGY on the northern edge of the University of British Columbia stands a three-storey-tall male figure. It is early evening just after the summer solstice when I first see him, and he glows new cedar golden in the long hot sun, an imposing figure against the western pillar of the museum. He wears a conical hat with a bulb like an onion on top. His stylized grin stretches across his face, and his arms hang at his sides, palms outward, giving him a gently unprotected appearance. A surprised frog contemplates up-lookers from the area of the man's navel, and below hangs his foot-long penis.

As I come down the steps toward him I see he has a blue rope looped twice around his waist and I smile at this whimsy. Some prude has dressed him up for tourists — a lot of tourists this Expo summer, cameras, and foreign voices. I angle past the man to the museum doors and I look at his feet, the adze marks making thick skin where he grows out of the cedar round he stands on. Someone has wedged pieces of wood under the round, and I suppose it was not flat on the concrete.

I look up, beside and behind him, past knees slightly bent and sawn vertically off for kneecaps, up his thighs into the careful thinness of his buttocks — again I'm jarred by the blue rope around his waist. Now I see it is knotted many times over his lumbar vertebrae, and the ends are tied to thick grey ropes encircling the concrete pillar. My sense of whimsy is cracked by chill horror, and slowly from this crack seeps sadness.

I had not yet seen the man at the museum the cold clear day I stopped my car for a red light and looked out the side window. Cigarette butts, too many to count, were scattered across the asphalt and onto the few blades of grass, brown and sickly green, trying to grow at the edge of the asphalt, the earth between the blades tobacco brown. Someone, while waiting for this same red light, emptied an ashtray. My mind's eye gazed under the asphalt and saw that nothing grew on that beaten, weighted earth. Earth that couldn't shrug the asphalt off. My shoulders shrugged themselves. The steering wheel was heavy in my hands. I could not take my gaze from the thin grass at the edge of the road, could see the asphalt expand like ooze between the cigarette butts, could hear the grass gasp in the fumes from waiting cars.

Suppose, I said to a friend, now is like then, that then the natives at Friendly Cove thought Captain Cook and his boys a passing phenomenon too. Suppose Maquinna and his gang gave them a few otter skins in return for guns and beads and a tour of the ship, and suppose they all had a party on the beach because the Europeans smelled too bad to be allowed into the longhouse...

The whites would have thought the natives smelled too, my friend interrupted.

But anyway suppose all the men and women went down to wave good-bye when the ship sailed out, and they rubbed their hands and thought that's that, now back to the business of canoes and fishing and collecting a few slaves. Suppose they thought we'll never see them again, those pasty-faced hairy men...

In Hawaii the natives thought Cook was a god, my friend offered.

But suppose the natives here thought they'd just come and gone and didn't have anything to do with their own lives — if they'd had TV they might have thought of them like a commercial interrupting the real program...

A commercial for a future movie?

Well anyway, I said, we know what happened. The Europeans came back and back and even if the natives wanted to, after the first few times they couldn't have stopped them.

Suppose then is like now, I said, what we've been talking about and calling a backlash, accepting it — the neoconservatives and corporate mergers concentrating power and star wars and free trade and fundamentalists with televised pipelines to a god whose views they report as if they were reporting their best friends' opinions — suppose all this too shall not pass?

I felt the lurch of possible truth in my stomach.

I saw it on my friend's face.

I go back to the Museum of Anthropology and discover the man is a twenty-seven-foot-tall Welcome Figure carved by Joe David. His name is Haa-hoo-ilth-quin — or else that means Welcome Figure in Kwakuitl. He is still tied to the pillar with the same blue rope. Hard to feel welcoming when you're tied up — or down.

I sit on the steps to look at him, trying to ignore the tourists stepping around me or taking pictures. He stares out of huge circle-within-oval Kwakuitl eyes. His head is larger than his body warrants — the way some people are disproportioned.

Perhaps the museum staff had to tie him down — maybe he'd stomped along Marine Drive the first few nights, scaring bikers and couples in cars. Or perhaps he's tied up to discourage pranksters, like the ones who stole the nine o'clock gun from Stanley Park some years ago. No, the ropes aren't thick enough to prevent a determined prankster. And they aren't thick enough to do much good in a strong wind. So maybe he did walk off some lonely night looking for people to welcome. Perhaps he still does — reaches around behind him with his wooden hands and slips out of the knots, steps down from his round and stomps off after the museum closes.

It's pleasant sitting in the sun, smelling the breeze from the salmonberry bushes and the dark rain forest and thinking how I can write about the Welcome Figure, except there's a food trailer slightly to the west, and I can smell frying onions too. I recall that last time I felt horror and sadness, but I'm not re-feeling those. There's no memory trace for feelings; each time is new. Pensive is the most I feel.

A man passing by says to a little girl, Look! That statue's tied up to keep him from getting away. The man sees me and smiles in embarrassed complicity: *I'm only doing it for the child.*

I smile back and think *down.* He's tied down.

A story starts with an image lodged in my — maybe — right parietal lobe like a niggle or an itch. I wriggle my shoulders and frown and wince as if moving those muscles will dislodge the image or sooth or scratch it. But all that happens is that my body becomes uncomfortable too. The image obsessively lurks on the edge of my consciousness, shifting sometimes to one side, sometimes to the other, and I fidget, grow irritable, and eat a lot. The image collects other images — or generates them — or both. I do not know what thought or images will adhere to the first, and it is only through writing that I find out.

I hear on the news of an attempted coup in the Philippines — some men took over the Manila Hotel and tried to establish a new government while President Aquino was "in the provinces." What would happen if a group tried that in Canada, I say. A friend laughs and says, maybe no one would even notice.

Last April I was up in the Yukon. There was still snow five feet deep, but I'd seen pussywillows that day and a patch of soggy ice on a creek. I had two hours until the bus left for the airport, so I went into the hotel bar to have a beer and make notes. The hotel was a log structure looking down the only street, and it was mostly full of men in untied boots and caps with peaks that said *John Deere* or something else in yellow. The only other single woman nursed a cider and looked glum. The inside walls were log, and I did not sit under the mounted moose, nor near the grizzly with his teeth, but chose a table by the ladies' room.

I was engrossed in writing: one goes *out* from the North, one never *leaves;* and a passage about thin pine trees rolling by, the *thin* related to my thick rain forest life, and the *rolling* to both camera (point of view-er as outsider) and the motion of the bus. A touch on my shoulder — I jumped and shrieked. A helpful man who'd been on the two hour trip before, telling me the bus was about to leave. I apologized, gathered myself, and went into the lobby where another bit of bear stared down.

A woman was standing by the desk. She asked the hotel woman when the bus went to __ which is where we'd come from. The hotel woman said that the bus first had to go to the airport, a half-hour run, before it came back to pick up passengers for __. The asking woman looked uncertainly out the window at three bags by the parked bus. It seemed to me she'd not done this trip before. The helpful man was silently unhelpful. There was some confusion then between the asking woman and the hotel woman and the hotel woman said, Where's Glen? The helpful man said, He's in the coffee shop. It was, after all, the bus driver's problem.

I rolled sympathetic eyes at the asking woman and she gave me a look of acknowledgement, and a small lip curl. She was slightly pudgy, about my indeterminate middle age, well dressed in a fortrel style with striking, shining hair pulled into a chignon and careful makeup. A competent woman going places.

Glen arrived from the coffee shop, looked her up and down and said what's the problem? She said I'm going with you to __; my bags are out there, and pointed. We don't leave till six, Glen said, in the loud voice one uses for the foreign or retarded, so get your bags. But they're out there already, she persisted, can't you load them now? Nope, Glen said, can't do that. You have to wait two hours and don't you drink, hear me? If you have anything to drink, I won't take you. I don't take drinkers on my bus.

But I've had two beer, I wanted to say, feeling suddenly guilty, does that mean you won't take me to the airport? Maybe it did, I thought, and tried not to breathe fumes out.

I won't drink the woman said. See that you don't, Glen ordered. I realized then — for the first time — everyone else in the bar had been white. Everyone on the bus coming out, I thought, had been white. Glen, hotel women, helpful man, me — we were all white.

A look was on the asking woman's face — rage, humiliation. She glanced at me, away. I felt hot with fury, shame, my cowardice, and guilt. I didn't say, I've had two beer, Glen, does that mean you're not taking me? I didn't say, load her bags and take her to the airport or load her bags on and pick her up on your way back. I didn't say, you racist pig. I said nothing. I could hardly look at her. She wasn't looking at me. Our glances caught: she didn't expect anything from me; I didn't give her anything she could use.

Finally the helpful man mumbled, I'll get your bags and raced outside.

I left the woman standing in the lobby with the bear grinning down and I — too humble and silently seething — went out to the bus. I thought: Glen is setting her up — a humiliated woman with two hours to kill in a bar.

On the bus Glen said to the helpful man who'd sat near him, I can't let them drink, they fight and puke all over my bus, I've had to stop fights and get hit myself and clean up the puke, she might be okay but you can't tell and if I take her bags and I get back and she's been drinking then it's like I'm committed to take her because of her bags and it's not worth it I'm responsible for my bus...

I wish I'd said something to let her know she wasn't alone (though she was), something to tell Glen I didn't agree with him or with the helpful man, something to show I'm the sort of woman I'd like to be, even if it meant two extra days in the Yukon before the next flight out. If I'd not had any beer I'd like to think I would have, but I don't know.

All I can do is write what happened and note my culpability. So that I will know it. Write my own story. Of her. Of Haa-hoo-ilth-quin. Emptied ashtrays and supposes. Hard to know what my story is.

The flight was delayed because the plane's heater wouldn't work. The wind chill made it 30 below. We passengers sat or paced in the prefab waiting room. A woman I'd noticed on the bus now had two boys with her. They were native, about 12 and 7, dressed in worn jeans and ski jackets. Each had a new toy car. The younger boy vroomed his around on the square-tiled floor; the older stood staring down at his finger, repetitively spinning the wheels of his, cupped on its roof in his left hand.

The woman smiled at me. She'd spent the bus trip talking vivaciously to some man I gathered she knew but not well. She was in her thirties and perhaps native, but I wasn't sure. She could have been of some other black-haired origin, Mediterranean perhaps or Middle Eastern.

She jerked her head to indicate the boys. I'm taking them out — I'm not the worker, it's just a favour for my husband. He's with human resources, but he's not their worker either. She rolled her eyes and clicked her tongue: it was important that I knew she was in no way connected to these boys.

The older boy glanced up, down again. I smiled at him, looked back at her waiting. I'm not from here, she said, I'm from Ontario, they've got things bad here. She shook her head, shaped her lips: a moue. The older boy was listening, head still down, wheels still spinning.

Going to stay with relatives? I asked him, brightly, stupidly. The woman shook her head, frowned, whispered, Group home. Then, Say hello to the lady, boys.

The younger one looked up. That's Brent, the woman said.

I smiled at the older one. What's your name?

The woman laughed. He's just called the chief. His name is...she searched. I waited, looked at the boy. He wasn't going to help her. She looked at him too, found: Jason.

Hello, I said, and told them my name.

I wondered what had happened that they were leaving the North, but I was afraid the woman would tell me in her confidential, defiantly disapproving tone. I looked out the window at the plane. She roughly straightened Brent's collar, smoothed

Jason's hair, and he jerked away. She frowned at him, at me, and tried to cover it with a smile, this native from Ontario, pressed into a disturbing duty.

I think of Jason and the two women as I sit in the sun staring at the tied down Welcome Figure. I think of distrust and power-lessness and privilege, disrespect for living beings, for living things, for life — my fingers itch to unknot the ropes, to let them drop to the ground like blue snakes he can step over...

Joe David carved Haa-hoo-ilth-quin to commemorate Meares Island. I've stood in March drizzle on a Tofino street and looked past the coop and the pier at the soft green lump of Meares Island rising out of the grey sea, like the onion bulb on top of this Welcome Figure's hat, symbols within symbols of symbols. I have a bumper sticker on my car: *hug a tree for Meares Island.* That's not hard to do: I've hugged many trees in my life, hugged them and cried when they were my only comfort, hugged them as friends when I played at their base. Of all trees, cedars are most huggable.

Hug a tree for Meares Island — not only Meares but also Lyell, not only Meares and Lyell, but *all* islands — on this coast are many islands — the scansion picks up Sunday school: in my father's house are many mansions — I wonder, does that mean rooms he can invade?

The first raising of the Welcome Figure occurred on the steps of the legislative buildings in Victoria. Odd to have a Welcome Figure for Meares Island — to welcome loggers? And to raise it where they did? Welcome to the government? Then I think of the injunction against logging on the island.

I've seen mountains freshly logged. Who hasn't on this coast? I remember from my gardening days: in decomposing, sawdust leaches nitrogen from the soil. There would be nitrogen-starved earth on a clear-cut hill, the feet thick tangle of left logs and chunks of bark all over the chain-saw-dusted ground. No grass growing, no fireweed, no trees for years. Asphalt and cigarette butts and clear-cut logging. And ropes.

Sitting in the sun on the warm bumpy concrete looking at the surprise of frog in the Welcome Figure's navel, I remember the attempted coup from the Manila hotel when the president had been "in the provinces."

What if, I thought to the frog, sometime when the prime minister is visiting the provinces, a group of women takes over Ottawa's Lord Elgin Hotel and declares a new government? What if there were a feminist convention happening in the hotel, and a native conference, and a Fate of the Earth one at the same time. And all the registrants agreed on this way of saying "no" to official desecrating policy? There'd be factions and subfactions, plots and subplots. I'd need plenty of characters; there are plenty of characters. I'd invite the two women from the north into my story, and Jason, and you, Haa-hoo-ilth-quin with your grin and your frog; you would not be tied down in my story. A short story? A novel? At the least, a script for the future with hope. I hope with hope, but I don't know how it will end. Or how it will middle. I must trust the itch in my brain.

I have no paper with me, nor a pen, and ideas always make me want to move. I stand up, brush the seat of my shorts, stamp my foot that's gone to sleep, and right then I know — I can't begin to write that vision until I change the title of this to: Images For a Story That Might Be.

Sandy Frances Duncan's latest novels are *Pattern Makers* and *Listen To Me, Grace Kelly*. She lives on Gabriola Island, British Columbia.

THE CALGARY TIME MACHINE

In Olympic City the contest between winners and losers is as old as the town itself

Katherine Govier

WHEN THE OLYMPIC GAMES came to Calgary the city got into a Stampede mood. It was one big party, in accordance with local custom; nothing new there. No, the new thing at Calgary 1988 was Olympic Square, where upwards of 50,000 people gathered nightly in the heart of downtown, outside in the winter air, to cheer and wave. Medal winners came on stage, and television cameras broadcast the scene to hundreds of millions of people around the world. Calgary discovered a centre, and the world discovered Calgary.

European cities grow from squares, places to buy and sell, to gossip, to preach. Squares were the centre of life in the city, and still remain to demonstrate to a visitor pride in architecture, commerce, history; in many all the energies are still at work. Public squares such as the Piazza della Signoria in Florence have seen martyrs and conquering heros; in the time of Savonarola wealthy women threw their jewels and wigs into "bonfires of the vanities" in the public square.

But Western Canadian cities are different. They seem to have no heart, no centre. In pure form, they are different because they grew up alongside railways. In Calgary everything was parallel lines and intersections. Avenues running east and west and streets running north and south. Cars carved these lines deeper and deeper and buildings grew taller and taller until the downtown from above looked like a fossilized checkerboard. Pedestrian malls encouraged foot traffic but they were no more than blocked streets; one still had the feeling one ought to be going somewhere.

But Olympic Square is not for going anywhere. It is for being there. The sunken meeting place is a kind of excavation in the once untouchable area east of Centre Street. A couple of streets of low rise shops, cafes and bars were razed to make room for it, but more of that later. Standing in Olympic Square one can see a mixture of old and new, culture and commerce. Old city hall, buffed and polished; new city hall built beside it; the Burns building which once housed the most glamourous meat market outside of Italy; several other heritage buildings have been restored and make the south side of the square. The Centre for the Performing Arts occupies space in that row. The public library, the Glenbow Museum and Archives, the Eighth Avenue mall all touch corners: a heart of the city has been uncovered.

I spent the better part of a day in the square in February. It is a curious combination of historical and modern style: the pit has an extended archway, a false canopy, around its rim; the steps down become seats. Olympic arches, erected in the centre for the medal presentation ceremonies, looked phoney in real life; like a set, they achieved reality only under television lights. But the action was real enough. Before noon it was empty save for media trailers and babies in strollers; school kids appeared in the afternoon. Children sold candles, tiny echoes of the Olympic torch. Foreign visitors traded Olympic pins with locals in ski jackets of mauve, turquoise, yellow, and pink. By six the square was full, every inch of space on its sunken steps crammed with spectators. As the sun went down, the girders around the core were lit with a blue neon strip. It matched the Greek blue of the stage. The giant torch burning over all this gave it a magical otherworldly feel.

The crowd was like some gigantic sea plant, the displaced members wavering frondlike around the edges and the main part of the solid mass rooted to the spot with necks craning. People balanced atop the old fashioned telephone booths; they clung to the sides of lampposts. The lights were round and clear, like trails of bubbles rising. And suddenly I realized that...

It was all happening underwater.

We were submerged and the square too and the arches. Those Devonian seas had come down again, and the water covered us over as high as the tallest building.

And then as I watched this Atlantis-on-the-prairie, the current began to pull everything backward. Slowly at first and then more quickly.

Until it was ninety-nine years ago, almost to the day. February 28, 1889. The neon lights were out; the flames, the flags gone. Even the chinook disappeared. We were all in this huge crowd suspended, and it was freezing cold, and there was nothing out there but a mud road, some wood frame buildings, and a couple of railway hotels.

It was ninety-nine years ago and one hundred metres from where I and 60,000 spectators stood (literally down the block and around the corner on McTavish Street, now known as Centre, outside the Turf Club Saloon). Rosalie, a Cree, was waiting for the man she hoped would save her from her predicament.

William "Jumbo" Fisk beckoned, and she followed him through the bat wing doors, and while we hold our breath everything happens the way it happened because this is the past we are writing and not the future, although that too is hard to rewrite, as Calgarians know.

Rosalie is found dead, and Fisk is charged with murder. But it was not so simple to get a verdict: he was the popular local blacksmith and drinking companion to almost every man who could serve on a jury. In the confusion which followed this urban murder — the death of the first and, to my knowledge, only martyr of Calgary — various remedies were tried. The little town of several thousand tried to clamp down on crime. Gun laws were enforced. The RCMP tried harder to keep destitute natives out of town. A man who slapped a prostitute was charged. The Turf

Club closed. More natives starved to death on the reserves to the south. Calgary stagnated a bit, and then began to boom. By 1911, it was the fastest growing city in Canada.

And somewhere along the way Jumbo Fisk was finally convicted of manslaughter. The judge who got this conviction was a hero of sorts, a French Canadian named Rouleau. Mind you, he needed three trials to get it. It is one of those third-time-lucky stories that, for some reason, turn up in Calgary lore. Another is the story about Deerfoot, the native runner, who was challenged by an Englishman named Stokes. Deerfoot beat him once, which they said didn't count, because it wasn't Stokes's best distance; Deerfoot beat him twice which didn't count either because Stokes claimed to be running for his own purposes and without reference to his opponent; he beat him finally a third time and got the prize.

As the water receded in gentle waves, boosting us forward the next seventy-five years, the stage set rose up again — arches, the mirror roof of the new city hall, the aircraft-warning lights on top of the office towers. But we were left with the consciousness of the past; clearly, many things have not changed despite the stage paste arches which after February remain only in the miles of television footage taken here.

The city is defined by the contest between winners and losers. Winners are celebrated; losers are wiped off the map. Urban natives, successors to Rosalie New Grass, have spent time in this part of town ever since it *was* a part of town. They were pushed out of this area to make Olympic Square. Nobody can tell me where they have gone. Cities have limits, people say, this space was too valuable to be left. They have their reserves to go back to — or have they?

A case in point is the Lubicon, who were, coincidentally, staging their celebrated boycott just down the block. In honour of the Olympics, Calgary's Glenbow Museum and Archives mounted an exhibition called "The Spirit Sings." Intended to demonstrate the "richness and diversity" of the native heritage, the exhibition brings back Indian and Inuit artifacts which were carried by explorers and enthnographers as far as Leningrad and Paris.

After trying for forty-seven years to resolve a land claim with the Canadian and Alberta governments, the 400 member Lubicon Cree band finally aimed its campaign at more sympathetic British and Europeans. The games provided an international platform. The Lubicon asked museums around the world to boycott the exhibit, persuading at least 12 to their cause, including the Museum of the American Indian in New York. Supporting actions were not without irony; Mohawks sued for the return of a false-face mask which apparently loses its power when seen by whites. (The mask has been displayed by the Royal Ontario Museum in Toronto for many years.) And local native sympathizers, caught between wanting to see the artifacts and wanting to show support, simply postponed their visits to the exhibit until after the Olympics had ended.

The Glenbow resisted pressure to politicize in what it saw as a threat to freedom of expression. To international media gathered in Calgary for the opening of the games, the museum looked like the enemy. But native grievances against the Glenbow are symbolic. Shell Canada, the oil company which gave $1,000,000 to sponsor the exhibit and is in fact drilling for oil on land which the Lubicon claim, was one target. But the main targets are the provincial and federal governments which between them managed to confuse the issue and stall a resolution.

In another way, however, museum mentality is the problem. The Glenbow exhibit celebrates the exotica of a way of life most of us believe is past. False-face masks and ball-headed clubs have little to do with how natives live today. The museum recognizes no responsibility to portray current native culture but sees itself as paying a debt to natives in another way. The exhibit is about pride, celebration of diversity, integration of European and native histories. But the position is hard to maintain without a certain forced naïveté. On my visit I heard a guide discussing Shanawdithit, the last of the Beothuks. "They wanted to take her back to her village but, when they did, they discovered they were all gone!" Surprise, surprise. She did not mention that the Beothuk were all gone because they had been shot for sport by settlers.

A celebration of the riches of the past looks like hypocrisy when contrasted with the deprivation of today. Can we claim as heritage that which we have systematically set out to destroy? With the Lubicon we are not talking about beaded coats, but livelihood. The Lubicon are hunters and trappers, depending on moose, beaver and deer which move over large tracts of wilderness land. A Canadian federal report had confirmed that the average annual family income from trapping declined from $5,000 in 1980, when oil and gas development in the area began, to $400 last year. Hunting grounds in northern Alberta and British Columbia are also invaded by sportsmen in pursuit of the Canadian dream of limitless wilds.

But the wilderness, like cities, has limits. Natives see that more clearly every year. Push comes to shove when natives find they can retreat no farther from the cities. This is the reason for the new mood of intransigence. Lubicon leaders know they must be guaranteed land or lose a way of life which is not dead but endangered. It is convenient to believe that native ways are history. But they are not. Not yet. The north is not infinite but surely it is large enough to keep these original people who want to continue a hunting life free from the intrusion of oil rigs and urbanites in search of weekend wilderness.

It was convenient to believe, as the lights came on in 1988 and Calgary welcomed the winning athletes of the world, that the past is behind us, and that all this movement forward has brought enlightenment. Most of the people who stood in the square had no idea Rosalie died there, and had only the faintest knowledge of the hundred year story of her successors among Calgary's natives. The Canadian Imperial Bank of Commerce now occupies the place where the Turf Club stood.

But the mood, at Calgary's triumph, was one of integration of past and present, of pride in red and white. The *Calgary Herald* was printing recipes for bannock, pemmican and Saskatoon-berry soup. Treaty Seven natives rode their ponies most convincingly across the imported sand laid in McMahon stadium (it looks whiter than snow on television) for the opening ceremonies. The image Calgary wants to give the world is that of a place which embraces its past and makes equal participants of all peoples. Would that this image lingers long enough to make itself real.

Looking at my feet I thought I too am standing on sand. Another layer has been laid over the earth by the intervening age of water. If you dug a little you could still feel the Turf Club and Rosalie underneath us. This is a geologists' city, after all. Some of this excavation has taken place. Like fossil hunters, the designers have scraped the dirt off the old buildings to expose the shape of the past. What I want to know is when this last layer will be lifted, the layer that gives us what really happened to the people like Rosalie, like Deerfoot the runner, all those who are not winners in history, but losers. Is their time coming? What happens next year in Calgary?

Katherine Govier was born in Alberta and lives in Toronto. A former magazine journalist, she is the author of two collections of short stories and four novels, the most recent of which is *Hearts of Flame* (Penguin, fall 1991). The death of Rosalie New Grass formed the framework for her novel *Between Men*.

The Birth of a Murderer

Fauzia Rafiq

IT WAS VERY EARLY in the morning. The sun was on its way up, or more accurately, the moon was on its way down. Mullahs were already calling the faithful to prayer. And the faithful were beginning to wake up to start their day. The city was engulfed by a sea breeze which the people had long stopped bothering to notice. The breeze became heavier as it went through the city, gradually loosing its breeziness.

It wasn't, of course, the fault of the breeze but Saeen' hated it as it reached him dust-laden and stagnant. Every morning he woke up to find it clinging to his half-naked body. He was used to the fresh, scented air of villages. The smoke-filled atmosphere of an industrial city depressed him. He had been living here for two years but was still far from getting used to it.

He worked in a prawn factory where he cleaned prawns, preparing them to be preserved and packed into small tins. He had to be there at 7 A.M. or someone else would be hired in his place for the day. He could not afford to stay in bed past five. Saeen' didn't have a clock and didn't find the need to waste his money on one since the mullah in the neighbourhood mosque was so particular about time. He would start calling at four A.M. and continued till five.

Like most mullahs, this one also had a dramatic way of saying things. His favourite words were "O Faithful," and "O Slaves of Mohammed." He told him every morning how sinful Muslims can be and how they will be punished in hell. And how when

Muslims were faithful and followed the word of Allah, Mohammed and Himself, they will be rewarded in heaven with beautiful, young and pure women, and streams of honey and milk.

Saeen' never had time or inclination to think about concepts. But unconsciously he felt afraid of burning in hell. He had problems with sunrays. They went right through his forehead and eyes. Sometimes, his body reacted to them so strongly he felt he might go blind with pain. Maybe working in the dark and damp of the factory basement had caused it.

On the other hand, his emotions were undefined about the situation in the Heavens. The mullah mentioned over and over again the pure, virgin, and beautiful women. Instead of finding the thought desirable, he felt intimidation and coldness from such women. Like the daughter of the owner of his factory. She sometimes came to get her father in her new blue car. She was so different from all the women he knew. She was beautiful like women in English movies. And she must be pure, Saeen' was convinced, because who would dare touch her? But the mullah seemed to think a large number of such women provided to men in heaven was a great idea and tempting enough for men to stay on the correct path of Faithfulness of Allah.

Saeen' knew most of the mullah's discourse was taped but even so, the mullah would have to wake up, walk to the mosque in the near darkness from his house and turn it on. Or would it turn itself on? Saeen' doubted a tape recorder had the capacity to do that. No matter. It worked for Saeen'.

He would wake up cursing the breeze; go to the public water tap in the square; take a bath trying to wash off the stickiness. Sometimes he could, sometimes he could not. Then he would walk back to his one room hut with his pail of water hanging effortlessly from his right hand. He would come into his room, start his small oil stove, pour some water into a pan, and set it boiling for his morning tea. Whistling softly he would turn his small transistor on, bring out his pack of cigarettes, empty two of them, heat up two generous measures of hashish, mix it with tobacco, and fill it back into empty shells. It would, by then, be time to throw three or four spoons of tea, a cardamom, and some milk into the boiling water.

This accomplished, he would go out and sit on the sill of his door, light one cigarette and smoke it devouringly, preparing for a hard day of work. He kept the other for whenever he needed it during the course of his day.

Meanwhile, the tea would be boiled to the hilt and ready for breakfast. He would fish out some dried sweet biscuits, dip them in tea, and eat slowly, enjoying every bite. He ate this because he liked it. It was cheap and filling. Most of all, it was easy to prepare. Then he would take some water from his pail and gargle thrice.

This was his amended method of preparation for his morning prayer. He then would start for the mosque, usually being the first one there.

But this morning Saeen' was groggy. He had gone for a rare splash of luxury last night. Pooling money with four other factory workers, he'd bought some *kuppi* (undistilled alcohol) and had hired a prostitute for one hour. It cost them a fortune. He wasn't sure exactly how much, but he knew he had had twenty-four rupees last night and didn't have a penny this morning. Either it was twenty-four rupees a head, or the others robbed him clean.

This last thought was making him uncomfortable. He postponed it until he reached the factory and could meet others. No one could cheat Saeen' out of his money. He went for his arm muscles in his sleep and, most reassuringly, found them there.

The prostitute had been very beautiful. She had good-sized boobs, sturdy thighs and a warm cunt. In fact, the warmest he had yet encountered. He felt all this and ejaculated in his sleep, overriding mullah's insistent attempts to wake him up in time for his work.

He had made sure that he'd be the first one to go in. The others objected to it, but he had the healthiest muscles and for the first time in months he was about to see a naked woman and penetrate a real cunt rather than doing it in the cup of his palm.

Her clothes were dirty but he hadn't noticed that. What he had noticed was her brown skin which had a rare shine to it. The shine typical of very young girls.

"Take off your clothes." He tried to hide the tremor in his voice and legs with the harshness of tone which he took as a right once he made the payment for her.

She looked at him with a steady and insolent gaze he was not expecting from a woman he had paid for. She went back to fumbling awkwardly behind her back, trying to open a pin.

"Are you a virgin?" he asked hopefully, forgetting her insolence.

"The hell I am, just like your mother."

She snapped and pulled out a pin she couldn't open without tearing part of her *kurta*. "Here this one goes, more expense." She took off her torn shirt and tried to determine the exact damage. She was oblivious of her suddenly revealed erect nipples, the shine of her young skin, and the sheer black of her long hair. He shuddered uncontrollably and snatched at her, bringing her down like an inconsiderate but forceful wave.

"Son of a dog! Can't you wait a minute?" she asked, going down with the wave.

"Only got ten minutes…" he felt obliged to give her a reply and nearly choked at her breast trying to take all of it in his mouth.

"Ouch," she said. "Not there, you son of a bitch, it's up here. Don't you know where to stick it in a woman?" She tried to guide him to where he needed to go. "Fucking bastard! How can you do it with your *shalwar* on?" She pulled him free from his clothes with a jerk. He grunted gratefully and went in.

It took him less than a minute. He lay panting with relief and a sense of loss. "Get off from over my *kurta*," she pushed him, trying to get her shirt back. She needed to know if she could mend it or if it was a goner.

Saeen' rolled over. He didn't want to go out just yet because the rest of the men might think he was weak and couldn't hold.

"So, what's your name?" He made a drunken but cautious

attempt to start a conversation.

"You don't know the name of your sister?" she retorted. "Get the hell out, it's over." She was busy inspecting her shirt. Then she folded it carefully and put it under the bed.

"How many are out there?" she asked.

"Oh, just four — yeah four," he mumbled, slowly putting his clothes on.

"Dirty bastards," she said most convincingly and Saeen' thought it best to take his leave. Also, ten minutes were over because the next in line was banging on the door impatiently.

"She was a virgin," he came out and announced solemnly. No one believed him but everyone was intrigued.

He got home sometime after three A.M. It was cruel to wake up at four. He gave himself another half an hour. He had a strong temptation to just keep on sleeping and not to wake up to go to work. But he was conscientious and his conscience was trained to work 12 hours a day, seven days a week. How else could he provide for his blind father, mother, and four sisters back in his village?

He sensed an unusual commotion in his sleep. He thought it was caused by a million bustling prostitutes, all free of charge. But even in his sleep, he realized it was too good to be true. The commotion continued, so he forced himself to open his eyes. He tried to concentrate and then determined that it was, in fact, a lot of men talking together in the next lane. The next lane — almost where the mosque was.

The noise was compelling. He got up and staggered towards it. He wouldn't see anything unless he rounded the corner of the narrow dusty street and faced the mosque. He was trying to regain his balance as he approached the corner. There was a small crowd of men. They faced the mosque. All he could see was their backs.

Doubtless, they were witnessing something captivating and most unusual. Saeen' was not one to be left so far behind. He had the muscle. His pace quickened, and he was within the crowd in moments.

"Get aside, get aside," he pushed and shoved a few men and reached the crescent created by the crowd around the gate of the mosque. The mullah was standing on the first step of the mosque and was saying something furiously. Saeen' couldn't hear him because everyone was saying something furiously, and somewhere a small baby was crying.

"What's happening here, in Allah's name?" Saeen' said furiously. But all this walking, shoving and pushing had weakened his legs and was sending sharp pain towards his temples. He squinted his eyes to see where everyone was looking. He focussed, with difficulty, at a small bundle on the second step of the mosque. The bundle was moving, most unnaturally, on its own. Saeen' had to hold his right temple in order to make an effort to discover what was going on over there. He strained, holding that fluttering vein in his temple. It was a baby. The baby was crying passionately, trying to get out of the bundle. There was a newborn baby on the second step of the mosque.

Saeen' felt dizzy. He could see a small fist banging aimlessly in the short circle of air that it could reach, forcing its tiny knuckles to go white.

"What's happening?" Saeen' mumbled weakly, forgetting how successfully he was advancing towards the centre of activity. People pressed around him. Again, there was a sea of men between him and the baby. He pushed himself up, but all he could see was the towering figure of a flustered and indignant mullah. The baby was crying and turning white, somewhere below his feet, beyond the sea of men. Why is no one picking it up? The baby is crying.

"The baby is crying!" Saeen' shouted with all his might as if people needed only to be informed of this fact and the baby would be picked up. The shout came out as a hoarse squeak. The crowd pushed him backwards. The imbalance in his body aggravated the move, and he was suddenly thrown out of the crowd onto the pebbly street.

The first rays of sun pierced his eyes as if aiming at him. He could not take it and retched out a yellowy stream of liquid. It seemed it would keep on coming out from his empty stomach until he did something about the sharp rays of sun searing through his eyes like needles.

He tried closing his eyes but the rays of the sun made their way through his forehead.

"The baby is crying," he mumbled again and was punished for it by a new throb of pain in his temples. The sun. I have to get away from the sun. He started to pull his body away from the crowd.

Shade, where is the shade? He looked around desperately. The baby was still crying.

"The baby is crying." He felt compelled to say it yet again.

"O Muslims   O Faithful," the mullah finally made an at tempt to get the attention of the crowd.

He can manage it, Saeen' thought with relief and crawled towards a small space under the west wall of the mosque where there was shade enough to protect his forehead and eyes.

"O Muslims? O Faithful! What is this newborn doing here?" The crowd suddenly fell quiet and thoughtful.

Saeen' reached the wall, pulled his body upwards and tried to put his back to the wall. He banged his spine into the wall, spreading unbearable pain through his body. But his forehead and eyes were protected.

"Is this a male or a female?" The mullah asked the crowd with full command over the chaos.

"Male, male," the crowd chanted.

"O Followers of Muhammad! Who owns this male baby? Whose baby is this?"

"Not ours," said someone.

"Not ours, not ours," cried the crowd.

Another wave of bile surged up to Saeen's throat; he stretched his neck, bumping the back of his head into the wall. His eyes snapped open with the fresh surge of pain. He thought he saw a woman standing a few yards away from him. He thought he was imagining her — a woman of stone. A real woman of stone. Her eyes were fixed at the moving and chanting mass of people. But she was not looking at them. It seemed she somehow had the power to look through them, beyond them. What was she looking at? What was beyond? With a sudden jolt of pain he realized it was the baby. The baby was beyond them. And she had the power to see through them.

"The baby is crying!" he informed her. She didn't hear him. A woman of stone with unmoving black irises.

"Who will leave a male baby, a baby that was born last night, on the steps of the mosque, with no one to claim it?" the mullah asked as if hosting an on stage quiz show.

No one was bright enough to answer this.

"Who?" the mullah shouted.

"Who?" shouted the crowd.

"Who else but a sinful woman?" the mullah answered triumphantly.

"A sinful woman," the crowd replied with force of revelation.

"A sinful woman who gave birth, in the dark of the night, to her sins."

"To her sins, to her sins."

"A sinful woman," Saeen' chanted with confusion. "A sinful woman and a sinful man! She is the sinful woman, where is the sinful man?" He strained his intoxicated brain cells. "I am the sinful man," he said. "I never saw her before — but why did she put the baby in front of the mosque?" He suddenly felt angry at her.

"The baby is crying — why?" He suddenly pulled himself forward and asked in a sharp whisper.

"Why did you put the baby there?"

The woman still looked at the baby.

"Hey, sister!" another sharp whisper.

The only thing which moved in the woman was her heart. It was banging so hard against her chest that he could actually see the violence of it.

"Hey, hey," he tried to distract her with a louder whisper, "why did you put it there?"

The woman's heart stopped. Saeen' panicked.

She tore her eyes away from her baby — the process took a long time. She then moved her black eyes, inch by every inch, from her baby, to the crowd, to the emptiness, to the front wall, to the corner, to the length of the shade, to Saeen', and to the shady space right past him.

She doesn't see me. Saeen' was desperate. She brought her eyes back to where he was — with difficulty — like a malfunctioning machine.

Saeen' flinched under her stony gaze — it hit him like the rays of the sun.

"Why?" he still managed to ask.

"This is a bastard!" the mullah screamed with indignation and horror.

"A bastard, a bastard."

"This is sin."

"Sin, sin."

"Sin is evil."

"Is evil, is evil."

"Allah sent us to eliminate all evil."

"To eliminate all evil."

"To eliminate, to eliminate."

The woman's eyes darted back towards the voice with a speed which was totally unexpected for Saeen'. He feared someone from the crowd had seen her. Hers was the eye of a wild animal identifying danger.

But no, no one had seen her, she was looking through them again. Not at the baby, but at the mullah on the first step of the mosque. Her heart was banging against her chest, ready to explode. It will, it might explode, he thought, and no one will know because she was a woman of stone and her heart will explode.

"So how, O Faithful! How will you eliminate this evil which is flourishing amid you? How?"

"How, how?" The crowd demanded a sign.

"Stone it to death."

"Stone it, stone it."

The stone suddenly became alive. Her hand went under her *ajrak* through to her shirt and within an instant came back with a long, sharp knife. A sharp butcher's knife. Her eyes stretched to limits, the woman of stone transformed into a woman of fire — a lioness — ready to pounce, ready to kill.

"No, don't," Saeen' picked himself up and threw his body between her and the crowd. "No, no."

"Stone it, stone it."

People were running around finding stones. Big and small; bricks, broken and whole. People were bumping into each other.

Suddenly fear gripped him; if they knew, they would kill the woman too. For sure, they would. He looked at her. The lioness was there. This time she was not looking at her baby. It was the mullah.

O God. It's the mullah, Saeen' realized, this was the man who...

"O my God," he looked towards her. She wasn't there. The woman of stone, of fire, had disappeared. With her weapon.

He heard stones falling, bricks big and small. The baby stopped crying.

"The baby isn't crying," he said to her who wasn't there.

The mullah had left the gate of the mosque and had gone inside.

People were going in to say their morning prayers.

The mullah was leading a special prayer worthy of the victory gained in the holy war against the evil.

People were crying with exultation and a deep sense of achievement.

Saeen' crawled back to the front of the mosque. The baby was nowhere. A small area in front of the mosque was filled with red blood and tiny pieces of skin and bone. The faithful had eliminated the sin. The baby was crying, no one picked it up. Saeen' felt the second step of the mosque with his trembling hand. The surface was sticky and uneven. He rubbed the surface, his hand came away red, as if it had no skin on it. Saeen' felt compelled to rub his hand on his face. His face too then looked as if it had no skin protecting it.

He rubbed his hand on his face again. To make sure, a death was mourned. To make sure. A birth was celebrated.

*To the woman whose baby was stoned to death
in front of a mosque in Karachi, Pakistan in 1982.*

Fauzia Rafiq is a Toronto writer and a member of the editorial collective of *Diva*, a quarterly journal of South Asian women. Her stories have been published in *Diva* and *Fireweed* as well as in *This Magazine*, and she is currently working on a collection of short fiction. She has edited and developed numerous handbooks and resource guides on anti-racism, wife assault and immigrant women for various groups in Toronto.

WOMEN, VIOLENCE AND THE MONTREAL MASSACRE

Lee Lakeman

IT WAS A TYPICAL WEDNESDAY at the Vancouver women's shelter. Upstairs in the attic meeting room, six rape crisis workers were busy reviewing November's reports, extracting and compiling statistics; on the main floor, five women residents who have fled the terror of their husbands' violence were cooking supper for their assorted children; downstairs in the basement, I was addressing leaflets to B.C. women's groups that assist sexual abuse survivors. Our transition house was, as usual, stretched to capacity with women quietly, methodically, trying to mend the damage wreaked by male violence. Into this humdrum quotidian activity came the phone call.

A volunteer who left the office earlier this afternoon calls from home, interrupting a collective meeting she knows is in session, with information she doesn't think can wait. "I've been listening to the news for a couple of hours now; I thought you might not have heard yet," she says. "Some guy has just shot fourteen women at the University of Montreal. He said he was killing them because they were feminists." Other phone calls follow. Bonnie, a ten-year veteran with the shelter movement, tells us, her voice gruff with emotion, "This is a momentous event." She suggests we turn on the TV.

"All the dead are female" a CBC "Newsworld" reporter is

saying from her post in front of the *ecole polytechnique;* meaning all 14 killed by the gunman before he turned the gun on himself were women. Anchor Whit Fraser is talking about the twelve injured students who have been taken to hospital. It's some time before it becomes clear that, of the 12, eight are women and four, men. It's hours before we understand the killer — later identified as Marc Lepine — took aim first at women and then only at men who interfered. The anti-rape workers at the shelter, who are familiar with how some men intimidate and victimize women, wait impatiently for details about the responses of the male students and professors during the rampage.

One man is asked by reporters why the women were abandoned. He says he thought the men were going to be robbed outside in the hall. Were all the men present so ignorant about violence against women not to recognize that a man ordering a group to divide themselves according to gender, while hurling insults at feminists, represents a greater danger to the women present than the men?

Interview after interview on the scene confirms that there was no resistance to Lepine's gender separation, that the "men left without protest." A man appeared in a classroom brandishing a deadly weapon and, though there are more than 50 other men there (not to mention the 2,000 others on the premises), not one refused. The reporters covering the event seem loath to pursue the point, implying that the only reasonable response was silent obedience. Imagine the male students fleeing through the corridors, yelling that a madman was shooting at people: if they had known enough to say that a man was killing women, would anything have been different?

And where were those in charge? Later, we discover that the university administrators and staff hid themselves in their locked offices. No one in the press corps investigates how these men came to believe they were at risk. In the evening, a saddened senior administrator admits the school's culpability. "They [the parents of the victims] gave us their daughters and we failed to protect them."

But what, exactly, made these particular women vulnerable to attack? Women entering "non-traditional" occupations do not represent a serious threat to the status quo until their numbers reach 15 or 20 percent. Until then, their presence is largely symbolic and does not imply any fundamental restructuring of the profession. In law and medical schools across the country, women students already account for close to half the enrolment. At the *ecole polytechnique* in 1989, 18 percent are female. Was Lepine's choice, therefore, a strategic one, designed to halt their progress?

It becomes clear that no one halted his. Students say the police arrived while Lepine was still killing. In SWAT team regalia, they surrounded the school, remaining outside. They evacuated no one and prevented nothing; Lepine ended his rampage at will.

Lepine was clear. "Women to one side. You are all feminists, I hate feminists," he shouted. One of the young survivors, Natalie, tells reporters how she pleaded at the time, "We are only women in engineering who want to live a normal life." She is unaware she had risen above her station. But her attacker, Lepine, was sure that it was not yet normal for Canadian women to become engineers.

Whit Fraser constructs the massacre as an "incomprehensible act of violence" and is soon echoed by reporters on other newscasts. Yet how incomprehensible is it, really? Unlike the coverage of rape cases, which usually allows for the possibility that the "alleged" crime didn't take place, or was unintentional, it's clear Lepine did it; we know he intended to do it, and we know why. Yet we're told it is all a mystery, way beyond the understanding of ordinary people.

Apparently, we are to believe everything about the case except the killer's own statement of his motives. In the coming days, acceptable experts will be produced to retrieve his act from the realm of the mysterious, to give it meaning. At the shelter, we predict they'll be psychologists, not feminists.

Fraser and his co-anchor, Carol Adams, continue the obfuscation, telling us how rare it is in North America for such a large number of people to be massacred at once. They draw comparisons to multiple murders of people, avoiding the connection to other acts of violence against women. Perhaps a closer parallel is the premeditated killings of 12 Vancouver prostitutes last year. That Lepine killed 14 women at once instead of one a month is hardly a key point.

Ninety-seven women were killed by their spouses in 1988. There is a similarity in those massive numbers and in Lepine's murderous belief that men can use whatever force "necessary" to control women.

But, having refused to accept the massacre as violence against women, Fraser, Adams, and their colleagues are unable to compare and contrast it with other forms of abuse. Lepine did not rape or assault women he knew; he murdered female students who, for him, symbolized a movement.

Feminists coined the phrase "violence against women" to open discussion. But, instead of starting there, what is asked in the media about Lepine's killing is, "What was his motive?" There is no room to explore the relationship between this man and his female victims. And so there's no way to respond to the event with action. But if "feminist" students constitute the new target of rage, should we not rush to university campuses to protect them?

When police search Lepine's body, they find a letter. Word gets out that he targeted fifteen women. While the police refuse to release the letter, the "hit list" is leaked to a few by a *La Presse* reporter. It will be several days before the media publish it, leaving many feminists in Québec and elsewhere in the country worried and wondering who has been targeted and who was in danger.

The named are: a feminist journalist; the president of a teachers' union (the CEQ); the vice-president of the CSN; the Canadian champion of the 1988 CA exams; the first woman firefighter in Québec; the first woman police captain in Québec; a sportscaster; a bank manager; a TV host and a transition house worker.

Marc Lepine indeed retaliated against women for taking liberties and creating liberty. But how did he compile the list? Had it ever been published before? As he didn't know the women personally, the most likely source was the media. And what was the slant of the articles in which he read their names? What other criteria did these women meet for him? If he saw them as economic achievers, why the transition house worker? And why did he name these women, but kill the students?

Since he was clearly attacking a movement, was it important to kill a group of women? Did the police refer to the names as a "hit list" because Lepine called for other men to kill the women? On Thursday, December 7th, Diana Bronson, a Montreal writer, tells the CBC "Morningside" audience, "Fourteen women are dead for one reason: they were women. Their male classmates are still alive for one reason: they are men." It is thrilling to hear her say this so directly, breaking open all the careful packaging and labeling of yesterday. She is eloquent in her expressions of fear and grief. But at the shelter, we begin to worry that all the female voices heard by the public will be limited to emotional identification with the victims. The situation also calls for leadership. So far, only half the message is being delivered.

The Canadian Association of Sexual Assault Centres, through the Vancouver office, issues a press statement: with a few exceptions, the media disregard this and other feminist press releases. It's beginning to look like a blackout.

Across the country, women are mobilizing; public vigils are being organized, starting with one last night in Montreal. More vigils will happen tonight. In the coverage, there are no details about the organizers and the speeches. All we get are ten second clips and one sentence quotes.

Instead, it goes like this: reporters fill time asking several women, "Does this make you more afraid?" and "Do you identify with the victims?" Asked to identify with the dead, the women are then photographed and filmed while they tremble and cry. This scenario becomes a litany. Some women manage to resist manipulation.

One young Montreal woman says firmly, "This is another event of violence against women, which is part of everyday life."

She is interrupted by a male student in an engineering jacket. He touches her arm and says softly, "Stay calm, okay? Just stay calm. That is not the point." Turning her eyes back to the camera, she is about to continue when he interrupts again. A chorus of women's voices rises to join hers as she insists, "But it *is* the point. Women are being killed. I am not safe on the street."

Women Against Violence Against Women rallies the community in Vancouver. On the steps of the court house downtown, speakers remember murdered wives and prostitutes and speak of the continuum of sexist behaviour from jokes to beatings. Bonnie speaks for Vancouver Rape Relief and Women's Shelter. "Many women have paid a high price for equality and liberty in our struggle," she says. "We call on men to tell each other that you have no permission to commit any act of violence against women."

Meanwhile, Kairn is holding the Rape Relief banner in the downpour muttering, "This stinks of classism," comparing the gathering of hundreds to the smaller response to the murders of twelve Vancouver prostitutes. She is suspicious of feminists, not just the media and the government. But she is here nevertheless because "the murder of any woman is a reason to organize." Others have stayed away, vowing that, until the murder of poor women, native women, runaways, and prostitutes causes public outcry, they will put their energy elsewhere.

It is a view that must be noted. For instance, by portraying this as "the largest mass murder in Canadian history," the massacre of native peoples is ignored. We can learn from the great American black feminist, Ida B. Wells, who revealed that lynchings after the abolition of slavery in the U. S., seemingly random, individual acts, were, in fact, another method of economic, social, and political control.

As the ceremony draws to a close, the organizers ask men in the crowd to move back, leaving women in the centre for a ritual in which they will hold hands. Few men move. A disheveled man storms around yelling. Every vigil has been harassed by verbal snipers. In Thunder Bay, feminists who asked men to stay home are denounced by Alderman Johannes Vanderwees as "sexist and extreme," guilty of "a kind of mind terrorism." On the eleven o'clock news, Robert Malcolm of BCTV accuses the Vancouver vigil of being "sexist and extreme compared to the legitimate mourning on campuses."

The vigils are also characterized as "spontaneous" gatherings, effectively hiding the people and groups behind them. Voiceless and apparently leaderless women are posited as fearful and passive. The anger and the analysis are both being censored by the media. The movement is portrayed as a loose, informal gathering of individuals, mostly white and middle class. The statements and theories of native, black, and immigrant women disappear.

In this moment of assigning public meaning to the Montreal massacre, women's history has to be brought forward. The American feminist, Jane Caputi, gives a political interpretation of urban multiple killers of women in her book *The Age of Sex Crime.* She observes that, during the nineteenth and twentieth centuries, as the church lost its power to regulate female behaviour, it was replaced by psychiatry, gynaecological surgery and Jack-the-Ripper-style killers, which she argues are the patriarchy's agents of social control today.

If feminists are correct in saying the fear and hatred of women in society at large is expressed in individual acts of rape, battering and killing, doesn't it follow that the antifeminist backlash has found expression through Lepine, a political assassin? But on "The Journal" the following night, Barbara Frum does not ask such relevant questions. "Surely this is a crime against humanity, not women," she insists again and again.

Friday, "Morningside" continues exploring the significance of the murders with an hour long panel, including Francine Pelletier, a founding editor of the defunct feminist magazine *La vie en rose,* who now writes for *La Presse.* She is one of the women on Lepine's list: she is making herself and all of us safer by staying public. Francine is at her radical best at this moment and speaks for many. She begins by saying that she sees the murders as a "reproach for feminist success," and speculates that "there will be more." Peter Gzowski glumly responds, "Yes, but isn't it time for mourning?"

As the discussion proceeds, Pelletier laments for the years of work that have been in vain, focusing more and more on the changes in attitude women want from the individual men in their lives rather than the transformation of the power structure and the culture. But it was that power structure and our culture which allowed and, in many ways, encouraged the killings. Why slow down the process of social change when we should be addressing the killing?

(By January 17th, Pelletier, who is on air regularly through the month, argues that the next ten years must be spent letting men catch up emotionally to women; she says feminists must drop the theory "all men are potentially rapists.")

Some men are afraid for women; some warn us to keep quiet so as not to attract the rage of other men. Some send money to the shelter, and others arrange a discussion group for men to work out their defensive responses. Many seem only to be seeking our approval; instead of asking themselves and each other what they can do to change, they are asking us to take care of them.

"Aren't there any nice guys out there?" the handsome "everyman" interviewer on CKVU-TV asks Bonnie. She gasps at the question, but recovers in time to answer, "Well, one in four of us is raped and not all by the same man. About half the women living with lovers are physically abused..." "Yes, but I'm asking you to make a concession, to say there are some good guys."

Why is this the central question for so many men? When half the population is unfairly treated, how can the other half be entirely innocent? It is true that not all men resort to violence, but men as a group do profit from higher wages, better jobs, less domestic work, and more control over everything. In this moment of candour, the anchor is asking Bonnie, and all of us, to fudge the facts so he can feel more comfortable.

In *The Globe and Mail*, after the headline "Killer's letter blames feminists," comes coverage of the vigils and the political responses, and commentaries by Emil Sher and Diana Bronson, along with an editorial which asks, "Why were women in the gunsights?" The editorial goes on to state unequivocally that "these executions emerge from a social context and cannot be disowned." It even recognizes the events as a backlash against "changes that are just and reasonable," and, although there is no credit or praise for feminists or the political movement that has promoted these changes, the editorial does state, "the arrogance of male dominance is to be found, naked and unashamed, at the heart of our democratic system and in centres of higher learning."

There is no call for affirmative action at Canadian universities, or funding of university women's centres; neither is there a demand for the reinstatement of NAC's funding, universal daycare, equal pay, or adequate federal funding for the work of rape crisis centres and transition houses.

Emil Sher writes what women have been saying about "the continuum of violence," repeating how individual men in various ways avoid facing their contribution to it by their refusal to talk about it with each other. His insistence that men must talk "about how we can give back what was never ours" seems appropriate but it still side-steps the specifics. (Assume your responsibility for the care of children, the sick, and the elderly; redistribute the 40 percent extra on your pay cheque to women until we achieve equality; be civil and supportive of one another; stop bullying women and children; organize to get other men to do this and lobby for women's movement demands.)

In another opinion piece, Diana Bronson evokes women's terrible fear of men's violence. She is diverted from a central point: these murders are not just expressions of the same misogyny that women experience every day; they are the product of a vicious new strain aimed at women who fight for women's rights — at feminists.

As does Stevie Cameron in her gut wrenching piece published the next day, Bronson omits to mention the value of women's groups, rape crisis centres and shelters in assuaging women's fear. When feminism is attacked, the first thing required is a reaffirmation of feminism and its political groups. But this does not happen in *The Globe and Mail* or anywhere else.

On "The Journal" tonight, Ann McGrath represents the National Action Committee (NAC), the largest women's rights organization in the country. McGrath is chair of NAC's Violence Against Women subcommittee. She is not, however, invited to share her knowledge and understanding of the issues sparked by the massacre. She is, instead, interviewed as a victim, the survivor of a classroom shooting in her high school. This story, the telling of which brings her almost to tears, is all Barbara Frum wants us to hear. "Are you permanently scarred by that event? Does one ever really recover?" she probes. Ann explains that she channels her grief and anger into changing the world by contributing her energy to NAC. It is the only political comment she is allowed.

Following the taping, McGrath says she is exhausted and debilitated from defending feminists against the criticism that we are exploiting this event for our own political ends. How could we do differently, we wonder, without betraying ourselves, our work and our responsibility to other women? How can we leave it to the antifeminist forces to define the event for us?

In Québec, there is more of everything. More angry resistance from men, more media sensationalism, more sympathetic columns, but the character of the gender struggle is the same. *La Presse* has run about a dozen statements denouncing the murders, some from unions, one by the association of engineers, one written jointly by the rape crisis centres and shelters of Québec, which is the only piece from the autonomous women's movement (their communique gets equal billing with a press release from Hydro-Québec).

La Presse has promised space to Madeleine LeCombe, past president of the transition house association. But no, the assistant editor explains in print, today he thinks, like Peter Gzowski, that this is a time for reflection and mourning rather than opinion. Feminist analysis, in his mind, counts as opinion rather than reflection.

Three months later, we still don't have all the facts about the massacre. The media peremptorily closed the door on the debate, but not before making sure that feminists were trivialized. Feminists could express acceptance of the emotional consequences of the massacre, but were not permitted to rail against it. Feminists were honoured as victims, but not respected as politicized participants who could constructively shape the event's meaning. There was some exploration of the environment of violence against women that produced Lepine, but no examination of the anti-feminist climate that created a political assassination.

Fifty years ago this year women won the vote in Québec. In that historic feminist struggle, no woman was murdered. For feminists, now, there is a before and after the Montreal massacre.

Lee Lakeman's ideas come from the praxis of almost 20 years of organizing with women in Canadian transition houses and rape crisis centres. She was coordinating one of the world's first women's shelters before she had the words: feminist, sexist-violence, social transformation. She has continued to answer the crisis line throughout the years, in belief that the work of connecting women, one by one, informs the coalition building and corrects the theory-making as no other work can. She has been a member of the collective operating Vancouver Rape Relief and Women's Shelter for the last 12 years. Lately, she has begun to record and preserve in writing the stories of actions in which she has participated with some of the fabulous women of this wave of the movement, exploring the liberating ideas which have emerged from their work.

DANGEROUS DETERMINATION

Moira Farr

"When I found so astonishing a power placed within my hands,
I hesitated a long time concerning the manner in which I should
employ it." — Doctor Victor Frankenstein,
          from *Frankenstein*, by Mary Shelley

Good health and male children — Italian saying, after a sneeze

First comes love, then comes marriage,
Then comes... in a baby carriage.
I wish you love, I wish you joy,
I wish you first a baby boy.   — U.S.A.

Eighteen goddess-like daughters are not equal to one son with a
hump. — Chinese proverb

A house full of daughters is like a cellar full of sour beer.
                    — German adage

When a girl is born, the walls are crying. — The Talmud

If the tenth too, is a girl child
I will cut both your feet off,
To the knees I'll cut your feet off,
Both your eyes too, I will put out,
Blind and crippled you will be then,
Pretty little wife, young woman.   — Bulgaria

IN AN ANGUS REID POLL on new reproductive technologies
conducted in June 1990, Canadians were asked, "Are you aware

of anything that can be done to human sperm in a lab to improve the chances of having a boy or a girl?" Seventy-two percent answered no.

The pollsters stated in their report that "Canadians are not yet aware of the applications of new reproductive technologies in the area of genetic screening. During the focus groups, it was discussion of sex preselection and gentic engineering that produced the most future shock in the minds of participants."

I hate to break it to 72 percent of Canadians, but future shock is not an appropriate response to something which has been around for a long time now. While we weren't paying much attention, sex determination (followed by abortion of the wrong-sex fetus) and sex preselection — through new reproductive technologies such as sperm separation, ultrasound, amniocentesis and chorionic villi sampling — have moved steadily from the realm of sci-fi to concrete reality. That makes it harder to deal with and more crucial that we do. The way old ideology allies with and thoroughly informs new technology is nowhere more evident than in the practice of gender preselection and determination. It has mostly been advanced through strong cultural biases against females and, in the name of population control, as a way of eliminating them.

It's easy and obvious to express repugnance, and apparently most Canadians do, at the thought of any technology being used to rid the population of people with traits society happens to devalue, now or in the future (femaleness, red hair, myopia, where would it end?). But the question of how to stop this from happening once we've said "isn't it awful?" seems so fraught with ethical dilemmas that until recently most of us, including feminists, haven't wanted to touch it with a ten-foot speculum.

Discussion of sex selection within the National Action Committee on the Status of Women (NAC) proved so contentious that only a passing reference to it appeared in the initial draft brief to the Royal Commission on New Reproductive Technologies (though the final document states that NAC is against sex selection and the licensing of clinics offering sex determination and preselection services). The brief presented by the Ontario Advisory Council on Women's Issues had 38 recommendations on new reproductive technologies, but not one of them dealt specifically with sex selection. The Toronto Women's Health Network, which also presented a brief, was under the impression that NAC would address it. In a newsletter, the network admitted it "heaved a mighty sigh of relief that someone else was including this issue in their written submission."

As NAC ultimately recognized, it is time for Canadian feminists to face the unpleasant and paradoxical aspects of this issue: is there a way to regulate sex selection technology without infringing on abortion rights? Do laws emanating from partriarchal governments have any place in the realm of women's health? Some feminists would answer no to both those questions, opting in case of sex selection for an ignore/disapprove-in-theory strategy. "No encouragement should be given to the uses of [sex selection] while recognizing that there is no way of enforcing a prohibition," argues sociologist Thelma McCormack in her 1988 article, "Public Policies and Reproductive Technology: A Feminist Critique."

Banning the technologies outright may not be the answer — they are capable of use for less sinister purposes than weeding out women, such as giving couples the choice of whether to bear children with sex-linked disorders or allowing families to "balance" the sexes of their offspring — though ethical arguments against both of these uses have been advanced by disabled activists and feminists; it should also be noted that these uses have never been and aren't now the chief focus for research and development of sex selection techniques.

Nor can we stop people who want to determine the sex of their children from employing methods which include everything from intercourse positions to vaginal douches. But we can start to examine the implications of the whole concept as it gains ground in Canada; a completely hands-off approach, in my view, amounts to encouragement. At the very least, restrictions on the proliferation of high tech commercial clinics offering sex preselection and determination services should be considered. India and Denmark have enacted legislation that limits the use of sex selection techniques. Germany, understandably sensitive about the eugenic capabilities of new reproductive technologies, is working on such legislation. One thing is certain: ignoring the problems won't make them go away. And misogyny, in the service of a patriarchal status quo, has a banal way of insinuating itself until we accept it as just part of life.

I first became aware of the notion of sex selection a couple of years ago, through a television documentary about the uses of ultrasound and amniocentesis in India for determining gender and, in virtually all cases, aborting fetuses which show up female. After swearing loudly at the TV (an ineffective form of protest which is nevertheless therapeutic in the short term), I did what I usually do when confronted with horrible things happening *out there*: felt gloomy and helpless, discussed it with a few friends, and gradually let it slip from my consciousness.

But last July, I was reactivated while perusing, of all things, Rosemary Sexton's society column in *The Globe and Mail*. Covering a benefit ball in aid of The Canadian Hemophilia Society, Sexton quoted a Toronto woman named Susan Bernstein, the mother of a hemophiliac boy (the disorder affects only males), who had gone to a gender preselection clinic in order to better the chances that her second child would be female. Of those using the clinic, Bernstein said, "I'm one of the few who wants a girl."

I called Bernstein. Yes, she had contacted a Toronto clinic (there is also one in Calgary), a franchise of a U.S. outfit, operated by urologist Alan Abramovitch. Susan G. Cole wrote an article in the Toronto weekly *NOW* when this clinic opened in 1987. She reported in detail on the sex preselection techniques offered: the Ericsson method, perfected and patented by American biologist Ronald Ericsson, involves separating sperm into those containing male and those containing female chromosomes (when being inseminated with female sperm, the woman must take the fertility drug Clomid); for selecting girls, the Sephadex method (by now gathering cobwebs), which filters female sperm through a tube.

Bernstein hadn't decided whether to go through with the procedure, which would cost about $1,800; she wasn't yet sure if the increased odds claimed for having the gender of choice were accurate. She was discussing her concerns with a geneticist at North York Hospital (in the end, she concluded that the clinic wasn't for her). She said that the clients had to sign a consent form saying they would accept either gender, but she also came away with the impression that the majority of Abramovitch's clients wanted boys. (Unfortunately, I was unable to verify this with Abramovitch, who did not return repeated phone calls. However, I subsequently learned that Ericsson's clinics operate in 46 countries in Europe, the U.S., Asia, and Latin America; Ericsson himself has stated that, in one study, 248 of 263 couples selected boys.)

I began doing further research and found that feminists throughout the world have done their homework on this one. In articles with titles like "Sex Selection: From Here to Fraternity" and "The Endangered Sex," they point to the overwhelming preference for sons evident in the folklore and customs of virtually all cultures. They show how the new sex selection technologies researched and developed in the past three decades have served that preference, in the most dramatic cases (in some areas of China, for instance) very clearly being seen as a "humane" alternative to female infanticide and neglect (sort of like the difference between public hanging and the electric chair, I guess.)

Even in Europe and North America, where son preference is generally less pronounced than in some Third World countries, study after study indicates that the majority of people who use sex preselection and determination do so to ensure the birth of males — if not exclusively, then at least as their first child, which leads feminists to speculate on the psychological and social ramifications of entire nations filled with first-born sons and second-born daughters. In India, where sex selection has been so rampant that males have begun outnumbering females in the population, women have rallied and won (as of 1989) acts of Parliament that seek to control prenatal sex determination.

Feminists have also revealed the repulsive ideas about global population control that have driven research into sex selection and other new reproductive technologies: Gena Corea, in *The Mother Machine*, outlines the ideas of a doctor in the 1970s who gained widespread coverage for his proposal that a "boy-pill" be developed; no less a personage than Clare Booth Luce endorsed this notion in the *Washington Star*. Corea also writes about an organization called The Good Parents Group of Nutley, New Jersey (I don't make these things up, I just report them), which "supports the practice of aborting the female fetuses of the poor in India (it calls this 'Therabort') and has offered to help finance a model therapeutic termination clinic. Women found to be carrying male fetuses would not be permitted abortions at the clinics unless the fetus were defective."

Rationales for the development of artificial wombs have also been based on ideas about the expendability of women. A man named Edward Grossman argued in a 1971 article entitled "The Obsolescent Mother," that with this technology "geneticists could program in some superior trait; sex preselection would be simple; women could be permanently sterilized." When this astonishing article was cited by Robin Rowland in a chapter she wrote in the book *Man-Made Women*, I thought at first, why highlight loony ideas from some grimy, marginal tract? Then I looked up the bibliography: Grossman's piece had appeared in *The Atlantic*. It's no wonder feminist writers have begun speaking about the unspeakable: femicide.

Absorbing all this stuff about the threat of female extermination, I thought I might perhaps be getting a little overwrought; other feminists I spoke with didn't seemed that concerned. And when I polled several hospitals, I was heartened to find that most Canadian doctors, such as Philip Wyatt, head of the clinical genetics centre at North York General Hospital, find the idea of gender selection "extremely distasteful." In other words, if you were to present yourself at a hospital ultrasound clinic today and say "tell me the sex of my fetus so I can abort it if it's female," you probably would not be accommodated.

But that "distaste," Wyatt makes clear, isn't part of some formal, written code of ethics. It's just a matter of how most individual Canadian doctors happen to feel. And one night last October, I heard an item on "As It Happens," in which Dale Goldhawk interviewed a doctor, John Stevens of California, who had patented an ultrasound technique he said could determine the sex of a fetus at nine weeks. Stevens spoke obnoxiously about protecting his "intellectual property"; he whined about unfair treatment in Canada. He had advertised his services in the Vancouver community newspaper, *The Link*, aimed at the South Asian community in that city. There had been an uproar; Goldhawk also interviewed a member of a South Asian women's group, whose protest to the newspaper had caused the ads to be withdrawn by the publisher. And a doctor from Vancouver's Grace Hospital expressed disapproval and scepticism about Stevens' technique, saying that the American doctor had not been granted hospital privileges (he wouldn't reveal why) and so would not be able to set up a clinic in Vancouver.

I tuned in the next night, wondering if the "Talk Back" segment of the show, where listeners phone in responses to what they've heard, would include some reactions to the Stevens item. It did, but not of the kind I'd anticipated. No outraged female voices that night. Both callers featured were men; one basically said: so what if this guy wants to operate in Canada, let him. The other seemed to have totally missed the point, harshly criticizing the piece for being biased because it didn't include an interview with a male member of the South Asian community.

Stevens got a lot of ink and air time across Canada after that initial "As It Happens" item. He thought it "authoritarian" of Canadians not to welcome him with open arms; it wasn't his responsibility, he argued, if clients went on to abort female fetuses his ultrasound technique revealed. In fact, he presented himself as a kind of hero, saving South Asian women from the shame of having daughters, which could result in violent reactions from angry husbands.

Charges of racist stereotyping ensued, and I wanted to find out what the situation really was in Canada's South Asian communities. I phoned Aruna Papp, director of a Toronto organization called South Asian Family Services and asked her if it was true that some South Asian women were so pressured to bear sons that they would seek out sex preselection and determination services, and abort female fetuses. "Yes!" She replied as though she'd been waiting a long time for someone to ask her that question. Could she cite examples? "Well, I've lived with it," she replied, with a mirthless laugh and proceeded to tell me some very painful details of her life.

She was born in Pakistan, the first of six daughters in her family (her parents finally got a boy on try number seven). "All my life, I tried to be the son that I wasn't," she says, explaining that Hindu cultural and religious beliefs hinge salvation on the birth of sons. "It's only in middle age that I've been able to feel it's okay to be a woman." Now divorced, she says some South Asian women in Canada do suffer abuse at the hands of their husbands when they bear daughters (she herself had two daughters, then "eventually" a son). According to Papp, pregnant women in these communities in Canada often go "for a holiday" to India and Pakistan where, despite legislation, it is still easier to obtain access to sex determination services and subsequent abortions, and return to Canada, female-fetus free.

Some feminists and doctors I've interviewed (including Philip Wyatt, who has referred people to the Ambramovitch clinic and says he has witnessed an East Indian woman having a "complete mental breakdown" when told she was carrying a female fetus) have argued that the pressure on South Asian women in Canada to bear sons and the abuse that can result when they don't, is reason enough to allow, however warily, sex preselection clinics to operate here.

But Aruna Papp is not the only woman of South Asian descent

who doesn't want to see these clinics, or the kind Stevens proposes, starting up in Canada. Sharmini Peries, a board member of the South Asian Women's Group in Toronto, argues strongly against them. While she makes it clear that not *all* South Asian families value sons above daughters (she herself was never so pressured, and she and her husband have "two beautiful daughters"), she doesn't deny the existence of such bias. But she is adamant in her denunciation of Stevens and his ilk. "Doctor Stevens has a gun to our heads as surely as Marc Lepine did," she states, in no uncertain terms. The same position is held by South Asian women's groups in Vancouver.

John Stevens may for now be thwarted from coming to Canada to "make a buck," as he puts it (though he is setting up a clinic in Buffalo, in hopes that residents of southern Ontario will make the trip across the border). But it isn't any law, or even the cry of outrage from South Asian women's groups that is keeping him out; he simply hasn't yet been able to persuade a Canadian hospital, for reasons which haven't been made public to affiliate with him (a licensing requirement of provincial colleges of physicians and surgeons).

Are the medical profession's rules, regulations, and codes of moral conduct enough to safeguard against the future use of technologies in ways that are injurious to the status of women? Medical licensing bodies in Alberta and Ontario have apparently had no problem giving the go-ahead to clinics offering sex preselection services. Wouldn't it have been more appropriate to have had some form of public debate about whether commercial operators of American franchises should be allowed to offer such services in Canada *before* they were up and running? (I realize this is a time honoured approach to women's health matters: barrel ahead, then say "oops, we goofed" when the casualties roll in.)

The Canadian Medical Association (CMA) has stated to the commission that it does not consider gender preselection or determination an ethical practice, except in cases where there is a family history of a sex-linked disorder, and CMA ethics committee director Eike Kluge told me he'd like to see gender clinics shut down. But the CMA is not a regulating body; it can provide guidelines but can't enforce them.

I'm dismayed when feminists downplay the current availability and appeal of sex selection techniques in Canada, and make statements like "This isn't India," as Canadian Abortion Rights Action League (CARAL) did in its brief to the royal commission. What exactly is that supposed to mean? Regardless of their ethnic origin, the people using sex preselection clinics here are Canadians, availing themselves of services open to all in the great, free, capitalist marketplace.

Beyond the issue of whether we should support the commercialization of reproductive health services, we are dealing with a trend primarily fuelled by the insidious power of hate-filled ideas; in this case, a patriarchal bias which utterly negates the value of daughters, blames females giving birth to females for overpopulation, and suggests that beyond their reproductive capacities — which we may soon be able to wholly duplicate in labs anyway — women have nothing of worth to contribute to the world. It shouldn't matter what group such ideas are aimed at, or how widespread we perceive their present influence to be. When James Keegstra taught high school students that the world was run by a Jewish conspiracy, did we say "What's the big deal? This isn't Nazi Germany. And it's only a few kids in rural Alberta anyway." No. Media klieg lights shone on Keegstra until he was brought before a human rights commission and then lost his job. When Philippe Rushton of the University of Western Ontario came forward with claims of a connection between race and intelligence, did we say, "Oh well, he's just one professor. Who cares?" No. People like David Suzuki denounced Rushton in public; CBC Radio's "Quirks and Quarks" won at least one award for a show which completely discredited his research.

As far as I know, neither Keegstra nor Rushton ever secured a platform for their views on the op/ed page of *The Globe and Mail;* but a Vancouver freelance writer named Graeme Matheson did, to argue in favour of eliminating women. In case you missed "What's Wrong With Choosing Your Baby's Sex?" here's one highlight: "Following the laws of supply and demand, as the numbers of available women fell, their value would go up...grooms [in India] could eventually expect to pay for brides, raising the value of girls..."

Fortunately, a rebuttal to both the racism and sexism of Matheson's Nutleyite views appeared four days later, written jointly by NAC president Judy Rebick, Sharmini Peries, and Judy Vashti Persad of Women Working With Immigrant Women. Their response was stinging and eloquent, but I couldn't help thinking that if feminists had been more vigilant on this issue, it would have been their view which appeared first and Matheson who would have been forced, if so moved, to write a letter to the editor.

In wading through the ethical dilemmas posed by sex selection, I've been torn between the stance of feminists such as Thelma McCormack who, though personally offended by the notion of sex selection, do not support *ad hoc* legislation on this or any other technology and the more interventionist approach favoured by some members of NAC and South Asian women's groups, who feel most threatened by sex selection technology right now. Ultimately, all feminists want the same thing: holistic, woman-centred, woman-run health centres accessible to all, where care does not revolve around drugs and high tech gizmos. We are a long way from such Utopian set-ups right now, but my feeling (and just like a woman, I'm trusting my intuition on this one) is that the existence of boy factories in Canada does nothing to further such a goal, especially when they appear to be aiding and abetting the victimization of women of a particular cultural group. At the very least, we should stand alongside these women and denounce such practices; call for government support services (shelters, education) to be chaneled towards women who are physically and emotionally abused when they give birth to daughters (ditto for the daughters themselves); monitor and study legislation in other countries (which regulates the use of sex selection techniques, *not* access to abortion) and think about how it might be applied in Canada; finally, seriously consider the virulently sexist legacy of this use of technology, and its potential contribution to the future of humanity, before standing aside in good liberal fashion and watching it flourish.

It beats swearing at the TV.

Moira Farr is a freelance writer living in Toronto; she grew up in Peterborough, Ontario, received a B.A. in English and History from University of Toronto and a Bachelor of Journalism from Ryerson Polytechnical Institute. Her work has appeared in *This Magazine* (of which she is an editorial board member), *Toronto Life, Canadian Business, Canadian Architect, Registered Nurse, Flare, Utne Reader.*

In 1991 she received a $5,000 "Protege Award," selected by journalist-activist June Callwood, from the Arts Foundation of Greater Toronto.

MUSE IN A FEMALE GHETTO

A Portrait of Elizabeth Smart

Rosemary Sullivan

I MET ELIZABETH SMART IN 1978 when I visited her at Bungay in Suffolk. I got to know her well when she lived in Toronto in 1983. She was one of the warmest, most generous, vital people I have known. She was also one of the most distressed.

Elizabeth was the kind of person one puzzles over: to understand her life seems as important as understanding her writing. She was a woman who tried to live the paradox of being female and a writer at a time when everything militated against keeping those two destinies together. When I try to figure out what made Elizabeth so extraordinary, I can see in retrospect it was her extremism. She refused half-measures, disparaged secured risks, and always went for the total gamble. She gambled with the myth of romantic love and the myth of art and the price of her fidelity to both was, I think, heart-breaking.

The outline of her writing career is stark. In 1945, when she was thirty-two she published *By Grand Central Station I Sat Down and Wept*. It came out in an edition of 4,000 copies, received minor attention, and was out of print in six months. Today it's hailed as one of the masterpieces of poetic prose in the English language. Thirty-two years later at sixty-four, she published a small book of poems called *A Bonus*, followed the next year by her second novel *The Assumption of Rogues and Rascals*. What happened to silence Smart during those thirty-two years? It's a puzzle I, as a woman, feel compelled to look at.

Smart was born in Ottawa in 1913, the child of wealth and privilege. Her family counted in the prime minister's set. She had governesses, long trips abroad, piano lessons in England at seventeen, a coming-out party. She was groomed for comfort, but she wanted to write. She published her first poem at the age of ten, and at fifteen gathered her writing into a volume she modestly called *The Complete Works of Betty Smart.* She was ambitious and wilfully idealistic about writing.

She was desperate to escape family and country. Her first attempt at a novel "Dig a Grave and Let us Bury our Mother" describes a flight to Mexico on a boat carrying refugees from European fascism in 1939. "I am escaping. I am putting miles of sea, continents of deserts and impossible mountains between us." The "us" refers to her mother, whom Smart describes as a woman who believed in the great class barriers. "One had a duty to stay where God had been pleased to put one. Naturally she had been put at the top. In Canada where nothing ever happens class must have been easier to believe in." Her idea of rebellion is pathetic. She slept with the refugees in steerage "taking my part with everyone else...anonymous, alive" until a cable arrived from mother with the price of first class passage.

Her rebellion was predictable. She wanted to shock and outrage (a lifelong need), and she turned to art in the bohemian tradition to make the blessed break from banality.

Believing great spiritual adventures could not happen in Canada, she looked to England. Her favourite writer was the young George Barker whom she loved because he "goes from the sheepish and shame faced to the roar of authority." There's the clue, the word *authority;* it's what she wanted for herself but never quite believed she had. From Canada she sent poems to Lawrence Durrell in Paris. A correspondence developed and she mentioned Barker. Durrell wrote: "Are you rich because I happen to know Barker needs money and has manuscripts to sell." So began her relationship with Barker, in which she played a supporting role for his art, the classic male/female relationship so dangerous to the woman writer.

In 1940 Smart was at a writer's colony in Big Sur. Barker was stranded in Japan, where war was imminent, and wrote asking her to send him fare. She managed to get him a quota number and the money and, in due course, he arrived in California — with a wife Smart had not previously heard of. Smart and Barker met on July 19, 1940; both were twenty-seven. "I am standing on a corner in Monterey, waiting for the bus to come in, and all the muscles of my will are holding my terror to face the moment I most desire." So begins *Grand Central,* the record of the first stages of her love affair with Barker. But the truth is that Smart had written much of it before she even met Barker. He arrived in time to fulfill her fantasy.

And what was her fantasy? It was the heroic myth of romantic love, the most outrageous, seductive, consuming myth a woman can fall captive to. Men have written about romantic love for centuries and managed to survive. One might almost say it's the male writer's first assignment: Neruda's *Twenty Love Songs;* Pasternak's *Doctor Zhivago.* Even Dante. But for men it remains a myth, never a stratagem for a life. Why was it deadly for Smart?

Ellen Moers in *Literary Women* has finally made clear what the myth means for women. It is an epic myth of power, the result of pride and ambition which focuses not so much on the object of passion, the man, but on the passion itself. Reading *Grand Central,* one sees the young Elizabeth Smart consumed by her own sense of power. "Virile as a cobra," she offers an exotic vision of what total love might be. And the man must be taught to believe in it; he must be converted to her will. "Eons have been evolving and planets disintegrating and forming to compel these two together," she writes. "I was born for this." She can no more resist her grand passion than the earth can resist the rain. The tone of the book is imperial, imperative, you might even say intolerant. "He is the one I picked out from the world in cold deliberation." And the point is rebellion: "Love offends with its nudity." The word is to be posed against all those other words — war, power,

prudence, comfort, thrust forward by the parade of taunting un-
believers. Love is sufficient to make the world anew, and Smart
will be its prophet.

And we are struck by this book because of the purity of this
extremism. It's a masterpiece of metaphoric, sensual writing.
Perhaps it awakens in us a kind of nostalgia, but it is a young
book, compelling in its unquenchable appetite, and yet lacking
in irony. Because, of course, the myth fails. For Smart, then, the
puzzle was to understand how to survive the myth, to tap the
source of her own creative longing.

In 1941 Smart was pregnant. She went to Pender Harbour,
B.C. to have her baby and write *Grand Central.* Her parents used
their influence to have Barker refused entry to Canada on grounds
of "moral turpitude." After the child was born, Smart promptly
returned to the U.S. and found work as a file clerk in the British
army office in Washington. Barker was then in New York. There
were "red nights under Brooklyn Bridge." But he was still with
his wife, a situation which weighed heavily on Smart. She fled to
England to escape him, but, in his way, he followed. Three more
children arrived in between his irregular visits. He lived with
three other women after her, and there had been several before.
Smart never demanded constancy.

If Smart's myth was that of romantic extremity, we might
ask what Barker's was. We can gather from his *True Confessions of
George Barker* that it was the male myth of fidelity to art at all
costs. Woman was the muse but also the distracting temptress.
Still, to see Barker's role as betrayer is irrelevant. We might better see both myths as literary myths. For isn't Smart's kind of love
an ideology learned from literature; as is the male myth of the
ruthless artist. And ironically the two myths are mutually exclusive.

The dangerous part of the myth for Smart was that heroic
love is all-consuming — she conceded to her partner the power
to absorb her identity; upon him depended her capacity to en-
dure. And perhaps the buried secret was what she sought; what
she most admired in the male was his ruthless autonomy, his

ability to sacrifice everything in life to his own genius. Smart may have had reservations about Barker the man, about what she called his roguery, but she never doubted that his fidelity to art was adequate justification for his weakness. And she always believed him the better artist. In my opinion, she was the more extraordinary writer. What she had done was project her own gifts onto the other, afraid to claim the loneliness of her own strength.

We know from *In the Meantime* (1984) that Smart continued to write in a painful desultory fashion over the years. Small pieces; nothing substantial. Perhaps four children is explanation enough for the silence, particularly with the loneliness and burden of raising them alone. She worked in advertising and as an editor and was at one time the highest paid editor in England. At times the children went to boarding school. There were also periods when she was desperately poor. Still, the deepest problem was, I think, that she had lost her confidence, her belief in herself, and she felt undermined intellectually. Certainly recognition would have made a difference. But *Grand Central* was soon lost from view. Her mother prevented its importation to Canada and bought up any British copies that made it into country and had them burned.

In England Smart became the writer who didn't write. For years her children didn't know she had published a book. She used to complain it was difficult to know what to call oneself. Sometimes she tried ex-writer. A kind of recognition did come in 1975 with the first North American edition of *Grand Central* and in 1978 with the publication of the two new books, but was it helpful? The truth is that by this time, Smart had become half afraid of her own ambition. She could envy plants: "The greed of plants to succeed doesn't seem at all disgusting. They don't need praise or encouragement or stimulation (though they often get it)."

After a thirty-year silence, Smart picks up the story where she left off. For *The Assumption of Rogues and Rascals* is the sequel to *Grand Central,* where she examines the cruel sexual bargain, and offers a portrait of the artist as a woman — not writing. She asks first whether writing and maternity are mutually exclusive. She complains that women like the Brontes and Virginia Woolf "bypassed the womb/and kept the Self." But she wanted children and "the womb's an unwieldy baggage. Who can stagger uphill with such a noisy weight?"

This could be the commonplace dilemma of the woman who can't write because of the claims of domesticity, but Smart is honest enough to see there is a deeper problem and it has to do with herself. Asked why she could not find a man after Barker, she said the answer is in *Rogues and Rascals*. Smart had to believe that love is "the mad moment, the electric revelation that causes the soul to seize up." Love is vertical. It is the great "iconoclastic ecstasy." When this fails, the only thing left is suffering. Smart remained attached to her own pain. But isn't there a terrible, perverse egoism in such suffering? Perhaps the power of such pain is that it confers a unique identity. The myth of romantic love becomes Smart's own myth of suffering. Moreover, she seems to have easily divided the world into two camps: the bourgeois who choose comfort, status, the postponing of desire and the rogues and outlaws, the artists who live free of the fetters of social convention. She chose desire over need; championed an ethic of feeling as the only true test of integrity. "All right. I accept. The price of life is pain, since the price of comfort is death and damnation."

Rogues and Rascals is a confession and its agonizing loneliness is unbearable. Why did love inflict on Smart so deep and debilitating a wound? This is the mystery that lies at the heart of the novel; the mystery of the writer's ego and what happened to it; the story of a gifted woman coping with her incapacity to write. For Smart, woman is "clitorically vulnerable." She talks of the "whory desire to please." She spent all her energy giving; she couldn't presume to demand. "Is ego a prick to the muse?" she writes, and is it male? "His pampered Muse/Knew no veto/Hers lived/in a female ghetto."

If Smart could not fully believe in herself as a writer, it was partly because she carried the male censor around in her mind: "the jeering inhibiting voices, the slappers down." But there was something else. She never found a solution to what she called her own "slushy need." To write, she believed, would mean being alone: "Could I stand up and say/Fuck off! or, Be my slave!/To be in a very unfeminine/Very unloving state/ Is the desperate need/ Of anyone trying to write."

But why should passivity be the sole model of the feminine? The answer, I think, may have had to do with the book she wanted to write and never did. It was to be about the mother and fortunately, we do have her notes; "I wasn't going to write about *my* mother — only the passionate relationship — serving nature." But is it her own mother who comes across in her sketches as an object of incredible venom. "Her long scenes of hysteria and crying, of pacing up and down the veranda, wailing in her uncanny voice, 'I'm going insane!' or moaning as she lay soft and whale-like on the bathroom floor." She still writes with bitterness at sixty-six: "The smug mother love walking around so self-congratulatory, so sure it won't be shot at; committing acts of super egoism under the guise of unselfishness and with the approval of the world." In her mother, Smart describes the classic archetype of the female who ruined five people's lives because of that need. Love which is tyrannical because it expresses itself as need is a form of control. Beneath this she saw "sexual fears hidden in her leather-bound Emerson." She battled this archetype, even having a lesbian affair in her twenties to sexualize the maternal image. To overcome the archetype she dedicated her life to the myth of sexual passion and refused to impose any need of her own on the lover with whom she could have four children and expect nothing. Ironically this did not free her but incarcerated her with a loneliness that was debilitating. Her charity, her generosity became a form of self-denial.

We should have had more from Elizabeth Smart, which made her death in March all the more painful. Too much contrived against her: a domestic life, an absconding male, the myths in her own mind and an isolation, part chosen, part endured, which kept her ego vulnerable. Still, she was heroic. She never gave up. And she produced two remarkable books.

Her story is an allegory, though we watch it now at a distance for there have been profound changes for women writers which are more than generational. I think woman writers can never again be quite as alone as Elizabeth Smart was. We may still wrestle with the problems of confidence, of intermittent silences, but because so much has been written about women writing we know where to go to find parallels to our own experience. Our themes have been validated as they were not for Smart. We have returned to a sense of female power and have defeated female solipsism. So much energy has gone into understanding the power politics of sexual relationships that love is no longer the female's sole responsibility. There is a larger world than the sexual, and women are entering it at long last, gratefully, and with relief.

Rosemary Sullivan teaches English at Erindale College in Toronto. She is the author of two books of poetry: *The Space a Name Makes* (1986) and *Blue Planet* (1991); editor of seven anthologies, including *Stories by Canadian Women* and *Poetry by Canadian Women*. Her biography, *By Heart/Elizabeth Smart: A Life* (1991) was nominated for a Governor-General's award.

POST-FEMINISM AND POWER DRESSING

Who Says the Women's Movement Has Run Out of Steam?

Susan Crean

POST-FEMINISM? DID I MISS SOMETHING HERE? Did feminism stage a revolution while capitalism was out golfing and we were away on holidays? For months I've been hearing the phrase, watching it crop up with increasing regularity in the mainstream, and finally, in the September issue of *Chatelaine,* I got to meet her myself: the Post-feminist Woman.

Suspending disbelief and holding my nose while I flipped past the photospread on Canada's ten sexiest men (Barry Callaghan: "It's his mind that's magnetic"; Pierre Trudeau: "His premiership was one long seduction of the Canadian psyche") and a vintage fifties piece on how to catch your man, (What scares men now? asks Sidney Katz. Answer: women who demand openness, earn more than they do, don't want a permanent relationship or kids, are sexually emancipated...) I arrive breathless at Bronwyn Drainie's article, to be greeted with: "The post-feminists of the mid-80s — women in their twenties and thirties are less concerned about waving a feminist banner than focusing on personal needs."

So here's what's been happening, according to Drainie. The younger generation of women are put off by feminism which they find old-fashioned and ineffectual. With so many of its goals still unrealized all it's got to offer is more of the same old struggle. Borrrring! These baby boomers are pragmatic, however, positive thinkers. They've decided to get on with it alone without a movement; to concentrate on their own priorities — finding a mate, raising a family and finding creative work which "breaks free of confining 'masculine' models" — which seems to mean having your own consulting firm at thirty and decorating your office in pink. Drainie doesn't seem fazed by any of this. "While they have lost the communal feeling so widespread among feminists, they bring something new and positive to women's complex evolution: a refusal to blame others for their problems. *Trying to make things work for me.* That's post-feminism in a nut-shell." Focus on the personal, to hell with the political. These people could make the Me Generation look self-effacing.

I have to admit when I first heard the word, I laughed. It sounded too much like those overstuffed terms we learned about in art courses — post-impressionism, post-painterly abstraction, post (and post-post) modernism — which I always suspected had more to do with the wiles of the art market and art critics than anything the artists were doing. (Did Gauguin know he was a post-impressionist? Did he care?) Well, we should care about post-feminism. Not only because it has arrived, the hot topic of the autumn season, but because it means a lot more than the word immediately suggests.

Not long ago a favourite antifeminist rant among popular chauvinists like Gary Lautens and Frank Jones in the *Toronto Star* and Robert Fulford at *Saturday Night* was that women's liberation had run out of stream. Some went so far off the edge of reality as to claim that it had achieved equality for women, the evidence being the almost universal acceptance of the moniker Ms. Usually these claims were made vehemently, in hope they would come true. But the movement itself didn't disband. It got older, broadened its base and has settled in for the long haul, which has entailed confronting its own shortcomings (racism and a middle class bias) as well as confronting sexism. Now, along comes post-feminism with an entirely different and craftier message. Far more devastating in the era of the eighties than merely being told you have outlived your usefulness is being declared passé, and post-feminism bluntly decrees that feminism and all its works are out of style, out to lunch and off the agenda of any right-thinking woman with get-up and ambition.

Well, we have known for some while that younger women have been receiving a warped image of feminism. A quick visit to a campus cafeteria or shopping mall will tell you all you need to know: feminism is seen as antifeminine, antifamily and anti-motherhood. Anyway, this is no time to be fooling around; jobs are scarce, and if you don't get married you'll soon find *men* are scarce. That is the message coming at young women from such unassailed authorities as American TV news. I am thinking here of the block-buster TV documentary "After the Sexual Revolution" aired recently on ABC, which depicted women in their thirties locked in a desperate and losing battle with the statistics, which say after thirty the chances of your ever getting married drop to an alarming ten percent. This was presented as the legacy of the sexual revolution and the bill of goods sold young women by Gloria Steinem. No mention of the failure of men in this connection. The failure of women to find intimacy in their lives was attributed to their own choices early in life (to have a career, to postpone marriage) and indirectly to feminism. And in what seemed to me a flashback to the fifties, intimacy and personal happiness were exclusively equated with marriage.

Post-feminism is cut from the same ideological cloth. It blithely accepts inequality and ducks the issue of why it has been so hard to get and why the social statistics describing women's lot have been so slow to improve. To put it mildly, post-feminism makes a mockery of feminism, giving the impression it is not antifeminist while actually pointing a finger at feminism, blaming it for society's failure.

If you were to reduce feminism to a set of demands and a political strategy for achieving them, you could perhaps make the case that seventies-style feminism has been bypassed by events.

(And that would, in any case, be a normal occurrence; society doesn't stand still, so strategies shouldn't either.) But feminism is more than a platform for social change. The writing, thinking, creating and researching done by women the world over in the past three decades — since Simone de Beauvoir published *The Second Sex* — have yielded something far richer and more important than a political analysis of power and gender politics. The feminist perspective has been brought to bear on virtually all activities of Man — history, sociology, religion, literature, psychology, business, law, medicine and just about everything in between, and it has given us a new way of understanding the world. A philosophy, a *weltanschauung.* For instance, my concept of history was utterly transformed the day I read this sentence in the introduction to a book on feminism and art history, subtitled *Questioning the Litany,* by Norma Broude and Mary D. Garrard: "Just as Renaissance humanists were able to define the Dark or Middle Ages for the first time as a separate transitional age, bounded at either end by differing cultures, and could therefore understand it as a distinct period with cultural characteristics that were unique to it rather than universal, so feminists have named as 'patriarchal' that period of more than five thousand years which reaches down to the present, and which began with the gradual replacement of a long-standing Goddess-worshipping culture by patrilineal and God-worshipping civilizations."

To even use the word post-feminism implies that we have entered a new age. Absurd, of course, for our society certainly isn't post-patriarchial.

Where then, does post-feminism come from? Well, not surprisingly there is a heavy dose of crass commercialism in it and the sugar-coated dreams of the marketing guys as they carve another notch in their demographics, the better to target a market. The post-feminist woman, you quickly discover, is inescapably upscale (no doubt about the second "p" in Yuppie) and ever-so-well-dressed. Which is to say she possesses a "wardrobe" and spends time and money on it. Another fondly held tenet of post-feminism, obviously, is that it's okay now to dress up and be feminine and no longer necessary for career women to wear those "ugly three piece suits" which the first women executives felt they had to. But is this actually true? Are dress codes for women really loosening up? Not by the evidence I see in the display windows of Simpsons. Nurses may still wear pantsuits, and factory workers can still turn up in jeans, but you won't see professional women in anything but skirts these days — with padded shoulders, high heels and painted nails.

There is a code out there all right; an expensive one which middle class women are buying into, some of them very consciously and with their accountant's advice, as a professional investment. It is getting so that some of us feel downright deformed and certifiably eccentric if we don't pad our shoulders and prop up our heels at least an inch. I think of it as power dressing and it was unmistakable at a gathering of Tory women in Ottawa last October, a year after the apotheosis of Brian & Mila and the glorification of the three "fs": fashion, family and friends in the right places. The transformation was startling to longtime observers. The crowd had lost the also-ran look of the Clark era and had arrived dressed to advertise their victory. It was actually possible to tell which women had the closest connections to power by the hierarchy of silk dresses and exquisite wool ensembles; to tell the back-room girls from the women's auxiliary types (Chanel vs. Yardley).

Shortly after the Conservative election there were several amusing news stories about the sartorial changes in Ottawa, from Liberal browns and earth tones to Tory pinstripe blues. Probably for the first time in the annals of political journalism male dress became an item for discussion. Interestingly, women's dress did not come in for comment, possibly because too few women were elected to spot a trend, but just maybe because the Press Gallery finally understood that they couldn't write about the dress of female politicians without being read as doing a *grand mal* putdown. Understandably in the last few years no serious journalist, male or female, has been anxious to take this one on. Yet there have been extraordinary changes in what women are wearing in the pantries and corridors of power, and it does have political significance. You can see it, moreover, in provincial capitals, head offices and bureaucracies everywhere. Drop into the Manitoba legislature and you'll find the same thing; political advisors and ministerial executive assistants walking around with a thousand or so dollars on their backs. They may look wonderful and feel great, but the point about a dress code is that it doesn't tolerate exceptions, and people who flout it usually have to pay a price. Wear comfortable shoes and someone is bound to comment on your "orthopedics," which is what happened to Deputy Premier Muriel Smith — who now wears a smart pair of heels like everyone else.

For women in public life just getting dressed in the morning can be a major challenge; the trick being to negotiate the poles of fashion and comfort so as to appear as unremarkable as possible (i.e., well groomed without attracting undue attention). So there has always been pressure on political women to conform, at least a little, to changing styles. But power dressing adds a new element (or rather an old one) by reintroducing dress as a form of pass key to certain circles. It is becoming more and more difficult for individuals to get away with any deviation, and I doubt that a woman would last long, even on Howard Pawley's payroll, if she turned up every day in Birkenstocks. The sixties may have loosened things up for a time, but even the counter-culture was turned into a style which eventually passed out of fashion.

For many feminists the return of killer high heels has been an astonishing and incomprehensible phenomenon. Given the choice, why would any woman even try to carry herself through a working day in shoes which so confined her movements and deformed her anatomy? (And never mind the symbolism.) For a time, it was at least a choice; but as trend became style became code it ceased to be. And today fashion and neoconservatism have women back in dress regulations as rigid as a set of 19th century stays.

Perhaps power dressing is the eighties revenge on the sixties. This decade certainly believes in surfaces, reads book covers and likes pretty well anything that's skin deep. Power dressing works on the principle that in order to be powerful you have to look powerful; so all the old theories of conspicuous consumption are coming back into play. You have only to think of the new, improved Flora MacDonald decked out in her regulation Holt Renfrew finery to understand the extent to which this decade is disappearing behind the looking glass of image makers. In 1976 when Flora was conducting her remarkable campaign for the Tory leadership (remarkable more for its success with the public than with her Tory colleagues) strangers would press dollar bills into her hands on the street, and people who had never voted Conservative sported "Flora" buttons. The public responded to her as a genuine hero — the party loyalist who laboured in the trenches and against all the odds rose from being a secretary at party headquarters to being a successful candidate. I think Canadian women looked at her and thought, "There with the grace of the Goddess goes any Canadian woman." And felt proud. But today you look at Ms MacDonald and know that the only women who will succeed in her circles are those with the right clothes.

On the one hand, post-feminism is about making feminism safe for the fashion industry; on the other hand, it signals the arrival of feminism in the mainstream. This is another way of saying that while some of the main tenets of women's rights have become socially acceptable (pay equity, easy divorce etc.), the impetus towards deep social change which has always been the energy source of the movement is being cauterized, or e-feminated (there being no female equivalent of emasculate in English). And therein lies the danger.

You can see this happening in *Chatelaine*. Although it is most assuredly a mainstream publication, the magazine did go through a unique period when Doris Anderson was editor. For the better part of twenty years Anderson never failed to deliver homemakers the goods on baked apples and homemade Christmas decorations. She also never failed to deliver strong features on all kinds of women's issues when all of them were news. (Why, you ask was she allowed to get away with it? Essentially because she doubled the magazine's circulation before the men in the Maclean Hunter boardroom noticed what was going on; then, being hip to bottom lines, they didn't want to tamper with a major success, one which for years actually "kept" *Maclean's,* as it were.) There was nothing remotely like *Chatelaine* in the U.S. at the time. More radical for its time than *Ms.* is in ours, *Chatelaine* was genuinely subversive, tilling the soil of public opinion to support demands for the Royal Commission on the Status of Women, pushing women candidates on political parties, encouraging women to organize for themselves. Ottawa columnist Stevie Cameron relates the story of working for a candidate who was running against Hugh Faulkner in the early seventies, and whom she discovered had no background whatsoever on women's issues. In desperation, she handed him a fistful of Anderson's editorials to read and overnight he became the best-briefed candidate of the bunch.

When Anderson left *Chatelaine* in 1978, the magazine lost this political edge. Under her successor, Mildred Istona, it has been editorially blenderized and, how shall we say it, custom coordinated. This month Barbara Frum is on the cover in a red leather jacket, hailed as "Queen of the Screen"; last year she was lambasted for being one of Canada's ten worst dressed women. *Chatelaine* doesn't encourage women to take charge of their lives so much as their bank accounts. Beating inequality is made out to be a matter of personal choice; women's politics is returned to the private domain, and feminism is patted on the head and relegated to nostalgia. Nothing says this so eloquently as the picture of Istona on the inside front of the magazine. In Anderson's day staff writers often complained about the anonymous young models used on the covers ("It sells copies," Anderson would growl.) Nowadays Istona poses above her editorials, beaming her whiter than white teeth and perfect bangs at us, every inch the anonymous, ageless model herself. Very post-feminist.

"It's a sign of the times," Istona editorializes, "that two diametrically opposed ideological camps — the feminist National Action Committee on the Status of Women (NAC) and the traditionalist REAL (Realistic, Equal, Active, for Life) Women of Canada

— have both been put on the defensive by the apparent sea change in womanthink, NAC affirming its dedication to homemakers and REAL Women proclaiming a woman's right to choose her own life role." It's feminism vs. family fundamentalism performing as equals on the lunatic fringe. And occupying the vast and lucrative middle ground? Post-feminism, presumably.

This is a gross distortion of the truth. In the first place, Istona swallows whole the myth that REAL Women is some sort of alternative to NAC, though it has consistently taken positions which run against the interests of the vast majority of Canadian working women. It has opposed publicly supported daycare, equal pay and most if not all issues to do with reproductive rights, including birth control. Moreover, there are very few Canadian women who can "choose" to stay at home devoting their "life role" to homemaking. Only 16 percent of all Canadian families now fit that fifties' mould; 84 percent are single parent families or families where both parents work.

Thus, to characterize REAL Women as a fringe group is apt; but to so characterize NAC is utterly misleading. NAC is in fact a broad coalition of 470 groups (running the gamut from the IODE to the Communist Party and including labour organizations and church groups as well as business and professional associations). It represents some three million Canadian women, which works out to an equivalent to the percentage of the Canadian work force represented by the Canadian Labour Congress (CLC). For this reason alone, NAC has to be countenanced as the major spokesbody of the women's movement. To equate it with REAL Women which, like the National Citizens' Coalition (NCC), is functionally a figment of someone's imagination, is tantamount to equating workers with management. Or for that matter the CLC with the NCC.

NAC is certainly a feminist organization and despite its mainstream makeup, it has managed throughout the determined and delicate efforts of its leadership to keep itself firmly to the left of centre. What commentaries like Istona's do, apart from trivializing NAC and marginalizing feminism, is to give legitimacy to REAL

Women it doesn't deserve and to perpetuate the lie that the women's movement denigrates homemakers and homemaking. Who, you wonder, is really on the defensive here?

Part of Istona's problem, finally, is that of trying to wedge square facts into a round theory. Post-feminism, like a growing proportion of Chatelaine's content, is an American import which ill fits the Canadian reality. NAC is not the elitist organization that the National Organization of Women is in the U.S. The history of feminism is very different here, to take Section 28 in the Canadian Charter of Rights and the defeat of the American Equal Rights Amendment as examples, and it is interesting to note that Drainie's article relies heavily on American data, only bringing in Canadians for "local colour." It may be that post-feminism has no relevance to the Canadian situation at all and that post-feminism is nothing more than flash journalism.

In the meantime, however, beware of post-feminists in beautiful clothes. Post-feminism is not an extension of feminism, as some try to claim; it is a denial of it; a label tailor-made for people who hate labels and would *never* have called themselves feminists in the first place. It is also a subtle denial of the very term feminist which more and more is being reduced to the radical feminist stereotype which Drainie defines as "lesbian, pro-abortion, man-hating, child-hating and shrill." If we don't call the post-feminist bluff we might someday face a situation where NAC and other mainstream women's organizations feel compelled to back pedal on their support of gay rights and other issues deemed too radical. Perhaps even abortion. It might one day again be a flagrantly antisocial act for women to wear long hair and pants. *The Handmaid's Tale* anybody?

Susan Crean is a writer and editor and long-time member of the editorial collective of *This Magazine.* She has written extensively about culture, politics, and the visual arts and for several years wrote a column, "The Female Gaze," for *Canadian Art*. She has published four books including *Who's Afraid of Canadian Culture?* (1976), *Newsworthy: The Lives of Media Women* (1984) and *In the Name of the Fathers* (1988), an examination of child custody, family law reform and the men's rights movement.

In 1989-90 she was the first Maclean Hunter Chair in Creative Nonfiction at the University of British Colombia's department of Creative Writing.

PEACE AND THE FEMALE PRINCIPLE

A Feminist Look at the Politics of Power

Bonnie Sherr Klein

Global politics is still a man's game. According to the United Nations, women comprise over 70 percent of the membership of peace and social justice groups worldwide. But women are almost totally absent from the official delegations which conduct peace talks and routinely excluded when conferences and panels of experts are convened to discuss disarmament issues.

Personally, I think there is a link between the goal of peace and the full participation of women in society, particularly in the media. Patriarchy is characterized by hierarchical thinking in which some people matter less than others and in which power is maintained by violence or the threat thereof. Women, who have historically been excluded from that system and assigned the role of caretaker (child rearing, homemaking, and volunteer work), have acquired specialized peacemaking skills only recently acknowledged even to ourselves. As a class, women have become society's expert custodians of ways to resolve disagreement between people resourcefully and usually without resort to violence. I hasten to add that I am not talking about biological or cultural superiority, but rather the accumulation of knowledge resulting from the division of labour according to gender and all the socialization by stereotype that ensues.

Let me be more specific by focussing on the two areas I know best: women and film. I work at the National Film Board in Studio D which was established in 1975 to bring the missing perspective of women to film. We produced *If You Love This Planet*. Terri Nash, who had never made a film before, saw Helen Caldicott speak and was incredibly moved. Kathleen Shannon, executive producer of Studio D, agreed the matter was urgent and approved a film proposal. Members of the NFB Program Committee, however, criticized the idea as uncinematic — it was just an illustrated speech, said most of our male colleagues. Besides, they added, Caldicott was...well, shrill. Strident. Hysterical. Words we'd come to recognize as feminists because we had heard them before. (I was called a "bourgeois, feminist fascist" by *The Globe and Mail's* film critic for making *Not a Love Story: A Film About Pornography*, which was an exposé of another manifestation of patriarchal violence.) Then, once *Planet* was made but before it was released, distribution officials at the NFB said we should remove the clips featuring Ronald Reagan as a bomber pilot in old war movies. They would offend the United States we were told, and, besides, it was a "cheap joke." What the men failed to understand was that women weren't laughing at the correlation being drawn between nuclear madness, machismo, and media. As Margaret Atwood succinctly summed it up in *Second Words*, war and rape are "two activities not widely engaged in by women." That's two good reasons for working toward a future society which derives more of its values from women. Indeed some women are developing an analysis of the connections between militarism and patriarchy, and between nonviolence and feminism. We are questioning and rejecting the "expertise" of those who have "led" us this far, questioning technology, for example, as an end in itself, recognizing the advantages of being generalists and jugglers, rather than specialists who can make munitions in the day and hug their children at night.

And, of course, as filmmakers, we come by our understanding of the interconnection of culture and power honestly. John Grierson, the father of documentary film and the first commissioner of the NFB, often talked about the power of film to "make people love each other or hate each other." Although the NFB began by serving the war effort, Grierson was challenged by the possibility of making peace as exciting and dramatic as war, by making films about "the everyday things of life, the values, the ideals which make life worth living."

In any case, we resisted the internal censorship and *Planet* was released. It has since become one of the most used films in Canadian history; *Planet* and *Not a Love Story* are by far the most popular documentaries to have emerged from the NFB in the last decade. The film has awakened more people to personal action and spawned more grassroots peace groups in Canada and abroad than any other single media event.

No doubt you remember the story about the United States Justice Department's attempt to suppress the film by declaring it political propaganda and requiring that distributors keep a list of everyone who saw it (an action which is currently before the U.S. Supreme Court). But you may not know, because the Canadian media engage so rarely in open self-criticism, that *Planet* was also rejected by our very own CBC because it was deemed to be biased and one sided. Terri's response to that was simple: how do you show the "pro" side of nuclear war? The night it won an Academy Award (an *American* award) it was finally aired on *The Journal* with no advance publicity and with a disclaimer about advocacy journalism

Which brings us to the question of bias and "objectivity." Reality is obviously a matter of individual perception; that is, it is dependent on a person's subjective interpretation of the external world (apprehended by the senses) and what is taking place out there. In the world of journalism, objectivity is usually defined as giving a balanced report of these events as they take place. In practice, it is commonly defined as presenting two sides of a controversy which, of course, assumes that all news stories involve a controversy and can be boiled down to two opposing points of view. The media's "reality" is described almost exclusively in terms of violence and confrontation. We hear about strikes, riots, wars, and terrorism. We do not see the conflicts that get resolved, the strikes that are averted because of successful arbitration, the wars that do not break out. These non-events, the evidence of successful peacemaking, are by their nature "unnewsworthy" and are rendered invisible. But are they any less real because of that? Certainly they aren't to the people affected.

At a certain point, therefore, you recognize that the media are engaged in the same either/or, win/lose kind of thinking that the superpowers and their representatives are. They participate in the same dualistic and polarized view of the world which is endangering our political (not to mention our natural) environment. In other words, the so-called objectivity practiced in the mainstream is another word for the status quo. Denying airtime for alleged bias to those who dissent or object in some way to the present scheme of things actually deprives the public of information about new and alternative ways to see and understand the world.

The rejection of Studio D films for television *really* means that our films reflect a bias other than that of those who control the airwaves. Their bias is so pervasive in the culture it has become invisible and has been declared nonexistent. It is a bias that sees itself as the standard and calls itself objective. Kathleen Shannon, Studio D's founder and recently retired executive producer, has her own interpretation of objectivity. In an address she titled "This is about Objectivity, Objections and some Objectives (or Some Sacred Cows are Bullshit)," Shannon suggested to the Women's Network of the Centre for Investigative Journalism that "objectivity" could simply be the contraction of "I object to your activity." This, she added, was another way of saying, "I'm objective and you're objectionable."

In 1985, at the start of its second decade, Studio D noted in one of its anniversary documents, "We believe in the films we make. The objectivity we practice is that of not letting one's own set of vested interests interfere with another person's telling of her own truth. But we do *not* believe there is value, at this time, in the kind of 'objectivity' that pretends detachment when dealing with matters of life and death, justice, truth and human well-being." As I see it, many well-meaning, liberal journalists mask fear of commitment behind a pose of amused or cynical detachment. But we, as feminist filmmakers, see emotion and reason as complementary, not contradictory, and the division between emotion and reason as schizophrenic.

In 1983, Terri Nash and I embarked on a film project about women, peace, and power (which became the *Speaking Our Peace* series) because we wanted to go beyond fear to look at the causes of war and the possibility of alternatives. We discovered a long, rich history connecting women and peace. We found that women have, all along, been asking different — and I think more fundamental — questions. Not about who has more missiles, who's got the strategic advantage, or where terrorism will stop if we don't retaliate; but about how we can secure a future for the planet. Women were linking domestic and public violence, defining peace and security as freedom from want and fear, defining "power" as power *to*, not power *over*: power to foster the development of others to a position of equality, to share resources and to resolve inevitable conflict nonviolently. As we made the film we were overwhelmed by the clarity, the strength and the imagination of the women we met around the world. We asked ourselves: "Where are these voices in the media? Can we afford not to hear them? Why have they not been acknowledged as 'experts' on questions of war and peace?"

Let me give you a few examples of the realities we encountered and how we saw them treated by the mainstream media.

Terri and I went to film the Women's Peace Camp at Greenham Common, England, and were awed by its power. Now Greenham has been news on and off. Mostly the stories have characterized the camp as a freakish bunch of women given to outrageous and theatrical actions such as climbing barbed wire fences to dance on the cruise missile silos under a full moon. But as Greenham became an international symbol and the women an inspiration to people everywhere, they came to be perceived as a serious threat to the status quo. British media coverage became increasingly vicious, repeating lies about the women's personal lives and hygiene, which in turn fueled local violence against them. When such intimidation didn't work, a kind of news blackout was employed which has left many people assuming Greenham was over. In fact, there are still a small number of women who continue to live there, resourcefully, occasionally even joyfully, under miserable conditions, and they have been doing so for *more than five years*. About a year ago, Greenham women reported medical symptoms that indicated they had been exposed to microwave radiation. This has been corroborated by radiation expert Dr Rosalie Bertell and there have since been further indications that the weapons used against the Greenham women were developed by Canadian university researchers under contract to the U.S. military. I haven't seen this reported in the mainstream press (CBC Radio's "Ideas" and Toronto's *NOW* magazine ran stories on it) which makes me wonder where the serious investigative journalists are hiding. Perhaps they are all at press conferences where the news is manipulated by highly paid spokespeople, themselves former journalists?

In June 1985, there was an International Women's Peace Conference in Halifax, which brought together some three hundred women from 34 countries. The significance of that event for anyone who participated was that, for the first time on such an international scale, white middle-class women from both Western and Eastern-bloc countries were listening to women of colour, from many of the so-called Third World countries as well as from our own countries. Because we listened, we expanded our ideas about peace and security, our sense of urgency was heightened, and we changed our agenda. Enormous political conflicts surfaced and were resolved in round the clock consensus meetings. It was an amazing event; I would say it was life-changing for myself, and I think it was the same for most of the women there. *The Globe and Mail* reported all this with a headline which suggested only that there had been some sort of confrontation, a power struggle between black and white women in which the black women had one-upped the uppity white women. It said nothing about how we had all hungrily listened and (sometimes painfully) learned. The CBC wasn't there at all. So in a certain sense, for most Canadians this important conference never happened. It never became part of our history of successful peacemaking.

The following month the End of the Decade of Women Conference, sponsored by the United Nations, was held in Nairobi. Seventeen thousand women from around the world, including hundreds of Canadians, spent two weeks together struggling to get beyond the divisions of national politics to reach consensus on essential issues for the future of the planet. Studio D initiated and organized a major component of the event, the International Film Forum, in which over 300 films and videos made by women from the smallest and poorest countries as well as the large and rich, were screened in a remarkable exchange of our differences and communalities. Over those fourteen days, we learned how little news we have of each other's lives, especially of the courageous and creative solutions to life-threatening problems. And, again, the same thing happened. The male press was busy elsewhere. Another major event in women's history and the peace movement ignored; another reality rendered an illusion.

One of the central ideas of feminism is to acknowledge, respect and celebrate diversity. White male ownership and control of the media, worldwide, has created an imbalance, a distortion which prevents us from hearing the multiplicity of voices which make up our world community. The voices of women, of old people, of young people, of working people, and people of differing class, ethnic, religious and geographic origins. These are the voices we have to hear if we are to have an accurate picture of the world and our place in it. If we appreciate that there is no one "objective" reality, then we have to understand that these different voices all speak their own passionately held truths.

We need to hear these voices, and we need to listen to what they have to say about making peace. In her book *Three Guineas,* Virginia Woolf answers the letter of a man who has written her to ask how she, as a woman, would prevent war. On behalf of women,

Woolf replied, "...by asking our help you recognize that connection; and...we are reminded of other connections that lie far deeper than the facts on the surface...to discuss with you the capacity of the human spirit to overflow boundaries and make unity out of multiplicity. But that would be to dream — to dream of peace, the dream of freedom. But with the sound of guns in your ears, you have not asked us to dream. You have not asked us what peace is; you have asked us to prevent war."

Contemporary peace activists like Dr Ursula M. Franklin, a professor of metallurgy at the University of Toronto who changed her field of academic research rather than accept "classified" research and who was a founding member of the Voice of Women, take every opportunity to encourage people to speak out about peace, and not, under any circumstances, to leave the debate to the "experts." Our situation, says Franklin, calls for more and more skillful conflict resolution. As she puts it, when you encounter a couple hurling crockery at each other in the kitchen, the answer is not to call in the crockery experts. Franklin also talks about the "dream of democracy." "If we no longer have a forum for reasoned discourse to debate matters of principle, to ask the big life and death questions, to chart our moral values as a people, then we've lost the dream of democracy. That forum should be the media. We must insist that we find ways in which those things are debated and debated genuinely, both in the constituencies and in Parliament. Because the solutions only come when there's discourse."

This suggests to me that we must urge our government to increase support for the public media institutions it is currently diminishing, the CDC and the NFB, and particularly efforts of diversity within these institutions, like Studio D, native programing and regional programing, all of which are threatened by funding cutbacks. Because in theory at least, if not in practice, these institutions, which do not have as their *raison d'être* the making of private profit and the exporting of their product to other countries, can ask the big questions which must be asked. They are endangered by the trendy view of Canadian culture as an industry, coupled by the desire for free trade which will make these industries farm teams for the U.S. media.

I can envision Canada combining its skill in communications technology, its tradition of public enterprise, and its leadership in women's media to take a leading role in the creation of change-promoting media. In Halifax and Nairobi we played a leading role in articulating a practical vision of an international peace network. The onus is still on us as citizens in a relatively rich and free country to voice our opinions. Margaret Atwood offers this poetic challenge: "We in this country should use our privileged position not as a shelter from the world's realities, but a platform from which to speak. A voice is a gift, it should be cherished and used, to utter fully human speech if possible. Powerlessness and silence go together."

This column is adapted from a speech, entitled "Illusion and Reality in the Nuclear Age," which Bonnie Sherr Klein gave at the McGill University international conference, after inviting herself onto an all-male media panel.

Bonnie Sherr Klein is a filmmaker on disability leave from the National Film Board of Canada. Her directing credits include: *Not A Love Story: A Film About Pornography*; *Speaking Our Peace* (with Terri Nash); *Mile Zero: The Sage Tour*.

She is writing a book about her personal experience of stroke, recovery, and living with disability.

WILL THE REAL NATASHA PLEASE STAND UP?

Women in the Soviet Union

Myrna Kostash

LAST MARCH, Heather Robertson tells us in *Chatelaine* ("Heather Meets Natasha," August 1986), Robertson flew to Moscow to interview Natalia Dolgopolova, a "typical" Soviet woman whose picture had caught her eye in a Toronto newspaper. Dolgoplova had attended a Halifax women's peace conference, is forty years old, has two daughters, works as a research historian and wears "googly glasses" just like Robertson's. Such a woman, she feels, is her "Soviet counterpart" and someone with whom she would like to exchange views. "What are Soviet women like?" asks Robertson. "Do they share our worries and dreams on the other side of the world or do they look at life differently?"

The questions are interesting. It is an arguement of the international women's peace movement that women must find a way to circumvent the male dominance of political discourse and to speak to *each other*, thereby breaking, it is hoped, the deadlock of ideas between the superpowers.

But Robertson's answers to her own questions are so inadequate, so naive and erroneous, that the questions remain in effect unanswered. Robertson wanted to have a "frank" talk with a "typical" woman about the world of women "from the other side of the looking glass" but what she has given us instead is an uncritical account of Soviet women's experience from the point of view of a member of the privileged elite.

Of course Heather and Natasha understand each other: they are both members of the intelligentsia, they both have access to their society's "good life," they both have the luxury of contemplation of problems beyond the struggle for daily existence. Fair enough. But to pretend that their genial dialogue in any way accounts for the experience of the great mass of Soviet women is profoundly insulting to those women in whose name Heather and Natasha purport to speak.

What is one to make of Robertson's blithe claim that "hard work is very highly regarded" in Soviet society — including, one supposes, the labour of peasant women pouring asphalt and shovelling snow for ninety rubles a month? With her assertion that the Russian revolution is rooted in the "prodigious scholarship" of Marxism-Leninism? Doesn't she know that same "scholarship" has come to be loathed by Soviet working people who are more or less compelled to march in offical parades carrying banners with slogans "people are sick to death of," in the words of a Soviet feminist, who goes on to write that "people are all the more resistant because they do not feel the slightest sense of solidarity with each other, much less with workers of the rest of the world?"

Robertson declares with satisfaction that "there is a tasty chicken in every pot in the U.S.S.R." — when, these days, there isn't even cheese to be had in one of Ukraine's largest industrial citites. "The cucumbers were delicious," she writes. "They disappeared in two days." Not surprising, as they are only to be found at that time of year at the private farmers' markets and, because there's no advertising (which Robertson finds so restful), it's anybody's guess when and where they're going to show up. How to take seriously her droll explanation of shopping queues — that Soviet shops are too small to fit all the customers in at once! (Things are improving, however. The Soviet press announced that the shortage of staple foods has become "less acute" over the last few years.) Robertson goes on to observe there are lineups in

Toronto too, "for buses, bank tellers, movies, restaurants," adding insult to injury by equating a Torontonian's few minutes' wait at a Green Machine with a Soviet woman's *hours* in line every week for the neccessities of life. Natasha, who likes to be a "little extravagant" from time to time with purchases of French perfume and imported clothes, informs a sympathetic Robertson that "accumulating material goods" is "frowned on" in Soviet society. Tell that to the millions saving for months for a winter coat, a pair of boots, a camera, a television set and other such extravagances. Frowned on or not, material goods aren't always to be had, even under Gorbachev. According to a recent visitor from Rostov, the working people's slogan these days is "Bring back Brezhnev!" In spite of Gorbachev's shake-up of the economy, the indispensable black-marketeering in goods and services — without which a housewife cannot find the parts and labour to fix her faucet, for instance — has dried up without any compensatory supply to the official market.

Natasha is a member of the Communist Party (an elite, less than ten percent of the population of the U.S.S.R.). She is married to a deputy director of the Institute of U.S. and Canadian Studies. She works as an assistant to its director. Is it possible that Robertson, normally a sceptical and perspicacious writer who does not suffer home-grown fools gladly, was unaware of what every Soviet citizen knows: party members are extraordinarily privileged, having access to their own imported goods shops — those French perfumes! — their own hospitals, their own resorts, and that institutes, especially those with international mandates, are riddled with KGB employees? Did Robertson not find it curious that she was granted in *two days* what it normally takes the rest of us *weeks* if not months to get — a visa to the Soviet Union? We can give her the benefit of the doubt, that she did not know. But this does not answer the question why she should have been so uncharacteristically ingenuous.

It isn't as though there is no readily available information about the actual conditions of women's lives. I count three anthologies in my own library, published by reputable publishers and purchased at my local bookstore, about women in the Soviet Union. I've consulted these books (in particular, *Soviet Sisterhood*, edited by the British sociologist Barbara Holland and *Women and Russia,* edited by the Soviet feminist in exile Tatyana Mamonova) as well as *Manchester Guardian Weekly* articles by the unhysterical Martin Walker, occasional clippings from Canadian newspapers and the English language *News From Ukraine* (a party publication) in order to argue that, contrary to Heather's and Natasha's complacent view, the conditions of everyday life in the Soviet Union burden and oppress women in ways which Western feminists would find all too familiar.

Take, for example, women's work situations. The Soviet press itself airs typical grievances: that health and safety regulations are routinely disregarded and female workers denied protective clothing, that night shift workers must find their own way home; that young women are expected to work illegally long hours and others work on their days off. Women are so badly underrepresented in managerial and highly skilled jobs that, for instance, only 16 percent of directors of enterprises are women but 90 percent of "laboratory assistants" are female. The consequences of job ghettos are predictable: for all their massive participation in the labour force — a full 86 percent of women of working age — Soviet working women earn 65 to 75 percent of men's earnings. Added to these endemic penalties are those peculiar to a highly bureaucratized economy: the "reference card" provided at the place of work or study, by which employers or supervisors rate an individual ("politically mature, morally unstable," for example) and without which it is impossible to change jobs or take a holiday outside the country; the work booklet, which employees must hand over to employers to be signed as proof of employment and without which a citizen can be arrested for "parasitism"; the residence permit, provided at one's place of work, without which a citizen is ordered to leave her city of residence within three days.

For the rural worker — 37 percent of Soviets still live in the countryside — the situation is even more harassing and exploiting.

The vaunted industrialization and mechanization of agriculture have failed to produce a revolution in farm women's lives. In the dairy industry, for instance, over 96 percent of milkers are women, working 12 and 14 hour days in processes only randomly mechanized; where they have been mechanized, they have been redefined as "machine operations" and reserved overwhelmingly for male employees.

But the largest group of women is employed in ordinary agricultural labour — seasonal, low-skilled and often back-breaking work. The mechanization of tillage and harvesting has left the manual drudgery of weeding root crops, stacking hay and sorting seed to middle-aged and elderly married women who lack any sort of professional training. Even without education they often have no choice but to accept such labour: child care facilities are woefully inadequate in the countryside, and many farm managers (forty-nine out of fifty are male) simply refuse to hire even those women specifically trained as machine operators. After 15 years of an official campaign to improve the vocational training of women, less than one percent of agricultural machine operators are female.

To what standard of living does an average working woman's wage entitle her? Take Nadia Khymko, 36, a bookbinder with three years' experience, earning 150 rubles a month. According to *News From Ukraine*, Nadia is most concerned with her accommodations — a crowded, two-room apartment for a family of four. But they are not in a position to make a 4,500 ruble down payment on a two bedroom cooperative (i.e., private) apartment and so must wait their turn for a more spacious state apartment, a wait of years in an economy with a chronic shortage of housing.

Food, in sporadic and uneven supply even in the large centres, is relatively expensive. A "weekly basket" of food for an average family of four in 1982 (based on an average take home pay of 170 rubles per month) would take Nadia 46.8 hours of work time to buy; in Paris she would have to work 19.4 hours, in Washington, 16.3.

A young couple with one child was interviewed by *News*

From Ukraine: Did having a baby represent financial problems for them? (He, an assemblyman, earns 330 rubles a month; she, a store clerk, 110.) Fortunately, they were given many items by family and friends. Otherwise, they would have had to spend 40 to 70 rubles for a carriage and 30 to 45 rubles for a crib (if they could find them in the shops: readers of women's magazines regularly complain about the "impossibility" of finding baby things.) They spend about 200 rubles a month on food (almost half their combined income) and live in a two room apartment with the wife's mother; they confess to feeling "a bit crowded," but say that a live-in granny is "indispensable." She is their babysitter and stands in queues for them.

To support a second or third child, however, even the Soviet press acknowledges that a family must be "well-off" and provided with "good housing." When the average industrial wage is 160 rubles a month and a sweater costs 75 rubles, a television set 650 and a small car 10,000 (all figures from the Soviet press), then it is indeed a well-off family which can afford to support itself in the style to which a working class family in Canada is accustomed.

Again, the situation of families in rural areas is worse than average. Two-thirds of housing on collective and state farms is without running water, indoor plumbing, or central heating. Half the family's food is provided from private gardens typically worked by women. Three-quarters of the children are without places in daycare or kindergarten. In the Russian Republic, it was found, rural women have less than half the free time of women in towns. In the Novgorod region, the average family spent 12 to 14 hours a week fetching water.

Soviet women spend an average of 40 hours per week on domestic chores — cooking, cleaning, child minding, and shopping. This is partly explained by the fact that only half of Soviet families have fridges. Only 45 percent of preschool children have nursery and kindergarten spaces, and consumer goods and services are undersupplied — all of which tax a woman's free time. But equally to the point is the expectation that it is *women* who will cook and mind children and shop. One study of 2,500 working women in and around Moscow found that in 50 percent of cases husbands took *no* part in looking after children, 67 percent did *no* cooking; 83 percent *no* laundry, and so on.

The size of an average Soviet family is shrinking, from 3.7 persons in 1970 to 3.5 in 1979, a rate of childbirth which does not even replace the population. This trend, for all its familiarity to industrialized societies, has alarmed Soviet authorities, who have countered with increased maternity benefits and provisions for unpaid leave. This is fine, but it does nothing to attack the reasons why women want to limit the size of their families: food shortages, cramped housing, inadequate childcare facilities and the double workload.

In 1965 the life expectancy of Soviet women was 74.1 years; in 1980 that had decreased to 73.5. (In Canada over the same period, life expectancy for women had increased from 74.9 to 78.6 years.) That being female in the Soviet Union is dangerous to your health is reflected in a number of ways, whether it's the official acknowledgement that Soviets eat "much more" bread and potatoes and less fruit and vegetables "than recommended" or that almost one-third of new mothers documented in a study in Leningrad had suffered toxemia in the second half of their pregnancies — a disorder associated with poor diet and inadequate antenatal care; or that pueperal fever remains a significant problem in maternity hospitals, or that women depend on abortions to limit family size (four or five abortions per woman not being at all unusual) with dire implications for their general health. Of course, a woman's chances to secure better than average health care increase with the amount of money she is willing to slip the doctor and nurses in this "free" health care sytem — for aspirin in the hospital ward, an episiotomy in the delivery room, for anesthetic during an abortion.

In a society which makes no commitment to provide reliable and accessible birth control (there are no spermicidal creams or foams, diaphragms are ill-fitting, condoms shred and tear, and only those with connections acquire Hungarian or East German contraceptive pills), thus forcing women to rely on abortion; in a society which avoids any sort of candid discussion about sexuality; in a society which has so trivialized International Women's Day as to make it the one day a year a woman doesn't have to do the dishes — in such a society it is not surprising to learn that the Five Year Plan has not allowed for the supply of cotton wool, indispensable for the making of diapers, sanitary napkins and tampons.

One would expect that Soviet women, organized politically as they are in local councils (soviets), in trade unions, and even in the Supreme Soviet — where they constitute one-third of the members — would act collectively to improve their situation. But such is not the case. For one thing, it is the *party*, not the government or the trade unions, which is the ultimate political arbiter, and women make up only one-quarter of party membership, 3.2 percent of the Central Committee, and 2.3 percent of the committee's candidate members. As *women*, these individuals have no political clout. For another, as dissidents organizing autonomously around women's issues, women are ruthlessly repressed. (The writers of the feminist *Women and Russia* were harassed by the KGB, interrogated, arrested and exiled or imprisoned, their libraries and manuscripts confiscated, and their typewriters destroyed.) Activist women in unofficial trade unions, in Helsinki Watch groups, in nationalist circles, in unofficial commissions protesting the political use of psychiatry, in nonconformist artists' milieux, have all been suppressed. It is only male-mediated women's organizations, such as the official Women's Councils, which are allowed to operate, which in effect function to isolate "women's concerns" somewhere away from the party.

The Soviet woman is caught — as are Western women — between two impossible ideals, in her case between the heroic, proletarian superwoman (skilled and successful, authoritative, responsible) and the selfless wife and mother ("a woman can only show her worth, her essence, when she...also fulfils her social role in the family," in the words of a Soviet academician) who unstintingly cares for the needs of her family, never being less than attractive, loving, kind, patient, and submissive. This is a familiar stereotype of femininity, and editorials and articles calling for the reassertion of husbands' dominance of their families have appeared in the Soviet press. "It is precisely those families in which the wife willingly relinquishes leadership in favour of the husband that are the happiest," to quote *Pravda* without the slightest hint of understanding that this can only be the "happiness" of the Boss and the Drudge.

Soviet style femininity is made, not born. Women's magazines piously reaffirm that "man is the defender and the woman the guardian of the domestic hearth" and columnists warn wives not to nag, and child psychologists advise that male children after the age of 14 should be fed more meat than girls. The corollary of all such "advice" is that it is precisely because women perform this role that they are denigrated and devalued; "women's" work is not the stuff of Bolshevik revolution. "To work on this great construction project, to launch rockets — that is what life is really all about. Day-to-day living, the home, cooking — all these concerns are [considered to be] petit bourgeois," to quote from Mamonova's *Women and Russia*. The means of women's liberation — the collectivization of the work force — has never had high priority economically or ideologically.

But what is so startling about this ideology of femininity, from a Western feminist's perspective, is that it seems the entire burden of reproducing everyday life and interpersonal relations were a woman's and that any difficulties she might have had in carrying it off were hers alone to overcome. Nowhere is it indicated that men, as men, benefit from women's prodigious labour — a benefit built right into the rigid structure of the patriarchal family.

How, then, is it possible to take Robertson seriously when she writes that "Soviet women have pushed social reform to the very top of the Communist Party agenda?" Where is her evidence?

Or did she simply take Natasha's word for it, Natasha, who is not about to risk disabusing this well-meaning *naif* from Toronto of her notions about Soviet ordinariness?

(In the same vein we have the spectacle of Germaine Greer, normally nobody's fool and acerbic critic of patriarchal relations in the West, travelling to Cuba [*Granta* magazine #16], heart in mouth lest Cuba be a "fraud" or "failure" of a revolution. What will she see? She takes in the Fourth Congress of the Federation of Cuban Women where she is impressed by the presence of Fidel Castro. She is impressed that Cubans' lives are not "soap opera" but "real," that Cubans don't seek to persuade or bamboozle but to "explain" themselves, and that Cubans do not share "our" interest in domestic and sexual affairs [which she calls "prurient"]. The Cubans, you see, are involved in a "much bigger adventure" in their society than we are in ours: we are hopelessly mired in "sex, speed, and smack." Against all expectation, Greer finds that the notorious Latin machismo of Cuban men is not a bad thing — it is an attempt to "counterbalance the dominance of women in family and kin relations." Well, we can't have that, can we? [Pass the muffins!] Anticipating the scepticism [Greer calls it sneering] Western feminists might feel of her observations based on a two-week trip, Greer labels us "feminist chauvinists" and carries on regardless. Cuban women, she tells us, "staunchly refuse" to base their policies on a notion of hostility between the sexes. Even when "Compañero Fidel" attacks male attitudes to woman's work, the women, writes Greer, "prefer" to stress "other, objective" factors. Furthermore, to point out that in a one party state like Cuba power is concentrated in the hands of an oligarchy [such as the Communist Party] is to argue as the "enemy of the revolution," according to Greer, thus encapsulating the argument of all fellow travellers everywhere, who have always found it easier to try to shut you up than to think and act their way through a contradiction.)

What is going on here? I think two important factors are at play in such suspensions of disbelief. The first is that anti-Americanism — and both Robertson and Greer are engaged in peevish

Yankee bashing — devoid of analysis of the structure of power relations *within* as well as between societies, is a perilous world view. Citations of the awfulness of American and/or Canadian society invariably accompany observations about the Soviet Union (or Cuba), as though to imply, illogically, that because *we* have fucked up, *they* (our ideological opposites) have done it right. Because American capitalism has manifestly failed to feed, clothe, and educate everyone to the level of its ruling class, am I to understand that none of us living here may make the point that Soviet socialism by comparison has failed to feed, clothe and educate the working class to the level of the party bosses? This is an indefensible argument: those of us who are capable of mounting a critique of Reganism and its discontents are surely likewise responsible to analyze and criticize how power works in the Soviet Union. It will not do to withdraw from that responsibility with the canard that any public criticism of the Soviet Union lends support to the agenda of the American hawks. This is to make the same argument as that of Stalin's cheerleaders in the West who hailed the achievements of the Great Falcon while millions were suffering outrageously in famines, purges, and slave labour camps. And it is to get drawn into that most unprincipled of arguments — that the enemy of my enemy is my friend.

Secondly, it is important to note how, in the debate between the superpowers or their proxies, even obstensibly pro-women journalists like Robertson and Greer abandon any feminist perspective on the actual, lived lives of women under patriarchy in order better to register their revulsion of Reaganism and their disgust with Western culture and values — as though to show sympathy with the bedraggled Soviet and Cuban wife and mother were somehow to betray one's commitment to nuclear disarmament! The result is that such journalists do not even ask the right questions — How is housework divided? Why are women concentrated in certain jobs? What is the infant mortality rate? What is the message of women's magazine editorials? — questions they would not hesitate to ask at "home." This gets Soviet patriarchy and its policies off the hook and allows the journalist to evade an indictment of these policies — offering instead apologies for the indefensible, made on the backs of women.

If Robertson really wanted to show her solidarity with Soviet women across the Cold War abyss, there are any number of themes she could address: the concrete conditions of everyday life and how they bear on women, the repression of unofficial peace movements, the cases of women political prisoners in the Gulag.

But none of these is as thrilling as the fervour of conviction that somewhere "over there" where the revolution has been "won" and the U.S. confounded — Cuba, Vietnam, the Soviet Union, Albania — women have been magically whisked into lives of authority, dignity, and self-fulfillment, and the struggle is over. But in the refusal of the glib and the wistful, the themes of Soviet women's real lives are more deeply respectful of their stupendous labour in constructing, against great odds, a human existence.

POSTSCRIPT

Happily, this piece is now dated. With the collapse and disappearance of the Communist Party of the Soviet Union and most of the structures of the U.S.S.R., the context of the lives and possibilities of women in the former Soviet republics has completely changed. All of society is in flux, is reflective and self-conscious, is experiencing democratization in the most mundane ways. Women can only benefit.

The context in which Western feminists studied and wrote about Soviet women has also changed utterly. Not only have archives and libraries and research materials suddenly been made accessible to us, and experts come out of the woodwork to talk about the "woman question," women themselves are now discussing their situation, their needs, and desires in an unheard-of contestatory and diverse manner.

In Kiev, in November, 1991, I observed for myself the emergence of a women's movement from within the scaffolding of an independent and democratizing Ukraine. This is not yet an *autonomous* movement (except for a handful of feminists at the Institute of Literature!); women activists are associated with one or another political party or grouping, including the former Communist Party. And the feminists are not so much a social movement as an intellectual current in the (male-dominated) academies.

But, wherever women are organizing by themselves to speak for themselves, wherever they are talking in public about themselves at work and in the family, themselves in the economy and in the political process, and making demands on all those sites of their exploitation, we can smell the whiffs of a women's liberation movement.

In deciding to keep this piece in print, I wanted also to make the point that we activists in the West should not too quickly forget how *we* used to talk about women in Soviet society. How easily we were satisfied by official assurances and private disclosures that the "woman question" was being taken care of. How speciously we accounted for Soviet women's rage and pain as "unprogressive" and "reactionary." How we chose to keep our silence on the subject of the oppressiveness of everyday life in the Soviet Union because to speak out against it was to lend comfort to the imperialist enemy. (There were even readers of *This Magazine* who cancelled their subscriptions in response to the initial publication of my pro-Reaganite article.)

This is probably a good time to remind ourselves of George Orwell's lugubrious assessment of political speech and writing "in our time" as "largely the defence of the indefensible."

Well, never again, I hope. And should we fall into such a trap again, we will stand corrected by the women of Eastern Europe themselves. — M.K.

Myrna Kostash is a full time nonfiction writer in Edmonton, the author of *All of Baba's Children, Long Way From Home* and *No Kidding.* She has another book forthcoming, based on her travels in Eastern Europe during the 1980 s.

IN HIS IMAGE

Science and Technology

Heather Menzies

THE ROOM WAS JAVEX WHITE. No, merely white: I was depressed because I'd just lost what would have been a baby. I had decided to postpone having children until I'd carved out a niche for myself in the work world and used the IUD so I could achieve this and be sexually liberated at the same time. The late childbearing resulted in a condition called endometriosis. The IUD resulted in pelvic scarring. Through the two effects, when I conceived, the embryo lodged in a fallopian tube instead of my uterus. A doctor had to cut it out before the fastgrowing fetus burst the walls of the tube and endangered my life.

Now, the morning after the emergency surgery, the doctor came into the room. He wasted no time in telling me that if I tried to get pregnant the normal way again, I'd end up back in the hospital or worse. The he smiled reassuringly and said that there was an alternative: *in vitro* fertilization. He could arrange this procedure for me as soon as I was up and about.

He stood at the end of my bed fingering the waxed tip of his moustache. I stared. Yes, it was wax-tipped.

The moustache was the only thing I could focus on for some reason. My mind had gone through the motions of acknowledging what the doctor had said. This having been my second ectopic or tubal pregnancy, not my first, I had to agree with his initial statement. But the second, about *in vitro* fertilization, flopped around like a fish out of water.

The latest in reproductive technology, *in virto* feritlilization involves extracting (or "recovering" as the medical practioners put it) eggs from a woman's ovaries, having first boosted their development through hormonal treatments. The eggs are then mixed with the man's sperm in a test tube (hence "test tube baby"), and when conception occurs, a live embryo is implanted into the women's uterus.

It wasn't just that the success rate is a mere 10 percent; actually, I only learned that later and not from my doctor either. Something more fundamental made me stare at this proposition as if from a great distance. It was like a jigsaw piece which, for all it might fit into the puzzle he was part of, was nonetheless alien to me.

Some instinct made me want to keep it that way. But the only way I could keep my mind from adjusting its focus to *in vitro* as a solution — even salvation — was to hang onto the gritty details of the present reality. I had to pull into myself, to immerse myself in my very personal, non-objective focus with the equal awareness of its being at odds with the doctor's. Perversely, willfully and almost subversively non-comprehending, I kept staring at the immaculate fingers stroking the waxed tips of the red-gold moustache. Eventually the doctor dropped his hand and left.

From then on, we saw each other as "one of them." Which is useful tactically at least. It's hardly a solution, but it's a good vantage point for starting to view science and technology through critical eyes.

I didn't immediately see the pill or the IUD as sinister in themselves; I began to see them, though, in context, as part of a larger system. The pill and the IUD did not spring Athena-like fully formed from the forehead of Zeus; they each had a particular pharmaceutical, social, and even political history. More to the point for me, they are part of a particular phrasing of the role of reproduction in society geared to production and consumption, and a particular phrasing of the problem of women's bondage to their own bodies. Hence the pill and the IUD came to be seen as *the* technologies of women's liberation.

Women didn't just buy the pill; we bought into a particular definition of women's liberation which named the pill as the golden key. Uncomplainingly, we bore the price — the actual cost of pills and the IUDs as well as the pain, the discomfort, and the mood swings. But lately, as the fallout from the "side-effects" has begun to accumulate, the price has gone up to include higher rates of strokes among women, with some preliminary evidence linking this to prolonged use of birth control pills; a dramatic increase in ectopic pregnancies — from 2,500 in 1971 to nearly 5,000 a decade later — and infertility, to be treated with hormones, *in vitro* fertilization, or simply suffered and endured.

Seeing technology as system rather than as a collection of tools helps us understand the paradox that, despite all the labour-saving technologies in the home, women still spend about the same time doing housework as they did fifty years ago. To a certain extent, one might argue that the paring knife is technology as tool; the food pocessor, however, is definitely not. The food processor is integral to a system which includes not only the kitchen utensils themselves, but also the images of labour-saving efficiency and the higher standard of cooking projected by advertisers. Having been sold on the image, we buy the food processor and set ourselves to making gourmet meals.

Coming to understand technology as a system that defines our choices, and even our identities as women "liberated" by household and reproductive technology, is a consciousness-raising experience of epic proportions. Additionally, it sheds new light on the cycle of women's peripheralization in the industrial economy, despite the 19th century claims of people like Christopher Sholes, the so-called "father of the typewriter," who congratulated himself for having liberated women from the drudgery of manual copying. "Whatever I may have felt in the early days of the value of the typewriter, it is obviously a blessing to mankind, and especially to womankind," he is quoted as having said more than a hundred years before the manufacturers of word-processing machines touted these inventions as yet another blessing to womankind. But wordprocessor use, defined within the social structures of a corporate wide management-information system, has even further standardized and mechanized information-processing work and marginalized most of the women doing it.

When I first wrote about technology, it didn't occur to me to consider the dictionary as part of a technological system — the technology of knowledge. *Webster's* informed me, value neutrally, I assumed, as befits a dictionary, that technology is the application of science especially to industrial and commercial objectives. There's no mention of the social structures of technology, the institutionalizaton of technology into a system so pervasive that it transforms even the language we speak in the so-called privacy of our homes. By excluding these dimensions of technology, by discrediting them, *Webster's* does its bit to make them invisible.

They were invisible to me when I began my research for *Women and the Chip* and *Computers on the Job*. If I thought at all about how much I was adjusting myself to the terms of reference of the established public discourse on technological change, it was only to congratulate myself for my maturity. I'd dropped my quirky habit of structuring my writing any old way that seemed appropriate to what I had observed and, in observing, felt. I'd finally familiarized myself with what others were saying on the subject and learned to position myself within their frame of reference.

I hadn't yet learned the distinction which my friend and mentor Ursula Franklin makes between "science as an enterprise and science as an establishment." Nor had I perceived its corollary in knowledge as an enterprise and knowledge accredited and "established" by the degree to which it fits with the theories and frames of reference and as adjudicated by the "experts."

The mainstream, international dialogue on technological change was decidedly economic, turning a great deal on the role of technological innovation in economic growth. The terms automation and modernization were used interchangeably. Productivity gains and competitive edges were valued in and for themselves. Technological change became synonymous with progress and progress, of course, is always a "good thing." End of discussion.

To question the technological "forces of progress" was to be a Luddite, which the old edition of *Webster's* taught us is a "misguided" fool. Yet the 19th century Luddites correctly identified the ideology underlying the so-called "forces of progress." They also regarded it as hostile to the values underpinning the traditional home- and commons-based English economy, which was life- and lifecycle-centred, not factory- and market-centred, and which cared about stability, not progress.

At the time I wrote *Women and the Chip*, however, I didn't understand that there were different ways of interpreting technology in society. Determined to integrate myself into the mainstream economic discussion so as to influence the policy making which would emerge from it, I did what was necessary to gain admission, to be accredited as an "expert" with a message for the press and the policymakers to heed. I didn't realize how much I was adjusting women's experience in the process.

By the logic of the mainstream discussion, the experience of technology was first turned into "social impact," and ranked as secondary, a "side-effect" to the main economic effect, just as pelvic inflammation leading to sterility is dubbed a "side-effect" of IUD use. Then the representation of the "impact" was made in strictly quantifiable, as well as economic-centred terms. By making job numbers the central measure of concern, the unbearable pain of individual women simply disappeared; it didn't belong in the discussion, therefore it didn't exist. This logic also marginalized issues demonstrating that the "debate" should really be about control over one's work and life, not about technology and jobs in the abstract. These issues include de-skilling (the computer controlling more of the work process), computer monitoring (the computer playing Big Brother and keeping a record of everything being done) and privacy, obliterated through such intrusive computerization.

By the final draft of my book, the women I was writing about were no longer whole women representing their personal experiences — saying, for example: "They treated the machines better than they treated us." That personal/political statement was voided as the women became statistical units in sociological categories — a transformation which sociologist Dorothy Smith likens to colonization, with the establishment of methodological pigeon holes representing "a sort of conceptual imperialism." (See "Women's Perspective as a Radical Critique of Sociology" in *Sociological Inquiry*.)

Moreover, I wasn't accountable to the "us" of that personal statement, for the women had been excluded along with their subjective observations and my experience of them. If I was accountable to anything beyond a front page headline, it was only for the correctness of my statistical analysis and only to the gatekeepers of knowledge at the research institute which made me an authority on technological change by publishing my report. Their Good Housekeeping seal of approval seemed to satisfy the various government bodies, unions, and profesional groups who convened conferences on technological change over the next few months and years, and breathlessly asked my advice on how women can overcome their math anxiety and adjust themselves to the world of high technology. A gratifying array of microphones, as well as speaker's honoraria, seemed to confirm that the answers I provided were appropriate.

When I regained consciousness, as Sergeant Renfrew would say, I discovered that if I hadn't deliberately sold out, I had certainly been bought off or had served as an accomplice in my own hostage-taking. The discourse had become an endless "debate on the long-term job impacts of technological change." Rising levels of unemployment and underemployment had polarized the working population into two tiers or even (as it's being described in Britain) two nations — the working rich and the working poor, the over-employed and the under- and unemployed — with women, young people, and older blue-collar workers ghettoized in the bottom tier. Canadian social policy is being adjusted to embrace this two-tiered (postindustrial) social reality (the proposed changes to the UIC program, and the revised talk of a guaranteed annual income can be interpreted in this light). But worst of all, not only had technology been marginalized as a social and political issue, and my message with it, but I had contributed to these developments by abandoning my own axis in favour of turning and being turned on theirs.

Barren, and partly by my own hand, I lay on the sidelines leafing through magazines. There was a cover story on big business getting into conservation by adopting birds and animals on the verge of extinction. Someone had sent me an article on environmental rehabilitation activities being turned into "eco-industries." But my heart didn't leap for joy. Instead, I checked the byline to see if it was the same person who'd been paid to rewrite feminism into "post-feminism."

But what about feminism? To me, a feminist is someone who is committed to equality between men and women, who believes that anything which denies this is wrong and must be changed and tries to do something about it. But feminism's been defined so much as integration into the status quo rather than transformation of the status quo that, in the media portrayal of it, women have to choose between embracing the traditional role of dependent wife-mother or embracing a skirt-and-kerchief version of the Horatio Alger executive type. The reality is that countless women experience dull, dead-end jobs and a double workload of paid plus unpaid labour as the measure of their so-called independence. To a large extent, the beneficiaries of the postwar women's movement have been governments which take our tax dollars, and big business which profits from us both as a cheap pool of labour and as a hyped-up market for more labour-saving consumer goods and services.

The French sociologist Jacques Ellul argues (in *Technological Society*) that the technological system is so pervasive that it is too late to reverse its effects. The rule of technique, the subordination of everything natural and human into parts of a technological system to be manipulated according to the values and priorities of the system (and those who control it) has reached the point of no return.

Knowing how I had lost the power to bear a child without technological intervention, and how in a strange yet real parallel I had relinquished the natural authority of my own impassioned voice and instead used the voice — objective language and methodological grammar — which would be recognized by those who would then accredit me as an "expert," I begin to lose hope as well.

But then I met Suzanne Bastedo Renaud, a graduate student in women's studies at Carleton University on whose thesis board I was asked to sit in my capacity as an adjunct professor. As a student trying to get her master's degree, she was accountable to the established disciplines and their representatives on her thesis board. But as a feminist, she felt accountable to the women whose esperience she was trying to represent through a questionnaire she'd "administered" to discover their attitudes toward technology. We talked about her "research instrument" as an example of technology in its own right: on the one hand, the user's manual advises the researcher to ignore the marginalia. On the other, Suzanne felt a responsibility to acknowledge what the many women who scribbled comments in the margins (includng myself, when I completed the questionnaire long before I met Suzanne) were saying, starting with the simple fact that they insisted on bursting out of the multiple choice boxes provided, demonstrating vehemently that the choices provided were inadequate somehow.

In the end, Suzanne chose to include only a minimal analysis of the collated, computerized results of the box scores. Instead, she declared that the marginalia had been as significant as the x marks. She described what she'd done — moving the marginalia out from the shadows into the centre of the discussion — as "transformed technology." And she got her degree.

But like feminism generally, it's the integration side that

gets the press, as well as the money and the backing of business, industry, and government. So, in schools where girls are under-represented in math and sciences such as physics, the question is why do girls drop math, not why do math and science drop (exclude) girls. Integrating women into science and technology is a laudable objective, and there's some reason to hope that once women's presence achieves "critical mass" women might begin to transform it from within.

But they'll only succeed if they take Ursula Franklin's advice and regard themselves as the equivalent of immigrants who must guard their customs and traditions against the pressures of assimilation. For the ideology of science and technology is out to transform them (into women who think like men) before they transform or even expose it.

In *Feminism in Canada*, computer scientist Dr Margaret Benston talks about the abrogation of responsibility that the pseudo-objective stance allows, "The idea of objectivity supports the actual use of science to gain control of and domination over a world viewed by those in power as being made up of manipulatable objectives — both human and non-human."

The roots of this desire for control and the ideology justifying it can be clearly seen in the writings of Francis Bacon, the "father of modern science." Coming of age at the height of the witch hunts, during which the denigration of women and women's ways of healing proceeded in tandem with the denigration of nature (which previously had been revered as a living female deity), Bacon urged that a new breed of applied scientists use the new "mechanical arts" to conduct an "inquisition" of nature, to "dissect nature," to "shape nature as on an anvil," to "bind" (nature) into service as a "slave" of man. Bacon referred to nature as "a common harlot" needing man's stern governance to control her wanton ways. But mostly, he saw nature as no longer as an autonomous organism, but as putty in the hands of technological man. Through "the art and hand of man," he wrote, nature could be "forced out of her natural state and squeezed and moulded...

to establish and extend the power and dominion of the human race itself over the universe."

Having named the ideology, the second half of the transformation includes reclaiming the history of women in science and technology which has been marginalized because the women were never accredited by the formal institutions or were discredited because they practiced science in ways that deviated from those of the establishment. It involves reclaiming methodologies which are subjective, participative, and intuitive. It means restoring context, agency (who's doing what to whom), and accountability.

Above all, it means asserting our authority to name things as we see and feel them. In other words, the personal *is* our politics, and it's our science too. It's our reference point, our home base. We must define reality for ourselves, not only reclaiming our "power of naming" but our power to be moved to action by what we see with our own eyes and articulate with our own voices; the power of conviction, the power of self-confidence, the power of magic.

Heather Menzies is an Ottawa-based writer, principally of nonfiction. Her books include *The Railroad's Not Enough* (about Canada during the 1970s unity crisis), *Women and the Chip* (case studies on office automation in service industries), *Computers on the Job* (more of the same, though enlarged to include factories, etc.) and *Fastforward and Out of Control* (about global restructuring and technological transformations of people and culture in Canada). A peace activist and a committed environmental democrat, Heather has written both about "getting women into science" and about "women's science and technology." On the latter theme, she has written the paper "Science through her Looking Glass" (forthcoming with Carleton University Press), plus written and directed a video documentary on Ursula Franklin called "The Soul of a Scientist." (Available through Magic Lantern distributors.)

OF MUFFINS AND MISOGYNY

REAL Women Get Real

Susan G. Cole

I DON'T LIKE DEBATING and never really did. I learned the rules in high school when a brave English teacher made me one of a three woman debating team which invaded the male club of Trinity College School, a private boys school which sponsored formal debates each year. They were fiercely competitive, a troubling factor which was aggravated by the atmosphere of the place, which reeked of hierarchy and repression. The debate, I discovered, was wholly suitable to that supermale environment. Debating is a quintessentially masculinist exercise: fancy verbal footwork is more important than ideas, and you can't win the debate unless you can argue both sides, which means you can't take a stand or get too emotional about anything. The assumption usually is that one and a half hours of debate ought to be enough to decide any issue, and the object is to win, which our all female debating team did, by the way, but that did not alter my conviction that I would never do it again.

Later on, when issues I cared about began to exercise the progressive community, I still refused to debate. Oh, I would talk, give my opinions, participate on panels and in seminars, but when audiences were looking for a circus, I always refused to provide it, never taking on anyone head on, but rather, trying to present ideas which veered away from the predictable. Debating,

I resolved, was incompatible with feminism. It was a word war which reduced complex issues to two "sides," and, as such, was essentially amoral and simply not useful.

So, last winter when I appeared on a podium to debate Gwen Landolt, the legal counsel for REAL Women, just about everyone asked me the same question. Why? Never mind that debates are irreconcilable with the feminist process, why was I giving those right wing, muffin-toting women a voice, and the legitimacy that goes with a public forum?

According to those critical of my decision, REAL (Realistic, Equal, Active, for Life) Women should be invited to fade into the woodwork, not to speak its mind. The three year old organization, which claims a membership of 30,000, has been recruiting disaffected women who resent the fact that their role as childrearers and homemakers is being devalued. In their view, public policy is bent on providing for working women, while mothers who are supporting the traditional family at home are left out. The leaders of the organization caused a furor in 1986 when they protested the decision of the Secretary of State's women's program to reject their application for funding. The din was so loud that the minister responsible, David Crombie, called for a reassessment of the women's programs' priorities. To get a sense of RW's increasing political clout, note that when the federal government's task force on daycare reported last spring, instead of recommending an increase in the number of daycare spaces, as the National Action Committee on the Status of Women (NAC) had advocated, the report supported RW-style tax credits.

Those tax credits have always been RW's panacea for policy. They allow husbands to write off a certain dollar amount per child cared for in the home. RW says tax credits will give mothers in the home a sense of well being and are a fair counterpart to the subsidies government is offering to working women. As I write, I imagine readers thinking that all this sounds quite reasonable. The problem is that hiding behind this sweet reason is strong opposition to the mainstays of the feminist agenda — affirmative action, equal pay for work of equal value. There is also the not-so-small matter of the hate campaign RW has waged against homosexuals, specifically against the inclusion of sexual orientation in the Ontario Human Rights Code.

To my knowledge these nasty tidbits of their platform had never been talked about publicly. While RW was distributing its slick brochures, the media, desperate for an opposition point of view, were inclined to accord the organization equal time, pitting it against NAC (and its three million members) with only a few questions asked. Suddenly RW's carefully crafted "reasonable" arguments were appearing more and more frequently on the op/ed pages of the nation's dailies. RW was gaining ground and worse, because its real intent was laundered; it sounded weirdly safe. Some feminists even began suggesting that it would be easier to support RW receiving a small women's program grant on the supposition that it would be satisfied and would fade from the headlines. It was at that point I began to suspect that the media attention and this feminist largesse were related to RW's refusal to tell the truth about its agenda. I decided to debate Gwen Landolt because I wanted REAL Women to get real.

The university campuses of the country, I thought, would be the appropriate venues. Worried that the feminist movement might be lost to this generation, I thought it would be worth while to make the case for feminism and equality directly and in person, as it were, so that students would get the straight goods, not from the press or from RW, but from someone who was committed to what is the most important movement for social change this century has yet seen. I also realized I wanted something out of it too. I wanted to know if we were getting anywhere, if the women's movement was still moving anything, making the changes we need at the level of attitude and culture. Was this generation different from ours? What I found out over those three winter months, debating Landolt at eight universities from Regina to Ottawa was more than I had bargained for.

I don't know if anybody has ever been able to explain feminism in a book, let alone in twenty minutes, but since the resolution of the debates was "Feminism: Boon or Bane," and as I was arguing for the affirmative, I had to go first, and twenty minutes was the limit. So I telescoped a little. Feminists noticed that the relationship between men and women is one of subordination, I began, and this inequality is one of the cornerstones of our social system. It goes on in the home, where women's work is undervalued; on the job, where women are paid less than men; on the street, where women fear sexual assault; in the family, where sexual abuse is almost normal. Feminists want to change the system and don't believe that it can be done until the subordination of women no longer exists. I provided all the dreary data — StatsCan's economic summaries as well as statistics on sexual violence. Feminists work to change these conditions, I continued, by creating safe places for women to recover from sexual and physical assault, by supporting policies that give women financial clout and access to decision-making positions, by supporting flexibility in family definitions and structures, by supporting autonomy for women and women's right to control our own bodies, by opposing the rigid sex roles that turn women into submissive nursemaids and men into corporate soldiers, and by transforming the educational norms that make male violence inevitable and female victimization a fact of life.

I may have been giving a hard line but I didn't want to soft-pedal the radical base of feminism. Landolt, on the other hand, was heavily into the soft sell. Her speech was designed to make the audience feel that life was just grand and with a few adjustments could become absolutely perfect. More and more women want to stay home with their children, she said, and then quoted feminists who said so. She added that when Swedish policies gave men and women equal access to parenting leave, very few men were interested; moreover, I and other feminists like me want equality on male terms, but that there were female terms to consider — children need unconditional love from a reliable source, and nobody has come up with a better living situation than the family. She went on to say that feminists are to blame for easy divorce and the misery that follows break up, that feminists do not have a right to speak for all women and that democracy has to leave room for other opinions. She used the word equality a lot and choice even more.

When I had arrived at the hall for the first debate, I had immediately reacted to the enormous size of the crowd and inwardly gasped. Everything I feared about debates was obviously about to take place. People were there for the two ring circus, to watch the spectacle of two grown women going at each other. But as Landolt spoke, I was amazed to hear the audience let go a steady stream of hissing. I began to realize that they hadn't come for the show, they had come to tell Gwen Landolt what they thought of her.

And did they tell her. During the question period, one woman stood at the microphone, swaying a bit as she told her story. "I brought up my children just like you say I should have, but I have now turned fifty, and I am bored to death chasing dust balls. So I upgraded myself and went out job hunting. But when I went for an interview, there I was facing a man across the desk. He looked at me and saw a woman over fifty and there was the discrimination the feminists keep talking about. So I did what you said I should do. I raised my children, and now what are you going to do for me?"

Throughout the eight city tour, the questions were equally breathtaking in their simplicity and clarity. They tended to reveal that RW is really doing very little for housewives, that it is actually betraying its constituency. While singing the praises of traditional housewifery, RW does not petition corporations on behalf of former housewives who decide to return to the paid work force after raising their children. They do not tell management that women who work in the home have developed extraordinary communications skills, can accomplish amazing things with limited resources, and handle a budget with a deftness which good managers would kill for. RW had not done anything to give room to mothers who choose to change their lives.

After just two stops on the tour — Regina and Saskatoon — I was already amazed at how much I had underestimated feminism's influence on campus. I don't know what I had been so worried about; feminism has made spectacular headway. I had been so afraid of a right wing swing at the universities that I was wholly unprepared for the intensity of the hostility Landolt managed to generate. At one point in Regina, when she was try to flog her pro-family ideology only to be met with derisive laughter, she grew flustered and exclaimed, "Oh well, maybe I am just a foolish old woman." "Yeah," came back the audience, clapping and hooting in a way that I found so abusive that I motioned for them to stop. I was terribly ambivalent about that fury. As the tour progressed I became more and more convinced that Landolt and RW are dangerous and are fighting against everything I have committed my own life to. But in that moment, and on a few occasions during the junket, I experienced the outburst of hostility directed at her as a disturbing act of violence. It reminded me of the time at a gay rights rally a few years ago when anti-gay rights crusader Anita Bryant was burned in effigy while the demonstrators chanted, calling her any number of flamboyant slang words for the vagina. My stomach turned over with the same queasy feeling.

It was at the end of the first debate that a woman pressed into my hand a copy of the RW pamphlet distributed to Ontario MPPs during the campaign against the inclusion of sexual orientation in Bill 7. I had known the campaign had been vicious, but I wasn't prepared for the venomous tirade of half truths and lies. I realized I could use it in the rebuttal portion of the debate at the next stop in Saskatoon. During my, count 'em, ten minutes of rebuttal I stressed that I didn't want equality in male terms, I wanted to change the terms altogether. I insisted that the traditional family was not working and that every time Landolt said it was paradise, she was making it harder for women terrorized in the family to leave their living hell; that feminists were not responsible for postdivorce trauma but that the 93 percent of ex-husbands who don't pay their maintenance and child support are; that working women do have a family life and are not neglecting their children. Does RW support affirmative action so the workplace will be even mildly more hospitable to women, I wanted to know. It does not. Does it lobby corporations, celebrating women's management skills? It does not. It spends its time distributing hate literature.

I don't think I am overstating the case when I call it hate literature. What does this sound like to you?

...Homosexuality is a psychosexual disorder...The homosexual seeks sex in a young age group. As he ages, he begins to lose his attractiveness and resorts to buying sex. The need has given rise to a subculture of prostitution of boys and younger men in inner cities...Homosexuals are a medical threat to their own sex, to those who require blood transfusions, to the promiscuous, and to their unknowing spouses. Homosexual food handlers are a frequent source of hepatitis outbreaks. Homosexual spouses expose their mates to a variety of diseases. The cost of medical research and treatment of AIDS is mounting daily and being paid for by the taxpayer...Many homosexuals because they cannot reproduce must recruit — often from the young. They promote recruiting straights. With new legislation, this seduction becomes permissible and acceptable...Any treatment of homosexuals should be weighed against the effects on their innocent victims, who are medically or psychologically damaged by them.

Dramatic reading of this text invariably sent audiences into paroxysms of rage. Landolt, however, argued that there was nothing wrong with telling the truth, claiming that the pamphlet was meticulously researched, quoting several studies and sources to back up her claim (and which my thorough bookstore search never uncovered). Of course, all this only underscored the need for legislation to protect gays, but Landolt didn't see it that way. One woman in Winnipeg explained that she had been fired from her job for being a lesbian and that Children's Aid workers kept watch near her home and harassed her when women came by to visit. Landolt looked her right in the eye and said, "You were probably neglecting your children," not even remotely aware that this was a monumentally hurtful thing to say to a woman in crisis.

With the gay issue began the process of my coming to terms with the debates. I began to feel glad I was doing them, if only so these audiences could hear some of the bigoted bile RW was capable of producing in the name of "equality." The issue of gay rights was easily the most explosive one, but while the audiences' consciousness got a terrific lift, Landolt seemed to get nothing out of the exchange. After the last debate at Queen's University in Kingston, she approached me at the train station in Toronto (we never travelled together and I had requested separate hotels). "Why," she asked genuinely, "do people get so upset about the pamphlet?" She was serious. I explained that because it was full of lies she was actually hurting people, making it harder for us to live what is already a difficult life. She just shook her head. Perhaps she had such an extreme stereotype of gays that she was not aware that her university audiences had a hefty gay contingent. She never seemed to grasp that by calling gays sexual abusers, carriers of disease, and mentally unfit that she was trashing a group of innocent people who are socially vulnerable and that she was saying these things about people sitting right in front of her. She still didn't get it.

Then again, maybe buried beneath her lawyerly facade is a religious fanatic capable of preaching compassion from one side of her mouth and hate from the other. I could never figure it out.

Were Landolt to sit down with Phyllis Shlafley, the American antifeminist who led the campaign against the equal rights amendment, they would have had a few things in common. They would have shared this loathing for gay people, a terror of affirmative action, a sense of resentment toward working women and a passion for the traditional family. But Landolt does not share Shlafley's tough-mindedness, or her intellect for that matter, though both are lawyers, and both had to leave home in order to argue that women should stay there. Landolt is not the type to take on issues head on but prefers to sidestep them. Had I not brought up the pamphlet, she never would have mentioned gay rights. Had audience members not brought up some of the employment issues, she might have convinced some people that all RW is after is a little respect for homemakers and a tax credit.

She bristled whenever anybody called her right wing, though in Ottawa, she did say, "What if we are? Democracy leaves room for a spectrum of opinion, doesn't it?" Here was some foreshadowing of Landolt's use of liberalism as a defence for conservative opinion. But ultimately, it was pretty hard to pin a political label on Landolt. Never once did she say women were naturally suited to the role of housewife and men born to run the world. She never sided with God. Her vision, at least the one she revealed on the podium, did not have any of that familiar fundamentalist fervour we tend to associate with the right wing. Yet, on examination, her views, if this is possible, were even more desperate. Men, she said, were not going to change. You could try, try, try, but they were never going to do the housework, never going to nurture children, never going to share homemaking and child rearing. Women are just going to have to adjust to that, and society had better do the same.

Saying such things produced some magic moments. On one occasion I had ended my opening statement by saying that men could get involved in the project of feminism, offering a list of ways they could get active. Then, on comes Landolt, saying men were hopeless. It was splendid irony. Here was the traditional female trashing men and the radical feminist — the supposed leader of man-hating hordes — explicitly telling the men in the audience that feminism meant them too. For the university audiences, and me too, Landolt's man-hating rant was a revelation.

Her woman hating, though, was a profound shock. A secretary at the University of Saskatoon campus came forward with some courage to describe her struggle to gain equal pay for work of equal value with the labourers on campus. Landolt retorted that if she wanted equal pay with the labourers she should become one. "The reason you haven't chosen to be a labourer is because you don't want the difficult working hours or working conditions." Dumbfounded, the woman allowed that she thought the working conditions of secretaries were not exactly great and then, unfortunately, the debate between the two was cut off by the moderator.

The exchange, limited as it was, was extremely useful. The truth was out. What Landolt was saying was that women choose lesser-paid jobs for their superior working conditions. What Landolt really knows about these conditions can't be much since as a lawyer she has never been confined to a pink-collar ghetto. But later it became clear that ignorance was not the operative phenomenon here, misogyny was. In London, she said that there was not a single shred of evidence to support the view that women are discriminated against in the workplace. Jaws dropped at the notion that if women do not have equality it is their own fault. They choose the jobs, you see. If they haven't equality it is because they didn't take it when it was offered. "Women have equality," Landolt said in Saskatoon. "The battle has been won. If you want to become a nuclear physicist, go out and do it. We won't stop you. We're not against that. We're for choice, for making it possible for women to stay home if they want to. Be a nuclear physicist if you must, but don't make all women go out to work if they don't want to."

Here Landolt was cheering for choice, but what was really happening was that she was dressing up old time misogyny with the old sloppy liberal sentiments: freedom of choice exists for women, equality is real, there is nothing stopping women from realizing their aspirations but women themselves. And now there is the Charter of Rights to underline the matter. There are no structural inequalities that circumscribe women's lives, no socialization that streams women into job ghettos training women for service as secretaries and men for service as labourers, no sexism in universities or sexist professors who might make life utterly miserable for women who are studying to become nuclear physicists, no built-in fiscal restraint that make women's economic equality prohibitively expensive and, heavens knows, no class interests to consider. There were only women choosing to be subordinated. Listening to Landolt, I learned that the politics of liberalism must surely be bankrupt if right wingers can use the language of liberalism to fuel their argument against feminism and to veil their contempt for women.

And I knew then that the debates, regardless of their occasional ugliness, had been worthwhile. I had discovered a population on campus committed to transforming sexual relations and women's inferior status. I listened to women who know their own lives speak their truth to a woman they thought could do serious damage to them. I was able to walk away and say to all those generous feminists who thought there was political room to accommodate REAL Women that blacks working against racism don't support funding for white supremacy and that we could not support the funding of such an antifeminist, antifemale outfit either. Can we imagine a group of blacks calling themselves REAL Colourful, claiming that because blacks like to dance and sing and are so darned good at it, that they therefore should be trotted out for the entertainment, but no one should think it wrong if they are excluded from the political sphere. For that matter, can we imagine a group supposedly advocating the interests of blacks saying that slavery was a matter of choice.

I doubt it.

POSTSCRIPT

The reference to Blacks in the last paragraph elicited an angry letter from Andonica Huggins who claimed that this comparison and the phrase "REAL Colourful" showed insensitivity to readers of colour. The letter and the author's response were published in *This Magazine.* — S.G.C.

Susan G. Cole is a long-time feminist activist, co-founder of *Broadside,* a feminist review published from 1978 to 1988, and the author of *Pornography and the Sex Crisis* (Amanita/Second Story 1989), a radical critique of pornography. Her play *A Fertile Imagination*, a comedy about lesbian reproduction, was produced by Nightwood Theatre in 1991 and remounted by Theatre Passe Murraille in 1992. She is senior editor of *Now* Magazine.

MONEY, SEX AND DEATH

The Return of the Warrior

Donna E. Smyth

MOGS IS THE DREADED MILITARIZATION DISEASE, Milito-Genital-Confusion-Dependency Syndrome. It was first identified in June 1986, in Halifax, as part of a satiric-action street-theatre event staged by the Never Again Affinity Group, a feminist peace group. We created a fictitious NATO general, Daniel O'Rat, who suffered from MOGS but wanted to be cured. We distributed a tabloid on Halifax streets describing, in intimate detail, the nature of the general's affliction. We made up a media kit which included the general's case history and copies of advertisements from various military and strategic studies journals which featured sophisticated systems such as the fire-it-and-forget-it type, using obvious phallic images and suggestive language. For our theatrical finale we dressed as clown doctors, carried fake MOGS testing devices and pictures of the weapons advertising and paraded through the streets, ending up at the World Trade Centre where the NATO foreign ministers were meeting under heavy security.

The objective of our action was to identify the psycho-sexual roots of the arms race, to call attention to the way arms manufacturers sell macho sex with weapons, and to satirize the masculine addiction to weaponry in the context of the NATO ministers' meeting.

The MOGS event touched off some curious reactions. On the street, most women who saw and heard us laughed. Some men reacted the same way. Others became very angry. In general, most men did not think it was very funny while most women did. More surprising was the reaction of the media. With the exception of one early morning CBC interview, the local media refused to cover the action. Some journalists became very hostile; even previously sympathetic ones accused us of "making up" the phallic weapons advertisements. We were variously accused of trivializing war, doing bad things to NATO, trespassing in the realm of male sexual fantasy and, worst of all, making fun of it. This last accusation was not explicitly articulated, but is the only one that makes sense of the anger the action provoked.

Clearly, MOGS describes one of the nerve centres of the permanent war economy and the ongoing militarization of our culture. Money, sex and death. We live in the world of the warrior where MOGS is so prevalent it is taken for normal.

Its primitive and crude manifestations permeate popular culture and are especially visible in the war pornography washing across the Canadian/U.S. border in movies, videos, and magazines like *Soldier of Fortune.* Its archetype is the primal warrior, Rambo.

Rambo has no mother. He springs, fully developed pecs, headband, and all from the forehead of his "father," a green beret colonel. Rejected offspring of the American war machine, Rambo, in turn, rejects high tech weapons in favour of hand-to-hand combat — just a knife and his balls between him and the Commies.

I think Stallone, consciously and unconsciously, tapped into two levels of myth-making with these movies. That's why "to act like Rambo" has become a cliché so quickly and why Rambo clones (movies and videos made by the likes of Norris, Schwarzenegger, Eastwood, Cruise) and even Rambo dolls have filtered the Rambo image/icon through multilevels of our culture.

The first, mostly conscious, level of political myth making in the Rambo set *(First Blood I* and *II)* reflects the neoconservative/new right version of postVietnam America. Symbolized on the high political ground by Ronald Reagan and articulated by ideological cowboys like Norman Podhoretz, editor of *Commentary* (which publishes all the right wing ideologues, including Jeanne

Kirkpatrick) this myth portrays an America wounded and humiliated by defeat. An America rendered impotent, a stricken warrior hero whose wound in the groin is inseparable from his masculine powers of fertility and strength.

The image comes from the medieval Romance legend of the Fisher King who is mysteriously wounded in the groin. His impotence renders his country sterile until he is healed by the deeds of the knight/warrior, Parsifal, in quest of the Holy Grail. In an ironic reversal, the Americans elected the old Fisher King to heal the stricken, young warrior-nation. During his 1980 campaign, Reagan described the Vietnam War as a "noble cause" which could have ended differently "if only our government had not been afraid to win." In *First Blood, Part II,* when Rambo hears his mission is "recon for POWs in Nam," his first response is: "Do we get to win this time?" At the end of the movie, Rambo again bursts into human speech. He says he loves his country — he is willing to die for it — and he only wants his country to love him and the other Vietnam vets. But he feels rejected and betrayed by the American people. America does not want him, does not understand him, and won't give him a job. He can't go home again.

It was Reagan's job to prepare an America to welcome Rambo home. Until the Iran-contra scandal erupted, it seemed as if he had succeeded. As the ad said: "The pride's back!" The Vietnam vets were treated to a ticker tape parade, and a revisionist remaking of America's role in that war is still apparent on every level of cultural activity from academe to the mass media.

In *First Blood, Part I,* another, deeper level of myth making emerges. After some sadistic treatment at the hands of the local law, the alienated Vietnam vet, Rambo, escapes and goes native. He fashions himself a monk-like garment and becomes the wild man of the forest who threatens to give the authorities "a war you won't believe." Having been cast out of a society where there are "no friendly civilians," the primal warrior returns to nature where he belongs. Society then determines to use its tools of coercion — the police and the military — to destroy him. But Rambo cannot be destroyed. In a redeemed society, he can be contained and controlled, but not destroyed as he is the libidinous violence at the very heart of the society which rejects him. At this point in the movie, Rambo is driven literally underground. The mine shaft where he hides is an equivalent for the underworld of the dead from which the sacrificed male demi-god will emerge to take vengeance on the unredeemed society. Explosive, spontaneous violence is thus pitted against the controlled violence of authority. Then the colonel father figure brings the message that the son must submit to discipline, must now assume human shape and significance. This transformation is once again signalled by human speech and a shift to the political level. Rambo reveals his obsession about having lost the war: "Somebody wouldn't let us win." He bursts into tears and reaches for the colonel's hand.

In this high tech, nuclear age when everyone, including women and children, is on "the front line," the eruption of the primal warrior myth figure is a phenomenon which demands attention. The idealization of the male body honed to perfection as a "fighting machine" in the image of Rambo is in stark contrast to the reality of war in the eighties. As weapons technologies become more sophisticated and complex, the human body actually becomes a clumsy hindrance to the functioning of the real war machines. Computers make the split-second decisions which determine if the weapon/plane works or not. They are more reliable than the human brain and eye and certainly more accurate than the human hand. (For example, a new "head out of cockpit" system called DASH has just been put on the military market. It features a "display and sight helmet" whereby the pilot can fire weapons accurately simply by looking at a target. The computer systems do the rest.) With these weapons, human skills are still necessary but not those of physical strength or macho toughness. The warrior body, moreover, is transformed into a monstrous creature, encased in radiation- and chemical-proof suits, with gas masks and goggles, and no human flesh exposed or visible.

Because most modern weapons can be tested only under simulated conditions, most modern military men have no idea whether their weapons actually work under field conditions. They have no idea, either, how they themselves would react under such conditions. It is therefore very easy to contemplate mega-kills, and other absurdities; the cool detachment of scientists in their weapons labs extends to the military men in their simulated cockpits.

Still they cling to the myth of the warrior which manifests itself in displaced desire. Gratification comes from the possession of more and more powerful weapons. Military and strategic defence journals such as *International Defence Review* and *NATO'S 16 Nations* sell weapons on the basis of potency, phallic thrust and ability to penetrate soft targets (human flesh). Nuclear-powered submarines are sexier than frigates. Generations of weapons are fathered without the need or the desire for the female.

On the political high ground, the cold warriors promote the star warriors. Neither the rhetoric nor the values differ significantly from the popular culture genre of the reel warriors. Think tough, talk tough, act tough. To be tough is to be a man. If you're not a man, you're a wimp or worse.

In 1977, Norman Podhoretz, wrote an article called "The Culture of Appeasement" subtitled: "A naive pacifism is the dangerous legacy of Vietnam." (In neoconservative rhetoric, pacifism is always "naive"; being "realistic" means being tough; i.e., macho/military.)

In his article, Podhoretz equates pacifism in England before, during, and after World War I with homosexuality and compares that period with the "homosexual apologetics" of contemporary America. In the warrior's code, pacifism equals impotence and/or a perversion of the normal male sexual drive which, according to this myth, must be allowed to express itself in violence.

Rambo symbolizes the instinctual eruption of this mythological figure and its fusion with far right ideology. Other crude manifestations on the popular level are magazines like *Soldier of Fortune,* (for the "professional adventurer") which glorify militarism and machismo while collecting money for contra brigades and a defence fund for Oliver North. They report on the maverick military, the covert military and the "mercs" (mercenaries) training and fighting with the contras, chasing SWAPO (South-west African People's Organization) terrs (terrorists) with the South African Security Forces. The down-market versions have names like *Eagle, Gung-Ho, New Breed* and sell the cult of the warrior with myth, fantasy, propaganda and weapons — guns, knives, swords. In this real man's world, male potency is magically associated with weaponry. It's like a mirror inversion of the high tech warrior's world. Weapons replace women as objects of desire, and they also function as phallic substitutes for the male conquest of the enemy.

It was no surprise when we learned that Oliver North slept in his office instead of at home and was self-righteously scornful about suggestions of a liaison with his secretary, Fawn Hall. Human sexual relationships do not tempt the real warrior. Always in bemedalled uniform, never repentant, often tearful in his sincerity, North's performance during the Congressional hearings into the Iran-contra affair was a skilled, TV-honed version of a Rambo who has learned to talk. "Olliwood" tapped the same level of mythical/political resonance as Stallone's productions. In fact, it's hard to know if Oliver North created himself or was created by this fusion of ideology and popular and mass culture which is the contemporary warrior's world.

In this neoconservative, MOGS-ridden world, women have three choices: they can either become real warriors in the military, symbolic warriors on the political/business battleground or they must be the wives and mothers of warriors. The recent Canadian attempts to "integrate" more women into combat jobs in the military is an official way to make sure women get MOGS too. In the 1980s the political and business worlds have been penetrated by the warrior rhetoric. Public space and public discourse are being interpreted in military/macho terms. The prime minister makes a joke about "nuking" whales and the opposition. The glossy business section of The *Globe and Mail* eulogizes economic warriors: tough guys who are aggressive, competitive, who win.

When Pat Carney sits down with Americans, she doesn't blink. She's tough, and all those who oppose free trade are wimps.

Maggie Thatcher's tough too. Her finest moment was the Falklands War, which was such a godsend to weapons manufacturers because they actually got to try out some of their weapons in "real life." The jingoistic passions aroused in Great Britain during this fracas show how vulnerable a media-controlled populace is to the ancient warrior's call to shed the blood of young men for the glory of a nation now occupied by U.S. military installations.

Jeanne Kirkpatrick, the ex-U.S. ambassador to the UN, is especially tough. It was Kirkpatrick who made it politically "acceptable" for the U.S. to support dictatorships in Latin and South America because these dictatorships were "friendly to American interests." Kirkpatrick marshalled the ideological assault against the UN in the United States which resulted in the withdrawal of crucial American funding. It was also graphically illustrated in the mini-series, *Amerika* by the prominent use of the UN symbol for the SS troops aligned with the evil Soviets, a deliberate attempt to discredit the UN and its agencies with U.S. viewers.

The wives and mothers of warriors are, of course, real women. They are supportive, like Mila Mulroney and Nancy Reagan and applaud their husbands' political-warrior exploits. They can be the power behind the throne, but they must not be too blatant about it, as Nancy Reagan was during the first topsy-turvy Iranscam days. Even an Old Fisher King president must be perceived "to wear the pants" in the family and the country. These first ladies are allowed to speak out against drug abuse and the drug trade, but what happens when funds for the contras are shown to be connected to drug trafficking? This more deadly addiction to military solutions to political problems is never questioned in public.

The patriarchal family is essential to the warrior's world. There must be a way of providing more warriors and there must be a "home" for the warrior to defend. Just as the neoconservatives in the U.S. have reached out to the so-called "pro-family movement," so have the Mulroney Tories promised to "enhance family values" in the last throne speech. At the same time, social services are being cut back to enhance defence spending. The "privatized" nuclear family will not need social services when they're huddled in their nuclear bomb shelters.

In a culture driven by these neoconservative values, women, children and non-warrior males are equally marginalized. The infinite variety of human activity becomes ever more narrowly focused on making profits and being tough. The militarization of the economy which began in the U.S. and is spreading to Canada institutionalizes the warrior's world in the academic-military-industrial complex.

MOGS, which is eroding our culture and will destroy our civilization, is taken as a symptom of health and well-being. During the MOGS action in Halifax in 1986, the media were not angry with the NATO ministers who actually endorsed the U.S. request for the resumption of chemical warfare weapons manufacture. They were angry with a small group of women who tried to publicly identify and criticize the psycho-sexual root of the arms race.

In 1936, Dorothy Livesay, a feminist woman of peace, wrote poignantly in a poem called "Day and Night" of what we stand to lose today:

We move through sleep's revolving memories
Piling up hatred, stealing the remnants
Doors forever folding before us —
And where is the recompense, on what agenda
Will you set love down? Who knows of peace?

Donna E. Smyth has published many short stories, poems and articles; two novels, *Quilt* (1984) and *Subversive Elements* (1986); a play, *Giant Anna* (1984); a historical novel for young adults, *Loyalist Runaway* (1991). She is an environmental and peace activist and teaches writing and English at Acadia University, Wolfville, Nova Scotia.

THE MEECH BOYS

Are Women Up the Lake Without a Paddle?

Susan Riley

FOR MANY WOMEN, the national debate over the Meech Lake accord has been a humbling, even depressing, experience. Whatever the ambiguities of the legal arguments — does the accord undermine equality rights in the 1982 charter or not? — the political skirmish was decisive. Women lost. The organized women's movement lost. On Parliament Hill, its representatives ran into an indifference more chilling than hostility. Women asked for a serious hearing and they got "trust me, sweetheart." When they persisted, they were accused of being hostile to Québec's desire to become a "distinct society," of being antiFrench. Their motives were questioned, their legal arguments ignored, and their political clout called into question. What we don't yet know is whether the events of the last few months represent a temporary reversal for women power — or a rout.

At first, a few liberal male allies, including Ontario Premier David Peterson, pledged their solidarity; they would never approve anything that threatened the sexual equality rights entrenched in the charter. Then, one by one, they defected, until finally most of the organized women's movement — along with a handful of federal MPs, some northerners, a few civil libertarians, and the odd crank stood alone in opposition to the accord.

You hear it argued by both left and right that the major

feminist lobby groups — the National Action Committee on the Status of Women (NAC), the National Association of Women and the Law (NAWL) or the women's Legal and Education Action Fund (LEAF) — don't represent real women, whoever they are. Feminist lobbyists are accused of being too well-dressed, too highly educated, too left wing to be credible representatives of mainstream Canada. They are said to be excessively lawyerly. But these groups, particularly NAC which never fails to mention that it speaks for 543 different women's organizations, come closer than anyone to representing the special concerns of 52 percent of the population. No lobby group is perfectly representative — indeed, no one group can speak for all women, since women's relationships with the state are so diverse — but NAC comes closest. In the last decade — and particularly during the 1981 constitutional discussions — its influence has been formidable. On the other hand, that was before Ottawa turned Tory. Nowadays it seems the Egg Marketing Board has more pull than the national women's lobby.

None of this shocks the cynics; they've been telling us for years about the limitations of liberal feminism. As for Meech Lake, what can you expect from an agreement signed by 11 men, drafted by men, and conceived by men, they ask? What can you expect in a country whose constitution has so many fathers and no mother? They have a point; women will never be taken seriously while they hold only associate membership in the country's ruling elite. But cynicism is neither emotionally satisfying nor politically effective. It will take something more if women are to stop the accord before it passes into law. Today they face their most daunting opposition ever: not the cranks and extremists, but the male mainstream.

No one ever accused Brian Mulroney of being a steadfast defender of equality rights for women, and he has lived up to his reputation. Mulroney isn't a misogynist and has no strong objection to having women in his cabinet — provided those women behave and think like men, and hold degrees from prestigious U.S. business schools. But it is obvious that feminist issues rank somewhere beneath solar energy on his personal agenda. Women shouldn't take this personally; Mulroney doesn't appear to care about anything these days except getting re-elected. Faced with a difficult moral choice, he consults Allen Gregg, not the Bible.

On Meech Lake, he made a typically cold calculation: he stood to lose more support in Québec by delaying the accord, than he would among women for refusing to fix it. Premier Robert Bourassa, who rushed the deal through the National Assembly with awesome speed, apparently convinced the nervous prime minister (his long-time personal friend) that the whole agreement would unravel if any part was touched. So objections from women and others were brushed aside. Mulroney didn't even bother giving a detailed explanation; he simply offered bland assurances that nothing in the Meech Lake accord would imperil women or minorities. It was left to Justice Minister Ray Hnatyshyn, an amiable westerner not known for his intellectual depth, to elaborate.

Unfortunately, Hnatyshyn had trouble sustaining a conversation on the subject beyond a sentence or two and resorted at once to diversionary tactics. When Liberal MP Lucie Pepin asked sober and pointed questions, she was twitted for being out of step with her party and her province. "I do not understand the purpose of the Hon. Member's question," said Hnatyshyn, all innocence. "Is she not in favour of bringing Québec into the constitution, into the mainstream of Canadian life?"

Senator Lowell Murray, Mulroney's minister responsible for federal-provincial relations, wasn't much more effective. He told one audience, to derisive laughter, that women shouldn't worry since they aren't discriminated against as a group. He later apologized for his awkward phrasing, but never really explained one of the glaring inconsistencies in the accord: why did the first ministers insist that nothing in the pact infringe on the rights of native people or multicultural groups, then refuse to offer the same assurance to women? Women's groups argued, persuasively, that the clause creates a "hierarchy of rights" in which some groups — natives and ethnic communities — get more protection than others. Murray explained that under the present constitution, native people and ethnic groups have only "interpretive rights" whereas women and minorities have "substantive rights." That means future courts may need guidance when deciding between native rights, say, and the rights bestowed by the "distinct society" of Québec. Women's rights, by comparison, are supposed to be transcendent.

But are they? Few legal experts — even those who defended the accord — were willing to swear that women's rights would never be overridden by the Meech Lake accord. Most said it was unlikely, improbable, "a remote possibility," to quote John Turner. The legal argument is dense and arcane, and neither case — for or against— is conclusive. Noted feminist lawyer Mary Eberts was careful not to overstate her side for the Parliamentary hearings. She said, carefully: "You cannot say there is no risk of harm to women's equality rights." So why not make a small change to eliminate that risk, Liberal MP Sheila Finestone asked one defender of the accord. Because, came the reply, women are already protected in two different places in the 1982 constitution: "We already have the belt and suspenders; why do we need galoshes, too?"

No one was surprised when Liberal Leader John Turner wearied of this complicated debate within days and decided to go along with the rest of the guys. Turner is a strategic feminist at the best of times; these days, he, like Mulroney, only wants to live to see tomorrow. His personal standing is already dangerously low in Québec. Besides, he had enough trouble within his fractious caucus over the way the accord treats immigrants, northerners, native people and the English minority in Québec without worrying about women. With the moral elasticity that is a venerable tradition in his party, Turner severely criticized the Meech Lake agreement for its threat to equality rights — then announced he was voting for it anyway.

That left the New Democrats (NDP), who have never been afraid to go to the wall for respectable liberal causes, even to the point of affixing the party name to those incendiary open letters on Latin America which run periodically in *The Globe and Mail.* Surely the New Democrats would speak up? *Pas si vite!* NDP Leader Ed Broadbent, the original strategic feminist, is busier being a strategic Québecer these days. He raised even less fuss about the accord than Turner. Even NDP constitution critic Pauline Jewett stifled her initial negative reactions. Perhaps the most devastating blow came when Queen Elizabeth II declared that even *she* likes the Meech Lake accord. To paraphrase that famous feminist Pierre Trudeau: who will speak for women? No one, it appears.

Since he first ran for the Tory leadership in 1976, Mulroney has favoured a style that can best be described as simple, partisan, and mean — and effective. He frightened an entire city (Ottawa) into silence by implying that anyone who opposes the Meech Lake accord is hostile to Québec. Instead of challenging this slur, the opposition parties, visions of power dancing in their heads, folded their hands.

Some non-Québec MPs from all parties were genuinely worried about the consequences of an English-Canadian rejection of this accord — about the consequences for their country, not just their party. Québec said yes to Canada in 1981, we were constantly told, now we must say yes to Québec. It is an attractive but misleading argument. It supposes that Quebeckers were clamouring to sign the constitution, holding candlelight vigils in front of the National Assembly, nursing bitter memories of the treachery of 1982. This may be true of some newspaper columnists, former Parti Québécois militants and various Québec academics, but there were no indications that the majority of the population felt slighted, ignored, or unrepresented; if anything, Quebeckers were bored with the subject of constitutional reform like everyone else. Besides, Québec has been legally covered by the 1982 document even though the late René Lévesque refused to sign it. Completing the deal was a formality — albeit a formality laden with political meaning for Robert Bourassa and Brian Mulroney.

In fact, the real urgency surrounding the Meech Lake accord

sprang from Bourassa and Mulroney's desperate need for an easy political victory. They could take joint credit for ending the destructive bitterness that marked Ottawa-Québec relations for so long and improve their standings in the polls. It has worked; Mulroney has climbed several points in the polls in Québec since Meech Lake. That alone should compensate for a bit of sloppy drafting.

To point to that sloppy drafting — to challenge the secrecy and haste that marked the Meech Lake deliberations or the errors it produced — isn't anti-Québec, any more than those who support the deal can be said to be pro-Québec. Are we to believe that Bill Vander Zalm is suddenly a champion of Québec's frustrated nationalist aspirations? Or does he, as Pierre Trudeau suggested, see this accord as a new way of cutting up the national pie: Québec for the French and the rest for the English?

As for Quebeckers, while a majority now support the accord, not all do. Nonetheless, Mulroney has been clever in exploiting divisions and particularly the division in the women's movement. A few Québec feminists, disturbed by some of the testimony coming out of Ottawa, accused their anglophone sisters of holding a prejudiced, patronizing, and outdated view of Québec. They had a point. While most of the women who spoke against the accord genuinely favour the recognition of Québec as a "distinct society," a few left a different impression. Some of the examples they cited sounded far-fetched, to say the least. What if a future Québec government, one Toronto feminist asked, became concerned about declining birthrates in the "distinct society" of Québec and outlawed programs directing women towards non-traditional roles? Or outlawed abortion? What if some future Québec government decided that in the distinct society of Québec, affirmative action programs based on language outrank those based on gender? Other English-Canadian feminists evoked the ghost of Duplessis — who persecuted Jehovah's Witnesses in the fifties on the grounds that Québec was a distinctly Roman Catholic society.

The point is, of course, that modern Québec is not a church-ridden, socially conservative province with fixed notions about the role of women. *Au contraire.* In her column in the Montreal newspaper La Presse, Lysiane Gagnon noted quite rightly that contemporary Québec is more secular, more progressive, and more tolerant of minorities than any other province. It has no lessons to learn from English Canada and particularly Ontario.

But that was not always the case, nor will it necessarily always be the case not because Quebeckers have some sinister liking for totalitarian rule, but because political regimes come and go. Isn't a constitution and a charter of rights meant to protect us from the whims and caprices of changing elites over all time? To imagine ways in which women's rights may be abridged in a "distinct society" of Québec is not to disparage modern Québec. A constitution must imagine every possibility.

Ironically, if it were left to the population of Québec, the shortcomings in the Meech Lake accord could probably have been corrected in a weekend. No one seriously imagines that modern Quebeckers would tolerate an assault on women or minorities, but the men who fathered this agreement have been extraordinarily reluctant to let anyone else near it. Apparently the accord is such a fragile creature, of such delicate constitution, it must be kept in intensive care until it is ready to go home. I have asked federal spokesmen: even if you don't think equality rights are necessarily threatened, why not make a minor addendum to mollify critics? Because to allow one amendment would be to open the floodgates, comes the reply. Floodgates of what? Democracy?

Now the battle shifts to the provinces. The accord doesn't become law until it is approved by all ten legislatures, plus Parliament (the Commons voted yes at the end of October, but the Senate may not decide until summer). All this must happen within three years. If one premier or province backs down, the deal is off. So far, only Québec and Saskatchewan have ratified the accord. Manitoba is planning hearings, as are Ontario and New Brunswick. In Ontario, David Peterson has shuffled the accord to the bottom of his deck for now, while he wrestles with the more immediate problem of free trade. But he has already acknowledged that he is unpersuaded by the "rather arcane legal arguments" put forward by women opposed to Meech Lake. For critics of the accord, their best hope now lies with Frank McKenna, the new Liberal premier from New Brunswick, provided he can resist the enforced male bonding of the typical first ministers' conference. His predecessor didn't. Richard Hatfield was a man of liberal views. But as spokesman for his fellow premiers, he encouraged women to keep arguing their case even after the premiers had rejected it. In other words, he offered therapy, not justice.

Before we write an obituary for the women's movement, though, we have to consider two things. First, the Meech Lake accord, for all its shortcomings, does not represent a direct, frontal attack on women's rights. Its dangers are more subtle. That makes it hard to attack; it is harder to rally people to fight a possible threat than an immediate one. It is even possible that other elements of the agreement hold greater long-term danger to the way we live our lives and order our society. Will the changes in federal spending powers, for example, preclude a national day care system?

Second, I am not convinced that what the constitution says matters that much when it comes to women's rights or anyone's rights. (Call this the George Baker school. Baker is the New-foundland Liberal MP who flipped a coin to decide how he was going to vote. His constituents, he said, couldn't give a fig: "You can't eat Meech Lake.") This is heresy in Ottawa, of course, and has been for the last decade. It also puts me squarely in the camp of former Manitoba premier Sterling Lyon and former *Saturday Night* editor Robert Fulford, and that alone should make me nervous. But you can argue that the way women are treated depends on the prevalent values of a society, on the way those values are reflected in democratic legislatures, not on cold words on a white page. A constitution is a blueprint, but it only works with the people's consent. If it clashes with accepted values, it will be ignored or changed. This is both good and bad — it means rights that are meant to be inviolable (the right to equality on the basis of sex, race, creed, national origin, or physical disability) are in fact subject to political mood and judicial interpretation, but it also means that an ill-considered constitution won't survive if it offends majority opinion. Defenders of the 1982 charter and its importance in our public and private lives argue that it already has resulted in a number of rulings that protect the minority from the majority — which is exactly what a charter is supposed to do. It is a compelling argument, one I can't readily dismiss. In fact, no one can dismiss it. We are all dragged into this constitutional debate — some of us protesting, some of us yawning — because our ruling elites believe it is important.

Even if we do view the argument over Meech Lake from a bemused distance; even if we remain unconvinced by any of the conflicting arguments, we cannot ignore one thing: the accord and the debate it generated was a bracing reminder of how male our political culture is. Of the fact that "the majority" is not necessarily the group with the largest numbers.

Susan Riley is an editorial writer and political columnist for the *Ottawa Citizen*. She also writes columns on federal politics for the *Vancouver Province* and the Southam chain and appears frequently on television and radio as a political commentator. She is author of a book on the institution of a political wife, *Political Wives: The Lives of the Saints* (1987). Riley has been a print journalist for 20 years, working at a number of Canadian newspapers and as a parliamentary correspondent and senior writer at *Maclean's* magazine in the mid-eighties.

LANA SPEAKS!

C-54, Where Are You?

Timothy Findley

ROUGHLY 50 YEARS AGO, in June of 1937, Lana Turner made her first appearance on the silver screen. All she did was drink a soda, make an exit, walk down a street. But more was happening than met the eye.

"I hadn't really understood the significance of the script," Lana Turner now recalls, "but I do remember what I wore: a tight-fitting sweater, a patent leather belt and a well-contoured skirt." Miss Turner, in her final scene, was required to walk away from the camera wearing this costume. Most of the men who watched from their darkened seats that night were never to recover. As exits go, it has its place as one of the greatest in motion picture history. "The walk," Miss Turner says; "was more than teasing....It was seductive. My breasts and backside were not that full, but when I walked, they bounced."

The film, as if to announce the career to follow, was called *They Won't Forget*. On seeing herself in June of 1937, Lana Turner was mortified. "Please," she said to the studio executive assigned to protect her from the public at the screening; "tell me that I don't really look like that."

"Fortunately," he said, "you do."

That's how it all began: the beatings — the bruises — the killing.

The character Miss Turner played in *They Won't Forget* walked off screen to her death, a victim of rape and murder. When engaged to play this role, she had been fifteen. "Thank God," the producers said, "by the time *They Won't Forget* is released, she'll be sixteen. We won't have to worry."

Lana Turner was not inclined to give this interview. Were it not for her surrogate, *Ms Lana* — a long-time resident inside the person of Timothy Findley, novelist, playwright, and closet postmodernist — the interview would not have taken place.

"There are bound to be some pretty strong questions," Miss Turner says. "I make it a point not to answer those. So I'd rather Ms Lana did the talking. She knows exactly how to tell what we've been through, whereas I," she shrugs a padded shoulder, coughs, and continues, "I tend to get all choked up. Next thing you know, I've said the wrong thing. I have my career to think about; my audience. I'm sure you understand. Besides," Miss Turner crosses her legs, uncrosses them, and smooths her skirt, "I like to hear Ms Lana talk. She gets so few occasions. No one you see — no *man*, at any rate — wants to hear what she has to say. They find it too upsetting...What Ms Lana has to say is what I'm not *allowed* to say. So, if you don't mind, I'll leave this one to her."

Miss Turner has asked the writer to stress that her name should be pronounced *Lahna*. "Lana with a short *a*," she said, "is a skin care product I do not endorse. It comes from lambs. And lambs are sort of like me: they're always being led to the you-know-what."

Ms Lana is not a figment of the author's imagination. She has been with Mr Findley ever since their first encounter back in the early forties. He was then a child of ten, and she came gliding (no more bouncing) across the screen in a film called *Ziegfeld Girl* — gliding, then stumbling down a staircase — falling to her death. What an entrance! But, at least she got to die on screen. No more hints of violence. The violence was there for all to see. Findley, the child, was distressed, and he asked Ms Lana if she needed help. Ms Lana replied: *I only want to get out of here. I'm sick unto death of always falling down.* After which she added, *Do you think I could hide for a while inside of you?* Findley — who was something of a romantic fool and already the repository of Peter Rabbit, Albert Schweitzer, and National Velvet — said he would be glad to offer her accommodation. She has been his secret sharer ever since.

The rendezvous that follows was prompted by Ms Lana's apprehension as the date approached for publication of her daughter's recent autobiography, *Detour: A Hollywood Story*, by Cheryl Crane and Cliff Farr. In her book, Ms Crane — who is Lana Turner's only child — tells in some detail how she came to kill her mother's lover, Johnny Stompanato.

Stompanato was a small-time gangster who had taken up with Lana Turner — just as he'd taken up with other motion picture stars — in order to sleep with her, gain access to her money, and — in the long run — make her a victim of his blackmail. in the course of doing all this, he had also toyed with the adolescent affections of Miss Turner's daughter. But he was a man of violence through and through and beat Lana Turner once too often in her daughter's presence. Cheryl Crane — enraged and frightened — had picked up a knife and, thinking to scare Stompanato, lunged at him with the blade. Fate was not with her — and he died. The killing took place in April 1958. Now, after many years of silence, Cheryl Crane has published her story.

A distraught Ms Lana appeared before Mr. Findley on December 16, 1987 at the Ritz-Carlton Hotel in Montreal. Slush was falling beyond the windows, and the muffled sounds of a traffic jam on Sherbrooke Street provided the scene with what Ms Lana termed "the usual background music of my life": shouted obscenities and grinding gears.

Ms Lana, who is sixty-six and really looks her age, was wearing a stylish suit of black raw wool with stains of mud, dried sperm and blood on the skirt. The artful jacket, with its modest neckline, was torn in three places, revealing undergarments especially designed by Break-a-Way Lingerie of Hollywood. Her hair, worn short, was white and her lips were pale for want of painting. The mask of her face was notable for its shocking lack of eyebrows, lost to a makeup artist's overzealous plucking early in her career.

Throughout the meeting, Ms Lana smoked incessantly and drank a moderate amount of Spanish wine. Angry, apprehensive, and nervous all at once, she stayed on her feet and paced the room. Everywhere she goes, Ms Lana takes along a CD player, plus a carrying case of compact discs. She does this to drown the sounds of the aforesaid "shouted obscenities and grinding gears." Her taste in music is eclectic — ranging from Victor Young (who scored her films), to the all time hits of Artie Shaw, to whom she was married in the early forties. "I was just a child," Ms Lana says of this marriage. "Artie was anything but. Make of that what you will..."

Soon as she'd made her appearance at the Ritz-Carlton, the first thing Ms Lana did was ask for Kleenex.

"Everything's running," she said. "My eyes, my nose, my knees."

The Kleenex was offered and Ms Lana wiped her face. "I always seem to be in tears," she said and then proceeded to dab at her blood-stained knees with another Kleenex dipped in wine. "When you spend your life getting beaten up," she explained, "it's always a good idea to have a drink nearby. That way, you've got an antiseptic handy..."

"You really are upset, aren't you," Findley said.

"Yes. And why not? Now that Cheryl is publishing her book, it's all going to start again."

"What's all going to start again?"

"The finger pointing. You know, the dark suspicion. Everyone thinks that I killed Johnny Stompanato."

"Maybe they do. But you didn't."

"You're much too kind to me, Findley. Deep in my heart, I sometimes wish I had. It would have saved Cheryl-my-baby, all those years of trauma: all that horror she went through — being a ward of the court — the psychiatrists — the reform schools." Ms Lana dried her knees with another piece of Kleenex and poured herself some more wine. "The point is, Cheryl-my-baby, shouldn't have had to bear such things. She only did it to protect me. Agh! The way Johnny beat me up in front of her — she must have been terrified. And the way he put the make on her. Kids shouldn't have to go through that."

"Agreed."

"I went through that myself, you know." Ms Lana looked at the falling slush on Sherbrooke Street and leaned against the window frame. "Women like me were made for violence..." she said in a husky voice. "Manufactured for it is what I mean," she said. "I don't mean born. Manu-fucking-factured." She fiddled with the venetian blind and wrapped its string around her finger. "That's what they did with me, you know," she went on. "Put me together, just like a Barbie Doll." She turned and looked at Findley. Findley was keeping his distance, sitting on the far side of the room nursing his own glass of wine. *"Barbie for the Barbarians!"* Ms Lana shouted at him, and he almost dropped his drink. Ms Lana laughed.

Findley lighted a cigarette and waited. Now Ms Lana was talking, he didn't want to interrupt. Everything she said was interspersed with gusts of traffic jam and shouted curses from the street below — underscored by the music from *The Bad and the Beautiful* playing on the CD player.

"The Bad and the Beautiful," now Ms Lana was serious again, returning to her reverie. "That's the one where I played a movie star, the one where Gloria Grahame played a slut and got to die in an airplane crash. She wasn't really a slut, of course. All she was doing was having an affair. But the sexier you are, the more you have to pay. Funny, isn't it: everyone uses you — then you die. That's the moralist's code. The very first role I played, I was a victim of violence. You remember that? That movie all about some guy who gets off on kids and killing. I was the kid he killed. The movie where they made me wear that sweater and I did that walk..." She took a sip of wine. "I wasn't killed on screen, of course. They had this rule, back then, you weren't allowed to show that stuff. They could show my tits and show my ass going wiggle-waggle down the street — but they couldn't show him

putting in the knife. They said it wasn't civilized to show a person things like that. Wonderful, isn't it?"

Wonderful, yes. And crazy.

Findley thought of Bill C-54, the censorship bill — the so-called "pornography bill" — currently before the House in Ottawa. He thought of its insane refusal to deal with reality — just the way the censors had refused to deal with reality back when Ms Lana had bounced her merry teenage way to rape and death — off camera. And he thought of Ms Lana, followed every legal inch of the way by all her avid fans who never got to see what bouncing did to a girl because it wasn't "nice" to show them what it did.

He also thought of what Bill C-54 would do to his work — the books he had written, the books he still intended to write. Certainly, it wouldn't be kind to Robert Ross, who was raped in The Wars. ("Men don't do such things!" Findley had recently been told; "Men don't rape one another." That's right, he'd thought; let's all run a little faster from reality. Nonetheless, he was now afraid. Such people and such thinking are gaining in ascendancy. That is precisely why Bill C-54 was drafted in the first place: to legislate the speed with which we're meant to run away.) Findley wondered what they would do — the boys in the pinstripe suits — if they ever found out that he met this way with his secret sharer, Ms Lana. Probably, they'd think she was a man in drag! What else is new?

Findley was just beginning to wonder if he could talk Ms Lana into going up to Ottawa to show her wounds to the suits who'd written Bill C-54, when she started to speak again.

"They dressed me up," she said, "in a sweater tight as a second skin for They Won't Forget. And they told me please to walk in front of the camera. *Walk in front of the camera, Lana. No one's going to hurt you*...No one's going to hurt you. Not while you're on screen. That's how my career began. Look how it ended!" Ms Lana displayed her spattered skirt and her bloodied knees as evidence of what has become of her after they had told her not to be afraid.

"Strange," she said, "when you consider what Cheryl-my-baby, was going to end up doing to Johnny Stompanato with her knife. Revenge, I guess, is a long time coming. And when it comes, they put the knife in all the wrong hands. I didn't want it that way. I didn't even know, back then, that what I wanted was revenge. How is a child supposed to know she wants revenge, when everyone is being kind, and they give you all that money, and they give you all that fame, and no one ever tells you it means you're going to end up being pig bait? Pig bait — that's what you are. And then you have to hire a bodyguard — at your own expense! — to ward off the pigs."

"I'm sorry."

"Why be sorry? All I'm doing is telling you the way it is!" Ms Lana's anger was in good condition.

Findley couldn't explain what he meant by "sorry." And, since he couldn't explain, he fell back into silence.

Now Ms Lana poured more wine and, while she held the bottle in her hand, she looked at it gravely and muttered, *"They only make you what you are because they want to make you.* Rita Hayworth said that. Someone else who was pig bait. And every time you tell them no, they call you a whore and beat you up for being disobedient. Now, I look at that Madonna person, and I wonder what she thinks she's doing to herself and all the rest of us and...Hold it! There I go, you see! Blaming *her,* for Christ's sake! If only someone could tell me what this means, I'd be most grateful."

Findley waited. Surely there was more. But now Ms Lana poured her drink and set the bottle back in its place as if she'd had her say.

It was true, he thought. Her whole career had turned on violence. So often dressed in white — yet she'd never played the official sacrifice. Ms Lana always asked for what she got. Or so it was made to seem. *The walk was more than teasing,* she had said. *It was seductive.* "I did all this to myself," she had told him once, "that's what they want you to think. *They* want *me* to think I did all this to myself!"

The record stopped. Ms Lana was silent for a moment.

"Sometimes," she said, "it's nice without the music."

"I never once," she said later, "got to put the knife in where it belonged. In the movies, they always made me kill some other man: innocent. That way, they got to send me to the chair. You know what I mean?"

Yes.

"If only someone understood, I'd give up — maybe — wanting my revenge. But no one understands it. Not even you. You think it's just some kind of story. Just another sad-ending story: *Love Goddess Caught in Trap*...That's crap."

Ms Lana put on her disc of Artie Shaw's classic hits.

She drank more wine. She smoked another cigarette. She smoothed the blood and semen stains on her skirt. All the prescribed behaviour. Outside, the slush continued to fall: the traffic jam and the obscenities made their bids for attention.

"You'll think it'll change when Cheryl-my-baby, has kids?" Ms Lana asked.

Findley didn't answer. He sat quite still, alarmed by his knowledge, shamed by his ignorance. *No*, he thought, *not the way we're going, it isn't going to change.* But he didn't say so. Saying so would have been too cruel and Ms Lana — like the lambs — had already gone too often to the you-know-what.

Timothy Findley first came to prominence with his novel, *The Wars*, winner of the Governor-General's Award and now a Canadian classic. Following his books, *Famous Last Words* and *Not Wanted on the Voyage*, his first mystery, *The Telling of Lies*, was given a coveted "Edgar" in New York. His most recent collection of short fiction, *Stones*, won Ontario's Trillium Award. His first book of nonfiction — *Inside Memory: Pages from a Writer's Workbook* — won a Canadian Authors Association Award in 1991. He is at work on a novel to be published in 1992.

TRUE NORSE

Iceland's Women Show the Way for Newfoundland

Dorothy Inglis

ONE NIGHT LAST MAY, as a chilly fog crept up the hills from the harbour, shadowy figures arrived in ones and twos at a house in old St. John's. While the gathering was not exactly secret, many of those attending hoped that some of their close associates didn't know they were there.

Inside, curses and incantations filled the air, with each new arrival adding a voice to the chorus — "They've bloody well done it again!" "How long are we going to put up with this?" "We can't let this go on." "We've got to do somehing."

A coven of witches, perhaps? A cell of dangerous revolutionaries? Well, no. But it was a remarkable meeting nonetheless.

The setting was a middle class living room, and in its light those shadowy figures were revealed as respectable St. John's women. Some were Progressive Conservatives, some Liberals, some New Democrats — some, indeed, were or had been officeholders in those parties and some had no party affiliation. What we had in common was a body of feminist ideology and a deep sense of frustration. We'd been brought together on this cold night because the three parties had finished nominating their candidates for the upcoming federal by-election in St. John's East, and — to no one's great surprise — the candidates were all men.

Many of us had worked hard to get a woman nominated for their own party and had failed. Was it time to run a women's candidate as an independent? Could we do it? And if we did, would it do any good?

What made the absence of women candidates particularly frustrating was the fact that the women's movement has been making important strides, affecting all of our social institutions but the most obstinate. A category which maddeningly still includes the political parties. As the women's movement in Newfoundland has tirelessly (and I'm sure some would say tiresomely) pointed out, no woman has ever represented the province in the House of Commons, and only one is at present sitting in the House of Assembly. Fortunately, Lynn Verge is a well-respected feminist as well as Canada's only female attorney-general. In spite of the pressure from women and all the changes in social attitudes, none of the three parties seem to regard this as an imbalance needing redress. And hence the semi-clandestine meeting.

Besides anger and frustration, the women attending also shared a source of inspiration: only a few weeks before, our friends of the Women's Alliance Party in Iceland had doubled their representation in Parliament and were holding the balance of power in a minority government. So between imprecations hurled at the power structures of our own parties, the meeting buzzed with the latest news of our sisters across the water.

There are many reasons why Newfoundland should feel a special bond with Iceland: both are small, isolated nations with a strong streak of independence which have made a living from fishing the cold North Atlantic. The differences are just as great and just as numerous, of course — Iceland has only a 2 percent unemployment rate, a stable economy, and one of the highest literacy rates in the world. By Icelanders' own boast, they have no beggars and no millionaires.

In the early seventies, the Conservatives, under Frank Moores, made a lot of noise about what they called the "Scandinavian model" of development. Politicians and civil servants were forever flitting over to Iceland and returning with glowing accounts of what was going on, though nothing ever seemed to come of it.

It was once remarked that to say something was done in Iceland was like saying that it was done in the Kingdom of Heaven — it was probably pretty good, but unlikely ever to happen here. In fact, the main difference between Heaven and Iceland was that some Newfoundland politicians had actually gone to Iceland.

While it may not be Paradise, this fascinating country of glaciers and volcanoes has been doing a lot of things right. Thanks to the work of the women's movement, peace is a major topic in political circles and Iceland's Parliament has reaffirmed a unanimous decision to keep the country nuclear-weapons free. And this in spite of a very large U.S. military presence.

The city of Reykjavik abounds with publishing houses and newspapers. A feminist publication, called the *Kvennalistinn (The Women's List)* is mailed to over half the women in the country over the age of twenty.

Two-thirds of women between the ages of 15 and 74 work outside the home, and legislation guarantees equality of the sexes on the labour market (although in spite of these progressive measures, women still hold the lowest paying jobs).

We feminists learned of Iceland and its wonders, not from politicians or civil servants, but from an article by Jan de Grass entitled "Reckoning in Reykjavik: The Icelandic Women's Movement Takes Power," published in the late and much-lamented Winnipeg feminist publication, Herizons.

What a story! Coming out of nowhere, the newly organized Women's Alliance Party first captured seats on municipal councils in two major towns in 1982, and less than a year later elected three women to the *Althing* — the Icelandic Parliament.

Iceland claims to be the world's oldest parliamentary democracy, which may help to explain why women there have been so forcefully active. It was at the beginning of thc UN Decade for Women, in 1975, that they went on strike for the first time. In the thousands they walked out of fish plants, offices and kitchens, handed their babies over to the men in their lives; held a mass outdoor rally to illustrate the importance of women's work in the economy.

Unbelievably, they pulled off the same stunt a second time, ten years later when the decade came to a close, to demonstrate that the same issues were still there to be reckoned with — equal pay, education opportunities, improved child care, and all the rest. Twenty thousand women took part.

The *Herizons* article swept us away. So we decided to invite one of the elected Women's Alliance members, Gudrun Agnarsdottir, to Newfoundland for a Women's Network dinner meeting, a day of workshops in St. John's and a trip through the Maritime Provinces to meet with other women's groups. That happened in September of 1986.

We've never been the same since.

Gudrun described for us the trepidation and lack of confidence she and the other women had felt when they first put themselves forward as candidates. She made us laugh with stories of the gaffes they made in their inexperience and inspired us with tales of how they drew strength from each other and the women around them who kept dusting them off and patching up their egos and sending them into the fray again.

And she built up *our* confidence with her accounts of how the Women's Alliance was putting new ways of handling power into practice. After the election, Gudrun said, the press simply couldn't believe when told the women had no leader of their caucus. Patiently the newsman explained to these simple-minded females that every caucus *had* to have a leader who would meet the press and speak for the party. Just as patiently, the women explained that there was no leader. Whoever was free on any given day would give the interview — and if it wasn't one of the caucus it would be another woman from the party.

Over and over, Gudrun spoke of empowering women — all women — encouraging them to find their own confidence, their own voices. Although she didn't say it in the same words, she constantly echoed Rosemary Brown's credo: "Until we've all made it none of us has made it."

She also satisfied our curiosity about a lot of other details — her name, for instance. Iceland preserves the ancient Norse system of personal names: her father's name was Agnar, so she is Agnarsdottir and her brother would be Agnarsson. By tradition, it is the father's name which is passed on, though single mothers pass their names to their children. And, by the same ancient tradition, women keep their own names when they marry.

One of Gudrun's most exciting stories was of the Women's Alliance's history-making bus tour. In a bus joyously decorated with symbols of women's lives — diapers, pots and pans, brassieres — twenty women toured Iceland's rural outports, visiting women wherever they could be found, in community centres, clubs, fish plants. It wasn't the old style campaign bus full of glad handing politicians passing out clichés; the women aboard came to hear about women's problems and needs.

In the wake of Gudrun's visit, Newfoundland women who had been inspired by the Iceland story formed an all-party-and-no-party group called the Fifty-Two Per Cent Solution, with the sole objective of working to get women into elected office.

During the winter the Fifty-Two Per Centers planned an Icelandic style bus trip across Newfoundland, and in July it travelled the island for several weeks. At one meeting, 250 women attended from small surrounding communities. (The name of one community gave a Memorial University academic one of the best titles of the year "Feminists Converge on Dildo.")

This, then is some of the background to that meeting last May and why the Fifty-Two Per Cent Solution debated running a woman against the three male candidates in St. John's East. It didn't happen, but it was a near thing, and talk of forming a women's party is still very much alive. Like our sisters in Iceland, many women here see such a move as necessary to prod the other parties to take women's involvement in politics seriously.

It's a big question, though, whether a women's party could work here. The Iceland example is inspiring, but theirs is a very different society. For a start, it's small — less than half the population of Newfoundland. (For Mainlanders, that's about the same population as London, Ontario.) Like many European countries, it has a multi-party system — six, at last count. Perhaps most significantly, it has a voting system that gives parties shares in the Parliament in proportion to their share of the popular vote. Without that, the Women's Alliance would not be in their present position.

The women's movement in Canada and Newfoundland is strong — but is it strong enough to create a women's party under the constraints of our political system? I don't know really. We've done lots of other things nobody thought we could do. Besides, maybe a full scale women's party with all the structural trappings wouldn't be necessary to get the other parties moving. Running an independent women's candidate in a by-election would be easy in most constituencies across the country — and only a little bit harder in a general election. If all three parties put up candidates who ignored women's issues — zap! There are a lot more strategies. And there'll be lots more meetings like the one last May.

The Fifty-Two Per Cent Solution had a letter from Gudrun a couple of months ago, bringing us up to date. After their spring election, the Women's Alliance found itself with six elected members who potentially held the balance of power. After some feverish negotiations with the two leading parties, though, Gudrun and her colleagues refused to be part of a coalition government because neither of the other parties would agree to the basic demand for an increase in the salaries of the lowest paid workers (mostly women) and an increase in pensions for the aged and the handicapped.

Other principles have also stayed intact. Gudrun writes, "I was standing for this election but will step down after two years, halfway through, to make room for a new woman. This we announced to the electorate before the election, so they knew what they were getting. We believe strongly in distribution of power and rotation, as you know, and it is important to live by your own rules."

The Women's Alliance has inspired women in many other

places besides Newfoundland, and they have been frantically busy responding to invitations from many countries. As Gudrun puts it, "We have sent many women spreading the gospel in the hope that a thousand blossoms will flower."

In Newfoundland, you might say she planted a blooming orchard. The question now is how we get the blossoms to bear fruit.

POSTSCRIPT

As of 1991, there are two women sitting in the House of Assembly: Lynn Verge in the opposition; the Honourable Patt Cowan, Minister for the Environment and for the Status of Women. — D.I.

Dorothy Inglis writes a weekly column, "Bread and Roses" in the St. John's Evening Telegram. She is a founding member of the St. John's Status of Women Council, a past vice-president of the National Action Committee, a co-winner of the Robertine Barry Award for journalism (1987) presented by the Canadian Research Institute for the Advancement of Women (CRIAW), recipient of the 1989 Governor-General's Persons Award, and a member of the Provincial Government of Newfoundland's Advisory Committee on the Constitution.

"NELLIE, WE'VE GOT WASHING MACHINES"

Working Out on the Family Farm

Susan Glover

JUST UP THE ROAD from where I live, at a crossroads called Clavering, is a dimly lit building which houses a used bookstore. On a recent trip there I found a first edition of *In Times Like These* by Nellie McClung, published in Toronto in 1915. In a chapter called, curiously, "As a Man Thinketh," she discusses the sorry lot of the farm woman and observes among other things, that "more than any other woman she has needed help, and less than any other woman has she got it."

She goes on to present the case for a farm woman buying a washing machine. Unlike the seeder or feed chopper, it shows no immediate financial return, but it would result in a substantial saving of womanpower. In my well-worn copy, someone (I wonder who, and when, and especially, why?) has bracketed with a pencil the paragraph which states "If men had to bear the pain and weariness of childbearing, in addition to the unending labors of housework and caring for the children, for one year, at the end of that time there would be a perfect system of cooperation and labor-saving devices in operation, for men have not the genius for martyrdom that women have; and they know the value of cooperative labor."

McClung argues for a new system of sharing the domestic work on a farm, with visions of cooperative laundries, bakeshops, dressmaking, "or perhaps even a butcher shop." This would lighten the load for farm women, resulting in happier homes, longer lives, and young people less eager to escape the drudgery. Again, the pencil has marked the lines, "The children feel an atmosphere of gloom, and naturally get away from it as soon as they can. The overworked mother cannot make the home attractive..." McClung concludes with a rather rosy picture of the superiority of country life and the people it produces, a life wanting only the lifting of the workload to make it perfect.

Well, Nellie, we've got washing machines. We've got dishwashers, vacuum cleaners and microwave ovens. We no longer make all our own butter, clothes, and bread, but somehow farm women are still working too long hours, still have almost total responsibility for all the housework and child care and are still watching their children leave for more prosperous, easier lives somewhere else.

On my desk, beside *In Times Like These*, is a paperback with a photograph on the cover of a woman wearing a hat and a flowered shirt staring into the camera from behind the wheel of a pickup. Titled *Growing Strong: Women in Agriculture*, it is a report released in November 1987 when the Canadian Advisory Council on the Status of Women belatedly addressed itself to some of these concerns. As I turn the pages, skimming through the now familiar litany of difficulties and needs, a surge of memories crowds the words from their pages.

"A large number of farm women, whether working in the fields or carrying out administrative duties, face the problem of access to child-care services." As a farmer and the mother of three small boys, I can only add a hearty amen. Whether I am working off the farm, or need to attend a meeting or appointment, child care is a constant problem. In the earlier years I used to wonder what other women did, and was astounded to discover that many women simply left their children — even babies — unattended in the house while they did the chores. There have been numerous attempts to determine the types of child care which might prove useful for rural and farm families, and several pilot projects have been conducted in our area. I remember once canvassing some women in the neighbourhood to see if there would be any interest in a local facility. One mother of four sat in her kitchen rocking her newest baby and explained to me that child care wasn't a problem for her. Now that her oldest son was able to drive the tractor, she wasn't needed in the field any more. Her oldest son was seven years old.

Another group of women in the south part of our county organized a child-care and resource centre for the area. When they approached the county federation of agriculture, not for money, but simply for a letter of support, they were turned down. Accompanying the refusal from the directors — most of whom were men and long past the child-rearing stage — were the usual grumbles that "my wife raised our kids and didn't need any day care — and did the chores besides." It would have been interesting to hear what those wives might have said.

Yet another attempt was a joint project prompted by farm safety concerns and sponsored by the Women's Institute and Concerned Farm Women. University students spent one day a week with each of five farm families for the summer. We were asssigned a terrific student and the program was very successful, but we had an unexpected and tragic reminder of the project's *raison d'être*; our student left our farm one evening for home to discover that her brother had just been killed, crushed by a tractor in a barn accident.

Further on I read, "The Farm Safety Association (Ontario) has produced a series of excellent fact sheets." I know. I keep one hanging at the side door, which describes in vivid detail, accompanied by drawings, "Caring for amputated tissue."

Despite recent federal and provincial initiatives, rural day care is still an idea whose time is yet to come for many families. I asked one of my neighbours, who has four children and has always worked part time as a nurse at the local hospital, what she did. "Oh," she replied, "I've always worked the night shift so I could be home with the kids." I didn't ask her when she slept.

Child care has become a more pressing problem for farm women in recent years as more and more of them take off-farm jobs to keep their operations going, even to put groceries on the table. A *Globe and Mail* article in July reported on the farm wife's triple workload, describing women who were taking day jobs in stores or cleaning motel rooms, coming home to the farm work, then working till midnight doing the laundry and getting lunches ready. It cited a 1985 study of Alberta farm families which found that the women worked an average of 11.8 hours per day. It also noted that experts observed that women suffer from "role over-load" from their multiple responsibilities. One farmer was quoted, "You get used to having your meals on time and having your wife truck the grain to the elevator. But now the wife comes home tired and no meal is made and the house is a mess and the kids are neglected. It's a real burden. It causes stress on the marriage." No kidding.

The low grain prices of recent years and this summer's severe drought have aggravated many of the problems for prairie families. But farm women all across North America are struggling with the same pressures. In 1983, a farm women's group in Ontario published the results of a survey of stress in farm families. The report sold over 4,000 copies, and the group received letters of support from farm women across Canada thanking them for documenting the realities of modern farm life.

"Working out" has become a buzzword for the eighties, re-ferring to exercise programs people take up to gain the physical fitness their daily jobs don't provide. On the farm, working out means taking off-farm employment, as in " Is his wife working out?" or "They keep pigs and cattle and both work out besides," to get the income farms don't provide.

Supplementing farm income with off-farm work is not new. Women went to work at jobs in town for the money to put run-ning water in the houses and new linoleum on the kitchen floors. A friend of mine, now a grandmother, runs a hairdressing shop in her farm home, and always did so, while farming and raising her five sons. She tells of putting a customer under the hairdryer, slipping into her overalls and out to the barn for a few chores, then back to the house for the comb out.

Traditionally, in our area, the men would go to the bush and cut wood all winter. That was back in the days when cows followed a more natural cycle and calved in the spring, which meant that they dried up about Christmas time and the milking hours were significantly reduced during the winter months. The off-farm work tended to be things which fit into the rhythm of farm life. The difference is now that paradoxically as the farm operations have grown larger, more complex, and demanding, at the same time the need for off-farm income often necessitates full time or year round jobs.

Another friend, who used to work at home on the farm, has had to take an off-farm job and now works in town six days a week. During last summer's heat wave she would come home at the end of the day, not to a cool drink and a lawn chair, but to wagons of hay waiting to be unloaded. When I talked to her on Labour Day, she recounted her husband's belated realization that their son was starting school the next day and would have nothing to say if asked where he'd been that summer — they hadn't had a day off.

Yet another friend, who taught school while her children were young, splurged on an in-ground swimming pool for her family."We never left the farm from 1962 to 1978," she would say, " so if we couldn't take a holiday at least we could take a swim." She and her husband lost their farm a year ago after a protracted struggle with their bank; at least she no longer feels guilty about the swimming pool.

I continue to turn the pages. "This publication is dedicated to the memory of Rosa Becker, in the hope that recognition of the work of women in agriculture will become a collective concern." After waiting in vain six years for her half of the value of the farm the Supreme Court of Canada awarded her following her separation, she finally committed suicide in 1986. The financial pressures of recent years, and the well-publicized skirmishes between farmers and bankers, have again brought home to farm women their tenuous position. The past decade has seen numerous changes to family law legislation, but farm women still find themselves in confusing or vague legal situations.

For example, many farm women have assumed that if their names appeared on the property deeds, and they worked in the farm operation with their husbands, they were legal partners, when such is not necessarily the case. At the same time, many farm women have found that even though they were not legally recognized as co-owners of the farm property, lending institutions expected them to take up their share when it came to the debts.

Frequently farm wives have found themselves in the untenable position of being asked to guarantee their husbands' farm loans with their off-farm income, knowing that to refuse would jeopardize the operations, and in all likelihood their marriages as well, but to accept meant pouring money into farm debts which would have otherwise gone to groceries, clothing, or even a non-farm investment. For women who see themselves as equal partners in the farm business, this is part of the risk. For women who have tried to separate their financial security from the farm, it is impossible.

There has been much hand wringing about the future of the family farm. Some trends appear irreversible: the ever increasing percentage of farm income earned off the farm, the growing size and capitalization of farms, the widening gap between "commercial" and "part time" farms. With every census, the number of full time farmers drops significantly, and they are becoming a minority even in the rural areas.

With this comes increased isolation, a major obstacle for women who are victims of violence. One of my neighbours works for a women's crisis centre, making its services more accessible to rural women. This has included the installation of a toll-free number, so there is no record of long distance calls, and a secret network of volunteer drivers who will bring women and children to the centre from outlying areas. Despite these efforts, the personnel at the centre continue to be frustrated in their efforts to reach farm women.

Farmers are also becoming isolated from one another. A dairy farmer who lived a few miles away was killed in a farm accident last year. The neighbours quickly assembled that evening to do his evening chores but none of them, not even the other farmers, knew how to run the milking equipment. Farmers no longer gather in bees to share each other's work and company; instead, fewer farmers with larger equipment work more land alone. Farm women now are also found driving children to town for hockey and piano lessons, taking farm- or job-related courses, or coming home from work with a video and something for the microwave. Or, more likely, all three.

As Nellie McClung pointed out, the life of farm women has its unique joys and enviable conpensations. On a perfect sunny winter morning, I can go out for a quick ski instead of plunging into commuter traffic. I don't have to spend hundreds of dollars on weathered country clothes; we have the real thing hanging at the back door. If I want organically grown food, I simply go to the freezer. I can load the children into the truck and drive into town in the middle of the morning, stopping to watch a turtle crawling into the swamp in a late spring rain. Our children early learn the harsh realities of cause and effect, the immutable laws of nature which we break at our own peril. (A lesson the rest of society is only slowly beginning to relearn.)

Of course there are lots of farm women whose lives are happy, relatively prosperous, filled with the activities of their families, farms, communities and churches. But statistics reflect the growing trends of increasing off-farm work: low incomes, poor financial returns, and rising levels of stress. Volunteer activities are strained, 4-H programs dropped for want of leaders. All of these issues — off-farm work, isolation, land use, child care and above all financial worries — are shaping the quality of life on today's farms, and it has been the farm women's groups which have taken the lead in addressing them.

The last chapter in the advisory council's book grapples with the difficulty of measuring women's contribution to Canadian agriculture. It begins, "Women's agricultural labour has long been one of the hidden costs of food production in Canada." Many farm groups, including the National Farmers' Union, have focused attention on the unpaid labour of women and children on family farms which in part enables Canadians to enjoy, with the exception of the United States, the lowest food prices in the world. This labour is being "donated" at a tremendous sacrifice, and as new farm women's groups begin to organize and finally demand changes, I truly hope that Canadian consumers and governments will listen. So, I suspect, does Nellie.

Susan Glover is a writer and editor living in Grey County, where she and her husband operate a dairy farm. She is the co-author of *To Have and To Hold: A Guide to Property and Credit Law for Farm Families* and editor of *On The Land*, a collection of essays on land use. Glover is a regular columnist with *Ontario Farmer*, and her work has appeared in numerous publications. She served as director of Concerned Farm Women for six years and is currently a member of the Ontario Farm Women's Network.

HUNGER

Maggie Helwig

CONSIDER THAT IT IS NOW NORMAL for North American women to have eating disorders. Consider that anorexia — deliberate starvation — and bulimia — self-induced vomiting — and obsessive patterns for weight-controlling exercise are now the ordinary thing for young women, and are spreading at a frightening rate to older women, to men, to ethnic groups, and social classes which were once "immune." Consider that some surveys suggest that 80 percent of the women on an average university campus have borderline-to-severe eating disorders; that it is almost impossible to get treatment unless the problem is life-threatening; that, in fact, if it is not life threatening it is not considered a problem at all. I once sat in a seminar on nutritional aspects of anorexia and ended up listening to people tell me how to keep my weight down. All this is happening in one of the richest countries in the world, a society devoted to consumption. Amazing as it may seem, we have normalized anorexia and bulimia, even turned them into an industry.

We've also trivialized them; made them into nothing more than an exaggerated conformity with basically acceptable standards of behaviour. Everyone wants to be thin and pretty, after all. Some people take it a little too far; you have to get them back on the right track, but it's all a question of knowing just how far is proper.

The consumer society has gone so far we can even buy into hunger.

But that is not what it's about. You do not stuff yourself with food and force yourself to vomit just because of fashion magazines. You do not reduce yourself to the condition of a skeleton in order to be attractive. This is not just a problem of proportion. This is the nightmare of consumerism acted out in women's bodies. This is what we are saying as we starve: it is not all right. It is not all right. It is not all right.

There have always been strange or disordered patterns of eating, associated mainly with religious extremism or psychological problems (which some, not myself, would say were the same thing). But the complex of ideas, fears, angers, and actions that make up contemporary anorexia and bulimia seems to be of fairly recent origin. Anorexia did not exist as a recognized pattern until the sixties and bulimia not until later than that — and at first they were deeply shocking. The idea that privileged young women (the first group to be affected) were voluntarily starving themselves, sometimes to death, or regularly sticking their fingers down their throats to make themselves throw up, shook the culture badly. It was a fad, in a sense, the illness of the month, but it was also a scandal and a source of something like horror.

Before this, though, before anorexia had a widely recognized name, one of the first women to succumb to it had made her own scandalous stand and left a body of writing that still has a lot to say about the real meaning of voluntary hunger.

Simone Weil was a brilliant, disturbed, wildly wrong-headed and astonishingly perceptive young French woman who died from the complications of self-starvation in America during World War II, at the age of thirty-four. She never, of course, wrote directly about her refusal to eat — typically for any anorexic, she insisted she ate perfectly adequate amounts. But throughout her philosophical and theological writing (almost all of it fragments and essays collected after her death), she examines and uses the symbolism of hunger, eating, and food.

Food occupied, in fact, a rather important and valued position in her philosophy — she once referred to food as "the irrefutable proof of the reality of the universe," and at another time said that the foods served at Easter and Christmas, the turkey and *marron glacés*, were "the true meaning of the feast"; although she could also take the more conventional puritan position that desire for food is a "base motive." She spoke often of eating God (acceptable enough in a Christian context) and of being eaten by God (considerably less so). The great tragedy of our lives, she said, is that we cannot really eat God; and also "it may be that vice, depravity and crime are almost always...attempts to eat beauty."

But it is her use of the symbolism of hunger that explains her death. "We have to go down into ourselves to the abode of the desire which is not imaginary. Hunger: we imagine kinds of food, but the hunger itself is real: we have to fasten onto the hunger."

Hunger, then, was a search for reality, for the irreducible need that lies beyond all imaginary satisfactions. Weil was deeply perturbed by the "materialism" of her culture; though she probably could not have begun to imagine the number of imaginary and illusory "satisfactions" now available. Simply, she wanted truth. She wanted to reduce herself to the point where she would *know* what needs and what foods were real and true.

Similarly, though deeply drawn to the Catholic faith, she refused to be baptized and to take Communion (to, in fact, eat God). "I cannot help wondering whether in these days when so large a porportion of humanity is sunk in materialism, God does not want there to be some men and women who have given themselves to him and to Christ and who yet remain outside the Church." For the sake of honesty, of truth, she maintained her hunger.

Weil, a mystic and a political activist simultaneously until the end of her short life — she was one of the first French intellectuals to join the Communist party and one of the first to leave, fought in the Spanish civil war and worked in auto factories — could not bear to have life be less than a total spiritual and political statement. And her statement of protest, of dissatisfaction, her statement of hunger, finally destroyed her.

The term anorexia nervosa was coined in the 19th century,

but it was not until sometime in the sixties that significant — and constantly increasing — numbers of well off young women began dying of starvation, and not until the early seventies that it became public knowledge.

It is the nature of our times that the explanations proffered were psychological and individualistic; yet, even so, it was understood as being, on some level, an act of protest. And of course symbolically, it could hardly be other — it was, simply, a hunger strike. The most common interpretation at that point was that it was a sort of adolescent rebellion against parental control, an attempt, particularly, to escape from an overcontrolling mother. It was a fairly acceptable paradigm for the period, although many mothers were justifiably disturbed; sometimes deeply and unnecessarily hurt. The theory still has some currency, and is not entirely devoid of truth.

But can it be an accident that this happened almost precisely to coincide with the growth of the consumer society, a world based on a level of material consumption that, by the end of the sixties, had become very nearly uncontrollable? Or with the strange, underground guilt which has made "conspicuous consumption" a matter of consuming vast amounts and *hiding it*, of million dollar minimalism? With the development of what is possibly the most emotionally depleted society in history, where the only "satisfactions" seem to be the imaginary ones, the material buy-offs?

To be skeletally, horribly thin makes one strong statement. It says, I am hungry. What I have been given is not sufficient, not real, not true, not acceptable. I am starving. To reject food, whether by refusing it or vomiting it back, says simply, I will not consume. I will not participate. This is not real.

Hunger is the central nightmare image of our society. Of all the icons of horror the last few generations have offered us, we have chosen, above all, pictures of hunger — the emaciated prisoners of Auschwitz and Belsen, Ethiopian children with bloated bellies and stick figure limbs. We carry in our heads these nightmares of the extreme edge of hunger.

And while we may not admit to guilt about our level of consumption in general, we admit freely to guilt about eating, easily equate food with "sin." We cannot accept hunger of our own, cannot afford to consider it.

It is, traditionally, women who carry our nightmares. It was women who became possessed by the Devil, women who suffered from "hysterical disorders," women who, in all popular culture, are the targets of the "monster." One of the roles women are cast in is that of those who act out the subconscious fears of their society. And it is women above all, in this time, who carry our hunger.

It is the starving women who embody the extremity of hunger that terrifies and fascinates us, and who insist that they are not hungry. It is the women sticking their fingers down their throats who act out the equation of food and sin, who deny hunger and yet embody endless, unfulfilled appetite. It is these women who live through every implication of our consumption and our hunger, our guilt and ambiguity, and our awful need for something real to fill us.

We have too much; it is poison.

It was first — in fact, almost exclusively — feminist writers who began to explore the symbolic language of anorexia and bulimia; Sheila MacLeod (*The Art of Starvation*), Susie Orbach (*Hunger Strike*), and others. However, as their work began to appear, a new presentation of eating disorders was entering the general consciousness, one that would no longer permit them to be understood as protest at *any* level.

For, as eating disorders became increasingly widespread, they also became increasingly trivialized, incorporated into a framework already "understood" all too well. Feminist writers had, early on, noted that anorexia had to be linked with the increasing thinness of models and other glamour icons as part of a larger cultural trend. This is true enough as a starting point, for the symbolic struggle being waged in women's bodies happens on many levels and is not limited to pathology cases. Unfortunately, this single starting point was seized on by "women's magazines" and popularizing accounts in general. Anorexia was now understandable, almost safe — really, it was just fashion gone out of control. Why, these women were *accepting* the culture, they just needed a sense of proportion. What a relief.

Now it could be condoned. Now it could, in fact, become the basis for an industry, could be incorporated neatly into consumer society. According to Jane Fonda the solution to bulimia is to remain equally unhealthily thin by buying the twenty minute workout and becoming an obsessive fitness follower (at least for those who can afford it). The diet clinic industry, the Nutrisystem package, the aerobics boom. An advertising industry that plays equally off desire and guilt, for they now reinforce each other. Thousands upon thousands of starving, tormented women, not "sick" enough to be taken seriously, not really troubled at all.

One does not reduce oneself to the condition of a skeleton in order to be fashionable. One does not binge and vomit daily as an acceptable means of weight control. One does not even approach or imagine or dream of these things if one is not in some sort of trouble. If it were as simple as fashion, surely we would not be so ashamed to speak of these things, we would not feel that either way, whether we eat or do not eat, we are doing something wrong.

I was anorexic for eight years. I nearly died. It was certainly no help to me to be told I was taking fashion too far — I knew perfectly well that had nothing to do with it. It did not help me much to be told I was trying to escape from my mother, since I lived away from home and was in only occasional contact with my family; it did not help much to be approached on an individualistic, psychological level. In fact, the first person I was able to go to for help was a charismatic Catholic, who at least understood that I was speaking in symbols of spiritual hunger.

I knew that I had something to say, that things were not all right, that I had to make that concretely, physically obvious. I did not hate or look down on my body — I spoke through it and with it.

Women are taught to take guilt, concern, problems, onto themselves personally, and especially onto their bodies. But we are trying to talk about something that is only partly personal. Until we find new ways of saying it and find the courage to talk to the world about the world, we will speak destruction to ourselves.

We must come to know what we are saying — and say it.

Maggie Helwig is a writer and political activist living in Toronto. She has published six books of poetry, most recently *Talking Prophet Blues* (Quarry Press) and *Graffiti for J.J. Harper* (Lowlife Publishing).

EXAMINING THE ELECTION ENTRAILS

Whatever Happened to the Gender Gap?

Thelma McCormack

EXAMINING THE ENTRAILS OF ELECTIONS may help settle scores for candidates who didn't make it. Losers want to know where and why and whom to blame, while winners simply want to confirm the wisdom of their strategies and their personal charisma. But in 1988 the defeated candidate was woman. Women's preferences in the most recent elections — in Canada, the U.S., Israel, and France — had little, if any, impact on the outcomes. The electoral power we thought we had in 1984; our confidence that we could control a large bloc of votes; the symbolic breakthrough achieved in the U.S. with the nomination of Geraldine Ferraro for vice-president: all have turned out to be blips on the pollster's screen in 1988.

Have the voices of women disappeared? What happened to the gender gap — the statistically visible difference between men and women on candidates and issues?

There *was* a gain in numbers. Thirty-nine women are in the House of Commons now; there were 28 in the previous session. But the disparity is still massive, and on issues that define women as electors, the results were discouraging. Free trade is one example, but an important one — in part, because so many women were unequivocally opposed to it on grounds of self-interest; in part because it became a symbol, the test of how far we had come in making the personal political. The energy that the National Action Committee and feminists like economist Marjorie Cohen put into defeating the free-trade agreement was a measure of our vision that someday the patriarchal state might wither away.

But the patriarchal state is intact, alive and well not just in Canada, Israel, France, and the U.S., but also in the minds of the pollsters. Women, an executive of Decima Research told me, are "risk aversive," by which he meant women were opposed to free trade and in favour of medicare. However, in a world where language counts for more than reality, the term risk aversive cannot be lightly dismissed as newspeak. It is, as the French feminists say, phallocentric discourse which barely conceals one of the oldest and most insidious stereotypes of women as backward, unenlightened citizens who obstruct progressive change by protecting hearth and home.

What is there about women which makes them risk aversive? And where does it start? A Freudian would say it begins in the womb and is part of female sexuality, the fear of pregnancy and death which haunts us and influences a wide range of social attitudes. Yet men, too, have their sexual anxieties; according to Freud, the fear of castration. The legacy of Freudian psychology to the understanding of politics has been the framework which compares women to men in terms applicable to men. Women are just like men only less so. And in most instances the difference reflects negatively on women.

The risk aversion thesis is a good example of male-centred thinking. It implies that there are, inevitably, political differences between men and women, but they are differences in degree, not in kind. Although the differences are anchored permanently in genital differences, they are not static. As women overcome their initial caution and follow the logic of men, the distance narrows so what started out at the beginning of an election campaign as a 30 percent difference is gradually reduced to 3 and may not even appear on election day in exit polls. It is not that men and women met their differences half way and influenced each other. It was women who closed the gap. As my Decima informant explained, there is a time lag between the final decisions of men and women: men decide earlier and women later. This might suggest that women are more thoughtful than men and don't decide impulsively or by habit. But the standard interpretation is that men, who are more in touch with the real world of the marketplace and less inhibited by the fear of change, lead and women follow. In other words, there is a pattern of women adjusting to men — never the reverse.

When politicians talk about the gender gap, they usually mean something less theoretical. They are interested in knowing the percentage variations between men and women on party preference or candidate choice. They want quick readings of the electorate as a whole and their constituents in particular as a method of planning campaign strategy and party policy. Pollsters broaden the definition of gender gap to include selected issues — taxes, defence, employment — which they and their advisors deem relevant to public opinion between elections. In addition, they are interested in rates of voter turnout: who actually votes and how. Academics, on the other hand, are more concerned with long-term ideological patterns. But they too are all looking at numbers; they all want some pay-off in the form of accurate prediction and they all assume, as Decima does, that the process which takes place over time is of women moving either in the direction of men or away from them by withdrawing altogether. And either way they all — politicians, pollsters and academics — assume that women are influenced by technology and history as designed and interpreted by men.

Women, however, define the gender gap differently. We are concerned with neither numbers nor predictions except as a useful bargaining chip with the established parties. For women, moreover, there are two gender gaps. The first concerns how much access and control we have to the political process. A distinction therefore must be made between party politics (where women 's participation is limited) and extraparliamentary political action where women have more control. It is in the latter sphere that women's political history is made. An example is the women's peace encampment at Greenham Common in England.

To the extent that women's political activity largely takes place outside of conventional political channels — by neccessity rather than choice — it is less routine, less visible and, as University of Toronto political scientist Sylvia Bashevkin has pointed out, less partisan. My own review of the academic literature suggests that women are much more problematic politically than men; it is more difficult to predict how we will vote and, since we have low expectations about what can be gained from electoral politics, it is more difficult to predict if we will vote at all. This combination of lukewarm party identification and low expectation shows up in polls prior to elections and is commonly misinterpreted as a lag. The same data can be read as alienation.

The second form of gender gap is qualitative and has to do with different cognitive processes. Men and women may arrive at the same conclusions, but we get there in different ways, through different reasoning. Although the choices presented to us are identical, we think differently about public life; our styles, reactions, and logic vary so that even if the polls show zero difference there would still be a fundamental difference shaping our political perspectives and expectations, a difference which informs and defines two separate political cultures. And within each of these political cultures are those people who for various reasons, again based on gender, are apolitical, apathetic and completely disengaged from the political system.

As you might expect, women's political culture is not a seamless web. Right wing women emphasize maternalism as the distinctive characteristic of women's approach both to private and public issues. Women, they say, extend traditional family-centred roles of caring and nurturing into public life. Feminists, on the other hand, emphasize contextual or holistic thinking based on more diverse and workplace roles. Neither, however, expects a convergence between men and women.

Why should there be, since our political socialization which

▼

starts early in childhood is different? In addition, there is biology. The range of attitudinal and behavioral differences that are a direct consequence of this fact can't be effaced by education or an androgynous pattern of socialization. And finally, as we all know, gender differences are deeply embedded in a system of structural inequality. Whichever explanation one prefers — socialization, biological determinism, or social structure — the differences are not accidental or chance variations. They are based in the reality of a gendered social system. The magnitude of difference may change but some measure of differences remains, regardless of context or historical moment.

Understandably, the women are skeptical of claims made by pollsters that the electorate is no longer stratified by gender. Nor do we accept the second half of the Decima dictum that over time women will catch up to men. As I said before, the shift that takes place during a campaign is a function of weak party identification by women and may reflect a higher level of rational thinking than the men who make quick decisions or simply go along uncritically with past habit. But the same idea that women lag behind men and are slow to arrive at a political position has been used to explain long-term trends. According to political sociologists, women are out of sync with the modern industrial world but will eventually fall into line. They must, otherwise it might be better for the polity and twentieth century democracy if women didn't vote at all. (And, indeed some political theorists have made that argument.) As women become better educated and more involved in the paid labour force, they are likely to internalize the instrumental logic of a techno-industrial system and, in due time, think like men. When that happens the gates of legislative assemblies and state bureaucracies will presumably spring open to welcome women, and the discrimination within these systems will, like the walls of Jericho, come tumbling down.

Consider, however, the reverse scenario. As more men share household tasks, child care, and other domestic activities, they might come to understand and adopt women's priorities. Elise Boulding, a peace activist and social economist, has described these priorities as "the peace-equity-conservation constellation." We could expect, then, that men will share this constellation only to a lesser degree; we could expect a lag that favours our way where we set the standard against which male deviation is measured. In the long run, they would catch up to us and the electorate would become feminized — although not necessarily feminist.

If the second picture (which, incidentally, is just as plausible as the first) seems less than convincing, it is because of the hidden factor, namely power. More women think like men than men think like women for the same reason the poor accept the values of the rich: both are dependent. Coercion and promises of reward keep us in line — a reserve army available for political consent when needed.

Feminists are ambivalent about electoral feminism. If your consciousness has been raised by street demonstrations, picketing and the rhetoric of anticolonialism, you are not inspired by all-candidates meetings or willing to put up with the stress and frustration of a candidature. You would rather criticize male-dominated party bureaucracies and a state which acts, to paraphrase Marx, as the executive committee of the male ruling class. Better a feminist *communard* than a faceless *apparatchik*.

But then there is a countervailing pull of daycare, pay equity, reproductive rights, child support enforcement, defence policies, and similar initiatives which came out of the United Nations Decade for Women. These social policies may look like tweedledee-tweedledum reforms (or worse, tokenism), but history will not forgive us if we take the high ground and ignore or sacrifice them for positions of doctrinal purity. The one talent we have acquired in our long history of patriarchial dependency is the ability to deal rationally with contradictions and to juggle both the abstract power structure and the concrete facts of daily life.

In 1988 there was another factor: a shift to the right. Religious fundamentalism, law-and-order justice, anti-unionism, cultural repression and supply side economics are some of the indicators of this neoconservative environment. It was one thing to stand on the sidelines and rail against liberalism and expose the limits of the bourgeois welfare state in the days when we had one or thought one was imminent. But the era of the welfare state is a memory, a few dollars wrung out of a budget for "safety nets." Realistically speaking, feminists are in politics today with the modest agenda of protecting what we have and preventing further erosion of the social entitlements we have gained.

But under whose auspices do we become involved? The party system itself has been responsible for and been weakened by "designer" politics; that is, by coalitions and single-issue lobbying which have diverted funds and organizational expertise. These activities, which are symptomatic of the entrenched hierarchies in the established party organizations, weaken the party system and make it a less attractive route for talented activists who want to make something happen. In addition, there is growing evidence that voters are less loyal to the parties of their parents or the parties of their youth and feel no binding commitment to the party of their choice.

Feminists have been caught in the middle. On the one hand, we distrust and are uncomfortable with the old line parties; on the other, we have invested too much in social, economic, and quality-of-life legislation to opt out altogether. Unlike Sweden, where the Social Democrats have fully incorporated the feminist agenda, Canadian women still have to negotiate with parties, and we give more than we get.

Given this situation, feminists have had to inflate a gender gap to hype it as a force to be reckoned with. This strategy was necessary to persuade parties with whom we were bargaining that the support of women was crucial to electoral victory or defeat. Women were no longer just one interest group among many; we could deliver a vote. It was only a partial truth, but what difference did it make if we could bluff our way into brokering some power? The strategy worked in the 1984 election and gave us our first (and last?) national women's debate. Nowadays, pollsters advise their clients that women's issues have peaked and that other items and other groups are more strategic to monitor. In the end women may have lost credibility with the very system we were trying to outsmart.

Until women have their own polls, gender will be either overvalued or undervalued, and women will continue to be the Other. Feminist polls, for and by women, would not be conducted for purposes of prediction but to ascertain agendas and explore the meaning of political issues that have been defined by women as salient. Feminist polling would draw on the same sampling methodology, but would be based on a concept of the gender gap which differs from that used by polling organizations, especially the commercial outfits which are more concerned with predictions than process. I suspect Decima, Environics, and other organizations would like nothing better than to have an all male electorate and a two party system — not just out of sexism or pro-Americanism but because it would improve the accuracy of their predictions, which is how their reputations and profits are made. What women want, at the very least, is a reliable picture of where we are in terms of public opinion and the changes taking place within our own frame of reference; at best, feminist polls could provide a kind of collective insight about women in Canada.

Meanwhile, the pollsters may themselves be victims of media politics. For example, in early January 1984, the *Toronto Star* carried a story on the gender gap:

> Amidst the otherwise dismal numbers in The Gallup poll released this week, federal Liberals found one bright spot. Statistical evidence of a growing "gender gap" that may loosen the Conservatives' hold on the voters.

Two weeks later *The Globe and Mail*, which had conducted its own polls, reported: "'Gender Gap' Not a Factor:"

> An analysis of party support by sex, age, income and other measures shows some interesting facts. First, party support does not vary significantly by sex — fifty per cent of women would vote

Conservative, and fifty-two per cent of men would vote Conservative.

The *Globe's* story continued by distinguishing Canada from the U.S. and Britain where it grudgingly acknowledged real gender gaps might exist:

> The so-called gender gap, which exists in the United States and Britain and reveals that women are less likely to support conservative-minded parties than men, does not exist in Canada. A further analysis shows no difference between working women and other women in party support.

Where do women stand on the political spectrum? Feminist spokespersons are usually to the left of centre, but the conventional wisdom of political science has placed women on the right. Much has been made of the British working class women who support Margaret Thatcher. True, they support her less than middle class women, but their support for her is stronger than working class men who vote Labour. Unionized women, who are mostly in white collar and service unions, however, prefer neither. In the 1987 election, they voted for the Liberal-Social Democratic Party Alliance. A new class looks for a new party.

In the French election of April 1988, there was a major difference between housewives (*femmes au foyer*) and women in the paid labour force (*femmes actives*): 43 percent of the housewives voted left, 54 percent, right; 54 percent of women in the labour force voted left, 46 percent, right. But it was men in all age groups, not women (except those over 65), who supported the ultraright wing Jean-Marie Le Pen. Le Pen's racist National Front drew its support from disaffected blue collar men. Women, then, may not follow the same trajectory based on class interests as men, and they don't support the extreme reactionary candidates no matter how "charismatic" they may be. Just as they did not support Le Pen in 1988, they did not support his reactionary predecessors of the fifties, the *Poujadistes*.

Canadian and American party politics are not conducive to the same type of extremism. We have centrist parties and pragmatic candidates who attempt to balance regional interests. But it is noteworthy that women seem to have a better sense of their economic interests than men. In the 1980 American election — Carter vs. Reagan — among the lowest income groups, 57 percent of the women voted for Carter; 57 percent of the men for Reagan. And Kathryn Kopinak, a feminist sociologist at the University of Western Ontario, has raised the question of whether the left-right division, which is based on economic justice and social policies, can adequately account for women. Other issues are more definitive.

Peace, for example. Several studies have indicated that in the U.S. the sharpest differences between men and women are over issues to do with defence policy: the kinds of actions that should be taken and the desirability of increasing military spending. Women have differed sharply from men in their opinion about American conduct vis-à-vis Communist regimes in Latin America and on the appropriate levels of nuclear freeze and military spending. On all of these subjects, women are doves. They may support the armed forces, believe women should be conscripted, and advocate women's having the same opportunities for promotion as men in the military; nevertheless, they are critical of aggressive threats toward putative enemies, nuclear build-ups and incursions into other countries.

To take another example — this time from the Middle East and the front lines, so to speak — Israeli women are more peace-oriented than their male counterparts. In a survey done last August by the Israel Institute of Applied Social Research, of those who intended to vote Likud, 67 percent of the women and only 33 percent of the men said "no" to the question: "Should the settlement of the territories continue even now?" In another question, "If the territories remain under Israeli rule what should be done to preserve the democratic character of the state?", 26 percent of the women agreed with extending civil rights to Arabs in the territories and only 18 percent of the men so agreed. Women have been active in the Peace Now movement in Israel, just as women have been prominent in peace movements around the world for several centuries.

Helen Caldicott, the distinguished peace activist, believes women are naturally pacifists; as life givers we are opposed to military actions which result in the death of others. Caldicott doesn't suggest men are by nature life takers. Diane Russell, an American sociologist who has done research on rape, does argue that men's attitudes toward war and military adventurism represent a continuation of their hostile attitudes toward women. Other feminists, however, maintain that the dovish altitudes of women can be attributed to our way of relating to others — more collectively than individually — and our notions of group rights. At home, at work, and in school we spend much more time resolving conflicts than competing for the brass ring or scoring points in some polarized debate. Arbitration, compromise, and peacekeeping come to us easily. So, although feminists are not in agreement about why women are dovish, there is a consensus that we are, and that this difference may be highly durable, semi-permanent and worldwide.

The peace issue demonstrates more clearly than anything else that there are two political cultures based on gender and that these separate but overlapping gender-based cultures are becoming global. Like our global economy we are developing a global political culture, a gendered global culture which is analogous to our national political culture. How desirable is it for us, either on the national or international level, to have two political cultures? From one point of view it is positive because it helps to validate women and legitimate our political personhood. On another, there is a large price paid for this dual system. The more pluralistic we are politically, the more we need a coherent and unifying political culture that defines us as a nation and a member of an international community. However, in order to have one authentic political culture, we would have to eliminate all forms and traces of gender inequality.

Polls don't create gender inequality, but they may reinforce it. Some critics would like to see them abolished altogether. Apart from depriving political junkies of their fix, it is not, I don't think, feasible. In a large scale popular democracy which depends on public opinion for guidance, polls provide a better, faster, and cheaper way of measuring public opinion than any other. Some regulation may be necessary. In France, for example, polls may not be published in the week prior to the election. That way, the theory goes, a bandwagon effect which reduces elections to self-fulfilling prophecy is avoided. Tighter controls are needed, too, on the methodology so that the public knows what it is getting.

Precisely because polls are critical to the political process, they should not be left to private enterprise and to men who are driven economically and psychologically to turn them into an instrument for prediction rather than understanding. The result is a distortion which turns up in their analyses of the gender gap. Pollsters are only interested in the gender gap when it is newsworthy (the media are often the clients), or they think they can weight it so as to improve the quality of advice they give their clients. Since their clients are rarely women, there is no incentive to restructure their thinking about women or their omnibus surveys.

Thus the old stereotypes in which men are the norm, the standard of political intelligence against which women are measured, persist. Women are still marginal members of the club. It comes down to this: describing women as "risk aversive" is one man's way of saying, "*L'État, c'est moi.*"

Thelma McCormack teaches Feminist Theory and Public Policy at York University where she is a professor of Sociology and Director of the Graduate Program in Women's Studies. Former

President of the Canadian Sociology and Anthropology Association, she was the first incumbent of the Nancy Rowell Jackman chair in Women's Studies at Mount Saint Vincent University. Her areas of interest are communication and cultural policy, political sociology, and medical sociology. Recent publications include *Politics and the Hidden Injuries of Gender: Feminism and the Making of the Welfare State,* (CRIAW/ICREF) and "Must We Censor Pornography? Feminist Jurispridence and Civil Liberties," in *Freedom of Expression and the Charter,* (Carswell). Some of the ideas in this article are more fully developed in the author's *Gender, the Media and the Polls* published by the Institute for Social Research, York University.

Scraping the Surface

Politics and the Pap Smear

Alison Dickie

If you're like most women, the Pap smear is an annual ritual you'd rather avoid. We try to calm ourselves as we lie uncomfortably on our backs with our legs apart and our feet in steel stirrups, breathing evenly while medical instruments held by gloved hands (usually male) go in and a scraping of our cervical tissue comes out. It's not just the discomfort which makes women dislike this test. In fact, because of the way medicine treats the disease the Pap smear detects, the test is in many ways a paradigm for the way male-centred medicine views female sexuality.

The Pap smear measures the degree of "dysplasia," or precancerous cell changes on the cervix. Women with moderate to severe dysplasia will undergo one of three types of surgery, depending on the degree of infection: cryotherapy (freezing), laser surgery, or knife-directed surgery. Women are usually told this surgery is preventive, removing infected tissue which might otherwise lead to invasive cancer. What we usually aren't told is that both dysplasia and cervical cancer are caused by a virus transmitted sexually by men.

For at least ten years the human papilloma virus (HPV) has been targeted as the cause of dysplasia and, ultimately, cervical cancer. This virus is transmitted during heterosexual intercourse. A man may harbour the virus on or in his penis without fear of anything worse than the almost microscopic warts or lesions which are often an effect of the virus in women as well. (While the warts themselves are benign, their presence often signals the presence of a more virulent strain of the virus.). HPV can lead to cancers of the penis and anus in men, but both are extremely rare. That men have little to fear from the virus may partially explain the lax attitude doctors have about telling women about the connection. The burden of treatment and prevention falls to women, just like the prevention of pregnancy. The same reasoning applies: women are the ones who get pregnant, so let them eat birth control pills. Women are the ones who get cervical cancer, so let them have annual Pap tests.

When Jessica, a teacher, went to a gynaecologist to have an abnormal Pap smear investigated, she was already afraid she had cancer. She arrived at the gynaecologist's waiting room just before nine o'clock to discover she was just one of the 20 patients he booked every hour for treatment on a "first come, first served" basis. When Jessica finally made it into one of the examining rooms, the nurse told her to drop her clothes on the floor and didn't even give her the customary sheet to wrap around herself. Jessica lay on the examining table, naked from the waist down, waiting for the doctor to come in. He finally arrived and, without looking at her, said: "So you're 32. When are you going to get married and have babies?"

During the exam, he refused to answer any of her questions. One part of the procedure involved a vinegar rinse of Jessica's cervix, and during this the doctor offered the instrument he was using to the nurse, with the words, "You should have one of these at home. That way, every time you ate chips you'd think of this." The nurse looked away, as she did when Jessica tried to catch her eye when the examination sent jabbing pains all the way to her throat. When the doctor finished, he pushed a tampon into her vagina and said: "No sex for you tonight. In fact, let's make that the whole weekend, and let you really suffer." When the nurse left he came around by her head and looked at her for the first time. "Sexual revolution — what are they talking about? It used to be when you slept with the wrong guy they pumped you full of penicillin — now they take you to the morgue." Mumbling something about AIDS, he left the room. Terrified by what he'd just said, Jessica dressed and followed him out to the reception area, where she tried again to ask him what was wrong. He ignored her.

One miserable week later, Jessica was told she had genital warts. The same doctor treated her with cryotherapy and said there was an 85 percent chance she'd have no recurrence. Although she felt battered by this experience, she got up the courage to see another gynaecologist.

This new specialist and his nurse acted like they didn't believe the brutal handling she'd received from a colleague, but they did acknowledge that his treatment had been wrong. It had done nothing about the real problem — carcinoma in situ, "cancer in place," the most severe form of dysplasia and the immediate precursor of invasive cancer. In fact, his treatment could have cost Jessica her life, because the cryotherapy cleared off the surface of the cervix so that future Pap smears would have looked normal, while the underlying cancer process proceeded undetected. Jessica underwent a cone biopsy and a D & C, the most severe form of surgery short of a hysterectomy.

It's difficult to know where to begin to analyze the first doctor's behaviour: the assembly line practice, the casual humiliation, the intentional pain inflicted, the brutality of the verbal assaults, the serious misdiagnosis. He clearly held Jessica responsible for her illness — making it clear that her non-married and therefore illicit sexual activity was to blame. Although he didn't say the warts were sexually transmitted, he left her with the overwhelming feeling that sex, or too much of it, was somehow the cause. Having proved her guilt to his own satisfaction, he treated her as if she were an object of disgust. At the root of his behaviour is the classic patriarchal fear that unless it is tamed by childbearing, a woman's sexuality will express itself in unbridled lust.

Jessica's case isn't unique. I spoke to numerous other women who reported similar if less extreme versions of this story from routine Pap tests. One woman said a doctor expressed surprise she didn't "come" during the preliminary breast examination, and then taunted her with sexual innuendo during the internal examination.

Even within the medical establishment it is acknowledged doctor's irrational attitudes towards sex interfere with their work. Dr Barbara Romanowski, director of a sexually transmitted disease (STD) unit in Edmonton, said recently that doctors find it difficult to treat such diseases because they believe only the poor or the promiscuous get them. Given the standard for promiscuity is different for women than for men, a woman who's labelled that way is likely to be badly treated by a male doctor.

Perhaps that's why the prevention of cervical cancer in women has never been a medical priority. The underlying attitude on the part of doctors has been that women who get cervical cancer deserve it. If medical science had been serious about preventing this disease, Pap smears for men or the equivalent would long have been routine.

When George Papanicolaou, a Greek cytologist, developed the test in 1929, cervical cancer was the leading cause of cancer death in women. The facts of the disease were clear: celibate women didn't get cervical cancer; it was uncommon among women whose husbands were not promiscuous; there was a very low instance of the disease among lesbians. Since the common factor clearly had to do with heterosexual intercourse, doctors should have gone looking for evidence of a sexually transmitted disease. It would have been reasonable to examine penises — or at least those attached to men whose wives were dying from this disease. Had penises and scrotums undergone the same scrutiny cervixes and vaginas have had ever since, then HPV might not be epidemic today. Given that the cervix of every sexually active woman in the country is examined annually, while the penises of men are examined only in the case of visible disease, the notion that women are the gate keepers of sexuality and are solely responsible for diseases they thereby contract is still reinforced.

All the pamphlets and hospital handouts on dysplasia focus

strictly on women. In a Toronto hospital handout called "Information About the Pap Test," the list of factors under the heading "Why Did I Get Dysplasia?" (notice it doesn't say how) includes: "infection with viruses such as herpes and the human papilloma virus, smoking, age at first intercourse, number of sexual partners, intrauterine exposure to DES, use of drugs which suppress the immune system, and family history of dysplasia." Nowhere does it say "the number of sexual partners your partner or spouse has had," or suggest that intercourse with a man who had venereal warts or lesions might be enough to cause dysplasia and even cancer. The only reference to the male role is with information that the HPV can also cause warts to appear on the male partner, without any hint they may well have come from him in the first place.

Dr Wendy Wolfman, an obstetrician/gynaecologist at Toronto Western Hospital, describes the incidence of HPV as epidemic. Of the 25 to 30 patients she sees daily, three or four will have abnormal Pap smears. Although Wolfman does ask that the male partners of her patients be checked for evidence of the virus, she is aware many doctors don't do this. Even at clinics specializing in the treatment of gynaecological cancer, a suggestion to test the male partner is usually made only when a woman has had repeated surgery without effecting a cure. This seems odd, since all studies done on the subject show cancers in the female reproductive canal are prevalent in women whose partners carry HPV-caused warts.

Some doctors think up to 25 percent of all women between the ages of 17 and 45 carry the virus, so it's likely an equal or higher number of men also carry it. Currently, it is the most common sexually transmitted virus, according to Dr Joseph Portnoy, a Montreal specialist in infectious diseases. It's not known how long HPV can lie dormant, but it is known some strains are more virulent than others. One family doctor I know told me he had a male patient who'd had two young wives die of cervical cancer. His third wife was being treated for it. The doctor described the man as a "stud" with "big balls." As far as I know, he didn't ask him to be tested, or even suggest he use condoms to prevent reinfecting his third wife. Portnoy says, unequivocally, such men are carrying a cancer-producing virus. In the trade they're known as "Cancer Charlies." In his own practice as director of the sexually transmitted disease clinic at the Montreal Jewish General Hospital, Portnoy insists all women infected with HPV should have their partners tested. He says it's stupid not to.

Yet of the dozen or so women I talked to who'd had surgery to remove precancerous tissue, not one had a doctor suggest their partner be examined. This applies to my own case too, although a nurse did tell me to examine my partner's penis for warts under a magnifying glass after dipping it in vinegar. If the situations were reversed, and men were developing cancer of the urethra because of a disease transmitted sexually by women, no one needs to wonder how fast checkups for women would become routine and how soon techniques for detection of the virus in women would be developed. Just imagine the literature which would have sprung up around any woman in history who'd had two husbands die of penis cancer.

As it stands now, three or four women per hundred will undergo specialized testing and surgery for this disease. What doctors rarely make clear to women is that not all forms of dysplasia will lead to cancer. It wasn't until after my surgery for severe dysplasia that I found out from my doctor that the condition I had wouldn't necessarily evolve into invasive cancer. This would have saved me considerable anguish had I known weeks before. What's especially galling for women is that the spectre of hysterectomy hangs over the treatment for dysplasia. Hospital handouts list it as having the lowest rate of recurrence of any surgical procedure used to treat the disease and, given the terror the word cancer evokes, it is not difficult to imagine circumstances where women are convinced to undergo unnecessary hysterectomies.

In an article on physician fraud, the *Canadian Journal of Criminology* lists hysterectomies at the top of the list of "overserviced" (read, unnecessary) surgeries, along with mastectomies and tonsillectomies.

Recent surveys of Toronto doctors by medical journals have concluded that more effort goes into solving male diseases than female ones and that the research itself is sex-biased. So it's not surprising an illness affecting only women hasn't seen more progressive testing and treatment. If men underwent such widespread preventive surgery for cancer of the penis, research would have blossomed long before now.

Consider Jessica's case again: she is reduced by the doctor to being nothing else but her sexual nature. The doctor prods and hurts this sexual nature, because he thinks it is disgusting, an attitude that in her vulnerability Jessica may well accept. The doctor's moral disgust at what he thinks is a "bad" woman causes him to completely miss what the barest professional competence would have made him see. And, at a deeper level, Jessica is left feeling that, really, it's all her fault: as she said to me during the interview, she wouldn't have believed her own story if her sister hadn't been there at the time and insisted she write it all down. This sense of it being the victim's fault parallels the experience of rape and incest survivors. (And given that some 20 percent of Canadian women avoid routine Pap tests, one can't help but wonder how many do so because of bad experiences with doctors. Almost 400 Canadian women still die each year from cervical cancer. And the number of cases of this disease has risen from 10 to 25 percent in women under 35.)

The Pap smear has meant women need not suffer the dreadful death of cervical cancer. But the prevention of HPV is the responsibility of both sexes. The way the Pap smear is currently administered makes it the responsibility of women and their doctors. Given the kind of intimacy a woman allows a doctor in the Pap smear, there could be no clearer place for male misogyny to show itself. It's not surprising many male doctors manifest the same attitudes inside their examining rooms which they share with men outside those examining rooms.

This misogyny easily displaces the facts of any disease, and not just HPV. More than a year ago, *Toronto Life* ran a feature story on AIDS. It began with what the writer described as an "apocryphal tale circulating in Toronto and the rest of the world," which was printed, for greater effect, on the front cover: a "great-looking woman...*really* comes on" to a man and they spend a *"really* wild night" in a hotel room. Next morning he wakes to find the woman gone and a message scrawled (predictably) in lipstick, on the mirror: "Welcome to the real world of AIDS." Of course the man discovers he has the AIDS virus.

If there's anything real about this tale it is the fear and earnestness of the telling. Apart from the lipstick, this woman resembles nothing so much as one of the beckoning figures who stalk the male literary landscape — sirens, lamias, Circe, "La Belle Dame Sans Merci" — promising sex, leaving death. Certainly no flesh and blood woman from this century or, for that matter, any other. No joke the tale is apocryphal — it adroitly captures the terror of female sexuality men have had for at least two millennia. The emergence of the AIDS virus is simply another conduit for that same terror. It's ironic that women, while actually more vulnerable to AIDS than men, are already being portrayed as its malicious transmitters — a tendency I expect we'll see more of.

For starters, AIDS began in North America as a disease among men, and at the time of writing it's still spread mostly by men. It's more difficult for a woman to pass the virus sexually to a man than the other way round: the virus is more concentrated in semen than it is in vaginal secretions, and men leave a lot more of themselves behind in a woman's vagina than what they take away on their penises. Of course it's men who routinely commit acts of violence around sex. And, while AIDS has become the number one killer of women in their twenties in New York City (Canadian statistics tend to follow suit), most of these women are poor and, not coincidentally, needle-users. It just isn't credible to portray an upscale male reader of *Toronto Life* as the innocent victim of AIDS inflicted at the hands of an equally upscale, if largely mythical, female in a context which neglects to convey how she got the virus in the first place. The omission leaves the impression the origin of the disease is the woman herself — a myth which underlies the politics of the Pap smear and ultimately inhibits a rational and humane approach to all sexually transmitted diseases — at great cost to us all.

POSTSCRIPT

Since this article was first published a Texas study has conclusively shown that this virus is the cause of cervical cancer in women. The study showed that this virus was present in over 95 percent of all cancerous cells. To date no comprehensive Canadian study into the modes of transmission of this virus has ever been conducted. — A.D.

Alison Dickie is a Toronto freelance writer. She was born in Scotland, and her family immigrated to Canada when she was one year old. She grew up in Hamilton, Ontario and studied literature and philosophy at Queen's University and the University of Toronto. She has travelled widely in Canada, living and working in Alberta and the Northwest Territories.

She is co-author of a collection of myths called *Mystic Voices*. She lives in Toronto with her partner Sean Armstrong, their teenage nephew and two young daughters. She is co-founder of the small educational publishing company Northern Nebula Productions.

ABORTION JUSTICE AND THE RISE OF THE RIGHT

Dionne Brand

FURY IS PROBABLY THE MOST FITTING WORD to describe my feelings about what has happened over the last several months in Canada and the United States around abortion and the right of women to reproductive choice. Any rights which women may have thought they enjoyed are threatened by teeter-tottering court actions and political machinations on the part of legislators both in Canada and in the U.S. Certainly over the last several years, we have seen the erosion of women's rights as a key feature of the rise and entrenchment of the right through the Mulroney and Reagan/ Bush years.

When the Daigle and Dodd cases emerged it became apparent that women's rights in this country are extremely fragile and that our reproductive freedom, the most important underpinning of those rights, was and still is in serious jeopardy. Despite the Supreme Court decision in Daigle's case, it is still hair raising to think that the ground can be cut out from under us on a boyfriend's wicked whimsy, or a judge's Christian fundamentalism, or a parliament's gratuitous shilly-shallying.

What also accounts for my fury is that I should have seen this coming. We have a tendency on the left and in the progressive movements to never quite believe the right is serious. We think they couldn't be that crazy or they're not strong enough to roll back those hard-won social principles. But of course they are that crazy and they are that strong and they are dead serious. Note well any number of their gambits — their rip-off of native rights and their successful free-trade deal, to name just two. Our miscalculations are a feature of living in a liberal democratic society inured to ideological traps about justice and equality, human rights, etc., etc. Even though we belong to groups (women, blacks, workers) which have, in fact, historically and consistently borne the injustices concomitant with liberal democracy such as racism, sexism and class oppression, we are nonetheless steeped in stuff and nonsense about justice.

This is not to underestimate the power of the system to drag us into its thrall through benign or brutal means. So, caught in the hoax of an egalitarian and just society, our illusions mediate our view of what is called the justice system — the mechanism to which we bring our claims of rights. The very justice system to which we bring these claims and that purports to dish out those rights equally is created by the class that controls the state and whose interest it is to protect private and corporate property. So you ask yourself: is the same justice system that let the killers of a native woman in The Pas go unpunished going to decide what will happen to my woman's body? Is the same justice system that put a bullet in the back of a seventeen year old black youth's head going to give me my rights? When the examples are not so brutal we ease up on the criticism; apply to the benign face of the law, spend years in court challenges, months lobbying politicians, centuries waiting for justice.

Liberals will say I'm being cynical. Too pessimistic. After all, didn't good win out in the end? But my history tells me that the oppressed always have to "watch their backs" as long as the machinery of oppression exists. The current socio-political climate remains one in which the right is expanding in influence and power.

The rise of the right has not been merely an ideological one, but an economic one marked by union busting, privatization, layoffs, falling real wages, de-regulation, so-called "retrenchment" of the work force — increase in part-time work and the "new division of international labour" — the changing of the North American economy from manufacturing to services and the creation of free-trade zones or *maquiladoras* in the Third World. Naturally this has meant the repositioning of women within the economy and a repositioning of the ideological terms under which we live. First the economic terms.

No fewer than eight labour actions and strikes by women have taken place in Toronto alone over the last five years. They include the bank workers, Eaton's workers, hotel workers, cleaners, garment workers and women in manufacturing. Anyone familiar with those battles realizes women have been fighting a rear guard action against attempts to lower the ratio of female to male dollars even further, never mind the effort to gain wage parity with men and equal opportunity to jobs. So in economic terms we are under attack.

In ideological terms, we see a resurgence of what is called family values: conservatism, selfishness, and bigotry. We see the flowering of groups such as REAL Women, Operation Rescue, Pro-life and other fundamentalist factions whose *raison d'être* is to herd women *en masse* back into the home, barefoot, pregnant, and silent. They are the ideological shock troops of the economic squeeze; the "scabs" in the workplace of progressive humanity.

Their significance for the current state of affairs in reproductive rights and freedoms is that women's reproductive capabilities have historically been controlled by the state in this "free market" system. As the free market developed, women were allowed somewhat more autonomy over their reproductive capacity because their labour, which is cheaper than men's, became more and more necessary to propel that system. Not accidentally, contraceptive techniques advanced as the free market economy developed. This development afforded women certain "privileges," like having more to do with the decision of whether to bear children. In reality, women have never had that freedom. No, I am not discounting the power of the ongoing and catalytic women's movement which most certainly sparked, agitated, and created the gains of women over the last century. Nor am I suggesting an overdetermining state apparatus which has total control, foresight, and power. What I am pointing to is the parasitic nature of capitalism; its ability to change and adjust itself, to go along for the ride, absorbing our claims and giving them back to us in a manner more palatable to the free market economy. The shock troops come out when that economy feels the need to cut back. Women must therefore be halted in their tracks and reminded of their tenuous position vis-à-vis men in society. This year, the funding to women's groups and services by the Secretary of State women's program was cut by 15 percent. It is also germane that a condition of funding from this arm of the state bureaucracy has been that groups funded by the women's program do nothing to "promote" abortion or lesbianism.

The Daigle and Dodd cases signal the new-yet-old confluence of the economic, ideological, and legal terms under which women in Canada and the U.S. are made to live. These recent court cases against women seeking an abortion in Manitoba, Québec and Ontario and the decision in Québec that would have forced Chantal Daigle to bear a child against her will, despite her constitutional right to choose abortion, indicate the repositioning of the legal terms of our existence. Always mindful of suggesting a conspiracy (as damning as the evidence is) between the men in the boardrooms, the men in the government, and the men in the courts, it is important to recognize that the judges making these decisions are not merely executing their personal agendas against women, but are actually carrying out the mandate (however ambiguous at times) of the power elite.

Even though the Supreme Court of Canada decided in Daigle's favour, it should not mislead the women's movement into thinking such a victory is permanent or irreversible. The weakening of the *Roe v. Wade* decision in the United States forewarns us of this fallacy. (Last summer, the U.S. Supreme Court watered down the constitutional right of American women to abortion by saying that states could decide individually whether state funds could be used for abortion.) Having one or two sympathetic judges who may wish to guarantee women's rights does not guarantee advancement for all women. Indeed, in Daigle's case, this reality was quite stark and resulted in what became a tortuous delay for Chantal Daigle. We must remember that last year we were fighting for the right to have abortions in free-standing clinics. This was with the assumption — and the law confirmed it — that we had a right to abortion. It was simply a question of access. This year we have been dragged into a struggle for the right to have an abortion at all.

The step-by-step erosion of rights we thought were fundamental is a feature of our lack of freedoms in general. The demonstration of acute hostility toward women by the state is, in fact, a reflection of that larger socio-political problem I have just described.

What has to be important in all this, therefore, is the role that the women's movement sees for itself. Under siege on all fronts — economic, ideological, and legal — we have to get back to a movement which understands the current alignment is hostile, even an anathema, to our aspirations. We cannot afford to assume that the government and judicial systems will necessarily work in our best interests as women; we must be cautious of "gains" made only when the interests of those in power are served or will not be unduly threatened. This means that, as compelled as we are to fight within the system, the courts and the legal system cannot be our weapon, since we have no control of these mechanisms and their outcomes.

It was sobering to hear a "campaign life" spokesperson say to a television reporter, "We don't have to mobilize anything." Maybe it was bravado, but it was telling in a way which might not have been intended. The right has lined up its economic, ideological, and legal forces, and so we must line up our resistance. It means regrouping and re-energizing the radical women's movement, agitating again in the most fundamental ways among women.

Daigle's actions are instructive. Though the Supreme Court struck down the injunction against her, making it impossible for men to stop women from getting abortions, Chantal Daigle did not wait for its decision. She exercised her reproductive choice against the will of the Québec court and the man who held her body hostage, telling all in no uncertain terms that it is a women's right to choose. Daigle is not a political activist, but simply a woman who was forced to fight for her life. In defying the injunction against her, however, she has shown us that women's rights are not given, but taken and at high cost. We in the women's movement owe Daigle a debt for this lesson.

POSTSCRIPT

Barbara Dodd and Chantal Daigle were both taken to court by ex-boyfriends seeking to prevent them from having an abortion in the summer of 1989. Very shortly after initiating a fight against the injunction, Dodd gave way to her boyfriend's wishes and the case was dropped. Daigle took hers to the Supreme Court. — ed.

Dionne Brand is a Black poet and writer living in Toronto. She has published six books of poetry. Her latest, *No Language is Neutral*, was nominated for a Governor-General's award in 1990.

She has also published a book of short stories, *Sans Souci and Other Stories*, and co-authored a work of nonfiction, *Rivers Have Sources Trees Have Roots — Speaking of Racism*.

Brand also works in documentary film. She was the associate director and writer of *Older, Stronger, Wiser*, a portrait film about older Black women in Canada, and she was co-director of *Sisters in the Struggle*, a documentary about contemporary Black woman activists in Canada. She is currently working on a third film, *Batari Wimmin's Blues*.

Brand was Writer-in-residence at the University of Toronto in 1990-91 and is now an assistant professor in the English department at University of Guelph.

OF MICE AND BATMEN

(or Woman as Wimp)

Judy MacDonald

I'M GENERALLY NOT AN ANGRY YOUNG WOMAN, or so it seems to me. And I'm no bra burner, hell, I've none to toss on that tired old flame. So what you have here are the musings of a post baby boomer. Born in the sixties but not of them. Musically weaned from early teens on Donna Summer and the Dead Kennedys. Woodstock known as a bird in the Saturday paper cartoons. You get the idea.

Popular thought has it that, in the West at least, we're an apolitical lot; ambivalent souls with no stronger conviction than what's found in the creed To Further One's Own Cause. In this postfeminist, postmodern and almost postmortem age of indulgence, me and my kind are seen as not interested in any possible message to be found in a medium. As long as the presentation is slick and glossy and rubs off a little so we feel slick and glossy for a while, we're sated. We even buy all sorts of mementos of the glitter: albums, T-shirts, buttons, posters, and now videos. They keep us entertained.

So, in examining a specific subspecies of the media — the action flick — you'll find this is where we look for *physical* movement, you know? Nothing of the social kind. (That notion brings with it connotalions of any number of nasty diseases we learned about from puberty on.) Besides, significance isn't necessary when all that's desired is the assurance a good safe time is being had by all.

Before going any further, it should be clarified I do get enjoyment from the finer things in life. This said, you'll find no apologies for romping escapism, which has always held a place dear to my heart. It's so dependable for a quick getaway from the day-to-day drudgery when finances limit the trip.

Or so it once seemed.

Then came *Batman*, the movie. More precisely, then came Vickie, the hero's foil. After watching her, I find myself at some remove from the hype surrounding the film (infecting young and old). In my case, a good time was not had; only a feeling that I was.

It was a shock to me, as it could have been to anyone, that this go-around I found myself offended by the usual vapid cliché character — here, Vickie — women are pressed in to playing in pop culture. My reaction begs the question: why this film and not innumerable others which have more flagrant and embarrassing examples of woman as wimp? Although they were vaguely annoying, other films didn't get under my skin the way this one did. The reason, perhaps, lies in the contrast between characters supporting the eighties superhero and those in the "Batman" TV series. The show was another sixties creation, one I fondly remember growing up with. One that left the impression on my 6-year-old self that women can be heroic, too.

While much from that decade is sniggered at by those just now come of age, the "Batman" series holds a kind of resonance. A few years ago it was reaired in the city where I went to postsecondary school. I am not elitist enough to think I was only one of a few kitsch connoisseurs rushing home to see it. No. In fact the TV series is known to many as a cultural classic to be celebrated. Unlike, say, Crosby, Stills, Nash, and Young ruminating on what it means to get a hair cut.

I was warned that the newest version of the caped crusader was not to be confused with the amiable klutz of the small screen. Supposedly, he is now more authentic to the original comic book character (though this is debatable). That is, Batman is tough. The "Pows" and "Whammos" flashing over fight scenes twenty years ago have been replaced with bodies dropping. Michael Keaton digs his fangs into the role; he's pumped it up and given it some balls. The more the merrier, said I. No harm in a little machismo here and there. Especially there, where it's not real and is certainly not to be taken seriously.

No one thought, however, to put out an alert on Vickie. Likely, no one thought of Vickie at all. What's there to think about? Vickie Vale, for those who've managed to miss this blockbuster so far, is the leading man's love interest. She arrives fresh from a job photographing war, hoping to capture Gotham City's rumoured bat creature on film.

Yet, as someone willing to go anywhere for a story, she seems to have great difficulty dealing with the situation at hand. Vickie is stupefied. Vickie is overwhelmed. Vickie stands helpless, knuckle-to-teeth like, full lips trembling, eyes wide.

Now, physically Kim Bassinger, who plays the lady, is no shrieking violet. This is a woman who liked a Texas town enough to buy it. She has a strong jaw, powerful walk, is tall, and has a determined voice. She is also, not-so-accidentally in the celluloid circus, blonde, beautiful, and buxom. Thus blessed, she is destined to play the bimbo.

What's new, you may ask. Save up the estrogen to get excited about a situation which has some hope of changing. We know Hollywoods North and South will always bring out a tape measure when deciding who should play the girly role. And proceed to poke and prod in appropriate places to see if a candidate emits the right kind of squeal, sigh, and scream.

But in this case, there *is* something new, an alternate view, which is found in the old. Bassinger's hollow example of the feminine is made more extreme because it contrasts badly with women in the TV series. True fans of Batman may pooh-pooh the oafish cartoon quality of both man and boy wonder on television. But there is one thing which cannot be denied: women could hold their own back then. Two examples to prove my point spring to mind.

While the villainous Catwoman was kept from succeeding in her criminal activities, there was little question who would win in hand-to-hand combat, good guy against bad. It was easy to see Batman and his unshakeable belief in the sanctity of the status quo kept her amused. Admittedly, she used traditional tricks of the sex kitten, but she pushed them to a point where the purr had too much of an edge, the curled lip went beyond coy, and the cocked head belied such pranks, exposing a real strength beneath them.

As for Batgirl, she was more efficient than Vickie could dream of being. When duty pressed, this heroine-cum-librarian finished filing, got on her motorbike and — quietly — cleaned up the trouble. Then she went back to work, no one the wiser. Unlike her male counterpart, she wouldn't launch into a self-aggrandizing pontification about what she did. She just did it.

Sure, she and Catwoman sported skintight get-ups, but for such active types they seem, in retrospect, to have simply been ahead of their time. They would hardly be noticed going by on bicycles or speed skates today. And don't forget, Batman and Robin were racing around in tights, too. Fair's fair.

I should mention the show also had coteries of pretty girls hanging around bad influences like the Joker, Penguin, and Riddler. This was in keeping with a spoof making light of the traditional good guy/bad guy entertainment genre. To be truly irreverent, "Batman" had to resemble the style to start with. The molls just had to be there.

Like everything, "Batman" on TV was a product of its time. The campy heroics were meant to amuse youth in an age which was anti-authoritarian; when a hero like Batman was the ultimate square, an upper class nerd out of his element and not quite sure what to make of the strangeness around him. For that matter, this description also applies to the 1989 version — of the hero; the audience is another matter.

Keaton's character is emotionally inarticulate, isolated and dependent on his butler (who is happy, thank you very much, with his position) for anything like camaraderie. But times have been a-changin' and, as Huey Lewis and the News announced some years ago in their upbeat song, it's now hip to be square. That's the eighties.

This film represents a decade which has seen a harking back to what was before all that liberal thinking addled us. Batman is again an exemplary millionaire who needs the support of a good woman; something he missed during the age of Aquarius.

Related to this retrogression, it's been a period when, more often than not, women's efforts to gain parity have been discreetly overlooked. Discreetly, that is, if only the more vocal gals would shut up about their rights and start to act like ladies.

Armed with examples like Vickie for the kids to look at and admire, however, society can almost rest assured the influence of these shrill activists will be minor among the upcoming crop of citizens. While living in a time when surface is everything, who wants to risk popularity by becoming what is perceived by peers as a frumpy women's libber protesting against sexual stereotypes which *look* perfectly fine? Stereotypes that look the way you want to. The way others want you to. (Youth has always wanted to be desirable among its own.)

While not pretending to have conducted a poll on the subject, it's nonetheless remarkable I can't think of many women my age and younger who wouldn't come out with, "I'm no feminist, but..." when discussing inequities they've come up against. If they discuss such things at all. It might seem too strident to notice any possible injustices against their sex. Glossing over disparities we operate under is another part of the hear-no-evil, see-no-evil, speak-no-evil school of social awareness doggedly studied these days.

Such an education makes social feminism appear overwhelmingly divisive with its us-them mentality and, truth be known, it strikes us as ultimately antifemale. In this new age, young adults assume feminism is geared to plow through differences they don't mind seeing between the sexes. Feminism is thought to reject the feminine as weak and undesirable, pushing women into taking on the trappings of men. Feminism is thus rendered into an ugly sister. It's undesirable.

But the women's movement didn't create sexual stereotypes, of course. If tomorrow protesters dropped their placards and NAC disbanded, joining the leagues of those who know their place, female characters wouldn't suddenly become something approaching human.

Vickie and her associates in the world of entertainment are too important to be given up so easily. Believing they could has to be as naive as believing communism smoothly leads to a stateless society free of bureaucracy. As with any kind of form we're handed to complete, she might be dull and seem to serve no purpose, but she does do a good job keeping us preoccupied, allowing those in charge to go about their business unmolested.

The attraction of her formula isn't lost on the creative people who have the burden of our culture to think about, either. It can be argued that, under such pressure, it's a good idea to plug at least one bimbette in for convenience's sake alone. Who knows, when the story line is lagging, she might just come in handy to liven things up with a smile. Such effortlessness! Such ease! It's disposable!

But those who use this device can't be thinking of any women they know. And it's too much to suggest they're all plotting to keep women down. They're just doing what comes automatically. It's sheer laziness.

What's missing from their picture-perfect logic is that half the audience has been ignored. Unlike the hero men are given to bolster the romance of what it is to be a man (upholding the good, saving the vulnerable), women are stuck with a heroine who presents yet another image they fall short of (impossible hair, gravity-defying figure). She doesn't do anything exceptional, she only looks that way. Vickie is no symbol of the feminine for women to embrace: instead, she comes across as competition — an ideal they're expected to aim for in themselves but can never hope to attain. She's a rival, pulled out any time someone wants to remind a woman she doesn't make the mark.

Men, on the other hand, don't have to deal with such physical inadequacies when they project themselves into the hero's place. Their heroes are meant only to allow for fantasy, to let them pretend they are the leading man and can do what he does. In other words, they won't be thought any less of if they demur at the chance to wear cape and mask. Or decline a solo mission to another land to kill a lot of foreigners for the sake of Truth. Heroes aren't there to remind them of what they aren't; instead, they allow for a momentary escape from what they are.

There have been films that allow for a strong female lead; but these are too infrequent. With the bias that women are around to create crises, distract heroes, and generally be great looking nuisances, the female audience is not getting what it paid for. The denial of women as active participants in the movie *Batman* and its ilk is a far cry from my Catwoman and Batgirl. And to me it is in no way a form of escapism. It's a form of oppression.

Damn, I'm sounding like some rabid feminist here, seeing significance where fun is meant to be. What would my peers say? It's just so…sixties, this talk about the oppressed. Not something we posties like to think about. But then it's hard to deny that not much has changed in real terms since women first started complaining. That was even *before* the Temptations, right?

Women's demands about pay equity, daycare, child support, abortion rights, sexual harassment, and the like are still being called into question. Nightly news still debates their validity during the blue moon when women's concerns are thought to be noteworthy enough to air. The issues have entered a twilight zone where time and circumstance do not change. And many seem not to be watching, anyway.

It's understandable these issues are met with a passive indifference. Not just by my generation — we must have started from somewhere — but by society at large. By the middle road; the safe route of thoughtlessness. Because ignoring them hasn't met with any strong reprisals yet, it's easier just to go on ignoring them than to change oneself, to analyze the situation and do something about it. Apathy is much more fun.

We go to a movie, my friend and I. It's *Batman*, and we're both looking forward to nothing more or less than great effects and some entertaining moments. He gets what we came for. I get angry. No humour, no irreverence, no *life*. Just the same tired stuff, making me feel ancient and used.

I mention misogyny. He doesn't understand. He finally admits he isn't familiar with the term I've used, this word misogyny. My reaction is not the intellectual response to his ignorance he expected. Instead, I feel sick. He is my age. We grew up together. Yet somehow he was able to miss misogyny, a daily reality imposed on women. Imposed on me. And if he were in South Africa, I think, would he know the word for apartheid? Would this liberal white young man be able to call it racism?

Standing in front of a downtown theatre, I understand what ate at me during the film. It was the gnawing realization that I was witnessing blind ignorance splattered explicitly on the screen. In that moment, explaining misogyny to my friend, I saw the need to admit my feminism. Feeling a little ridiculous about reading so much into such an unsubstantial movie, I nonetheless knew there was a reason for doing so. Because it's there. Still. Maybe if we think about it, not always.

Judy MacDonald was born a post-Diefenbaker era baby. She is the Managing Editor of *This Magazine*.

JOCK TRAPS

The Locker-room Door is Still Closed to Women

Helen Lenskyj

THE EXPERIENCE OF CANADIAN GIRLS and women in the male world of sport has been short, but not sweet. Until 1986, women's exclusion from male sport in Ontario was sanctioned by the Human Rights Code. Athletes could file complaints of racial discrimination but had no recourse to the code when they encountered sex discrimination. Given *carte blanche* to hang a "No girls allowed" sign on the clubhouse door, male-dominated sports-governing bodies rose to the occasion. It was only after the implementation of the Charter of Rights and Freedoms, and Justine Blainey's winning the right at the Supreme Court of Canada to play hockey with the boys, that the Ontario code was revised to make sex discrimination in sport illegal.

This state-sanctioned discrimination against female athletes was illustrated in countless stories of girls who were not allowed to play on school or community teams, despite their success in the tryouts, because they were the wrong sex. It is difficult to imagine another context where the courts would have considered such primitive, pseudoscientific arguments to justify the denial of human rights protection to a disadvantaged group. For example, there were references to girls' lack of "fighting hormones" and warnings about the "distorted" personalities of female athletes, whose feminine helplessness and passivity, it seems, were irrevocably damaged in the heat of sporting competitions.

A recent incident in the U.S. Boy Scout movement may shed some light on male opposition to sex-integrated team sport. In Maryland a few years ago, a woman with forty years' association with scouting asked the Boy Scouts of America to appoint her as a scout leader. "No way," the association replied, "it takes a man to build character." When she took her claim to court, the judge articulated what it is to be a man "He speaks with a male body motion, the pursing of a man's lips, a snort...a welling of tears of mirth or pain, a strictly male bellowing of outrage, disgust, commendation, warning, encouragement...all a matter of speech and communication in its male role manifestations...the way a male might look at one of the Scouts — just the look itself might be enough."

It comes as no surprise that scoutmasters are seen as builders of male character, but to reduce that character to a series of mannerisms which could be learned by anyone with a gift for mimicry seems a rather narrow interpretation of masculinity. True, much of what constitutes our idea of femininity has to do with movements and mannerisms, but surely masculinity — the bedrock of western civilization — goes beyond such simple formulas. What happens is that men in scouting, like men in sport, have taken insignificant sex differences, such as deepness of voice, built up an ideology around the masculine form and subsequently convinced male judges that these are *bona fide* requirements of the job.

We can see the same rationales operating in sport. The vast majority of activities defined as sport in the western world are in fact tests of physical strength and endurance, rather than tests of such attributes as flexibility, coordination, artistry, and grace. The guiding principle of the Olympic movement reflects this preoccupation with speed, strength, and endurance. These are areas in which men as a group outperform women, although there is a significant overlap in performance and a rapidly closing gap between the sexes. In their dominant role in sport circles, men can maintain the illusion of athletic superiority by identifying strength and endurance, not coordination and grace, as the pre-requisites of a *real* athlete and, by extension, a *real* man, a hero; someone who gets his picture on cereal boxes. And it is no coin-cidence that sport metaphors and sport mentality are rampant in business and politics. The boys are wearing pinstripes now, but they think they're still playing football.

Obviously, a lot of energy is devoted to keeping females off male turf, so that the serious work of teaching boys how to play like men can proceed. Yet why is it that, in a society where men as a gender group have power and privilege, and where hetero-sexuality is institutionalized, the masculine, heterosexual iden-tity appears so vulnerable to the tempering effects of women? Some psychologists have attempted to explain this in terms of object relations theory, which suggests that separation is a major developmental task of boys because they are mostly raised by female care givers. According to this theory, boys need to estab-lish a separate, masculine identity in the presence of men. Girls, on the other hand, have a clear sense of their femininity because of women's role in teaching and caring for young children.

The correspondence between this psychological explanation and the common-sense view of the "man in the street" should be an immediate cause for concern. Consider some popular rationales given by men like a former Etobicoke Parks and Recreation Com-missioner who oppose mixed-sex recreational or educational ac-tivities. "Boys don't know they're boys any more"; boys will feel inadequate if there are "sweet little girls around to crush them"; "a girl who comes second will try harder, a boy will give up trying." What boys have to learn is not simply that they are different, but that they are superior to girls. And this myth is a bit hard to swallow if reality suggests otherwise. The solution: change reality.

Object relations theories of masculinity development ignore the more sinister reality of power dynamics between the sexes. Masculinity and femininity are not equally valued in patriarchal society, nor are heterosexuality and homosexuality. Male heterosexual privilege is often maintained by violence: sexual harassment, sexual abuse of children, wife beating and sexual assault. The transmission of masculine identity is not simply a harmless developmental task, like learning to shave. It is a complex enterprise aimed at maintaining male power and privilege. Boys and young men have to learn who they are, and who they ain't: they are men, they ain't girls and they ain't queer. By failing to exercise the male prerogative of dominating women, at least in his private life, the gay man is obviously letting the side down. So what are men to think when some well-known sportsman — NFL running back David Kopay, for example — lets it be known he is gay? Where are the good old days when girls were girls and men were men?

The ideology surrounding sex differences allows sport to play a key part in maintaining male power and privilege. Human physical capacity is one remaining area where female performance measured, of course, by the male yardstick — seems to be deficient. At a time when most other rationales for male superiority and exclusivity are losing ground, at a time when women's achievements in the male preserves of politics, science, higher education, etc., are matching or surpassing men's, they can be sure of one thing: women will never make it to the NHL. In male hands, sport provides an ideal means of entrenching the myth of male physical superiority. But if sex equity in sport were ever a reality, we might see women competing on equal terms with men in a variety of sporting contexts. And, if a feminist transformation of sport ever took place, the whole nature of sporting competition might be called into question, with fun, friendship, and cooperation replacing the violence and the win-at-all-costs mentality.

Let's look at the other side of the coin, when men have attempted to gain access to women only activities. A Toronto man, Michael Celik, was recently refused entry to a women only self-defence class conducted by the Wen-do Women's Self Defence Corporation, which has been teaching such classes in Canada for over ten years. The man got support from a so-called men's rights group, In Search of Justice, which claimed that men are in greater danger of assault — presumably physical attacks by other men — than women. (By the way, Celik had a black belt in judo.) The men's group filed a complaint of sex discrimination with the Ontario Human Rights Commission. In Search of Justice belies its name: for example, it has criticized the women's movement for using the human rights route to get sex-integrated hockey, and it has publicly stated that most women cannot be trusted in their charges of rape.

It seems probable that the affirmative action provision of the Ontario Human Rights Code and the charter will protect this women only program, which is clearly intended to promote women's equality. Of course, these men's actions are not motivated by their profound concern for sex equity in sport. Nor is it just an instance of the "sour grapes" mentality; that is, using anti-discrimination statutes to turn the tables on women only activities. It is sexual harassment, pure and simple.

Consider the verbal and sometimes physical abuse directed at women who symbolically reclaim the streets in October in annual Take Back the Night marches. Consider that, a few years ago, a Metro Toronto police officer told women *not* to fight back, since, he said, it was safer to let the rapist have "his few minutes of pleasure." The idea of women taking matters into their own hands by learning how to fight back is hardly welcomed by the men who abuse and exploit their wives, daughters, girlfriends and co-workers, and get away with it. Nor can we be sure that the so-called average man, who prides himself on protecting "his" womenfolk, would be supportive of women's new capacity for self-defence. Male interests are well served by keeping women out of team sports, opposing women only wen-do and thus minimizing the opportunities for women to work together to develop their physical capacities, as well as their mental toughness, to the full.

It is clear men put considerable effort into defining and defending the boundaries around sport. Male only scouting is okay (but women only self-defence is not). Initiation into masculinity would apparently be diluted or contaminated by the presence of women in scouting. Similarly, combat sports, the military, and the police force have long been sites of struggle for male exclusivity — in short, any context where there is a premium on the worst features of aggressive and violent masculinity and where the exercise of this machismo would allegedly be diminished even by routine interaction with women. The rules against (heterosexual) sex the night before the big game no doubt stem from the same mentality. Women — cheerleaders, girlfriends, wives — are the spoils of this war without weapons.

Members of college football and basketball teams, like their counterparts in men's fraternities, have on occasion carried the battleground analogy to its most violent conclusion by gang raping young women on campus. And in case you think it doesn't happen here in Canada, consider the behaviour of the football team at a North York high school: the school's cheerleaders can no longer travel safely in the same bus as these young men, who seem to view cheerleaders as communal sexual property. After reading the testimony of former high school football players at the Dubin inquiry, we might be tempted to explain some of this adolescent male behaviour as a combination of steroid use and testosterone poisoning. And yet when progressive physical educators like Bruce Kidd called for an end to high school and university football a few years ago, we heard the usual outcry about "tradition" and "school spirit." Whose tradition? Whose spirit?

Finally, let's turn to some incidents which seem at first glance to be more isolated and individual, not so clearly a function of institutionalized misogyny. Let's begin with the infamous Professor Hummel and his practice of leering at women swimming in a University of Toronto pool. Was he just unusually insensitive and arrogant, or was this typical male behaviour?

What about the incidents of sexual abuse that female athletes experience at the hands of male coaches? There has been very little investigation of this problem, but girls' and women's testimonies suggest it is rampant. There have been accounts of a male coach in the U.S. who "seduced" most of the young women on the university team, allegedly to "motivate" them. And the young athlete in a smaller community cannot simply shop around for a new coach, as one Alberta athlete, likely to become a national competitor in her sport, found out. Her options were to respond to the male coach's sexual overtures or to quit the sport and so she quit. Her story, no doubt, is a common one.

One aspect of coaches' behaviour which has come under scrutiny is the psychological pressure they put on young female athletes regarding weight. This ranges from mandatory daily weigh-ins to the public humiliation of girls who fail to satisfy the coaches' demands for thinness. The fast growing incidence of eating disorders, especially anorexia nervosa, among young female athletes is in many cases directly attributable to coaches' abusive behaviour.

A final note about the violence issue: we cannot ignore the fact that significant numbers of female joggers have been attacked and raped, sometimes murdered, while they were out running; nor should we forget the murder of young track athlete Alison Parrott in Toronto three years ago by a man who presented himself as a photographer. The police have evidence that young female athletes in Toronto have been targeted by a known child molester, and many of these girls and their families have also been terrorized by men making repeated harassing phone calls, claiming to want to "represent" the girls for publicity purposes.

From these apparently isolated incidents a picture emerges: "You're on my turf and you take your chances." The results have often been tragic.

Helen Lenskyj is a feminist activist, writer, and researcher with a major interest in women, sport, and sexuality issues. She is now an Associate Professor in the Department of Adult Education at the Ontario Institute for Studies in Education. She has written two books, *Out of Bounds: Women, Sport and Sexuality* (Women's Press, 1986) and *Women, Sport and Physical Activity: Research and Bibliography* (Fitness and Amateur Sport, 1988 and 1991).

THE SAGA OF SPACE DORKS

Technophilic Flying Boys from Planet Earth

Joyce Nelson

IN NOVEMBER OF 1989, I attended a small Toronto conference organized by members of Science for Peace to bring together people from a wide variety of disciplines. The purpose was to discuss the crisis we are in during this last gasp of the fading millennium — a crisis encompassing ecological, social, spiritual, and political dimensions. The hope was that, out of the alchemy of our combined insights, some sort of synergystic approach to solutions might arise.

During this weekend event, two eminent white male scientists rose to address the gathering as keynote speakers. Not coincidentally, each made reference to the moon landing of 1969. Until that moment, I had forgotten that, in certain circles, 1989 had been earmarked as the 20th anniversary of the Apollo mission (or "The Boot on the Moon," as I call it), rather than any number of other events in that extraordinary year of 1969. *Chacun à son gout.*

In any case, the first scientist informed us that the moon rocks have turned out to be "no different from any other rocks" you might find in an alley in Moose Jaw but, he said, the $28 billion spent on the project was "justified" because "for the first time human beings were able to look at the earth and see it as a beautiful jewel shining in the firmament." The second scientist also waxed poetic about the Apollo mission, calling it "a turning point in the history of humanity." "For the first time in human history," he exclaimed, "we were able to see that the earth is whole, an intricate ecosystem that is our beautiful home."

By this point, my blood pressure was rising fast and I was having serious doubts about the alchemy which might arise in our gathering. I wanted to interrupt both eminent speakers and say, "Hey, guys, it's white suburbanites who were the last to know." Ancient non-patriarchal and native cultures have known for millennia that the earth is a living and intricate ecosystem, and they have certainly considered it "our beautiful home." For such pagan heresy they were killed off in droves, especially in the centuries following the Cartesian revolution in science.

While I was trying to decide which was more galling — the unconscious racism expressed in the rhetoric about "the first time in human history," or the attempt to "justify" that $28 billion price tag for putting "whitey on the moon" — an Ontario organic farmer-writer named Chris Scott stood up and reminded the eminent scientists about a member of their fraternity, Giordano Bruno, who had been burned at the stake in 1600 for coming to the same ecological insights 350 years before The Boot on the Moon.

But of course the real payoff of the Apollo Mission was the ideological and psychological — summarized by that other object brought back by the astronauts that, unlike the moon rocks, has not been demystified by analysis and time. The object is the photograph of the planet which now graces the covers of "environmental" editions of many mainstream magazines, which has become the potent symbol used in every form of corporate/governmental ecobabble, and which is the numinous logo for the new Earth Flag ("Because Every Day is Earth Day") available in "full-size or child-size," screen-printed on blue polyester with brass grommets and retailing for a mere U.S. $39.

The $28 billion photograph is also displayed on the editorial page of *Scientific American*'s 1990 special issue called "Exploring Space" — an edition sponsored entirely by Lockheed (one of the world's prime weapons suppliers), with fourteen pages of the company's ads. Under the Apollo photo of earth, editor Johnathon Piel reiterates the rhetoric about "a vision unseen and unseeable before the space age" — don't these guys read anything about science? — and calls the photograph "a symbol of the millennial human achievement in exploring space. The human eye, drawn close to the planets and their many moons, has now seen the earth in new perspective. It is a perspective which also enables us to glimpse cosmic beginnings and ends." (It's those "cosmic ends" which have me worried, especially with Lockheed and all the other military-industrial space dorks running the world. These guys get billions of dollars of government handouts and unlimited planetary resources to fire their ambitions.)

Anyway, as a mandala for our time, that $28 billion photograph of the blue-green planet is getting a lot of mileage these days. Before we examine the meaning of this photograph, however, we must delve into the murky realm of psychology: specifically, the psychology of the space program, and even more specifically, the psychology of what the Jungians call the *puer aeternus* archetype; what American men's group leader and poet Robert Bly calls "the flying boy" and what Peter Pan apologists might refer to as the psychology of the Lost Boys.

The Latin *puer aeternus* means "eternal boy" and as an archetypal pattern of behaviour and attitude, the *puer* has been studied extensively. The literature ranges from the wonderfully readable work of Jungian analyst Marie Louise von Franz (*Puer Aeternus*), to the less accessible prose of Jungian James Hillman (editor of *The Puer Papers*), to the pop psychology of Dan Kiley (*The Peter Pan Syndrome* and *The Wendy Dilemma*), the more personal approach of John Lee (*The Flying Boy*) and the increasingly popular (and very important) work of men's group leader Robert Bly, who focusses on various aspects of this psychological pattern.

The *puer* (pronounced "pooh-air") archetype is a rich one and difficult to briefly summarize, but the above experts would likely agree on this: a person who is possessed by and thus living out this archetype has profound difficulties being a grounded adult living in the mundane, daily reality of the world. The *puer* is the dreamer, the romantic, the restless wanderer, the high-flying dare-devil in every field (well, usually they don't go into accounting) who refuses to be "tied down" by conventional ways. Bly contrasts "the flying boy" with what he calls "the plodder" and says most North American males fit into either of these two categories, but that currently most boys and men are "flying boys."

The positive and negative qualities of the *puer* are expressed in such literary classics as *The Little Prince* by Antoine de Saint Exupery (analyzed by von Franz) and *Peter Pan* by J.M. Barrie (which Kiley's work addresses). A more recent example of the *puer* can be found in the movie made from Isak Dinesen's book, *Out of Africa*, where the Robert Redford character is a classic *puer*: a flyer-pilot reluctant to commit himself to anything except the never-never land of his adventurous exploits.

Always appealing for his youthful exuberance, the *puer* is nevertheless likely to die young, usually by becoming ungrounded — whether from the "high" of drugs (like Jim Morrison, Jimi Hendrix, John Belushi) or by actually flying and crashing (like Saint Exupery himself and the Redford character) or some other tragedy which replicates the fate of Icarus (that mythic *puer* who ignored the advice of his father and flew too close to the sun, thereby melting his artificial wings and crashing to his death). Coming down is the hard part for a *puer*.

These examples remind us that there is a female equivalent called the *puella aeterna*, an equally rich archetype (explored in Linda Leonard's *The Wounded Woman*). But here I'll focus on the *puer*, since not that many women become space dorks. We do, however, imitate the negative Icarus pattern in the form of addictions whose high flights and crash landings can kill as surely as they killed those lovely *puellas*, Janis Joplin, Karen Carpenter and Marilyn Monroe.

Perhaps the essence of the archetype is expressed in Saint Exupery's *Wind, Sand and Stars* where, on the one hand, "He who would travel happily must travel light," and on the other "We all yearn to escape from prison." Thus, the *puer* is usually unburdened by the conventional baggage (in every sense) and can thereby reach heights of vision, insight or ecstasy denied to the "plodders." Not surprisingly, good artists are usually working from the "eternal youth" side of themselves, which knows how to travel light. But at the same time, there is the danger of perceiving the mundane world, daily life, earthy groundedness and even the body itself as a prison from which one yearns to escape.

The necessity of being grounded in the body as the balance for high flying is precisely what troubles the typical *puer*. Reconciling the highs and lows, flight and ground, "the sacred and the profane," is the challenge in this archetypal pattern. As Robert Bly says (commenting on his own career as a "flying boy" poet), "Changing the diapers brought me down" to earth. For the *puer*, the impulse is to "stay up" all the time, like the Lost Boys led by Peter Pan who don't know how to take care of daily routine (like eating and sleeping) until "the Wendy" arrives to play surrogate mother.

Turn of the century author J.M. Barrie thus provides a clue to the neurotic form of the archetype as it functions in a patriarchal culture: women are stereotypically supposed to supply the earthy grounding (like Wendy) for the high flying *puer* who, as the bumper sticker says, "would rather be hand-gliding." The work of men's groups is important in helping men to ground themselves and each other, rather than to rely on women to try to do this for them — since it rarely works.

The perennial popularity of *Peter Pan* throughout this century (the play recently finished yet another successful run in Toronto) indicates the centrality of of "the flying boy" in our cultural zeitgeist. But I would argue that the *puer* is caught in those false dichotomies which characterize Western patriarchy — mind versus body, spirit versus matter, sacred versus profane — with the first term in each "opposition" scripted into our society to triumph over the other. Although the Jungians don't say this, I will: the extreme expression of the *puer* archetype is the space dork — the technophilic "flying boy" (completely at home in B.C. novelist William Gibson's cyberspace) whose dream is to soar off and colonize space.

As the predominant archetype of Western patriarchy, the neurotic *puer* advanced into techno-think by the turn of this century, which began with both *Peter Pan* and the success of the Wright Brothers. It went on to deify flyers like Billy Bishop, Charles Lindberg, Amelia Earhart and will likely end with a permanent lunar base for even further Dorky exploits.

On July 20, 1989, President Bush (an aging "plodder" who wishes he were a puer) voiced his support for such a project in his speech commemorating the 20th anniversary of The Boot on the Moon. Soon afterwards, the Canadian feds expressed their space dork complicity by giving massive financial injections to the aerospace industry. By March 1990, *Scientific American* was providing details of the plans to mine the moon and also set up observatories there, for which the April 24th Shuttle "Discovery" blastoff was the next neccessary step.

But the ultimate living space dork is probably Marvin Minsky, founding father of artificial intelligence (AI) at the Massachusetts Institute of Technology. Minsky has influenced many space dorks, instilling the belief not only that the planet earth is passé, but that the ultimate human goal is to download the human brain into a computerized robot which will live forever and make wonderful journeys into the farthest reaches of outer space. "I think it would be a great thing to do," says Minsky. "I think people will get fed up with bodies after a while."

Thus, the problem with the space dork patriarchy is that it has completely "concretized" its high flying *puer* impulse: pouring trillions of dollars into a space program which is a tragically literal-minded expression of the archetype by which it is possessed. By contrast, we need only consider the fate of the earth during the same historical period: treated as a sewer, a toxic dump, mere "resources" for the great patriarchal goal of, in *Scientific American*'s words, "embarking on more ambitious and challenging manned missions, such as those to Mars." But Robert Bly's work suggests the really challenging mission for our space dorks would be to do something simple and mundane, something respectful of embodied daily life — like changing the diapers.

Which gets us back to that planetary mandala, that ubiquitous Earth Flag logo, that $28 billion photograph said to signify "a turning point in the history of humanity." Taken from the astronautical perspective miles from earth, it shows us where we're at as a culture; spaced-out, in orbit, ungrounded, virtually disembodied, lost and flying like that *puer* Peter Pan, who has a horror of growing up. Paradoxically, growing up can only be done by growing down; reconnecting to the planet, to the body, to the space-time of the divine human animal; respectful of limits and of those not to be discounted but lesser flights of the embodied soul.

Thus, the photograph of planet earth illustrates the choice we're all being asked to make in our time. We can continue to soar off into never-never land (which is where the space dorks of every First World country wants to go, though they may call it Mars or Venus) — a goal which is wasting the planet daily. Or we can return to the earth where we started and get to know it for the first time; a pretty blue-green planet (now much the worse for wear) trying to make it through the latest round of Space Dork millennium fever.

Joyce Nelson has written numerous articles and essays for Canadian magazines and is the author of *The Perfect Machine: TV In The Nuclear Age* (1987), *The Colonized Eye: Rethinking The Grierson Legend* (1988), *Sultans Of Sleaze: Public Relations And The Media* (1989), and *Sign Crimes, Roadkill: From Mediascapes To Landscape* (1992), all published by Between The Lines in Toronto.

TWIST AND SHOUT
A Decade of Feminist Writing in *This Magazine*

FEATURES

Vol. 13 #5/6 Magaret Atwood, "Nationalism, Socialism and Feminism" (1979)
Vol. 18 #4   Linda McQuaig, "Reflections of Reality" (1984)
Vol. 18 #4   Libby Scheier, "Creativity and Motherhood" (1984)
Vol. 19 #3   Theadora Jensen, "Roots of Dissent" (1985)
Vol. 21#2   Carole Corbeil, "Ivan the Advertised Infant" (1987)
Vol. 21 #3   Lenore Keeshig-Tobias/David McLaren, "For As Long As the Rivers Flow" (1987)
Vol. 21 #6   Sandy Frances Duncan, "Notes For a Story That Isn't" (1987)
Vol. 22 #3   Katherine Govier, "The Calgary Time Machine" (1988)
Vol. 23 #3   Fauzia Rafiq, "Birth of a Murderer" (1989)
Vol. 23 #3   Lee Lakeman, "The Montreal Massacre" (1990)
Vol. 24 #7   Moira Farr, "Dangerous Determination" (1991)

FEMALE COMPLAINTS

Vol. 20 #3   Rosemary Sullivan, "Muse in a Female Ghetto" (1986)
Vol. 20 #4   Susan Crean, "Post-Feminism and Power Dressing" (1986)
Vol. 20 #6   Bonnie Sherr Klein, "Peace and the Female Principle" (1987)
Vol. 21 #1   Myrna Kostash, "Will the Real Natasha Please Stand Up?" (1987)
Vol. 21 #2   Heather Menzies, "In His Image" (1987)
Vol. 21 #4   Susan G. Cole, "Of Muffins and Misogyny REAL Women Get Real" (1987)
Vol. 21 #5   Donna E. Smyth, "The Return of the Warrior" (1987)
Vol. 21 #7   Susan Riley, "The Meech Boys" (1987)
Vol. 21 #8   Timothy Findley, "Lana Speaks!" (1988)
Vol. 22 #1   Dorothy Inglis, "True Norse" (1988)
Vol. 22 #5   Susan Glover, "Nellie, We've *Got* Washing Machines" (1988)
Vol. 22 #7   Maggie Helwig, "Hunger" (1989)
Vol. 22 #8   Thelma McCormack, "Examining the Election Entrails" (1989)
Vol. 23 #1   Alison Dickie, "Politics and the Pap Smear" (1989)
Vol. 23 #3   Dionne Brand, "Abortion Justice and the Rise of the Right" (1989)
Vol. 23 #4   Judy MacDonald, "Of Mice and Batman" (1989)
Vol. 23 #5   Helen Lenskyj, "Jock Traps" (1989)
Vol. 24 #4   Joyce Nelson, "The Saga of Space Dorks" (1990)